ABSOLUTION

THE ABSOLUTION SERIES #1

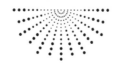

AMANDA DICK

Absolution
The Absolution Series #1
Third Edition
Copyright © 2014 Amanda Dick
www.amandadick.com

Cover Art and Design by Fiverr.com/Germancreative
Editing by Sarah Widdup

ISBN-13: 978-1719321327
ISBN-10: 1719321329

DEDICATION

For Bette Luksha-Gammell, Bobbie Pene, Abigail Andersson,
Sandi Laubhan,Sharon Goodman, Tracy Skerratt,
Lillybeth Melmoth, Tara Horak, Diana Houkamau, Jennie Coull,
Sherralynne Dewhirst, Kate Gissell, Susan James, Amanda Edwards,
Emma Spicer, Stephanie Davis-Linkous, Joanne Tolhopf, Sarah
Widdup,Raewyn McCormack, Lisa Horton, Sarah Gullett, Patricia Lee,
Vicki Waters, Verna Stock, Vanessa Macdonald,
Susan Marie Schoch, Johanna Rae
and
The Booknatics, A Literary Perusal, Summers Book Blog,
Amazeballs Book Addicts and Electively Paige

... for believing in me.

PROLOGUE

"You cannot find peace by avoiding life."
- Virginia Woolf

"Eddie Vedder is a god," Ally announced from the back seat. "No doubt about it."

Jack nodded at her in the rear-view mirror.

"And not only is he a god, but he has to be *one* of the sexiest men on the planet."

"Good save, babe," Jack winked.

"He's the guy that chicks want and dudes want to be like," Callum said, turning around to face her from the seat in front. "But I don't blame you. If I was a chick, I'd do him."

"Ugh, now I need bleach to scrub that mental image from my brain."

"You're welcome."

Ally leaned forward between the seats.

"Okay, favourite song from the concert tonight."

Jack sucked in air through his teeth, eyes on the road ahead as he thought it over.

"*Oceans*," he said.

"*Crown of Thorns*," Callum said. "I never got to see Mother Love Bone live so it's the next best thing. Although *Why Go* was pretty freakin' amazing."

He broke into a frenzied air guitar session in the front seat, his expression rapturous.

Jack chuckled as Callum turned back to Ally.

"Yours?"

"*Black*," she said, without hesitation. "With *Release* a close second. And I got it all on video. Can't wait to get home and upload it!" She squealed, leaning back again. "I cannot believe it's taken so long to see them live, but tonight was worth the wait."

"Definitely."

"He has the sexiest voice ever," she said.

"Hello?" Callum turned around in the seat again. "Do we have to spend the entire trip home hearing about how sexy he is? I'm sure that, given half a chance, he'd prefer to be known for his talent than his looks or his… general sexiness."

"Jealous?" Ally ribbed.

"When I have all this at my fingertips?" he ran a hand through his short, dark hair. "Not a chance. And come on; he may be sexy, and he may be a rock god, but I'm sure it's not fun and games all the time. I mean, he probably has those paparazzi bottom-feeders chasing him wherever he goes, splashing his visit to the pharmacy to buy haemorrhoid cream all over the front page. That's gotta suck."

Ally leaned forward to swat him around the head.

"Don't you dare drag him down to mortal level like that! Anyway, I'm sure he has people to do all that stuff for him."

"True. That's a job description I'd love to see."

Ally leaned forward to slap him again but he ducked out of the way with a chuckle.

"Quit it, you two," Jack grinned, taking his foot off the gas in anticipation of the approaching corner. "Don't make me the grown-up here. You know I hate that."

The road was still wet, even if the rain had stopped. The country road had been lined with trees for the past half mile, trapping the light from the headlights, bouncing it off the undergrowth and back out onto the road again. The effect was eerie and he was grateful when the trees gave way to the open countryside again.

"You need to put a leash on her," Callum grinned. "She's outta control tonight!"

Jack glanced at Ally in the rear-view mirror and she smiled back, winking wickedly. She was in a playful mood tonight, still on a high from the concert. He could relate. Adrenaline hummed through his veins and his ears still rang from the noise. It had been worth the long drive there and back but he suddenly wished they were home already. The ring tucked safely into the pocket of his jeans dug into him as a physical reminder of what lay ahead.

Distracting himself, he leaned over to turn the music up and Eddie Vedder's sultry voice filled the car. Ally swayed to the music in the back seat, a satisfied smile on her face. He turned his attention back to the road as they rounded the corner.

Headlights cut through the dark, directly into their path, blinding him momentarily. His heart leapt into his throat and his gut knew instinctively what was about to happen mere seconds before the car hit them.

Callum yelled as Jack automatically wrenched the steering wheel away from the blinding light. It all happened so fast. He didn't even have time to slam on the brakes.

The impact was mind-blowing, sending a shuddering jolt throughout his entire body that turned his limbs to jelly. Time stopped as they skidded across the road, the buzzing in his ears blocking everything else out. Then they were upside down. He squinted out through the windshield, his brain struggling to process what was happening. He felt like he was moving simultaneously in slow motion and fast-forward, and it crossed his mind that this might be how he died. A strange calmness washed over him. His fate was completely out of his hands.

The car suddenly bounced as it left the road, ripping through a fence, the trees ahead rapidly filling the windshield as he mentally braced himself for the impact. The crazy rollercoaster ride ended as abruptly as it began, jolting him again, throwing a spear of pain through his shoulder and neck that left him breathless.

And then there was silence. Buzzing, humming, vibrating silence.

CHAPTER ONE

"There are four questions of value in life; what is sacred?
Of what is the spirit made?
What is worth living for, and what is worth dying for?
The answer to each is the same. Only love."
- Johnny Depp

*J*ack McKenna bolted upright, bathed in sweat, his heart racing. When he was a child his mother would soothe him with "It's alright, it was just a nightmare. It wasn't real." But this wasn't just a nightmare. It was a memory, a very real memory. He fell back onto the pillow and ran a clammy hand down his face. He was on the brink of exhaustion but apparently sleep was a luxury he was being denied tonight.

No light spilled into the room from the tiny window and he lay there in the dark, listening to the sounds of the night. Traffic from the street below, cats fighting somewhere nearby, a distant sound of smashing glass followed by shouting. His current neighbourhood was more war zone than suburbia but afraid to close his eyes again, he lay there and listened to all of it.

Four years had passed and still he could recall every last detail of that night. In his waking moments he had control for the most part but when he slept it was a different story. Grief and guilt soaked through him like acid, eating away at him.

Frustrated, he pushed the covers off and swung his legs down onto the threadbare carpet. His entire body ached. The trembling hand he ran through his short brown hair left it standing on end, the nightmare still nipping at the edges of his subconscious. Ally's face flashed in front of his eyes. He squeezed them shut, trying to block her out as he fought to regain control.

In, one thousand. Out, one thousand. In, one thousand. Out, one thousand.

Slowly, he opened his eyes again, staring blearily at the stained carpet beneath his feet. The day hadn't yet begun and already he was bone-tired. He stood up, his shoulders still sore from the fight the week before. The recovery time was longer these days but he didn't care. He needed somewhere to channel his frustrations and inside the ring suited him just fine. He was fighting again tonight, instructed to take a dive and being paid good money to do it. Wearily, he pushed his pride aside one more time. The fact that it had become easier to do these days sat like a lead weight across his aching shoulders.

Padding across the room in his boxers, he grabbed his sweats and pulled them on. He took the stairs from his shabby apartment down to the street two at a time. Running through the streets, cloaked in despair, almost invisible in the dark, he tried to block out the world. The sun had begun to rise by the time he ran back towards his apartment.

He showered quickly, unable to ignore his battered reflection in the mirror as he prepared to shave. The skin was still healing over the bridge of his nose and he had a dark bruise around the cut on his cheekbone, the result of last week's fight. His green eyes were dull and hollow and he had a haunted look about him that made him look much older than his thirty-one years. Disgusted, he threw the razor into the sink instead.

After changing into his work clothes - faded jeans, checked shirt, padded jacket, work boots - he threw down a cup of strong, black coffee which did nothing to settle his stomach. Driving to the work site, he cranked the radio up loud in an effort to silence the voices in his head.

The day passed much like any other. He put in a solid day's work on the building site and declined an invitation from his workmates to hit the local bar after their shift ended. One day soon they would stop asking. He had held plenty of jobs just like this over the past four years and the invitations always dried up eventually. The less they knew about him the better.

That evening, he sat at the tiny table in the dingy apartment that had passed for home over the past few months and ate lukewarm pizza in silence. The light bulb had blown in the living room a couple of days ago but he hadn't gotten around to replacing it yet. The borrowed light shining through from the small kitchenette gave everything a sombre glow that suited his mood.

He felt like he was running in circles. Just when he finally felt like he had made progress, that the memory of what happened that night was fading, he would have the nightmare again and everything would come flooding back. At first it frustrated him, but then he realised that this was how it was supposed to be. The guilt he carried around with him like a chain around his neck, belonged there. Sometimes he thought that this was God's way of punishing him for what he did. Leaving like that was an act of cowardice and cowards deserved to be punished. He wasn't an idiot; he knew that he looked for that punishment every time he got into the ring. He was grateful for every punch that found its mark on his body. He deserved it.

Of course, his father would disagree. Tom seemed certain that forgiveness awaited him - from Ally, from Callum and from everyone else he had left behind. The truth was, as much as he loved his father and appreciated his support and loyalty, he knew some things were unforgiveable.

One day, he promised himself, he would go home and apologise in person. But not yet. Four years had passed and he was no readier to face them now than he was back then.

He took another swig from his beer bottle and set it down on the table in front of him, staring at it as if it would provide him with answers. He had fantasies about going home, about just turning up on his father's doorstep out of the blue. He imagined talking to Callum, hearing him say that he understood why he left and that he didn't blame him for anything. He fantasised about Ally forgiving him, throwing herself into his arms and everything going back to the way it was.

But they were just fantasies. The reality was that he would never be able to go home, Callum would never understand why he left and Ally would never be able to throw herself into his arms again.

Sometimes, in the moments just before waking, he almost felt her warm body tucked into his on the bed, her hair tickling his nostrils. He could swear he felt her long, smooth legs entwined with his, his hand curled around hers beneath the pillow.

And then he woke alone, his arms empty, his bed cold.

He had taken something from her that she would never be able to get back. As she lay in the ICU that night, he remembered thinking that she looked whole. But she wasn't. A shattered spinal cord did invisible damage, damage that could never be repaired. She would never walk again and it was his fault. He carried that knowledge around with him like an anchor that simultaneously tied him to her and tore her away from him.

The brief conversations with his father were torture. Questions haunted him but he was afraid to ask them. He convinced himself it would be easier if they didn't talk about her but the delusion was paper-thin. Just because they didn't talk about her didn't mean she was far from his mind. He shook off the musings, taking another swig of beer. He didn't deserve to know.

Staring down at the untouched slice of cold pizza on his plate, he saw his whole life stretched out before him. Alone in some grubby little apartment, working a dead-end job miles from home. Throwing himself into harm's way - tempting fate, but too much of a coward to take matters into his own hands. Working himself to the brink of physical and mental exhaustion as he tried to block out all of his sins. How had he ended up here? The sense of hopelessness was so strong he wanted to scream.

Instead he took what was left of his beer over to the couch and sank into it, running his fingers over the fabric on the arms, smooth with the ingrained grease and dirt of previous tenants. His gaze crawled over the faded, peeling wallpaper as he tried to psyche himself up for the fight tonight. He had been instructed to take a dive in the third round, which got under his skin. He knew his opponent, had seen him fight. He was bigger but he was clumsier too. He knew he could take him if he put his mind to it but he had his instructions. It didn't matter if he could take him or not. He needed the money and he needed to do what Ben wanted.

The trill of his ringing cell phone broke into his thoughts and he picked it up off the stack of pizza boxes that passed for a coffee table. An unfamiliar number blinked at him from the screen.

"Hello?"

"Jack?"

The hair on the back of his neck stood on end.

"Who is this?" he asked tentatively, although the voice was far too familiar to be mistaken.

"It's me. Callum."

His heart thumped in his ears.

"You still there?" Callum asked.

"I'm here."

How the hell did Callum get this number?

"I've got some bad news. It's your Dad."

The words hung in the air between them, Jack's heart breaking as if it knew the truth before he did.

"He's dead, Jack. He had a heart attack."

Jack stared at the wall opposite him, unblinking. There was a humming in his veins, in his blood, deep inside his chest, that made it difficult to concentrate.

"When?" he mumbled.

"This afternoon. I came over to –" Callum's voice broke and he cleared his throat. "I found... he was in the living room. Your number was in his phone. I thought you'd want to know."

Jack nodded blankly, unable to find the words.

"I'm sorry. Funeral's on Friday."

The pause was long and uncomfortable. He imagined Callum's face on the other end of the phone but that just made it worse. Imagining Callum's face also conjured up Ally's. He had never felt emptier or more alone.

"Are you coming home?" Callum asked.

His heart hammered in his chest, fear pulsing through him at the thought.

"Jack? Are you planning on coming home, for the funeral?"

The harshness in Callum's tone shocked him into answering.

"I don't know."

"It's your call, obviously. I don't care one way or the other but I just want you to know that if you do decide to come back, Ally doesn't want to see you."

Jack froze at the mention of her name.

"So, come or don't come, that's up to you, but stay away from her - I mean it. She doesn't need this shit from you, not now. Funeral's on Friday at eleven. Father David's handling it. You can call him for all the details."

The anger in his voice was unmistakable. He rattled off Father

David's number as Jack scrambled for a pen and scrawled it on top of the nearest pizza box.

"Thanks," he mumbled, his hand shaking so badly he could barely read his own handwriting.

"I mean it, Jack. Stay away from her. You owe her that much."

The line went dead.

*J*ack pushed the conversation with Callum into the back of his mind, compartmentalising it as he had done so often over the past few years. Shadowboxing, he bounced on the balls of his feet. He didn't want to think about anything right now. He just wanted to get into the ring and fight.

The warehouse was on the outskirts of the city, tucked in behind a factory that looked like it had shut down years earlier. Grass sprung up from cracks in the broken concrete outside and most of the windows were smashed in. It was the poster child for urban decay, abandoned and forgotten, a reminder of better, more industrious, days.

It smelled like sawdust and oil and it reminded Jack of long hours spent with his father, working in their garage on his motorbike. Tom wouldn't have understood why he was doing this, Jack was sure of that. Jack could almost hear how that conversation might have gone in his head, his father's voice firm and unwavering in his disapproval.

Just then Ben arrived with one of his heavies, strolling straight into the small storeroom out back that served as the locker room. He didn't bother with any preamble and got right to the point, clarifying the details with him before the fight. He was to go down in the third round. Jack nodded, ignoring the giant standing behind him.

"Third round," he mumbled. "Got it."

"Payment after the fight, as usual," Ben said, preparing to leave. He turned around in the doorway. "There's a lot riding on this so don't screw it up, for either of us. You go down in this fight and your next one will earn us both double, trust me." He paused, giving Jack the once-over from his feet up. "You look tense. Loosen up."

Jack clenched his teeth, nodding. As much as he hated to be told, Ben was right. He needed to concentrate on keeping his father out of his head if he was going to make it through this. So, he pushed the pain down deep, just like he'd been doing for the past four years. He didn't have the luxury of dealing with grief right now.

The general buzz of the amassing crowd outside was slowly building. Moments later, the place erupted in a loud roar. There had to be at least a couple of hundred people out there. By the time he climbed into the ring to the deafening sound of cheering, Jack was in a trance.

Let's do this.

Standing up inside the ring, the smell of sweat, stale beer and liniment was overwhelming. He bobbed up and down, rolling his shoulders, ignoring the crowd and concentrating on his opponent. He had clearly been spending a lot more time in the gym since he last saw him. Jack's ribs ached just looking at him.

"Just another day," he mumbled to himself above the cacophony, throwing punches into the air in front of him.

He never even heard the bell above the roar of the crowd but he saw his opponent heading straight for him. He shook his head to clear it and headed into the centre of the ring to meet him head-on. They were fighting for money and the crowd was betting large. There was no meeting in the middle to touch gloves, no agreeing to abide by the rules. There were no gloves and no rules. Strangely, he felt at home there.

He ducked the first punch and snapped back to reality in time to feel the second punch connect with the side of his head. His ears rang but he kept his hands up and his feet moving. He stole a quick glance ringside. Ben stared back at him, his face expressionless. Jack diverted his attention back to his opponent, dancing around him for a few seconds before bearing down with a series of one-two combinations, ending with a sharp jab to the ribcage. His opponent staggered but stayed on his feet, Jack's arms and shoulders burning from the recoil. Over the next minute or so stray punches found their mark but Jack shook them off.

At the end of the first round, he retreated to his corner and took the squirt of water offered greedily. Panting, he was fairly certain that was more from the effort of trying to keep his mind on the job rather than any physical toll on his body. His father's voice kept overriding that of the crowd. Blinking, he grabbed the water bottle, squirting it over his face in an effort to wash the voices away.

Heading into the centre for round two, he was anxious and hyper-alert. He dodged his opponent's first couple of punches easily, swinging his body away from the right hooks - his most powerful. He was too slow to avoid the sudden left swing that hit him out of nowhere though, and it reverberated throughout his body, leaving him staggering.

Ally's face flashed in front of his eyes and he shook his head to get rid of her, an overwhelming sense of guilt hitting him with the same power as a well-placed roundhouse kick. Groaning, he knew she would never have let him put himself and his body on the line like this. She would hate it if she knew, they all would.

A thunderous blow to the head saw him falling to the floor as the lights went out momentarily. He lay on the floor for what seemed like hours, his head ringing. Slowly his vision cleared and he saw his father standing inside the ropes, staring at him. Jack held his breath. Then he blinked and the image was gone. Scrambling to get up, he shook his head and tried to ignore the screaming crowd. He was being driven to the point of insanity. Maybe he was finally losing it?

This had to stop.

He shot upright, barely thinking about what he was doing, heading straight for his opponent, hands up, eyes focused. He didn't even feel the first punch connect with his opponent's ribs but he saw him double over all the same. The next punch came straight out of the blue and into his opponent's face, front and centre. The grief and guilt tore out of him at a hundred miles an hour and rained down on his opponent because he was there. For a split second, he felt sorry for him.

Catching him as he rebounded off the ropes, he slugged him again and again and again, until the man was a steaming heap at his feet.

The crowd roared. Slowly, Jack came back to himself. Realisation slammed into him. Adrenaline fired through his system as he frantically sought out Ben. It was like staring into the eye of a hurricane. He stood in the centre of a baying crowd, unmoving, silent.

Jack bolted from the ring, fighting his way through the crowd. He had been in more establishments like this than he cared to remember and one thing he routinely did before the fight was check for possible escape routes, just in case. More than once he'd had to escape an unhappy crowd when the fight didn't go their way. He snatched his bag, jamming a chair beneath the door handle. Heading straight for the small anteroom at the back, he tried to force the window open. When it wouldn't give, he dug into his bag and pulled out his shirt, wrapping it around his fist and jabbing it into the window-pane, shattering the glass. He cleared the jagged glass around the edges of the frame and climbed through, glancing behind him once he was out in the alley.

Panting heavily, he ran along the alley, not stopping until he was clear of the building, steam pouring off him into the chilled night air. He jumped into his car and gunned the engine, heading for his apartment, blood pounding in his ears. Checking the rear-view mirror every few minutes, he looked for signs that Ben or his henchmen might be following him. He took the long way, just in case, and bolted up the stairs to his second-floor apartment.

Throwing his meagre possessions into his duffle bag, he checked his cell phone battery and ripped the lid off the pizza box, jamming that in too. After giving the small apartment a quick once-over, he headed straight back to his car. There was no time to waste. Ben would be looking for him.

Throwing his bag into the car, he glanced quickly up and down the street. He climbed in, pausing to take a deep breath. His lungs pushed painfully against his bruised ribs. His muscles screamed and his hands shook uncontrollably.

"I'm coming Dad," he whispered into the silence. "I'm sorry I'm late but I'm coming."

CHAPTER TWO

"Regret for the things we did can be tempered by time;
It is regret for the things we did not do that is inconsolable."
- Sydney Smith

SIX HOURS EARLIER

*A*lly Connor hummed to herself, lowering her paintbrush and staring back at the canvas in front of her. A smile played on her lips and she found her concentration waning. She had tried to put this morning's meeting out of her mind in order to get back to work, but the distraction tactic had clearly worn off. Giving up the pretence, she let her gaze wander to the workbench - more specifically, to the draft exhibition invitation on top of the workbench.

Linda Frostmeyer wanted to exhibit her work - the proof lay in that invitation. It wasn't a dream. Years of work, of pouring her heart and soul into her art, were finally coming to fruition. What had always been a private matter, a sanctuary for her, would now be shown to anyone who cared to look. The thought made her slightly queasy but she pushed it aside. All artists went through this transition at one time or another. For once, she was no different.

The exhibition was three months away and she still had to finish the current painting she was working on, the last in a series, and make the final decision on the other paintings to be included. She reached for her crutches, sliding her arms into the cuffs. Pushing away from the padded frame propped in front of the canvas, she made her way slowly over to the workbench and picked up the invitation, running her fingertips over the gold-embossed logo of the Frostmeyer Gallery on the front.

Four years ago, she would never have thought this moment would have been possible. After the accident and Jack's sudden disappearance, while nursing a broken heart and a broken body, her genetic stubbornness had deserted her. Doubt, frustration and the shock of Jack's betrayal had intermingled with anxiety, hollowing her out. It had almost consumed her. If it hadn't been for the support of her friends, her family, she knew she would have lost herself. They had held her up when she felt herself falling, both physically and emotionally. They taught her that acceptance didn't mean giving up, or giving in. The trials and tribulations of rehabilitation and recovery had been a team effort and she was eager to share the moment with them. Luckily tonight was movie night and she planned to fill them in then.

Placing the invitation back on the workbench, her gaze wandered around her studio. Beneath the window, finished canvases were stacked in front of each other against the wall in several piles, waiting for her to decide if they were to be included in the exhibition. Like dancers lining up at an audition, they waited patiently, each one speaking to her, mentally extolling its merits.

One in particular spoke so loudly it stood out, even though it was partially hidden behind another canvas. Linda had been insistent that this one was included but Ally still wasn't convinced. It laid her soul bare and she wasn't sure she could face knowing that the world would see how damaged she really was. Linda had argued that the portfolio would not be complete without it and, in principal, Ally agreed. On an emotional level however, it was a different story. The fact that it was part of her 'Evolution' series made the decision that much harder to make.

It was the most personal of all her work, documenting the various stages of her physical and mental recovery following the accident, and it held a special place in her heart. It was the series she was simultaneously most afraid of and most proud of. It exposed her vulnerabilities - her insecurities, her heartache and fear - but it also showed her overwhelming desire to conquer this new life and to emerge stronger than ever. In a moment of clarity, she realised that the last four years had been a journey and now that journey was coming to an end.

A sense of peace and tranquillity grew within her, rising up from the ashes, empowering her with a feeling of acceptance and confidence. Her studio seemed to be full of promise, offering up the vibrant lime green walls as a symbol of growth and new beginnings. Her finished canvases adorned every space that wasn't already occupied by a door, window, storage shelf or workbench, a visual confirmation of her accomplishments. A large shelving unit along one wall held supplies while a dual-height workbench took up another entire wall, littered with materials. The workbench had been custom made by Callum and Tom with space for her wheelchair to fit comfortably underneath on one half, while the other half was higher so she could stand in front of it if she was wearing her braces. Between them, they had thought of everything including padding the front of the higher end, minimising the possibility of bruising she may not be able to feel.

Without them, she knew she literally wouldn't be standing here now.

Callum's face had been the first thing she'd seen when she

woke up after the accident. Over the months that followed he never left her side. She had long suspected that he had been trying to fill the hole that Jack had left out of some sense of moral obligation, but as time passed it didn't seem to matter anymore. She needed him, he was there and she was grateful.

But he wasn't Jack and they both knew it.

Initially, she decided that Jack must have left because he felt guilty about the accident. That frustrated her because she didn't blame him at all. As time went by, she wondered if perhaps he just didn't want to be with her because of her injury. That hurt went much deeper. In the beginning she thought she might go crazy from the constant speculation. It was so unlike him to just disappear, to leave not only her but his father, his friends - everything.

Tom had been honest with her from the beginning. Jack had called him. He had stipulated he would keep calling him as long as it was on his terms. He was not to give his number out to anyone - not to Callum and especially not to Ally. That was like a hammer blow to her already fragile heart. He didn't love her, not anymore.

As to where he was now, that was anyone's guess. She stopped asking and Tom stopped telling her when he'd called. It was easier that way. She had her own life to live and so did he. Life went on and she decided that she wasn't going to let the past haunt the present. It wasn't easy but she took back control of her life. She lost herself in her art and she concentrated on getting the most out of each and every day. Finally, the path ahead was clear and it wasn't as lonely or as dark as she had once feared. In fact, today it was brighter than it had been in a long time and she was going to nurture that feeling as long as she could.

The doorbell chimed, interrupting her thoughts. Making her way slowly out into the hall, she planted her crutches first, then using the power in her hips, she propelled each braced leg forward one at a time.

"Ally, it's me," Callum's muffled voice carried through the door.

"I'm coming!"

Perfect timing. She was so excited about the exhibition, she could barely contain herself. Arriving at the door, she balanced on her crutches and reached out to open it, grinning in anticipation. The moment she saw Callum's face, however, the smile died on her lips.

"What's wrong?"

He stood in the open doorway, red-rimmed eyes downcast as he fidgeted with the car keys in his hand. Finally, he shoved them into his pocket.

"I think you should sit down," he said quietly, turning to close the door behind him.

Her heart raced.

"Tell me."

"I didn't want you hearing it from anyone else," he said, turning to face her, his voice barely above a whisper. "It's Tom. I went over there this afternoon and I found him in his living room. He'd had a heart attack."

"Is he okay?"

He shook his head slowly, his chin quivering.

"He never even made it to the hospital."

Suddenly everything seemed to stop. Callum's face blurred. Blood pounded in her ears. She felt the floor shifting beneath her and then his arms were around her, holding her up.

"He's gone Ally."

Her heart ached with a loss so familiar, she felt like it had never really left her.

---

*J*ack stared at the road ahead and once again considered carefully what he was about to do. He was scared to death but he owed it to his father. If nothing else, he had to say goodbye.

He replayed the conversation with Callum in his head, followed by other conversations, countless ones with his father, running on an endless loop. He shook his head to try and clear it, the muscles in his neck and shoulders twinging at the movement. He had been caught squarely between a rock and a hard place. Not showing for the fight would have brought Ben's wrath squarely down on his shoulders, so he had fought. But losing control like that in the ring was another matter. Ben would not take that lightly. He had screwed up, nothing new there. He'd resolved it by leaving town, also nothing new. Grateful again that his obsessive need for privacy meant Ben only had a phone number rather than a contact address for him, he still glanced at the rear-view mirror again out of habit.

He was going home.

Home.

The word conjured up a sense of dread with it. Despite Callum's warning to stay away from Ally, he couldn't help but think of her. Would she change her mind and want to talk to him? Would Callum? Would anyone, after what he'd done?

He pulled over onto the hard shoulder as soon as he left the highway, retrieving his phone from his duffle bag and dialling Father David's number from the scribble on top of the pizza box lid. Father David offered his condolences and Jack quietly informed him that he would be coming home for his father's funeral. He thanked him for organising things on his behalf. The words of comfort offered down the phone line washed over him, barely making an impression.

Driving through town after town, the road ahead seemed longer, not shorter. There was no turning back now. Fate had taken over, clearly sick of waiting for him to make the right decision on his own. Pressing harder on the gas pedal, he went over the last conversation he'd had with his father, turning it this way and that. It had started out as always; pleasantries exchanged, the conversation slightly awkward. For the first time in a while, his father had mentioned Ally and Jack had interrupted him, reminding him of their pact; don't ask, don't tell. The conversation had taken a swift dive and thinking back on it now, he couldn't remember who had hung up on whom.

He pulled over to refuel just as the sun was coming up. Sitting in the deserted gas station forecourt for several minutes afterwards, he stared at the horizon as it changed colour. He closed his eyes, trying to recall his father's face. It had been four years since he had last seen him and his face seemed blurred at the edges.

All that wasted time.

He leaned forward and rested his head on the steering wheel. At this time of the morning, on this lonely stretch of road, he felt like the only human being on the planet.

His phone rang, breaking the silence. He stared at it suspiciously and picked it up off the passenger seat. Ben's name stared back at him and he cancelled the call immediately, throwing the phone back onto the seat. He glanced in the rear-view mirror, just in case, but the road was clear.

He didn't stop again until later that night, at a cheap motel with a broken neon light flashing intermittently in the darkness. The tiny room reeked of cigarette smoke and he lay down on the bed fully-clothed. Staring at the ceiling, he wondered for the hundredth time what awaited him at the end of this road.

In the twenty-four hours since he had learned of his father's death, he had come to the terrifying - and, if he was completely honest with himself - slightly liberating conclusion that it was now or never.

He had to fix this.

His father had been right, only he had been too damn scared and stubborn to see it. He still had the chance to do the right thing by Ally and he needed Callum to know that he was sorry. He would do it for his father and for them because it's what they deserved.

He shifted irritably on the hard bed. His muscles burned and he felt every split and bruise as if his body was on fire. The ceiling blurred in front of his eyes. He didn't even have the energy to reach over and switch off the light behind his head as his eyes slid closed.

---

*C*allum helped himself to a fresh cup of coffee.

"Sure you don't want one?"

Ally shook her head, her long, dark hair falling loosely around her shoulders. She was refusing coffee. Things were worse than he thought.

He had spent the night on the couch because it didn't feel right leaving her alone. Movie night had been forgotten as they gathered in Ally's living room and tried to process Tom's death. After a lengthy discussion, Callum picked up Tom's cell phone from the table and walked out into the back yard to call Jack. They had argued that Father David would do it but Callum had an ulterior motive.

He stood in her backyard after the call, staring up at the night sky.

"I'm sorry, Tom," he whispered.

He knew that Tom wouldn't have approved but there was no way that he was going to stand by and let Jack rip her apart all over again. He would do everything in his power to protect her. If Tom didn't approve of his methods, he knew he would approve of his motives.

Taking a seat across from her at the kitchen table, he knew

he'd been right. She fidgeted with her grandmother's ring, a nervous habit. She had that same haunted look in her blue-green eyes that she'd spent so long trying to exorcise. And she was grieving.

Losing Tom was bad enough but knowing Jack was coming home made everything worse. He missed Tom already. With things about to get messy, they needed him now more than ever. It was up to him now. He needed Ally to know that whatever happened, he was going to be there. They would get through this, probably not unscathed, but they would get through it.

"Everything's gonna be fine," he said, trying his best to sound convincing. "Don't worry."

"You're a crappy liar."

She stopped fidgeting with her grandmother's ring and planted her elbows on the table, resting her head in her hands. Her face was instantly hidden behind a curtain of dark hair and Callum didn't like it. She was hurting and she was hiding it and it made him nervous.

"Okay, you caught me," he admitted. "I just thought that's what you wanted to hear."

"It's not. I want the truth," she said from behind her hair. "I want to be prepared and I can't be if you start lying to me now."

"Prepared for what?"

"For when I see him."

"Hang on, I thought you'd decided you didn't want to talk to him?"

She looked up, smoothing her hair away from her face.

"I know but I'm not sure anymore. I don't know what to do."

"What's going on?"

She shrugged, dropping her hands to the table and staring at them.

"Come on, let's hear it."

He couldn't help the feeling of dread that rose up from deep in his gut. It would've been much simpler if she just stayed away from the funeral - and Jack - but he couldn't ask her to do that. Besides, she had as much right to be there as anyone. Tom was like a surrogate father to her, to both of them.

"Talking to him and seeing him are two different things," she said, still staring at her hands. "I can't avoid seeing him, I know that."

"Unfortunately. Doesn't mean you have to talk to him, though."

"I know." She looked up, her eyes pleading for understanding. "But I can't shake this feeling that I need to."

He didn't like the way this conversation was going.

"What should I do?" she asked.

She stared back at him as if he had all the answers. Was she crazy? Did she really expect him to give her an unbiased opinion on this?

"What do you want to do?" he hedged.

"Please don't do that," she groaned. "I just want a straight answer."

"But – "

"Please, Callum? Just tell me what you think I should do. I need to know."

"Fine, you really want to know what I think? Here it is then. I think that he's gonna want to talk to you and I think that whatever he says is not gonna make a blind bit of difference. It's too little, too late. If anything, it's gonna hurt you more to hear it and I just don't know why you'd go ahead and put yourself through that."

Judging from her expression, Callum didn't think that was what she wanted to hear. Everything about her screamed that she was vulnerable and in pain and he blamed Jack for that. She should be allowed to grieve for Tom without having to worry about what Jack wanted or what Jack was going to do. The realisation riled him even more.

"You know what else?" he added before he could stop

himself. "I also think I want to punch him in the face as soon as I get the opportunity. I think I'd feel a whole lot better if I did that."

"For God's sake," Ally groaned.

"Hey, you asked."

She sighed, absentmindedly stretching gently from side to side.

"Your back hurt?"

"Just a little, nothing serious."

"Would a massage help?"

"No, it's okay. But thanks."

She reached up to rake her hair back from her face, holding it behind her head for a moment before releasing it with a heavy sigh.

"I don't know what I'd say to him anyway," she said. "I guess I just want him to know that I'm alright, that I've moved on."

He had no idea who she thought she was convincing. She had to know that was a lie just as he did but he didn't call her on it. If that's what she was hanging on to, he didn't want to be the one to take it away from her.

He picked up his coffee mug and took a long sip. If the betrayal was still raw for him, he knew it'd be worse for Ally. He and Jack been inseparable since they were eleven years old. He knew how guilty Jack felt after the accident - hell, he was there - but he hadn't expected Jack to react the way he did. None of them did. You didn't let guilt get to you like that, not when someone you loved was suffering. You pushed it deep down inside and you did what you could to help. You didn't let it tear your life apart, that was just plain selfish. He'd thought Jack was stronger than that.

"I dreamt about him last night - Tom," Ally said, interrupting his thoughts. "I miss him so much."

Callum reached across the table for her hand. "We'll get through this."

"He should be here. With Jack coming home, I always thought he would be here."

She was right. Somehow, Tom had a way of making sure everybody kept their heads.

"I know," he said. "Me too. But it's gonna be okay. I promise."

---

*J*ack pulled up in front of his childhood home and the memories rushed in. The house looked the same as when he left. How could that be? How could this symbol of family remain intact when the family within had been torn asunder?

He climbed out of the car, singling out the one key he had kept even as he moved from town to city, from job to job. He stared at it for a moment in the palm of his hand before slinging his duffel bag over his shoulder and heading up the path towards the house.

The wooden stairs creaked ominously beneath his feet as he climbed, and he glanced around behind him. It felt like the whole street was watching. He was sure he saw Mrs Watson's curtains twitch. His father had always called her 'The Neighbourhood Watch'. His heart ached as he unlocked the front door and stepped into the hall.

Home.

Everything looked the same, it even smelt the same. For a moment, all he could do was stand there and let the memories wash over him. Finally, he pushed the front door closed behind him and placed his bag on the floor beside it. Jamming his hands into his pockets, he walked the few steps to the living room doorway and stopped.

A heart attack, Callum had said. In the living room.

It was so quiet, he felt like an intruder. There was no noise, save the slow, rhythmic ticking of the clock on the mantelpiece above the fireplace. It was the room that time forgot. Nothing had changed and yet everything had changed.

Looking over at the kitchen doorway, he half expected his father to come through it at any moment. Suddenly he found himself sagging against the door frame.

What if he wasn't strong enough? What if he messed things up even more, just by being here?

He stared at his father's empty armchair.

What if I can't do this?

---

*M*aggie put away the last of the dishes and leaned against the counter, surveying the tidy kitchen with a critical eye. There were a lot of things she would have no control over in the next few days but she had control over this. She was all too happy for the distraction.

She started aimlessly wiping down the kitchen table for the hundredth time. Tom's funeral was tomorrow and Jack could turn up at any time. Unless Ally sent her away, she was going to stick to her like glue. Ally hadn't even argued with her when she had told her that. After the past four years she would not just stand by and watch as Jack blew back into town and turned everything upside down again. She and Callum were in agreement. Once was enough.

Dropping the dishcloth finally, she headed towards the bedroom to check on Ally. Peering around the corner of her bedroom door, she saw her sitting on the bed, crutches propped up beside her, a small wooden box on her lap. She held the box as if it were made of glass.

"What's that?" she asked, walking over and sitting on the bed beside her.

Ally reached in to pull out a photograph, staring at it for a moment before handing it over.

Maggie took it from her, recognising it immediately. It was a photograph of the four of them - Ally, Jack, Callum and herself - taken at a party a couple of years before the accident. They had their arms around each other, grinning at the camera. They looked so young, blind to what the universe had in store for them in just a few short years. It was like staring into the faces of strangers.

With quiet determination, Maggie reached over to put the photograph back in the box on Ally's lap, closing the lid and lifting it gently from her.

"It's gonna be okay," she said.

The anxious expression on Ally's face told her that she didn't believe it either.

---

*J*ack sat outside Ally's house, trying to muster up the courage to get out of the car. He had to do this today, before he lost his nerve. Life was too short, too unpredictable. He knew that now. He could get hit by a bus tomorrow and she would never know how sorry he was. Steeling himself, he closed his eyes for a moment and allowed the memories to rush in.

She was laughing, those beguiling blue-green eyes twinkling, her long dark hair falling over her shoulder as she tossed her head back.

She was standing in front of a partially painted canvas, deep in concentration, humming to herself while she worked.

She was clinging to him on the back of his motorcycle, laughing as the wind whipped her hair around her face.

She was lying on the side of the road in the dark as the paramedics worked on her, pale and broken, deathly still.

His eyes shot open. Even with all their history, all the years they spent together, calculating out to literally thousands of happy moments, whenever he thought of her, that was the image that always came to mind eventually. It was guilt that repeatedly brought him back to that wet roadside. Guilt and shame.

He got out of the car before he lost his nerve altogether, walking up the familiar path to her front door. He climbed the steps slowly, distracted by the new addition off to his left. A wooden ramp led from the path to the porch, dog-legged in the middle. He stood rooted to the spot, staring at it. He had expected this, so why did it come as such a shock to see it? The answer came back immediately; because it was real. It was tangible, solid; not a fantasy, not in his head, but reality.

He drew himself up to his full height, six feet and one inch of pure fear and remorse. His heart began to beat so fast he felt like it was trying to pound its way out of his ribcage, one hammer blow at a time. He hesitated for a moment before finally pressing the doorbell, wincing as the sound reverberated through the house.

What am I doing here? What if I make it worse?

His father's voice echoed in his head, as clear as if he were standing right beside him.

"It wasn't your fault, son. You need to come home. Just talk to her - explain. It's going to be alright."

He was under no such illusions. Yes, he was here but that was only the first step in a long journey. Standing at her door, petrified, he was ready to ask for forgiveness but he had no idea where he would find the words. He tried to breathe normally, jamming his hands into the pockets of his jeans to stop them from shaking.

It took every ounce of strength he had to stand on her doorstep and wait. It seemed to take an eternity before the door finally opened. When it did, it wasn't Ally's face he saw but Maggie's. Her hair was longer and blonder and her brown eyes were red-rimmed and ice cold. It shouldn't have surprised him but it did.

"You're here," she said.

Speechless, he nodded.

"I'm sorry, about your Dad."

A mechanical offer of condolence. All he could do was nod again.

"I can't believe you actually came," she said.

His mouth was dry although his hands felt clammy. He clenched them into fists inside the pockets of his jeans.

"I had to."

"Took you four years but you got here eventually."

He winced, willing himself to remember why he was there. His entire body tensed as if barricading itself against a physical onslaught. He had to end this before his strength dried up.

"Is she here?" he glanced past her, down the empty hallway.

"Yes. But she doesn't want to see you."

His heart sank.

"I can understand that." He took a ragged breath and tried again. "Look, I'm not an idiot. I know… I mean, I was just hoping that maybe she might talk to me? Just for a few minutes."

"She doesn't want to see you," Maggie repeated.

He was being stonewalled and he knew it. He couldn't blame her.

"You shouldn't have come," she said.

His mouth and throat were barren and aching from the effort of trying to keep a lid on his emotions.

"I'm sorry."

"It's not enough," she shook her head, eyes suddenly brimming with tears. "It's not nearly enough, Jack."

"I'm sorry," he said again, turning away, fighting the urge to run back to his car.

He could barely see straight, the road swimming in front of him crazily. He didn't even remember the drive back to his father's house, just the desperate need to escape.

CHAPTER THREE

"The brave man is not the one who has no fears;
he is the one who triumphs over his fears."
- Nelson Mandela

*P*ain nudged Ally awake, the intensity building slowly until fiery tendrils licked up and down her spine. Holding her breath, she lay on her side, miserable and motionless in the dim light of early morning. The pain held her physically captive as she mentally struggled to fight off the last vestiges of the nightmare she had been in the middle of when she had been so rudely awakened.

Sometimes she woke with the uncertainty of not knowing if she was awake or still dreaming, the phantom sensations shooting up her legs confusing the two. It took a few moments for reality to crash headlong into her, the sensations giving way to the familiar numbness as disappointment settled like ice in the pit of her stomach. Most nights she was lucky to get five or six hours sleep, often waking with a dull ache where the steel rods were surgically fused to her spine. Occasionally she woke like she did this morning - in agony. She had gotten used to the lack of sleep but the pain seemed to take her by surprise every time.

This morning was a double whammy. Pain had woken her out of the recurring nightmare she referred to as 'the running dream'. It had felt so real. She could actually feel her feet hitting the ground as she ran, her body jarring with the impact. She swore she felt the soles of her feet tingling. Not phantom pain, not some kind of muscle memory, but actual sensation. Adding to the torture, there was usually some twisted reference to the accident.

She steeled herself against the pain squeezing her spine. She had lain awake half the night thinking about Tom, about Jack and about what might happen at the funeral. She relived moment after moment as they played through her head like a movie, years of familiarity reduced down to snippets and echoes, some clearer than others. Tom was gone. Jack was here. Everything had twisted around again.

She had cowered in her living room yesterday while Maggie had talked to Jack on her doorstep. She had hidden from him as if she was afraid of him. In a way, she was.

It was strange, hearing his voice after so long. He sounded different. Anxious, unsure of himself; not the Jack she thought she knew. It threw her. She tried to feel some empathy towards him, putting herself in his shoes, but it didn't last. Before she knew it, the old anger and betrayal began rising to the surface. It had taken years after his disappearance to convince herself that she didn't need to see him again to put everything behind her. It had allowed her a kind of closure. She needed to move on so she struck a truce; forgive to forget, although the last part was never really true. The memories lingered.

Now he was back and he brought the truth with him. It was intoxicating. Ignore him and the truth or saddle up and ask the question she was so afraid of hearing the answer to? She didn't know whether the courage, independence and sheer willpower that she had built up over the past few years would be enough. Suddenly it all seemed like smoke and mirrors.

Occasionally, in moments of weakness, when she was worn out and disheartened, she allowed herself to imagine that Jack had never left, the accident had never happened, and she was still whole in mind and in body. But then reality rushed in and it hurt more than ever.

The truth was she didn't feel whole anymore and deep down she knew it wasn't just because of the accident. It was because Jack had left and taken a piece of her with him. His rejection cut deep and it didn't seem to matter how determined she was to ignore it or what she tried to fill it with, that hole had never gotten smaller. In her darkest hours, she was afraid that, despite her best efforts, everyone else could see it too; ugly, ragged, raw and bleeding.

Taking a careful breath, the hot knives digging further into her spine, she mentally prepared herself to move. Counting silently to three, she reached over for the medication and bottled water on her bedside table. Her body automatically tensed against the movement, bringing a new wave of pain down on her. She rode it out, counting the seconds until it eased. Then she opened the small bottle and tipped a pill out onto the covers. She picked it up and slipped it onto her tongue, taking a clumsy sip of water to wash it down. Capping the bottle, she let it fall onto the bed beside her. Then she closed her eyes and waited.

Helpless, immobile and slightly nauseous from the pain, her thoughts drifted back to Jack. He couldn't see her like this, ever. She was desperate to show him how strong she was, how capable, but still she wondered what he would see when he looked at her. Would he look deep down, past the wheelchair and the crutches and the braces, and see that she was still there?

The pain began to ebb, the medication leaving her light-headed. Normally she would give it a few more minutes before attempting to get up but she needed a distraction. The pain would push all thoughts of him out of her mind and she was prepared to put up with it if it meant a reprieve for a few precious minutes.

Gritting her teeth, she reached down to remove the pillow from between her knees. She awkwardly pushed herself up onto her elbows, a low moan escaping as she grabbed a fistful of sheet. Pushing herself further upright, she breathed through her teeth, sitting motionless for a couple of minutes until the pain eased again. Then she reached over to pull her wheelchair closer. Manoeuvering her body to the edge of the bed, she slowly transferred into it, breathing through the pain.

She was determined to wear her braces to Tom's funeral today even if she had to take more pain medication to do it. It wouldn't be a popular choice but no one needed to know. For the first time since he left, Jack would see her standing. That was not negotiable.

Tom's funeral.

Part of her still couldn't believe he was gone. It was so tempting to sit this one out and she knew no one would blame her for that. She had been to enough funerals to know how much it would hurt but she also knew she needed to be there, as much for Tom as for herself. She could still see her father's funeral - the glossy wooden casket glinting in the sunshine, the flowers almost completely covering it, her grandmother sitting beside her, sniffing into a pristine handkerchief, soft blue eyes brimming with tears.

She was so tired of losing those she loved. Her mother had taken off a couple of months before her second birthday. Her father had raised her until his own death from cancer when she was fourteen. Following his death, she had come to live with her grandmother, whom she adored. She made friends quickly and settled into small-town life. Then, six years ago, her grandmother had also passed on. Her death had left a huge hole in Ally's life, but by then Tom and Jack had become her family, too. They both played a big part in helping her pick up the pieces.

And then the accident happened, Jack vanished and everything was different. She was different, and not just in ways she could quantify, either. Something had changed inside of her. Her perception of the world had altered. She felt both wise beyond her years and more frightened than she had ever been in her life. She was lost and, for a time, she wasn't even sure she could be bothered finding her way back.

The fact that she had was partly due to Tom. Putting his own grief and disappointment aside, he had made sure that nothing changed between them. He was still there for her, he still loved her. Losing him so suddenly was somehow worse than watching her father's slow death from cancer. At least then she had known what was coming. He had wanted to prepare her. Having Tom ripped away from her like this was cruel, like some kind of bad joke the universe was playing on her; yes, you can be happy, but not for long. Don't get too comfortable.

Tom's funeral was her chance to say goodbye, to say thank you, and as much as she dreaded it, she hoped it would help the emptiness to pass.

FOUR YEARS EARLIER

Tom sat watching the clock on the waiting room wall. The minutes ticked by, each seeming longer than the last. After a brief consultation with the nurses' station, they had asked him to wait while they found someone who could tell him what was going on. That was half an hour ago. In the meantime, his son was in there and he had no idea how badly he was hurt. All he knew was what they were able to tell him on the phone - that Jack's car had been involved in an accident out on River Road and that he, Callum and Ally had been brought in by ambu-

lance and were currently being assessed. He stood up, rubbing his neck to try and ease the tension that settled there.

"Tom!"

Jane and Maggie ran across the waiting room towards him. Jane threw herself into his arms as soon as she was close enough.

"Where are they?" she demanded. "What's going on?"

He pushed her away gently as Maggie stared at him over her shoulder, wide-eyed and shaken.

"I'm still waiting for someone to come out and talk to me," he said, rubbing her arm. "Hopefully it won't be much longer. In the meantime, let's just try and stay calm, alright?"

He steered them over into a corner of the room and they sat down, huddled together in a row of chairs. An uneasy silence spread over them, punctuated only by incoming patients and their entourages.

"I don't have a number for Callum's mother," Jane said. "What if we need to call her?"

Tom put his arm around her.

"Let's just wait and see what the doctor says first. If we need to call her, we'll worry about it then."

He wished Lucy were here. This was one of those moments where, as parents, they would comfort each other, talking through the uncertainty, holding each other up. Instead, he sat here, surrounded by Jack's friends, who needed comfort just as much as he did. For now, he concentrated on that.

When the doctor finally arrived, she led them along the hall to a private waiting area and invited them to sit down. She was young and clearly nervous. He would have felt sorry for her if he wasn't so worried.

"Sorry to keep you waiting this long," she began. "We were waiting on the results of the MRI. I know how you must be feeling so I won't beat around the bush."

"Thank you. We'd appreciate that."

"It appears that Jack was driving," she said. "He sustained an injury to his collarbone, probably from the seat-belt, however the x-ray

revealed no broken bones so he's very lucky. He'll be sore, and he has a few abrasions, but he'll be fine."

Tom breathed a sigh of relief.

"Thank God," Maggie whispered, reading his mind.

"Callum?" Jane asked breathlessly.

"He has a concussion," she glanced down at the clipboard in her lap. "It's fairly minor but he lost consciousness at the scene, according to the paramedics that brought them in, so we're taking the precaution of monitoring him overnight. He's sustained a bit of bruising but all going well, he'll be released in the morning."

Maggie put her arm around Jane and held on tight as Tom offered up a second prayer.

"That's good. He's going to be alright," Maggie smiled through the tears, rubbing Jane's shoulder encouragingly.

"What about Ally?" Tom asked.

The doctor seemed to take a moment longer to answer. She checked her clipboard again before crossing her arms over it, a slight frown creasing her brow. The mood turned sombre and the young doctor seemed to take on the appearance of someone much older and wiser than her years. A chill crawled up his spine.

"I'm afraid she hasn't been as lucky."

The next few sentences that came out of her mouth were jumbled. His brain struggled to make sense of them, turning the words over like puzzle pieces, trying to fit them into place. It didn't matter which way he turned them, nothing seemed to make sense.

"I don't understand," he said finally, his heart pounding.

He turned to Jane and Maggie, sitting beside him. They stared back at him in silent horror.

The doctor calmly continued.

"Ally's spinal cord has been badly damaged. She has fragments of bone protruding into her spinal column that need to be removed and her spine needs to be re-aligned and stabilised with surgery."

Tom's heart pounded in his ears. He shook his head.

"I'm sorry - for a minute there I thought you said she was paralysed?"

"That's right," she said gently. "I did. I'm so sorry, I know this must be quite a shock."

Tom stared at her, his brain struggling with the implication of the word.

"It's permanent?"

"I'm afraid so. The blunt force trauma that occurred as a result of the accident caused irreparable damage."

"You said that the surgery is to remove bone fragments. Won't that fix it?"

"Removing the bone fragments is only part of the problem. The damage has already been done. To give Ally the best chance of recovery, we'll be surgically fusing metal rods to her spine to stabilise it and allow her to heal faster, so her rehabilitation can commence as soon as possible."

No one spoke. Tom barely dared to breathe.

"I'm very sorry. I know it's a lot to take in, and as you said, it's been a long night - we'll talk more in the morning. Right now, we have her heavily sedated but she's stable. We'll keep a close eye on her overnight and prep her for surgery in the morning." She paused briefly. "There's no doubt this is a life-changing situation for her but she's twenty-six years old and she's in good health otherwise. There's no reason she can't continue to live a very full life."

Tom couldn't think of a single thing to say. Instead, he nodded, swallowing back tears as Maggie slipped her hand into his.

"The best thing you can do right now is take your son home," the doctor suggested gently. "There's nothing more you can do for Ally now. We have an excellent medical team here, we'll take care of both her and Callum."

Tom nodded again. This was every parent's worst nightmare; something you couldn't fix. Something no one could fix.

Suddenly, all he wanted was to hold Jack in his arms.

*J*ack had lain awake most of the night. Unable to turn off his brain, he had gotten up a little after two. He shuffled into the kitchen in boxers and a t-shirt, bare feet padding against the cold hardwood floor. He opened the fridge and stared at the food stacked neatly inside. Maybe his father's death had been a dream? It seemed so normal; food in the fridge. How could something so normal belong here?

Closing the fridge door, he poured himself a drink of water and leaned back against the kitchen counter. In the moonlight that flooded the room through the kitchen window, he could barely make out the folded note that Father David had left for him on the small kitchen table. It included all the details of the funeral arrangements that had been made on his behalf. As grateful as he was that he didn't have to do that himself, he was still concerned about the eulogy that the priest had assumed he would deliver.

Delivering a eulogy was an honour - one he felt he didn't deserve. The thought of standing up there in front of his father's friends and neighbours, not to mention Ally and Callum, made his blood run cold.

If he looked hard enough, he could still see his father sitting at the kitchen table, reading the newspaper. He could see him standing inside the back door, taking his boots off and hanging up his coat. He could hear the match strike and smell the cigar smoke as his father relaxed in his armchair after work in the evening. He could see his mother standing at the kitchen counter, kneading dough. Her hands were white with flour and his father came up behind her and put his arms around her, resting his head on her shoulder as he whispered something in her ear that made her smile. He missed her. He knew his Dad had missed her, too. He seemed to be just a shadow of himself in the years after she died.

Suddenly he realised he was an orphan; worse than that, he was alone. He had felt lonely and adrift over the past few years but never alone.

Memories tumbled over one another as he padded through to the living room and sank into the couch. He looked over at his father's armchair and he could see him sitting there, TV remote in one hand, cigar in the other. He glanced at the table beside the chair and noticed for the first time the book his father had been reading, a worn leather bookmark poking out from between the pages, reading glasses perched casually on top. It was as if he wasn't really gone, he was merely not here at this moment. He could come back at any time and pick up where he had left off.

Jack leaned forward, buried his face in his hands and cried. The heartache poured out of him, the first time he'd allowed himself to cry since he learned of his father's death. Sitting in the darkness, he let it all come tumbling out, sobbing until his throat was raw and his body numb.

Eventually he sat up, sniffing and running his hands down his face. The emptiness inside was still there, as he knew it would be. As his vision cleared, he found himself staring at the framed photographs perched on top of the mantle, just as they had always been. Sniffing again, he dragged himself up off the couch and made his way over for a closer look. Standing in front of the mantle, his gaze roamed over the photos, one by one.

He shook his head in amazement. Was it loyalty or pure stubbornness that made his father keep them there? Their world had been turned upside down yet his father had obviously refused to concede defeat.

Faces smiled out at him from their frames, oblivious.

His parents on their wedding day; his mother holding him as a toddler; he and Callum, their arms around each other, grinning; a group photo of himself, Ally, Callum, Maggie and Jane; his graduation; a photograph of he and Ally.

He picked up the frame and ran his fingers over her face.

They were both smiling, carefree, glowing with happiness. It was a snapshot from another life.

He recalled his conversation with Maggie earlier, the empty hallway behind her and the wooden ramp leading up to Ally's front door.

Things were perfect one minute and then suddenly they weren't. In a split second their world had come crashing down.

---

*A*lly yawned blearily at her third cup of coffee. The pain in her back had gone, thankfully, and the medication had left her more or less clear-headed, which was both a blessing and a curse.

The doorbell woke her out of her reverie. At this time of the morning it could only be Callum. Also an early riser, he had a habit of calling in for coffee, or so he said. She knew it was really because he was checking up on her. She sighed, rolling back from the table and making her way slowly up the hallway.

Reaching up to open the door, Callum's tired face greeted her and she made an attempt at a smile.

"Morning," he said, leaning down to give her a quick hug before standing up and heading straight for the kitchen. "I can smell coffee."

She closed the door and turned to follow him.

"Come in. Help yourself."

He poured himself a cup in silence as she resumed her place at the table.

"Refill?" he offered, holding the jug aloft.

She nodded, pushing her cup towards him and watching as the steaming liquid filled it.

He replaced the jug and turned to lean against the kitchen counter, taking a brief sip and running his eyes over her face, into her soul.

"You look like hell."

She shrugged, hands wrapped around the cup in front of her.

"Thanks, that's always good to hear. They teach you that at charm school?"

He shrugged, unfazed.

"Rough night huh?" he asked, settling himself in the chair opposite her.

"Yeah, you could say that."

She sighed, glancing up to find him watching her closely. She had no intention of expanding her answer but she knew by the way he was looking at her that he had already guessed something was up. It scared her sometimes, the way he seemed to read her mind.

"I had the running dream again."

The moment the words left her lips, the dream came flooding back.

"I wondered," he said. "It's probably to be expected, given Jack's sudden reappearance. Do you want to talk about it?"

If anyone else had asked, the answer would've been no but this was Callum. Apart from Jack, he was the only other person who could fill in the blanks in her memory from that night. Having lost entire days from around that time, her brain had seen fit to conjure up false memories, filling in the gaps between what she knew and what Callum had told her about that night in any number of ways, often both disturbing and unnerving her.

"I started off in the park," she said, recalling the dream in as much detail as she could remember. "Then I ran along River Road. I saw the ambulance from the turn-off. The lights were flashing and as I got closer, I saw that the ambulance was empty. Then I saw the car."

The image of the pile of mangled metal that had once been Jack's pride and joy was suddenly burned into her brain.

"And I saw us. You were trapped under the car and Jack and I were trying to get you out. There was blood everywhere."

Callum reached across the table for her hand.

"That's just your over-active imagination again," he said softly giving it a squeeze before letting go. "It didn't really happen like that. You know that."

"I know," she nodded. "I do, it's just… it always seems so real."

"I bet. You okay?"

"Yeah. I just wish today was over."

"You sure you want to do this today? There's still time to back out if you want to. I mean, we don't have to go."

"Yes, we do. We owe it to Tom and I'm not letting Jack scare me away. I just want to get it over with. Get in, get out, come home."

"Okay," he said after a few moments. "Whatever you want to do."

She knew Callum had to be dreading this as much as she was, and for the same reasons. Seizing her moment, she jumped in.

"Can you do something for me? If you do see Jack today, can you promise me you'll stay away? Don't start anything, not today."

He looked about to object so she cut him off.

"I know how you feel, you know I do. I just think that we need to make an effort to keep things under control, for Tom. Today is about him, not me or you or even Jack. We need to respect that."

"What do you think I'm gonna do?"

"I know you, remember? I know how hard this is for you, I know how you feel about him. I'm asking you to promise me. Please?"

Callum didn't answer immediately.

"I won't go looking for him," he said finally. "That, I can promise. But if he tries to talk to me - if he comes anywhere near you - I'm not sure I'll be able to stop myself. I'm sorry but that's the best I can do."

"Thank you."

She loved him like a brother but Callum had a temper. Not so long ago, he had been involved in an altercation of some sort in Barney's bar. He wouldn't tell her what happened exactly but the matter had ended up in court. He'd been lucky to escape with anger management counselling and what was tantamount to a good-behaviour bond - a miracle in itself, taking into account his existing record. The last thing she wanted was for him to end up in court again, even though she suspected he would think Jack was worth the jail time.

"Y'know, I never really thought he'd actually come back," Callum said. "Not even for the funeral. I really wish he hadn't, to be honest. It's just messing everything up."

"I know," she said quietly. "All that time I wished he'd come back and now that he's here it's just all wrong. It wasn't supposed to be like this."

CHAPTER FOUR

"Be not afraid of growing slowly;
be only afraid of standing still."
- Chinese Proverb

allum left Ally's place nursing a sense of impending doom coupled with an overwhelming desire to hit something due to pure frustration. Despite what he'd promised Ally, he had the powerful urge to rip Jack's head off his shoulders and ram it down his selfish neck. Instead, he climbed into his car, slammed the door shut, gunned the engine and pulled away from the curb.

He had already been keeping a lid on his simmering anger that Jack had ignored his warning to stay away from Ally. Now she was nightmares again, too. Did he have even the slightest idea about what his presence here was doing to her? One thing was for sure, she sure as hell wasn't ready to face him yet. Maybe she never would be. She seemed to flip-flop between wanting to talk to him and hiding from him. Personally, he was hoping for the latter. No good could come out of the two of them getting together over coffee. If anything, that would make things a whole lot worse. What the hell was Jack playing at?

She was right about one thing though - today was about Tom, and yet Jack's return had overshadowed even that fact, which only served to ratchet up the frustration level. He felt as if he hadn't even had a chance to grieve properly yet, another thing he blamed Jack for.

From the very beginning of his friendship with Jack, he had taken a shine to Tom. He was everything his own father wasn't and he was a little jealous of Jack at first. After his father left, Callum began to spend more and more time with Jack and Tom, appreciating the stable home environment and relationship that they shared, wanting to share it with them. Tom took over as the role model he never really had, even when his drunken father had been around. It was Tom who had sat with him when he broke the news to Ally about her injury. Tom had been the one to help organise her rehab placement and later, her release. He had spent many a night with Tom as they talked and drank into the early hours of the morning, discussing the best way to help her.

The day Jack disappeared, Callum had been with Tom when Jack had called him, after they were all going crazy trying to find him. He had tried to wrestle the phone off Tom but by the time he had, Jack was gone. He called him back immediately - against Tom's wishes - only to go straight to voicemail. Jack's phone had gone to voicemail from that moment on.

Looking back, it must've been tough on Tom. He had refused to divulge Jack's new number because he said it's what Jack wanted and he needed for Jack to trust him. No amount of shouting, needling or taunting had moved him and eventually a tentative truce had been struck. Tom's loyalties remained with Jack but that didn't mean he wasn't going to be there for Ally or Callum. Not being in any position to argue, Callum accepted that.

Those early days were tough. Jack was gone but he was there and Ally needed someone she could count on. Unconsciously, he had stepped forward. At times, he had nearly buckled beneath the weight of that responsibility but with Tom's help, he never did.

Watching Ally tentatively navigating her way through her new life nearly tore him apart and no matter how courageous she tried to prove she was, he knew deep down that she was scared. He could see it, plain as day. Jack vanishing like that had done things to her soul. How could he just walk away from her?

Knowing that he was back just scratched away at the scab. Unlike everyone else, he knew why Jack had left. Unexpected? Yes, but not a mystery. He had seen it tear Ally apart and he desperately wanted to enlighten her but he couldn't. He suspected the truth would be harder for her to stomach so he kept quiet. It wasn't his place to tell her.

He slammed the palm of his hand against the steering wheel, wishing he had never made that promise to Ally. The thought of having to watch in silence as Jack stood up in front of everyone to deliver Tom's eulogy made him sick to his stomach. Tom deserved better.

***

*L*ater that morning, Ally sat in the passenger seat of Callum's car, staring out the window. She wished the church was further away than just a fifteen-minute drive. She would have happily sat in the car for another hour if it meant she could avoid the inevitable for a while longer.

"You okay?"

The concern in Callum's voice was evident but the question was so ridiculous she ignored him. To his credit, he didn't push the issue. Maggie and Jane sat in the back seat in silence. By the time they pulled up in front of the church, she was so tense she wasn't sure she could move even if she wanted to. As they parked along from the church, cars already lining the street, her anxiety mounted.

"Come on," Callum said, to no one in particular. "Let's get this over with."

She found herself glued to the seat. She stared out through the windshield, searching desperately for courage. One thought rang out louder than the others.

He's here, somewhere.

Callum opened the passenger door and crouched down beside her.

"It's not too late. You don't have to do this."

"Yes, I do," she said, carefully controlling her voice.

"Okay," he murmured. "If you're sure. We're gonna be right beside you."

He hung her crutches over the car door and stepped back to give her room. Willing her hands to stop shaking, she pulled herself up and out of the car, locking her braces and slipping her arms into her crutches without a word.

Maggie appeared at her side, gently draping her arm around her shoulders.

"Come on, let's get inside and find a seat."

Callum pushed the car door closed behind her and together they headed down the street towards the church. Ally found herself having to concentrate harder than usual to co-ordinate her movements. Her shoulders were tense, making progress slow. She wanted to cry, such was the frustration.

"Remember your promise," she heard Jane whisper to Callum.

Her stomach knotted up tighter but she kept moving. Her eyes were fixed determinedly on her legs as she threw each hip forward, her legs following suit. As they got to the front steps of the church, she froze. The thought of walking inside made her blood run cold.

"I need a minute," she said.

"It's okay." Callum squeezed her arm gently. "We'll wait. Take your time."

"I just need to get my head around this."

"It's fine," he urged Maggie and Jane. "I'll wait with her, you go ahead, save us a seat - near the back, preferably."

Ally opened her mouth to protest, but Callum was quicker.

"I'm not leaving you out here by yourself."

A group of people walked past them and Callum nodded towards the garden laid out beside the church.

"Come on, let's go find somewhere to sit down for a minute."

With mature trees and pretty flowerbeds, the garden was sprinkled with benches donated by parishioners in memory of loved ones. The perfect place to find some solitude and take a breather from the chaos in her head.

---

*J*ack arrived at the church and sat in his car for several minutes, watching people arrive. They huddled together in small groups before they made their way inside. He spotted Father David at the church door, greeting folk as they entered, reminding him painfully of his mother's funeral.

When he could finally bring himself to get out of the car, he headed straight for the church door before he could change his mind. He allowed Father David to usher him to the front pew, keeping his head down as he tried to block out the whispers that seemed to follow him. A few of the more direct friends of his father came up to him and shook his hand, offering their condolences, their expressions caged. He thanked them woodenly. Surrounded by people he knew, he felt more alone than ever.

Just when he thought he couldn't take any more, the service began. He silently prayed for strength, in the same breath knowing he hadn't any right to pray for anything. His hands were wet with perspiration as he wiped them hard against his thighs, trying to ignore the fact that his father's coffin lay mere feet from where he sat. An unfamiliar photo of his father stood proudly on top of it. He looked weathered, beaten down. Old. It tore at his heart.

Did he do that? Did he make it so hard on him by not being here, that he wore him down until he couldn't take it anymore? Did he die not of a heart attack, but of a broken heart?

A hymn was sung then Father David stepped up to the pulpit to speak. Jack couldn't hear a thing for the pounding in his ears. A hand patted his shoulder lightly. It was time for him to step up and give his eulogy. He stared blankly up at Father David and received a smile of encouragement. Getting unsteadily to his feet, he made his way over to the pulpit, where the priest shook his hand firmly and stepped aside. His mouth was so dry he could barely swallow and he worried he wouldn't be able to speak.

As he turned to face the body of the church, the sea of faces swam in front of him. He unconsciously searched the congregation for Ally until self-preservation kicked in. If he saw her, he would never get through this. Tearing his attention away, he found himself staring again at his father's coffin. The unfamiliar photograph gazed back at him.

Then he was barrelling down the aisle with his head down, aware only of the knot in his chest drawing ever tighter, threatening to choke him. He burst through the double doors of the church and out into the sunshine, gulping in air like a diver resurfacing. Searching wildly, his need to escape took precedence over everything else. Locking onto the garden alongside the church, he stumbled towards the nearest bench and sank into it, frightened that at any moment his lungs might burst.

*A*lly sat on a bench next to Callum, her pulse racing.

"Just breathe," he said.

"I'm sorry," she murmured, her fingers finding her grandmother's ring and turning it in endless circles. "Maybe you should go inside. No point in both of us sitting out here."

"I'm not going in without you. Either we both go in, or we both sit here. Either way is fine by me."

She nodded, trying to reason with herself. Tom would be so disappointed in her. She couldn't let him down.

"Alright," she said, reaching down to straighten out one leg, locking the brace.

She pulled herself upright, locking the other brace and sliding her arms into the cuffs of her crutches, automatically adjusting her centre of gravity.

"Are you sure about this?" Callum asked, standing up and straightening his tie.

"If I don't go in now, I never will."

"Okay then. Let's do this."

She began walking, placing her legs carefully on the uneven ground. The last thing she needed right now was to face-plant. She felt Callum stiffen beside her and she stopped walking to look up. Jack stood just a few feet away, staring at her.

Suddenly, she forgot how to breathe.

---

*T*heir eyes locked.

She's standing.

Jack wanted to ask her how but he didn't have the words. Her body language, the look on her face, everything about her screamed that he needed to be careful. He searched relentlessly for an opening, a sign, anything. She shook her head slowly, her eyes clouded with emotion so thick that he couldn't penetrate.

He lowered his gaze to her legs. She was using crutches, her hands gripping the handles so tightly that her knuckles glowed white. But she was standing - no wheelchair. His heart soared.

"You're walking."

The words hung in the air between them. Every time he had imagined this moment, he had never thought that she would just be standing in front of him like this. It was a miracle.

"You need to get out of here," Callum interrupted, taking a step towards him.

Jack put his hands up in self-defence, automatically taking a step backwards as he tore his gaze away from Ally to face Callum's anger head-on.

"Fair warning, Jack."

Hatred spilled out between each word as Jack's body reacted, breaking into a cold sweat.

"I'm sorry," he said quickly, taking another step backwards.

Callum pushed him roughly and Jack stumbled back, caught off guard.

"Don't make me say it again."

"I'm sorry, I – "

"Save it," Callum hissed. "Bottom line here? Not interested."

Jack had difficulty thinking straight as confusion, guilt and fear swirled in his head and his heart, pulling him off-centre. The fury that rolled off Callum did not surprise him. He opened his mouth to speak again but Callum immediately shut him down.

"You need to go."

"I didn't mean to – "

"Where the hell do you get off?" Callum demanded, close enough for Jack to see the fire in his eyes. He pointed at the church beside them. "Your father's in there, Jack - his *coffin* is in there! And you stand out here and say you're sorry?" He shook his head, almost foaming at the mouth with the effort it took to keep his temper under control. "It's a little late for sorry, don't you think?"

His heart sank, the truth slicing through it like a knife through butter.

"Callum, please!" Ally cried.

"I don't want to fight," he said. "I just… I wanted to say I'm sorry."

"You have no idea, do you?" Callum frowned, shaking his head. "You just thought that if you couldn't see what was going on here, it wasn't happening? Do you even realise how selfish that was, what that did to him? To Ally, to me?"

Jack struggled to keep it together. Every word weakened his resolve, wearing him down. He took another step backwards, closely followed by Callum.

"Look, I know – "

"You know nothing!" Callum shouted, bearing down on him.

"Stop it!" Ally begged. "Please don't do this!"

"Why couldn't you have come back last week? Or last month, or a year ago? What the hell is the point of coming back for his funeral?"

"Hey!" Maggie demanded, appearing out of nowhere. "What's going on here?"

Jack glanced over Callum's shoulder at Maggie, standing with her arm around a shaken Ally. Jane stood behind them, watching closely.

"Stop this, right now!" Maggie hissed at Callum.

Callum glared at him, struggling to control his temper, before finally turning to re-join Ally, Maggie and Jane. The four of them stood there, watching Jack in stony silence, united against him.

"You've got every right to be pissed," he said, addressing Callum.

"You think?" Callum's nostrils flared. "I have no idea why you even came back here. It's too late for Tom and we don't need you anymore - we needed you four years ago but you disappeared like the coward you are and left us to deal with everything, which we did - without you."

Faint strains of a hymn carried out on the wind from the funeral service still progressing inside the church.

Callum took a step towards him.

"Do you even know what that did to him, you running off like that? Do you have a clue at all?"

Jack's heart hammered in his chest and he opened his mouth to speak, but Callum wasn't interested in anything he had to say. Callum took another step towards him and grabbed the collar of his jacket. Backing him up against the nearest tree, Callum drew his fist back.

"Don't! Please!"

"I'm sorry," Callum said, addressing Ally while keeping his eyes firmly on Jack. "I know this wasn't what you wanted but it's what he deserves."

His fist hovered in mid-air, his grip on Jack's shirt so tight that it left him with no choice but to take whatever was coming to him.

"You walked out on all of us that day, not just her," he said, to Jack this time. "You don't get a second chance after something like that."

Jack's heart raced, the bark from the tree digging into his back.

"Don't do this - not now, not like this," Jane begged, walking over to them. "You promised."

Callum turned to her and Jack felt the grip on his shirt loosen. He held his breath. Slowly, Callum released his shirt altogether and took a step back. Jack straightened out his jacket and shirt and stole a quick glance at Ally. She stared back at him in silent desperation, Maggie's arm around her shoulders.

Jane had managed to position her body between himself and Callum, forming a physical barrier. She snaked her arm around Callum's waist and tried to draw him away but he stood his ground.

"I never meant for any of this to happen," Jack said, addressing Ally.

The weight of their collective gaze fell upon him. Ally had tears rolling freely down her cheeks, which only added to the ache in his heart.

"Are you okay? I'm sorry, I – "

Callum shoved Jane aside and threw a punch that knocked Jack back into the trunk of the tree so fast he never even saw it coming. There was a roaring in his ears as he slid to the ground. Before he could get to his feet, Callum threw another punch, his fist connecting with Jack's cheek and jarring his entire body. He barely had enough time to register what was happening before he was hit a third time, making his head almost literally spin. Callum reached down to grab his shirt front and hauled him unceremoniously to his feet.

"You selfish bastard!" he yelled, only inches from his face. "Not one damn word from you in four years and *now* you ask if she's okay?"

Jack shook his head to clear it of the ringing in his ears. His vision swam, and he had a flashback to one night a lifetime ago, recalling the power behind Callum's right hook.

His head was on fire. Acting entirely from instinct, he threw a desperate punch that caught Callum off guard and sent him reeling backwards, staggering to stay on his feet. Seizing his chance, Jack flew after him, tackling him around the waist as they both hit the ground, scrambling to get a decent grip on each other. Frustration and anger boiled over, finesse giving way to raw emotion. Voices in the background became white noise as he fought to gain the upper hand. Guilt was pushed aside, super-seded by the desperate need to survive. This wasn't like any fight he had ever been in before. Yet despite the fact that he felt he deserved it, his survival instinct was too strong to be suppressed.

Out of nowhere, rough hands on his shoulders forced him bodily upwards. He scrambled to maintain his equilibrium, panting heavily. Callum was facing him, restrained by men he didn't recognise. The noise was deafening but he couldn't distinguish the ringing in his ears from the multitude of voices that surrounded them. Callum spat fresh blood out of the corner of his mouth.

"Get the hell out of here," he panted, glaring at Jack. "And this time, don't come back."

Jack heard every word, crystal clear.

With some difficulty, he shrugged out of the hold on him and pitched to the side, straightening up and wiping his hand across his mouth. Pain rocketed through his body. The metallic taste of blood welled up in his mouth and he spat it out, pulling feebly at his ripped shirt. He glanced down to see blood splattering the front of it, spilling over onto the torn sleeve of his jacket. He was suddenly aware of dozens of faces staring at him.

He searched out the only one that really mattered; Ally.

She stood next to Maggie and Jane, tears streaming down her face as they tried to comfort her.

He'd just made everything worse.

"I'm sorry," he mumbled, staggering away from them all.

He ignored the stares as he made his way back to his car, shrugging off the offers of help. He fell into his car and sat there, hanging onto the steering wheel as if it would save him.

I'm sorry Dad.

CHAPTER FIVE

"A coward is incapable of exhibiting love;
it is the prerogative of the brave."
- Mahatma Gandhi

$\mathcal{M}$aggie drove home, snatching the keys off Callum
and giving him a filthy look that quickly silenced
him when he tried to protest.

Ally stared out the window, ignoring Callum's numerous
attempts at an apology. What was the point of apologising now?
It was too late for that. The two goals she had for today were to
say goodbye to Tom and make it through the funeral without
losing her shit in front of Jack - neither of which she accom-
plished. She felt sick. It didn't help that the air was so thick with
tension that she could barely breathe.

She replayed the scene over and over in her head.

Jack looked so different. He looked battle-weary, as if this
wasn't the only fight he'd been in recently. He had a cut on his
cheek and fading bruises near his hairline. His hair was shorter

and his green eyes held an empty, haunted look that broke her heart. What had happened to him? Was it grief? Was it the guilt he carried? Was it his conscience torturing him? Whatever it was, it was so deeply ingrained in him now that it physically changed him. He looked older.

He also looked surprised to see her standing. Didn't he know? Why didn't Tom tell him? If he had known, would he have come home sooner? Her head ached as she turned the questions around and around, only coming up with more questions.

By the time they pulled into her driveway she was near breaking point. She just wanted to get inside and lock the door before she lost it completely. As soon as the car came to a stop, she threw open her door and leaned her crutches against it, lifting her legs out.

"Ally - come on, just wait a minute, please?"

She ignored Callum, pulling herself up using the back of the seat and the door, throwing her hips forward as she heard her braces lock. Reaching down to check them, she grabbed her crutches and slid her arms into them, taking a couple of shaky steps before pushing the door shut behind her.

"Do you want me to stay for a while?" Maggie called after her.

"No thanks. I just need some time to myself," she called back over her shoulder, not bothering to turn around.

"I'm sorry, okay?" Callum called. "Oh, come on! You saw him, the smug bastard! He just expected an apology would be enough, after everything he did?"

"You promised," she said tightly, making her way up the front path towards her house. She could feel his gaze burning into her back as the conversation continued behind her.

"Go talk to her," Maggie ordered.

"I've tried, you heard me! She won't – "

"You made a promise and you broke it, what the hell did you expect?"

"That is such bullshit, don't pretend he didn't deserve it!"

"Of course he deserved it! For what it's worth, I don't blame you, but that's not the damn point is it? The point is she asked you not to do this today and you promised, then went ahead and did it anyway!"

"I only promised not to – "

"Just stop making excuses and go talk to her!" Jane hissed.

"Fine!"

Ally heard him starting up the path behind her and she gritted her teeth, wishing she could walk faster. He caught up with her as she climbed the front steps. She tried to ignore him, placing her crutches on the step above, pulling her body upwards and watching as her feet swung onto the step.

"Please, will you just listen?"

He wasn't going to let this lie. Drawing in a ragged breath, she stopped but she didn't turn around.

"I really mean it, I am sorry, and you have every right to be pissed off at me. If he'd just stayed away from us, I could have handled it, but that bullshit apology of his? He should've backed off. I gave him enough chances."

The sincerity in his voice wasn't enough to diffuse her temper.

"So, screw the fact that you made me a promise - it's all his fault?" she demanded, trying her best to glare at him over her shoulder without losing her balance.

"No! Well, yeah, but – "

"Save it, this is getting us nowhere."

She resumed her climb up the steps but he marched up and stood in front of her, blocking her path.

"Just tell me what it is I did that was so wrong!" he demanded. "I never promised this wouldn't happen - he deserved it!"

"That's not the point!" she blurted out, angry tears barely held in check. "And what if he goes to the cops and you get landed with an assault charge? Will it be worth it then?"

"He's not gonna go to the cops!"

"How the hell do you know that?"

"My moneys on him packing his bags as we speak. He's got a shitty track record for sticking around when the going gets tough, remember?"

Ally's heart sank to hear him give voice to her fears.

"It's obvious you've never had to bury anyone you love," she said. "I've been there - twice - and let me tell you, it never gets any easier. What you did today - worst possible timing."

"I'm sorry I broke my promise to you and I'm sorry about my shitty timing. But I'm not sorry for what I did. He had it coming."

"I was dreading today," she said as she choked down the disappointment and fear. "I was dreading the funeral, seeing Jack, all of it. But it was Tom's funeral. That's why I asked you to promise not to do this. Not because he didn't deserve it but because it was Tom's funeral and we were there to say goodbye. And we never even got to do that."

"I'm sorry about that, I really am. But did you expect me to just let Jack do whatever the hell he wanted today? Even though I could see what it was doing to you?"

"Don't make this about me!" she cried. "You were thinking about yourself! I know you're pissed at him but taking out your frustrations on him at his father's funeral was just wrong! Why can't you see that?"

Callum rubbed his forehead with the tips of his fingertips as if trying to massage the problem away. She knew she had hit home and she was glad he'd got the message but it didn't take any of the fire out of her temper.

"Look, I – "

"I don't want to do this now. I'm tired and I just need some time to myself."

"Come on, can we just – "

"Just move, please."

"Ally – "

"Move!" she glared up at him until he finally stepped aside.

"I'll come by later," he said as she climbed the final two steps in silence. "Maybe we can talk properly then."

"Don't bother. I'm tired, I'm gonna take a nap. I just want to forget this day ever happened."

"What if he turns up here again?"

She stopped in her tracks and took a deep breath, fighting the anger that rose up inside her.

"Then I'll deal with it," she said, turning to face him. "I suggest you do the same."

"What the hell does that mean?"

"It means you need to get a handle on this. Don't let it consume you. You need to let it go."

"Right," he nodded. "Let it go. You mean like you have?"

She glared at him and he shoved his hands into his pockets, wincing at the movement.

"You look like shit," she mumbled, her brief glance indicating his battered face and dishevelled clothing.

"I'm fine. It was worth it."

She shook her head and turned her back on him.

"See you tomorrow."

She heard him talking to Jane and Maggie as she unlocked her front door, but by the time she got inside and closed the door after her, the car had pulled out of her driveway.

*J*ack didn't remember driving back to his father's house. He seemed to snap out of the haze as he stumbled through the front door, collapsing against it as it closed behind him. Callum's words echoed in his ears, each word beating against the inside of his skull like a hammer blow. Running a hand over his face, he winced as his fingers brushed over the cut Callum's fist had opened up in his cheek.

Calling on all his remaining strength, he forced himself to stand up and make his way into the bathroom.

He grabbed a towel and held it under cold water, dabbing cautiously at the cuts and bruises on his face. He stared at his reflection, holding the wet towel against his cheek. It was as if a stranger stared back at him.

Callum was right, about everything. He didn't deserve to be at the funeral, his apology was outrageously inadequate and he had no idea what Ally had been through.

He replayed the moment in his mind, seeing her standing in front of him again, no wheelchair, heartache etched into her face. He still couldn't believe his father hadn't told him, despite their pact. How long had she been walking? How did it happen? What changed?

He rinsed out the bloody towel under more water, pressing it back on his cheek in a futile effort to reduce the swelling.

Once again, he saw the pure hatred in Callum's face, the sense of betrayal and anger tumbling out of him.

It was exactly how he feared it would be.

---

*a*lly sat at her kitchen table, watching through the window as the breeze lifted the leaves on the trees in her backyard. She couldn't get Jack out of her head. The hope and relief written all over his face when he saw her standing; the sorrow as he apologised; the reluctant acceptance as Callum landed that first punch. But what hurt most of all was the raw pain and guilt as he had walked away, bleeding.

What if Callum was right? What if he thought that, after today, there wasn't any point in staying? What if he had gone back to Tom's house, packed his bags and taken off again, for good this time? She may never get the chance to talk to him.

After all this time, all these years of wondering, he was back, only to disappear again just as quickly?

From deep down inside of her, through the pain and the anger, a desperate need welled up. Where had he been all this time? What had happened to hollow him out like that? She wanted to tell him that she was alright, that he didn't need to feel guilty about the accident. She wanted to ask him why he left, and now she didn't care if the truth hurt more than the unsettled ignorance of the last few years.

She straightened her shoulders and took a deep breath. Last time she didn't have any choice, she was unconscious in a hospital bed, broken and helpless. But not this time. This time she was awake and determined not to let it happen again. She deserved answers and she deserved to be heard. He owed her that.

"*H*ey - watch it!"
"Don't be such a baby."

"Some bedside manner you have there," Callum grumbled, wincing.

Maggie handed him a beer, peering over Jane's shoulder as she treated the cut on his cheek with antiseptic. She popped her own beer open and took a mouthful before flopping down on the couch beside him.

"You're welcome to do this yourself, you know."

Callum frowned and pushed Jane's hand away.

"It's fine, just leave it."

"Suit yourself."

Jane picked up the antiseptic bottle and medical kit and took it back to the kitchen. He stood up and began to pace the room, taking a long swallow from his bottle. Okay, so Ally was pissed off at him. Wouldn't be the first time. She'd get over it. In the meantime, what the hell were they going to do about Jack? He had half a mind to head over to Tom's place right now and make sure he was packing his bags.

Jane came back from the kitchen, scooping up her beer and dropping onto the couch beside Maggie.

"So," Jane said. "Do you think he'll stick around for a while?"

"I can't see it."

"No way, not after today. The truth hurts," Callum snapped, hoping like hell he was right.

An uneasy silence filled the room.

"Can you believe him?" he demanded. "Jack? I mean, what the hell was he thinking? He just shows up here and thinks 'I'm sorry' will magically fix everything?"

"He came home for Tom, for the funeral," Jane said, nursing her beer in her lap.

"Well, the funeral's over so if he's got any brains he'll be out of here by morning - if he hasn't disappeared already," Callum said.

"Don't you want to talk to him? Find out where he's – "

"I'm not interested in where he's been or what he's done. He chose to leave, no one made him go. He doesn't get to stroll back here and try to pick up where he left off. He made his choice."

"I'm not saying I disagree with you," Maggie said. "But I just think it took a lot of guts for him to show his face today. It can't have been easy. He gets credit for that in my book, not that it changes anything."

"Like I said, he came for Tom's funeral," Callum snapped. "That's it."

"Yeah, I know, but he did try to talk to Ally yesterday. He didn't have to do that."

"And?"

"Well, I just think that if he had intended to come home, go to the funeral and then leave straight afterwards, he wouldn't have bothered."

"What's your point?"

"Just that maybe he didn't plan on coming home *just* for the funeral? Maybe he's planning to stick around for a while?"

"Do you think so?" Jane asked, sitting forward on the couch.

"Maybe. Who knows?"

Callum sank down into an armchair and peeled at the label on his bottle nervously.

"I don't know. If I'd gotten the reception he did today, I probably wouldn't be hanging around for long," Jane said quietly.

"Well, if he knows what's good for him, he better stay the hell away from me - and Ally. She doesn't need this shit, she's been through enough."

"Yeah, well you're hardly helping the situation," Maggie said.

"What the hell does that mean?"

"It's not exactly a secret. I've lost count of the amount of times you've said you'd rip his head off his shoulders if you saw him again."

"Yeah? So?"

"No one blames you for feeling like that," Jane said. "It's only natural, you have every right. We're just saying that Ally knows how you feel too, and she's bound to be worried about how you're gonna deal with all this."

"I'll tell you right now how I'm gonna deal with this, I'm gonna make damn sure he stays the hell away from her!" Callum shook his head, annoyed at the shift in focus. "So, you just leave Jack to me. It's her we need to keep an eye on, not me."

He took another swig from his bottle, wishing it were something stronger than beer.

---

*A*lly made her way to the front gate and paused, staring at the unfamiliar car in the driveway at Tom's house.

Jack's car.

The realisation was quickly followed by relief that he was still here and a wave of anxiety about what might happen next. Slowly, she made her way up the path.

How many years had she been coming here? She knew this house as well as her own. It was unnerving, the thought of walking inside knowing that Tom wasn't going to be there. Drawing herself up straight, she tried to put him out of her mind. It was Jack she was here to see.

She paused briefly at the bottom of the few steps leading to the porch that swept across the front of the house. Slowly, she began to climb. It only took her a couple of minutes but by the time she got to the top, all the bravado and determination she had felt in her kitchen half an hour ago had evaporated. What was she going to say? Where was she supposed to begin?

"Hi."

She looked up to find Jack standing in the doorway. She froze. She had been lying to herself, she realised too late. She wasn't ready for this, not by a long shot.

"Come inside," he said, his desperate gaze holding hers. "Please?"

He had changed out of the torn shirt and jacket and stood before her in jeans and a dark blue t-shirt. Looking very much the worse for wear, one of his eyes was slightly swollen and the cut on his cheek she'd noticed earlier looked much angrier.

Her heart pounded against her ribcage and she fought the impulse to turn and make her way back to the car. As if he could read her mind, he moved aside, silently pleading with her. Slowly, she followed him. Standing in the hallway, she fought back tears. It felt wrong, like they were trespassing somehow.

"I wasn't expecting you," Jack said quietly, closing the door behind her. "But I'm glad you're here."

He stood facing her, shoving his hands deep into his pockets. Had his eyes always been that shade of green? They seemed darker, heavier somehow. God, what was she doing here?

"Ally…"

Her hands gripped the handles of her crutches even tighter. The questions bolted out of her before she could stop them.

"Why'd you do it? Why'd you leave like that?"

The silence seemed to buzz in her ears, seconds stretching out.

"Why do you think?" he whispered, his eyes brimming with tears.

"That's not good enough," she shot back, tilting her chin in defiance. "I need to hear you say it - you owe me that."

"You're right, I'm sorry," he said, running a hand through his hair. "Look, I... this could take a while. Come through to the living room, I'll get us something to drink."

She frowned, afraid of losing her resolve if she moved any further into the house. Before she could answer though, he walked into the living room and she had no choice but to follow.

She had last been here two weeks ago, for dinner. The house looked exactly the same except for the glaringly obvious fact that Tom was missing. Her heart ached for him. If he were here, he'd be the buffer she felt they desperately needed now. Without him it was too raw.

Jack poured the drinks, his back to her. To his left, on the side table, was an almost-empty glass that he topped up. Clearly, it wasn't his first drink today. She couldn't blame him.

He turned back to her, holding a glass in each hand, indicating the couch. "Shall we sit down?"

She ignored the couch and headed for the small dining table at the end of the room instead. She wanted to put something solid between them, hoping it would help her concentrate. She could feel his eyes burning into her back as she lowered herself into a chair, leaning her crutches against the table beside her. He set the glasses down on the table and pulled out the chair opposite her. As the chair's legs scraped against the hardwood floor, she silently begged her trembling hands not to betray her. Reaching for her glass, she took a quick sip.

Tom had been the one to teach her about whisky. He'd taught her about the good, the bad, the difference between blended and single malts, when to have water with it and when to have it neat. It was yet another reminder that he was missing from her life, from all their lives.

"What do you remember about the accident?" Jack asked quietly.

A black void where her memories should be. She stared into the glass she held with both hands on the table in front of her, not trusting herself to look at him.

"Nothing. I don't remember a thing. Callum told me what happened, after."

"What did he say?"

"That it wasn't your fault."

Why did she sound so frightened? She cleared her throat, mustering up the courage to look across the table at him.

"He said there was nothing you could have done, that the other car came out of nowhere."

His expression was guarded and she waited for him to elaborate but he didn't. She seized her chance, before she lost her nerve completely.

"I want to know why you left like that, if it wasn't your fault. Was it because of what happened to me?"

He shook his head and she tried to distance herself from his obvious pain. She couldn't afford empathy if she was to get through this. She needed answers.

"Was it?" she pressed. "You were gone when I woke up from surgery, Jack. You knew what happened to me. Did you leave because of that, because you didn't want to be with me? I want the truth. I can take it."

He shook his head, swallowing back tears.

"No."

"You're lying."

"No, I'm not. I – "

"You're lying!" she cried, anger bursting forth.

"No! I'm not lying, I swear to you," he insisted desperately, leaning forward. "I left because of me, because of what I did!"

"What the hell does that mean?"

He looked like a deer caught in the headlights. Something was going on behind his eyes that she couldn't read and she frowned, searching deeper.

"I was driving. It was my fault."

"So, you left because you felt guilty?"

"I left because I was scared."

"I was scared too - I woke up and you were gone!"

Breaking it down like that hurt much more than she expected. All the things she couldn't say - the fear that had overwhelmed her and pulled her under and nearly destroyed her - manifested as tears, overflowing and running down her cheeks.

"I'm so sorry," he whispered, staring at his hands on the table. "I thought you'd hate me… I thought you'd all hate me."

"So, you just decided to run away instead?"

He didn't answer, and anger and betrayal overwhelmed her as his face blurred.

"I wish I could take it all back, I wish I could change everything," he whispered.

"You can't."

"I know. I'm so sorry. I should've stayed, I should've – "

"I'm not interested in hearing about what you should've done," she snapped. "I know what you should've done, but you didn't, did you?"

Jack looked devastated but she couldn't help the words that came tumbling out.

"I lay in that hospital bed, counting the holes in the ceiling tiles, thinking about all the things that I would never be able to do again, and I kept thinking that if you were there, it would be okay - that you being there would mean that everything was going to be okay. But you weren't." She held his gaze, binding him to her as surely as if she had used ropes or chains. "I hated you for that. I hated you for leaving, I hated you for not even saying goodbye, for not having the guts to talk to me before you left, for being such a coward."

Tears spilled down his cheeks but she wasn't finished.

"Why didn't you call? Or write or email - why didn't you at least try? Did you even think about me at all?"

"I never stopped thinking about you," he whispered, chin quivering.

It was on the tip of her tongue to call him a liar again but something stopped her. His eyes searched hers and for an instant, he invited her inside his heart, his soul. What she saw there took her breath away.

"I'm sorry," he whispered. "I never meant for any of this to happen. I was weak and I was wrong and I'm so sorry."

She hung her head, her hair falling forward to shield her expression as she swiped a tear off her cheek with a quick flick of her finger.

"I always meant to come home," he said. "I just never thought it'd be for Dad's funeral."

Her heart seized at his reference to Tom and the hole in her heart magnified. Out of the corner of her eye, she saw him running a hand down his face.

"The longer I stayed away, the more I thought you'd hate me. And after a while, I didn't think that coming home would do any good."

The silence mounted around them. She stared at her drink, not having the strength to lift the glass and take another sip.

"It took me a long time to realise you weren't coming back," she said, her hair falling away from her face as she looked up.

The air around them crackled with words they couldn't bring themselves to say, or hear. Sometime over the past few minutes her anger had dissipated. The disappointment and betrayal, the heartache - all of it had gone, withered inside of her. What remained was an intense sadness, a longing for the lost years and the road not travelled. She wasn't the only one who had suffered. He had suffered too, she could see that now.

Jack reached over to lay a trembling hand on hers. Her skin tingled, memories flooding back, stealing her strength and adding to the overall sense of emptiness.

"I never meant to hurt you," he whispered. "Please Ally. I'm so sorry."

*J*ack sat at the table and stared at the space across from him that Ally had vacated. The sun had gone down an hour ago, plunging the house into darkness, yet he didn't move. He could still feel her hand beneath his and he flexed his fingers, longing to touch her again.

His heart had soared when he had seen her standing outside the church, but from what he had seen since, it was clear that all was not as it seemed. He had been so close to throwing his bag into the back of the car and taking off again. And then he saw a car pull up in front of the house. He felt like a voyeur, watching as she got out of the car, walked up the front path and up the steps. His heart beat so loud in his chest that he thought it might break a rib. Yes, she was walking, but obviously it wasn't as simple as that. She seemed to have limited control over her body and he desperately wanted to ask her about that but he wasn't sure he had the right to and he was terrified at what she might tell him.

His self-respect plummeted to an all-time low. He had lied to her by omission. That wasn't part of his plan. He had planned to tell her the truth, he was going to lay it at her feet and let her decide then if she would forgive him or not. He had not planned to give her half-truths and echoes.

What have I done?

After everything that had happened over the past few days, all his noble intentions, his promises to his father, the bargains he made with himself, why lie now? Why not tell her the truth - all of it? The answer seemed simple enough: what if, when she knew the truth, she turned him away? It was as if he had returned to the same crossroads of four years earlier. Stay or go?

She didn't want to talk about the accident at all. She barely mentioned it, she said she didn't remember it. Was that a blessing or a curse? She wasn't angry about it either, she was angry that he had left the way he did, without saying goodbye. He groaned, berating himself once again. If only he had stayed and talked to her then. Maybe she would have forgiven him. Maybe she would have hated him even more. Maybe she still would, when he told her the truth now.

A knock on the door startled him. If Ally had come back, he needed to tell her now, before he lost his nerve. He pushed the chair back and headed for the front door, flicking on the porch light on the way. Readying himself mentally, he opened the door.

"I thought I made myself clear earlier," Callum said, his voice laced with anger.

Jack's heart sank.

"I told you to stay the hell away from her, didn't I?"

"I don't want to fight again," Jack sighed. "It's been a long day. Can't we just take this up again tomorrow?"

"What was she doing here? What did you say to her?"

"She came to me - I didn't go to her," he frowned, shifting his weight as he made the connection. "And how the hell did you know she was here anyway, are you stalking me?"

Callum just raised his eyebrows.

"You're *stalking* me?" Jack was incredulous, his blood boiling.

"Don't flatter yourself," Callum huffed, planting his feet on the doorstep. "I saw her car outside earlier. I want to know what you said to her."

"You want to know if I told her about what happened that night."

Callum glared at him.

"The answer is no, I didn't. But why the hell didn't you? You were there, you knew."

"Because it wasn't my place to tell her - it was yours."

"Jesus, Callum! You just let her think God knows what, all this time?"

"What the hell do you care what she thought? You weren't here, remember? I didn't tell her because what would be the point?"

"What would be the point?" Jack repeated indignantly. "She would've known the truth!"

"That you were a coward? She figured that one out for herself when she woke up and you were gone!"

Jack opened his mouth to speak, but Callum cut him off.

"Don't you dare come back here and start blaming me or anyone else! No one told you to go, you made that choice yourself! You did the wrong thing then and by coming back now and stirring it all up again, all you're doing is making it worse. You're here for your own selfish reasons, not because of Tom or because of her!"

"I'm trying to make it right!"

"How?"

Jack was dumbfounded, knowing that he had asked himself that question a million times and come up empty.

"She doesn't need you anymore. The best thing you can do now is just crawl back into whatever hole you crawled out of and leave her alone."

"No. I'm not going anywhere, not this time."

"That's your master plan? Seriously?"

Jack glared at him in silence, his anger mounting.

"Oh, come on, you gotta admit, that's a reckless statement,

especially for you. You disappear when the going gets tough remember?"

"That's not what happened and you know it."

"Do I? Because that's what it looked like from where I was standing!"

"You know damn well why I left!" Jack blurted out. "You knew what I did - you were there!"

"Yeah, I knew what you did. Big deal! You were trying to save her life, she wouldn't have blamed you!" he said hotly. "You did the wrong thing Jack, you should've stayed."

Jack stared at him, his heart racing. He thought about the relationship they used to have, how close they were. Like brothers. And now this; strangers. Worse than that; enemies.

"I made a mistake. I won't make that mistake again."

Callum shook his head, eyeballing Jack as he took a step backwards, forcing his hands back into his pockets.

"Here's the thing, you made your choice, now you have to live with it, just like the rest of us. You can't change what happened and if you stick around you're only gonna hurt her again. Is that what you want?"

Jack opened his mouth to reply but Callum wasn't finished.

"She was just starting to get her life back together, after everything she's been through. Don't rip it all apart again. Do the right thing this time. Leave."

Devastated, Jack couldn't think of a single thing to say in reply. He watched Callum walk down the steps and along the street to his car, get in and drive away. He was still standing frozen in the doorway, watching the space where Callum's car had been, several minutes later.

CHAPTER SIX

"Your future is not determined by others but by your own choices - the choices you make today and tomorrow."
- Maori Proverb

The morning sun splashed columns of light across Ally's living room. From her place on the floor, she watched the light play across the wooden beams above her and tried to recall every word of her conversation with Jack the day before.

She spent half the night sitting at her dining room table, trying to imagine just what Jack might have been going through over the past four years. It was clear he was a changed man and, except for that brief glimpse, the fact that she couldn't see beyond the façade bothered her.

Callum knelt beside her on the floor, gently manipulating her right leg at the knee before pushing it up towards her hips and then back down again. The usual feeling of detachment gnawed at her. He might as well have been holding someone else's leg in his hands for all the sensation she felt. She had a friend from rehab who had sensation below his injury point although he had no movement. She often wondered if that would be better or worse than the numbness. Her friend suffered with spasms whereas she did not. Perhaps it was some kind of cosmic balancing act? Either way, facts were facts. Wishing things were different didn't change anything.

Should she tell Callum about her conversation with Jack last night? After his heartfelt apology this morning, she was tempted to but now he seemed so withdrawn. She couldn't blame him. The funeral yesterday was brutal, on all of them.

He laid her right leg down on the yoga mat and picked up the left, positioning it carefully in both hands before repeating the motion: bend knee, push towards hips, lower leg to mat, repeat. Range-of-motion exercises were necessary to keep her lower body supple and healthy. They were as much a part of her life as massage, swimming, pain meds and everything else. She thought that it would get easier over time, just like the other aspects of her new life. She had been wrong. As grateful as she was for Callum's help, it didn't take away the dull ache in the pit of her stomach as she watched him push and pull, rotate and extend. Annoyed with herself, she pushed the self-pitying thoughts away once again. She had fallen down that pit once before.

"I saw your car outside Tom's place yesterday," Callum said.

She looked over at him sharply. He had laid her leg back on the mat and was sitting on the floor at her feet, staring at her.

"I came over to talk to you," he said. "After what happened at the funeral, I wanted to apologise again. When I saw you weren't here I drove by Tom's place on the way home."

"I'm sorry," she adjusted her arm beneath the pillow, suddenly uncomfortable. "I couldn't figure out how to tell you... and I didn't want you to get mad."

"I'm not mad, I just don't get it. One minute you don't want to see him, the next minute you're going over there?"

She blinked back tears.

"Come on," he said, his expression softening as he got to his feet. "We're done here. Let's get more comfortable."

She sniffed and sat up, grateful for the distraction. Callum pulled her wheelchair closer and she reached back for it, adjusting its angle to her body and pulling on the brake. Bending her knees and pulling her legs in close to her body, she counted silently, pushing herself upwards on the count of three and aiming her backside towards the seat.

Callum rolled up the yoga mat and set it down on the table behind him.

"I needed to see him," she said, hoping her voice wouldn't betray her. "I needed to talk to him about what happened."

"I get that. It was probably the right thing to do."

"Was it?" she murmured, fighting back tears. "I'm not so sure anymore."

He walked over to the armchair and sank into it wearily. She turned her chair to follow him, trying to rein in her fears.

"I thought it would help," she said, trying her best to explain. "I thought that if I told him how much it hurt, it would feel better to have said it, owned it like that. And I thought maybe if he told me why he left, I could deal with it and put it behind me."

"Do you?" he asked quietly. "Feel better, I mean?"

"No. Not really. I didn't get any answers, either. Just a boat-load more questions."

"What do you mean?"

She shook her head, trying to unwrap it all over again and failing miserably. "It didn't seem to matter that I didn't blame him for the accident. He still said he felt responsible for what happened, that's why he left. I kinda guessed that part already."

"No surprises there, then."

"I guess not," she said, fidgeting with her grandmother's ring. "I just get the feeling there's more to it, that there's something he's not telling me."

"I'm sure there's a lot he's not telling you."

She winced.

"Look," he said, leaning forward. "Here's a recap of the situation; he left four years ago and he only came back for Tom's funeral. Does he feel guilty about that? Sure, why not. But did he even try to call you or me or anyone apart from Tom in the past four years? Did he make any effort at all to come home during that time? No, because he didn't give a shit. I know it hurts like hell and I'm sorry, but it's the truth. I don't know about you but I'm all out of second chances. I don't think he deserves one, not after that."

"I know how you feel about him. I know how much it hurt when he – "

"This isn't about me, it's about you."

"No, it's not. It's not just about me. I wasn't the only one he left behind."

"Yeah, well, you were the only one he left behind in the ICU."

She felt as if she'd been kicked in the chest.

"I'm sorry," he said, running a hand down his face with a heavy sigh. "I didn't mean it to come out like that."

"It's okay," she murmured, trying hard to recover. "You're right."

She could feel herself losing ground, the past and present overlapping, getting mixed up in her head. Just a week ago, things had seemed so simple.

Callum was staring at her, waiting. Suddenly she felt guilty. He didn't need this. He was having a tough enough time as it was. She sat up straight, taking a deep breath and conjuring up a fleeting smile that she hoped would be convincing.

"It doesn't matter now, does it? It's all water under the bridge. What's done is done."

Internally, she cringed at the forced indifference in her voice. He wouldn't be fooled. She would have to make more of an effort. She opted for a diversionary tactic, giving herself time to get herself together.

"I need coffee. You want one?" she asked.

She didn't wait for a response, turning abruptly to head for the kitchen.

FOUR YEARS EARLIER

The impact was mind-blowing, sending a shuddering jolt throughout his entire body that turned his limbs to jelly. Time stopped as they skidded across the road, the buzzing in his ears blocking everything else out. Then they were upside down. He squinted out through the windshield, his brain struggling to process what was happening. He felt like he was moving simultaneously in slow motion and fast-forward, and it crossed his mind that this might be how he died. A strange calmness washed over him. His fate was completely out of his hands.

The car suddenly bounced as it left the road, ripping through a fence, the trees ahead rapidly filling the windshield as he mentally braced himself for the impact. The crazy rollercoaster ride ended as abruptly as it began, jolting him again, throwing a spear of pain through his shoulder and neck that left him breathless.

And then there was silence. Buzzing, humming, vibrating silence.

He hung by his seatbelt upside down for several moments as his mind and body tried to comprehend and compensate.

"Callum?"

His voice was croaky and weak and it scared him. He reached behind for Ally but his sense of direction was wonky and he watched his hand waver in mid-air, mesmerised for a moment before terror took over.

"Callum? Ally!"

The silence buzzed in his ears. He reached for Callum again, the seatbelt restricting his movements. Gravity toyed with him. He took a moment to draw a deep breath and assess the situation, forcing the panic down into his gut. His hand groped blindly at his waist, finding the seatbelt release and popping it open. He collapsed heavily onto the inside roof of the car, a low groan escaping as a stabbing pain shot through his shoulder. He tried to breathe through the heavy air, something sharp digging into his knee.

"Callum?"

He was unconscious, hanging limply in his seat. Reaching over with trembling fingers to feel the pulse in Callum's neck.

"Thank God." His heart raced wildly. "Come on, wake up."

Turning his attention to the back seat now, he saw Ally. She was also suspended by her seatbelt, long dark hair almost touching the roof beneath her. Her arms and legs dangled, reminding him of a rag doll. He twisted around, pain shooting through his arm and shoulder as he jammed himself between the seats, feeling for the pulse in her neck, praying under his breath the whole time. Finding it at last, he fought back tears of relief.

He had never felt so helpless in his life. A constant hum filled his head until he could barely think straight. None of this seemed real. They were coming home from the concert. They were safe. They were together. So, what had just happened? He had to get them out of there, had to get them to safety and call for help.

"Callum, wake up. Come on man, please - I need your help!" The panic in his voice scared him as he shook Callum's arm. "Callum!"

Callum stirred and the breath he didn't realise he had been holding escaped in a rush.

"Hey!" he said, shaking Callum's arm again. "Come on, wake up!"

Callum groaned, feebly pushing Jack's hand away.

"The car flipped," Jack breathed. He shook him gently again and Callum offered resistance this time, pulling his arm away.

"What happened?" he mumbled hazily. "Oh man, my head."

"Another car hit us. We're upside down. I'm gonna try and release your seatbelt, but you're gonna have to help me here. Brace yourself - hey, can you hear me?"

"What? Yeah. I'm here. I'm okay," he mumbled, sounding a plane ride and a taxi journey away from okay.

"You're gonna have to brace yourself. Stay with me. Do you think you can stop yourself from hitting the deck?"

Jack twisted around to get into a better position. He leveraged himself, reaching around Callum to fumble blindly for the release button.

"You okay? Are you hurt?" he asked, wanting to keep him talking in the meantime. His shoulder cried out with every move he made but he gritted his teeth against the pain.

"No, I think I'm okay," Callum mumbled, both arms reaching down to brace for the landing. "The car flipped?"

Jack grimaced, reaching over as far as he could, ignoring the pain in his shoulder.

"Yeah, looks like it," he grunted, finally getting his fingers to work. "Okay, I got it. You ready for this?"

"Yeah."

"On three, okay? One, two, three."

Jack pushed on the release and Callum landed on the roof of the car with a strangled groan. Jack tried his best to help him right himself as he mumbled a string of curses under his breath.

"Sure you're not hurt?" Jack demanded, casting a worried glance behind him at Ally.

"No, no I'm good. Just my head... I think. You okay?"

"Yeah. Shoulder hurts like hell but I'll live."

"Jesus - Ally?"

"She's out cold. I can't wake her."

The silence seemed to scream at them.

"We've gotta get her out of here."

Jack turned his back on Callum, twisting and crawling to gain access to the back seat. He fought his way through to kneel beside her, breathless with the effort. She was pale but he checked her over and couldn't see any blood. He felt again for her pulse, relieved to find it once more, although weak.

"You're gonna have to help me here," he said to Callum, his eyes tracking the seatbelt to the release button at her waist. "I'm gonna let her down as easy as I can but you need to hold her so she doesn't hit her head."

"Hang on, we don't know if she's okay." The urgency in Callum's voice stopped him dead. "We shouldn't move her, just in case. What if she has internal injuries or something?"

"We can't just leave her here like this!"

"Just hang on for a few more minutes. I'll see if I can find some help, maybe that other car, maybe they can help."

Callum reached for his door, trying to force it open but it was stuck fast. He grimaced but gave up, twisting himself around and crawling towards the driver's door instead. He shoved at it but it wouldn't budge so he rolled over onto his back and kicked at it. One, two, three times before it finally gave.

"Just wait, okay? Don't do anything yet," he breathed, clambering out of the car.

"Okay."

Callum took a moment to get himself together outside before he stood up. Then he promptly collapsed onto the damp grass.

"Hey!" Jack crawled between the seats and out through the driver's door, the twisted metal giving way further with a sickening screech. He scrambled across the grass to Callum, who was already coming around.

"Are you okay?" he demanded, turning Callum over.

"Oh shit."

Callum rolled away and vomited, his body bucking with the effort. Jack grimaced, giving him a moment to catch his breath. Callum ran a trembling hand across his mouth and squinted up at him.

"Man, my head. Feels like it's been run over by a semi."

"I bet."

Jack glanced around them, the moonlight turning everything ghostly. It was cold and it was dark and they were in a field beside River Road. There were no streetlights along this stretch of road and there was no one around, not another soul. His heart sank.

Turning his attention back to his car, he caught his breath. He traced the trajectory of the car backwards to the road via the tell-tale gouges in the soft ground, visible even in the moonlight. The car had apparently slid across the road, through a fence and over a culvert, coming to rest against the side of a tree. Jack remembered the almighty jolt and a chill crawled up his spine. The car was a mess of mangled metal and broken glass, Callum and Ally's side taking the brunt of the impact.

"Holy shit," Callum breathed, following Jack's gaze.

"Where's the other car?"

Jack laboriously got to his feet, scoping out the tree line. He couldn't see it anywhere. He took a couple of steps towards the road and suddenly spied it on the opposite side of the road, on its side, half-buried in the trees. Callum was by his side, leaning forward, bracing himself on his knees.

"I'll go," Callum panted. "You stay with Ally."

"But you – "

"I'm okay, just stay with her."

Before Jack could say anything more, Callum stumbled across the grass towards the road. Jack watched for a few moments to make sure he wasn't going to collapse again, then turned back to the car. He crawled in the open door, the mere movement sending a stabbing pain through his shoulder that stopped him in his tracks. He breathed through it and pushed on, crawling through the car until he had positioned himself next to Ally. She looked so helpless. He brushed trembling fingers across her cheek and took her hands in his, sniffing back tears.

A jolt of fear stabbed at his heart. He sniffed again, a sickly-sweet smell catching in his throat. Horrified, he sniffed a third time, wishing it away.

No. No!

Gas.

His heart raced.

The possibilities played out in his mind as he fought hard to breathe. Searching the car desperately, he spied Callum's jacket, now strewn haphazardly behind the steering wheel. He reached over for it, ignoring the pain it caused him. He rolled it up as best he could and reached up, *tying it carefully around Ally's neck in a makeshift neck brace, just in case. He had seen that on TV once, a towel used as a neck brace for a swimmer who had dived head-first into shallow water. Callum was right, they needed to be careful, there was no knowing what damage had occurred internally, or where.*

"You're gonna be fine," he mumbled, more to himself than to Ally. His voice boomed in the silence as he reached up to find the seatbelt release button at Ally's waist.

"I'm sorry babe," he whispered. "I gotta get you out of here. Just hang in there, okay? I love you. We can do this. It's gonna be alright, I promise."

The smell of gas was getting stronger, making him sick with fear. He turned and tried the door behind the driver's door, looking for the fastest and easiest way out. Pushing against it with all his strength, it gave way a little. He put his back into it, pushing it all the way open with a screech of metal. He crawled back to Ally, stretching his legs straight out beneath her. He reached up to release her seatbelt and she landed on top of him, the weight of her temporarily forcing the air out of his lungs. Recovering quickly, he crossed her arms over her chest and started backing out of the car, her upper body sprawled on top of him, her legs trailing behind.

"See? That wasn't so bad was it?" he grunted, moving them backwards.

He glanced behind him, easing her out through the door, desperately pushing it open further to allow them passage. The smell of gas soaked the air.

"Hang in there, okay? Nearly there."

He dragged them both free of the car and across the grass, his shoulder screaming in pain, his teeth clamped tight. His head swam and at one point he thought he might pass out but he didn't stop. Ally's head lay cushioned on his thighs, her neck still wrapped in Callum's jacket. He glanced up fearfully at the car, half-expecting it to explode into flames at any moment.

"Just a little further."

The ground was wet and uneven beneath them but he only had one thought in his head; keep her safe.

Finally, he collapsed back onto the wet grass, certain they were out of harm's way. Breathing heavily from the exertion, his shoulder burning, he threw his good arm over his face and wished they were home. A few moments and several deep breaths later, he sat up, favouring his good side. He gently re-crossed Ally's arms over her abdomen and checked her pulse. It was there and she was breathing. Beyond that, he didn't know.

Reaching into his pocket, he pulled out his cell phone. The screen was cracked but it still worked. With trembling fingers, he dialled the emergency services, giving their location and details to the operator. There were three of them, plus the other car. No, he had no idea how many were in the other car or how badly they were hurt. He had checked Ally's pulse but no, she hadn't regained consciousness. The operator told him to keep her warm and immobile and check her airway to make sure it was clear. She kept asking questions, trying to keep him talking while help arrived, but all it did was aggravate his already-fragile state of mind. He yelled at her to hurry the hell up and snapped the phone shut. The resulting silence was overwhelming. Where the hell was Callum? He couldn't do this by himself.

No cars had come along the road since the crash and the night was clear and crisp. He shivered slightly as the adrenaline wore off and shock began to set in. He stared down at Ally, silent and still. The weight of responsibility began to feel uncomfortably heavy.

He peeled his jacket off, trying to keep his screaming shoulder immobile as much as possible, and gently tucked it around her as Callum half-stumbled, half-jogged towards him.

"You shouldn't have moved her," he panted, collapsing down on the grass beside them.

"I didn't have any choice, the car's leaking gas. I had to get her out of there."

"Jesus."

"What about the other car? Could you get to it?" he asked, his stomach knotted in fear.

Callum shook his head, lying down on his back. Jack glanced over at him, noticing for the first time that there was a trickle of blood stemming from a gash in his head. More blood, dark in the moonlight, matted his hair.

"Callum?"

Callum rested his forearm over his face.

"I could only see the driver," he said. "I don't think there were any passengers. I couldn't reach him."

Jack wanted to scream. They needed help now.

"He's a real mess," Callum said, shifting his hand away and peering up at Jack. "I think he's dead."

"Shit."

Jack looked down at Ally, stroking her cheek gently. He checked her pulse and breathing again to reassure himself and prayed silently for the ambulance to appear. He glanced over at Callum. His eyes were closed and he reached over to shake him gently.

"Hey, wake up. You have to stay awake okay?"

Callum's eyes shot open and he blinked rapidly several times.

"Sorry. Just so tired. My head's killing me."

"Come on, sit up," Jack said, shaking him again. "You hit your head, you gotta stay awake man, come on."

Callum sat up slowly, leaning forward to hang his head between his knees.

"You good?"

"Yeah."

"Where the hell are the damn paramedics?" Jack muttered under his breath, smoothing hair away from Ally's face.

The wait seemed tortuously long and he checked her breathing and her pulse again, tucking his jacket carefully around her.

"You're gonna be okay," he whispered. "I promise."

---

*T*he sun woke Callum early the next morning. The moment he sat up, he instantly regretted it. He ran a hand over his throbbing head and squinted at the living room window. Looking around him, he deduced that he had spent the night on Maggie's couch. He peered towards the kitchen, where she sat at the table, watching him.

She raised her mug with a sympathetic smile.

"Coffee?"

He tried to nod but it felt as if the action would cause his head to separate from his shoulders.

"Stat."

Slowly the details of last night came back to him. He remembered calling Maggie after he left Ally's, meeting her at Barney's some time later. He told her about finding Ally's car outside Jack's house the night before, about confronting Jack after she had left and about his conversation with Ally about it earlier. He was bordering on frantic by the time the third round of beers had been ordered. He remembered the conversation detouring onto the funeral, Tom and a kaleidoscope of other subjects that escaped him right now. Whatever followed remained a blur.

He didn't remember coming back here after Barney's and he sure as hell didn't remember swallowing the small furry animal that appeared to have crawled into his mouth overnight and died there. Ditto the battalion of tiny miners who were trying to hack their way out of his skull from the inside. He rubbed his forehead again and reached up to take the mug of coffee that appeared in front of him, indicating the window with a wave of annoyance.

"Can you do something about that?"

He heard her tilting the blinds and risked opening his eyes again, enormously relieved when the morning sunlight no longer hit him squarely in the face.

"You might want these, too."

She handed him a glass of water and a couple of pills. He put the coffee mug down on the table in front of him, anxiously placing the Aspirin on his furry tongue while suppressing his gag reflex.

"I guess it's a waste of time asking how you feel."

He gave her a withering look and rolled his shoulders, wincing as his body recalled the fight with Jack outside the church two days ago.

"Sexy, huh?" he quipped, squinting up at her.

"Hot," she deadpanned. "Just so damn hot."

She sank down into the armchair opposite him and he peered over at her.

"Why don't you look how I feel?"

"Well, maybe because you drank enough for the both of us last night?" she smiled sweetly. "Besides, someone had to drive us home."

He stood up, stretching carefully. His stomach churned but he had a feeling it wasn't only due to the bar he had drained the night before.

"I have no idea what happened last night but I'm really sorry," he said, by way of apology. "Something tells me I wouldn't have been pleasant company."

He caught a vague whiff of toast. Could he stomach food yet?

"Why didn't you tell me before, about Ally?"

"What about Ally?"

"Oh, I don't know. Maybe the fact that you're in love with her."

He was going to deny it but one look at her face told him he'd be wasting his time. He sank back into the couch, a wave of nausea washing over him. Definitely 'no' to the food thing.

"Ancient history," he mumbled.

Just how wasted was he last night? It was Jack's fault. If he hadn't come back, all of this would still be buried, where it belonged.

"It didn't sound like ancient history last night," Maggie said, ignoring his dismissive tone. "Does she know how you feel?"

'Ancient' was possibly a stretch, although he didn't say that aloud. It was a couple of months earlier when he had tentatively told Ally about the way he felt. He had needed a few beers under his belt that night, too.

"Yeah, she knows," he said, staring down at his hands.

He hadn't spoken to anyone about it, preferring to just sweep it under the carpet. He hoped that one day everything would just go back to normal. Ally was the strongest, most determined person he had ever known, there was no doubt about that. Deep down he hoped that some of that strength would rub off on him, as if being near her would somehow allow for that. Other days he wished he was a million miles away, the ache in his heart was so great.

"What happened? What did she say?"

"So, she didn't tell you?"

Maggie shook her head. He hesitated, tempted not to elaborate but reluctantly acknowledging there was no turning back now.

"What do you think?" he said, the memory still raw. "She said she was scared. She said she wasn't ready, that she didn't want anything to ruin our friendship."

He picked up his coffee mug and took a hasty sip.

"Did she mention Jack?" she asked.

"Nope, but I did. She denied it - obviously. Said it had nothing to do with him."

"But you knew she was lying, right?"

"Of course I did," he snapped. "It was written all over her face."

His head ached and impatience gnawed at him. This was exactly why he didn't want to talk about it. What was the point?

"That's what I thought. She's been pretty stoic about it up until now, but I always got the feeling she was hiding something.

We stopped talking about him after what happened, but I don't think she stopped thinking about him."

Callum stared blearily at the floor. He suspected the same thing.

"Does Jane know?" Maggie asked. "About you and Ally?"

"There's nothing to know. It has nothing to do with her, anyway. We'd long since broken up."

"I get that. I just thought maybe you'd talked to someone about it."

"Right. Because talking about how humiliated... never mind."

He didn't even try to keep the sarcasm out of his tone. He concentrated on his coffee, taking a big gulp and ignoring the fact that it burnt his throat and tongue. He and Jane had been on the verge of splitting even before the accident happened. Then, after the accident, things had gotten complicated. He had spent the majority of his spare time with Ally because she needed him. Even without the accident, he and Jane would have split anyway. As it was, it just seemed to delay the inevitable, putting their relationship woes on the backburner as they dealt with Ally's situation and the long list of battles that followed. Eventually, their relationship had become one of friendship and mutual support.

There was no animosity when they both finally faced up to the fact that it was time to move on. The night they had officially ended things, he found himself at Tom's and they had talked long into the night. Thinking about Tom now, the ache inside seemed to intensify.

"How do you do it?" Maggie asked. "Doesn't it hurt? Being around her after that, I mean?"

"What am I supposed to do? She needs me, I can't just walk away because it's too hard. That's Jack's calling card, not mine."

"You're right. She's lucky to have you."

"Yeah," he snorted cynically. "Obviously."

"She loves you. Maybe not the same way you love her but she does love you. You know that, right?"

"Is that supposed to make me feel better?"

"I'm sorry. I know it must be hard for you, after everything that's happened. I can't help but wonder how close she came to actually getting him out of her system, though."

He had doubted she was anywhere close to getting Jack out of her system then, and that was only a couple of months ago. Anger welled up inside of him. Jack didn't deserve her love. He had deserted her in her time of greatest need and left him to pick up the pieces. Didn't that count for anything?

"I'm worried about her," Maggie said. "You saw how she was at the funeral. What are we gonna do? How are we supposed to help this time?"

He sat forward, anger pushing aside the headache, the nausea and the general sense of helplessness. He had a few ideas but he didn't think Maggie would approve.

"Do you think your little chat with him did the trick?"

He remembered what Jack had said last night, through the haze of several beers and a killer hangover.

I'm not going anywhere - not this time.

"I don't know." He ran a hand through his short dark hair.

He needed a shower and a shave. Maybe then he'd be able to think clearly.

"Are you gonna be seeing her today?" he asked.

"I thought I'd call her and see if she wants to meet for coffee, see how she's holding up."

"That'd be good. She was pretty upset yesterday. I mean, she tried to hide it but it was obvious, y'know?" He rubbed the back of his neck. "I wouldn't mention my little chat with him, it'd only upset her. I told her I'd seen her car outside his house but she doesn't know that we talked and it's probably better she doesn't, especially if it turns out he's taken off again."

"Okay, yeah. I think that's probably best."

"I hope he's gone," he said, staring at his coffee. "I gave him plenty of reason to. I just hope he did the right thing this time. She doesn't need this crap."

"You know we're gonna have to clean up his mess again if he has?"

Callum took a gulp of coffee before leaning back into the couch.

"Yeah. I know."

CHAPTER SEVEN

"It has been said 'time heals all wounds'. I do not agree.
The wounds remain. In time, the mind, protecting its sanity, covers
them with scar tissue and the pain lessens.
But it is never gone."
- Rose Kennedy

Callum drove slowly down the street as he approached. If he'd been a religious man, he would've prayed. As he got closer to Tom's house, he almost forgot to breathe. The neighbour's tree obscured his view of the driveway from this angle, but as he got closer he saw Jack's car was still there.

"Damn it!"

He debated whether or not he should pull over and talk to him again but he jammed his foot down on the accelerator instead. He roared past, head down, eyes fixed on the suburban street once more. He gripped the steering wheel tightly as he pulled up to the intersection at the end of the street.

"Now what?" he mumbled to himself, glancing in the rear-view mirror.

The silence was deafening.

---

*T*he little diner was busy. Ally glanced around, there in body but not in spirit. The peace of mind she'd craved when she'd decided to go and talk to Jack still eluded her. Her mood seemed to see-saw between relief that they had been able to talk alone finally, to confusion at what he had to say. Smack in the middle of that war of emotions was the almost maternal need to protect him - from Callum's anger, from the guilt he seemed determined to shoulder, from everything. It was a heady mix.

She found herself reflecting on the complexity of the universe during the hours before dawn. After the accident, everything changed. Every day was a challenge and once the dust began to settle, she realised how far-reaching the consequences of what happened really were. Jack left. Callum spent almost every waking moment with her, and if he wasn't there, Maggie or Tom were. Callum and Jane broke up. Callum sold his beloved van. She couldn't help but feel responsible.

The only way she could control things was to try and minimise the negative effect she was having on the lives of everyone she loved. She stopped venting her frustrations and began internalising them instead.

She understood why everyone seemed determined to keep her and Jack apart but it wasn't helping. She needed answers, not the half-hearted, vague explanations he had offered the other day. The only thing she took away from that conversation was that he shouldered an insane amount of guilt over the accident. She needed more. What happened to him over the past four years? Where did he go?

"Hey, you gonna eat that cake or not?" Maggie asked.

"Help yourself, I'm not really hungry."

She slid her plate across the table. Glancing casually sideways, the quiet chatter at the next table over stopped momentarily. Guilty looks accompanied the silence and anger bubbled up from inside of her. She tried to ignore it, watching as Maggie helped herself to her slice of cake. The chatter started up again in hushed, exaggerated whispers. She heard Jack's name and she turned her attention back to the window, trying to block it out.

The street outside was busy with people going about their daily routine. Cars pulled in and out of the parking lot outside the diner. An elderly man walked his dog across the street. A mother scolded a toddler with bouncing blonde curls, holding onto her hand tightly as she scanned the busy street for a safe time to cross.

"Okay, enough," Maggie demanded. "Feels like I'm sitting opposite a cardboard cut-out. Speak."

"I hate this," Ally said, watching the mother and daughter cross the street.

"Hate what?"

"This," Ally said, tearing herself away from the window. She leaned forward, frowning as her gaze encompassed the crowded diner. "The gossiping, the idle chit-chat. Can't they just leave it alone for once?"

Maggie pushed the plate away and dabbed her lips lightly with the paper napkin, balling it up and throwing it onto the plate with the remnants of the cake.

"In this town? You've got to be joking. This is big news. Anyway, it's Jack's problem, not yours. Just ignore it."

The coffee Ally had been drinking only moments ago turned to ash in her stomach.

"This is your home," Maggie said. "You belong here. He doesn't, not anymore."

Despite everything, Ally couldn't help but feel that Jack didn't deserve this. It was no fun being the subject of gossip. Had everyone forgotten that he had just lost his father?

"Do you realise how hard it must've been for him to come back here, after what happened?" she pleaded, trying to make Maggie understand.

"Of course I do. That takes guts, I know that," Maggie said, keeping her voice low. "But on the other hand, it should be hard for him. Do you really think he should get to waltz back here, no questions asked, and just pick up where he left off?"

Ally could feel tears welling up even as she fought for control.

"What happened the other day?" Maggie asked, sitting forward. "One minute you don't want to talk to him, and the next minute you're going over there for a chat?"

Ally stared across the table at her friend, trying to figure out how to explain it.

"I needed to know," she said.

"Know what?"

She searched for the right words. When they finally came, tumbling out in a rush, she saw things clearly for the first time since Tom's death.

"How could he just leave me like that? I thought he loved me. Was what happened to me so awful that he couldn't stand to even look at me? Why didn't he come home? I mean, where's he been all this time?" Her voice caught in her throat. "I tried pretending it didn't matter, believe me, I tried, but that's a lie. It matters, it matters a lot. I want answers. I think I deserve them and now that he's here, I finally get a chance to ask him."

"So, what did he say when you talked to him? Did he tell you what you wanted to hear?" Maggie folded her arms in front of her on the table.

"Not really. I did most of the talking. He didn't really say much except how sorry he was."

"Good. He should be sorry."

"Yeah, but it's not what I wanted to hear, not really."

"You didn't want an apology?"

"Not like that. I wanted answers. I need to talk to him again but I'm worried about Callum."

"He's trying to protect you, you realise that, right?"

Ally nodded, tucking her hair behind one ear.

"I know that, but I need to do this. It's the only way I'm gonna find out what really happened. I think Callum needs to talk to him, too - but with his fists tied behind his back."

"I get it. You have more guts than I do, I'll tell you that much. Are you sure you're ready to hear whatever he has to tell you? What if knowing all the details makes it worse, not better?"

"It won't," she said, even though deep down she wondered the same thing. "Anything's better than not knowing."

"He broke your heart, he wasn't there when you needed him most. In my book, that makes him a pretty lousy human being. Just prepare yourself, okay? What he has to say may not be what you want to hear." Maggie picked at her cuticles for a few moments. "I'm going to tell you something now, something that I promised Callum I wouldn't. But given everything you've just said, I think you need to know."

By the time Callum arrived at the pool, Ally's car was one of only a handful in the parking lot. He hauled his swimming bag out of the back seat and headed inside. Maggie had called to warn him earlier, filling him in about her conversation with Ally over coffee. He had been dreading this moment ever since, unsure about what he was walking into but pretty sure it wasn't going to be pleasant. He took a deep breath as he approached the main doors of the old grey building that housed the town's pool.

It had taken a while to get Ally interested in swimming as part of her exercise routine. Jogging had been her endorphin rush of choice before the accident and he knew she missed it. Swimming was part of her rehab and he had pushed her into taking it up once she was home, joining her at the pool every Sunday night for moral support. At first, she was shy about swimming in public but he had done his research. He asked around, attended a few swim sessions on different days and times and had a couple of casual chats with one of the admin women at the pool. He eventually pieced together that Sunday night from about 7pm was by far the quietest time. Ally was more relaxed without an audience.

Swimming was great for her mental health as well as her physical health and in the pool, without the constant pull of gravity, she was able to exercise much more freely. Callum was hoping that the endorphin rush following a good workout would help smooth things over tonight.

He changed into his trunks in the deserted changing rooms, the smell of chlorine clinging to the wooden benches and wet concrete floors. Stashing his clothes in a locker, he grabbed his towel and headed out to the pool. Ally waited for him in her wheelchair near the door, a towel draped over her legs. He forced a smile and threw his own towel haphazardly at the bench running along the wall behind her.

"Hey," he said, smiling to break the ice.

"We need to talk."

He had been hoping to delay this until after they swam but she clearly had other ideas. He mentally prepared himself for the onslaught he knew was coming.

"You were way out of line," she said. "You had no right to go storming over there, and what made it worse was that you didn't even have the guts to tell me. I had to hear it from Maggie!"

Her voice echoed through the building, bouncing off the walls and causing a few stragglers to look over their way.

"Let's just dial this down a notch, alright? People are staring."

She took a ragged breath, glancing around self-consciously. A man dried himself off nearby and a couple of middle-aged women chatted quietly as they exited the pool.

"Come on," he said, making his way over to the bench lining the back wall.

Ally followed, albeit reluctantly.

"I'm sorry," he said, sitting down. "I should've told you. When I drove by and saw your car there, it freaked me out. I didn't go in then because I didn't want you to get stuck in the middle. What I had to say was for Jack's ears only. It was between us."

"Except I am stuck in the middle, aren't I? You're trying to help and I get that and I'm grateful, but you're not. If you really want to help, you can stand behind me, not in front of me."

Stand behind her? He'd done nothing but stand behind her for four years. Why couldn't she see that all Jack would bring her was a world of pain - and that was if he stayed? When he disappeared again - which he knew he would, eventually - then what? Suddenly he felt squeezed between a rock and a hard place. However, this played out, she was going to hurt and he was going to have to watch.

Already the cracks were starting to show. The carefully constructed façade that she had spent years building up was starting to crumble. He could see it falling piece by tiny piece, the despair seeping through. Tears gathered in her eyes and he had to try to warn her once more, to try and slow the downward spiral he could see was coming.

"Whatever he has to say to you isn't going to fix anything," he said. "I promise you that."

"How do you know?"

She was strong, there was no doubt about that, but Jack was her Kryptonite and he always had been.

"He's only been back a few days," he said, keeping his voice level. "And already I can see what that's doing to you. You think I don't? You try to hide it but you're only human. You want to know the truth? I don't trust him. I don't think he's gonna stick around, despite what he says. I don't think he's strong enough, he doesn't have the guts. You think it hurts now? I guarantee you the longer he stays, the worse it's gonna get. You know me, you know I'll do everything in my power not to let that happen. So, if you're asking me to back off while you throw yourself under a train, the answer is no. I won't do it. I'm sorry. I can't."

Their eyes remained locked and he could see the turmoil within. He could also see the anger, the frustration and most of all, the resentment. He took it all deep down and buried it. One day she would thank him but today was not that day.

"I love how everyone seems to think they know what's best for me," she snapped. "Like I can't be trusted to make my own decisions, like I need to be wrapped in bubble-wrap and protected from the world. I may have made some mistakes in my life, but newsflash - I'm not made of china, I won't break."

Releasing the brake on her chair, she turned abruptly and headed towards the pool.

"Hey!" he called, hurrying to catch up. "Hang on a minute."

"I don't want to talk about this anymore," she said, stopping at the edge of the pool. "There's no point."

She pulled the towel off her legs and lay it down in front of her, clearly done talking. Lowering herself onto the towel, she lifted her legs into the pool, leaned forward and fell into the water. Bobbing to the surface a moment later, she began swimming the length of the pool, leaving him to stare after her.

Not knowing what else to do, he slipped into the pool himself, sprinting a couple of laps to burn off the residual anxiety. His brain was in overdrive and he was soon exhausted. He kept an eye on her at each turn before finally giving in and pulling himself up to sit on the edge of the pool.

He smoothed his wet hair back and tried to catch his breath, watching her. Her stroke was smooth and graceful, powerfully pulling her body through the water. To the casual observer, she looked like any other swimmer.

But she was only human. If he had used swimming as a distraction to work off anxiety and frustration, he knew she had too. While it wasn't a problem for him, it could be a big problem for her. Her pace had slowed. As he weighed up how to intervene without copping another roasting, she began swimming towards him. The closer she got, the more evident it became. He slid back into the water and swam towards her.

"I think I might need a hand," she said.

Without further comment, he stood up, scooping her into his arms and carrying her through the water to the concrete steps at the far end of the pool. Climbing up the steps and out of the pool, the cool air pricked his skin, in stark contrast to the warm water.

She weighed next to nothing these days. She had lost a lot of weight since the accident and gaining it back wasn't as easy as it used to be, especially since she was using her braces most days now. She never commented on how her body had changed but he could see it in her eyes every time he performed the range-of-motion exercises with her. That faraway look that told him she was trying to distance herself from everything. Self-preservation, he assumed.

He set her down gently in her chair, bending down to pick up her towel and hand it back to her. She took it without a word. She looked so vulnerable, sitting there, shivering. Knowing how much she would hate the observation, he immediately pushed it aside. She had fought so long and so hard to regain her independence. She was strong and she was determined and she had a stubborn streak in her that had driven him to drink on several occasions. But she wasn't invincible.

He pushed her over to the bench and sat down with a heavy sigh. Reaching over to snag his own towel from where it had landed earlier, he wiped his face and rubbed his hair dry. She sat facing him, staring at the empty bench, shivering.

"I know you thought you were helping," she said finally. "But I really need to do this. I need to talk to him, I need to know, and I need you to back off for a while. Please?"

He continued to dry himself off, then stood up and wrapped the towel around his waist, tucking the end in to hold it in place. She wasn't going to give up, he realised, watching as she rubbed at her legs half-heartedly. He wasn't surprised.

He sat down again and reached over to turn her chair around and drag it backwards so she was in front of him. He started kneading her shoulders firmly, the muscles taut beneath his fingertips. After a few minutes, he eased off slightly. Her shoulders were shapely and toned, testament to the strength of her upper body. Also, testament to the strength of her spirit.

"Okay," he said, standing up and bending low to take hold of the handles of her chair. "If that's what you want."

She let him push her towards the changing rooms, something she rarely permitted.

"I do," she said, the words laced with both relief and fear.

An ache rose up in a wave from his gut, lodging in his throat. He was going to regret this, he could tell. He stopped beside the entry to the women's changing room.

"I wish Tom were here," she said quietly, taking control of her chair.

She propelled herself slowly into the changing room, her head bent as if the weight of the world rested on her shoulders.

CHAPTER EIGHT

"Some choices we live not only once, but a thousand times over,
remembering them for the rest of our lives."
- Richard Bach

*J*ack stood up and paced the length of Ally's porch before sitting down again in the same spot. He turned his hands over, studying the bruised knuckles.

One question plagued him: was Callum right?

Maybe he really was staying for his own selfish reasons. Maybe he was blinded by his desire to prove himself, to his father, to them, to himself, and to hell with what his presence here was doing to Ally. Was it really possible to make a difference now, after all this time? There was only one person who could answer that and he was impatient to talk to her.

Talking about the accident with Ally was much harder than he had thought it would be. Her pain was still raw, as if it had just happened yesterday. That was one thing they had in common.

Callum hated him and he didn't blame him for that. Deep down he had hoped for some sign that there might be a chance he could claw their friendship back from the brink, that he hadn't screwed it up for good. He knew now that wasn't going to happen.

He felt like he was drowning. He wished his father was here. He would know how to stop everything from falling apart. This morning, desperate for guidance, he had decided to go to the cemetery to visit his father's grave. He got as far as the cemetery gate but he couldn't make himself get out of the car. Back at the house, he sat at the kitchen table and stared at the notes on the fridge door. Church newsletters, shopping lists, articles from the local paper, appointment reminders in his father's handwriting. Everything looked normal, yet in reality it was just the opposite.

Then had come the epiphany, of sorts.

Glancing up towards the road, he saw tunnels of light punching through the darkness. His gut clenched as the car turned into her driveway. This was her decision, not his. He just had to let her make it. He owed her that, at the very least.

He stood up, raw knuckles grazing against his jeans as he shoved his hands in his pockets, hunching his shoulders against the chill. From the shadows, he watched her unload a wheelchair from the back seat, unfolding it and clipping on the wheels. She hoisted herself out of the car and into the wheelchair, so preoccupied that she didn't even notice him.

He felt like a voyeur. Considering he had expected to see her in a wheelchair all this time, it shocked him to see it now. Before he lost his nerve, he stepped out of the shadows and made his way down the path towards her. She grabbed a sports bag from the back seat of the car and dropped it into her lap, turning to close the car door.

"Hey."

She whirled on him, clearly startled.

"Sorry," he held up his hands. "I didn't mean to scare you."

His shadow engulfed her as the security light from the outside of the house illuminated them.

"I hope you don't mind me coming around like this, I know it's late."

"No, it's okay," she said, recovering quickly. "I just didn't know if you were still... never mind, it doesn't matter. Do you want to come inside?"

She thought he'd disappeared again. The realisation cut deep but he didn't blame her. He tried to smile, to reassure her, but he wasn't sure how convincing he was.

"Thanks."

He followed her up the path in silence, hanging back as she navigated the ramp alongside the steps with practiced ease. She reached up to unlock the door and used the doorframe to pull herself over the threshold. He closed the door behind him as she deposited her keys on the hall table. Dropping the sports bag onto the floor beside her, they stared at each other in awkward silence.

"Do you want coffee?" she asked finally. "Or maybe a beer, or something?"

"Coffee would be great, thanks."

She smiled, a nervous smile that didn't quite reach her eyes, and turned to head down the hallway. Following her, he fought not to stare as she powered her wheelchair with smooth, even strokes. He struggled with the image, pushing aside a flashback from another time - Ally striding down this same hallway wearing purple boots with two-inch heels and a long, flowing dress.

Watching from the doorway as she prepared the coffee machine, his resolve began to crumble. Was it fair to make her decide?

She pulled out two mugs and set them on the table before flicking her wet hair over her shoulder. Desperate to fill the silence, he gave small talk a shot.

"You've been swimming?"

"Yeah, with Callum. It's kind of a Sunday night ritual," she said, lifting a handful of wet hair and sniffing. "I stink of chlorine. I should probably go rinse my hair. Help yourself to the coffee, I won't be long."

He stepped into the kitchen as she moved to pass him and his hand shot out, latching onto her shoulder.

"I need to ask you something," he blurted out before he could stop himself. "I really want to do the right thing here and I thought I knew what that was but it's all kinda blurry and I'm just... I'm not sure anymore."

She stared up at him, clearly confused.

"What I mean is, it's not just up to me. I know that now. I don't want to make it harder for you - that's the last thing I want - so I'm asking you what you want. If you want me to stay, I will. But if you think that it's just screwing everything up, me being here, then I'll leave."

Silence descended on them, the grandfather clock in the hallway marking the seconds as they passed.

"Do you want to go?" she whispered, her blue-green eyes holding his.

"No. But if you want me to, I will."

Her chin trembled and she looked so frightened, he fought the urge to reach down and take her in his arms.

"I don't want you to go."

FOUR YEARS EARLIER

Callum sat on the step outside Jack's house, waiting. When Jack finally came outside, tugging a Pearl Jam t-shirt down over his jeans, he grinned at Callum and slapped him on the back, sitting down next to him.

"Cool shirt, dude. That new?" Callum asked, grinning back at him.

"Present from Ally."

"Nice. You all set for later?"

"Yep." Jack patted the pocket of his jeans.

"Nervous?"

"Kinda."

"You know she's gonna say yes."

"Yeah, I think you're right."

"Wow," Callum raised his eyebrows. "Marriage. Dude, don't look now but I think you're a grown-up."

Jack chuckled.

"You'll be getting a mortgage next. Just seems like yesterday we were setting fire to Jolene Parker's hair," Callum mused. "And now it's all over. Marriage, mortgage, then kids and all that other scary shit."

"Funny, I thought a best man's job was to keep the groom calm? Not freak him out."

"Best man," Callum beamed. "I'm gonna be a best man. This is gonna be the best bachelor party ever. Ever - I swear to you, I won't let you down."

"If you have anything in mind that's gonna see me naked and tied to any traffic sign anywhere in town, just forget it right now."

Callum just grinned wickedly.

"I mean it," Jack warned. "Not cool. At all."

Callum feigned seriousness for a moment.

"Okay. Got it. What about strippers? Where do you stand on strippers?"

Jack fumbled over his words, trying not to smile.

"You worry too much. You're like an old woman in a dude's body. Chillax, okay? It'll be fine. Leave it to Uncle Callum."

"Jack! Where are my purple boots?" Ally called from inside the house.

"In the kitchen, where you left them!" Jack called back, shaking his head. "I swear she's the quintessential artist sometimes - completely *oblivious to mundane things like time management. Just as well she's got a damn fine ass."*

"I'll remind you about this conversation on your fiftieth wedding anniversary, right in front of everyone, grandchildren included. I'm sure they'd love to hear about the damn fine ass grandma had, back in the day."

Jack chuckled, blushing slightly.

"I might slip that little anecdote about her ass into my best man speech, too."

"Shhh, keep your voice down!"

Callum feigned horror, then he jumped up and stood on the path in front of Jack, clearing his throat.

"Ladies and gentlemen, thank you for joining us here today. As some of you may know," he indicated an imaginary crowd with a wave of his hand, "the groom and I have known each other pretty much forever."

"For God's sake, will you shut up!" Jack hissed.

"Settle down, grandpa, she can't hear us," Callum grinned, climbing the steps and sitting down next to him again. "What do you think she'll do, when you ask her? Scream? Cry? Jump you, right then and there? Is there such a thing as post-proposal sex?"

Jack shook his head, a smile playing on his lips.

"God only knows."

"I bet there is. In fact, I'll bet my van on it."

"That's not much of a wager - you can't even drive that piece of crap yet."

"Not far off it, though. Just one more pay check and she'll be good to go. Thanks for the lift tonight, by the way. I feel like I'm cramping your style though. Are you sure it's okay to come with you guys? I can get a lift with Mitch – "

"No, it's fine. You can help take my mind off it till we get home."

"So, what are you gonna say? Have you got a little speech worked out in your head or what?"

"Yeah, kinda, I think," Jack scratched his chin. "I don't know. I'm going to drop you off first, then probably take her down by the river."

"Nice," Callum nodded. "Classy. Take her back to the place you took her on your first date."

"First date was to the prom - first real date, anyway."

"Whatever. Chicks dig that romantic shit," he grinned. "You gonna do the whole 'get down on one knee' thing too?"

"Dude, you're getting into this way too much."

"What can I say? Cheap thrills."

"I'll be your best man when you tie the knot, so you better watch it with your damn speech, too. I hear karma's a bitch."

"I'm not worried."

"Well, you should be. I've got a long memory."

"You're off the hook. I'm never getting married."

"What?" Jack stared at him incredulously. "Where did that come from?"

"I don't know. Just can't see myself doing it, that's all."

"You're not your father."

Callum shrugged casually but Jack decided to leave it for now. The timing was all wrong. Callum would need a few beers under his belt before they broached that subject again.

"Do you and Jane ever talk about it?"

"Not really."

"Why not?"

"I don't think she's into the whole marriage idea either."

"In general?"

"I don't know." Callum studied his shoes. "It's complicated."

"I can't find my coat!" Ally's voice rang out from inside the house. "Jack!"

"Hanging on the hook by the back door!" Jack yelled back, rolling his eyes. "Jesus, I'm in for lifetime of telling her where her shit is, aren't I?" he mumbled under his breath.

"Hurry up!" he yelled. "I'm going grey out here!"

"Yeah, you are," Callum grinned.

*a*lly stood in her bedroom, surveying herself in the full-length mirror. She had pulled her freshly rinsed hair up into a high ponytail and changed into her favourite t-shirt. Her most comfortable jeans concealed her braces. For reasons she didn't dare explore, this was important.

After overdoing it at the pool tonight, she would normally have stayed in her wheelchair and given her sore muscles a chance to rest, but with Jack here that wasn't an option. She needed to show him how strong she was, and to do that she had to be upright.

All she heard after *if you want me to stay, I will* was a resounding *yes!* blazing through her subconscious. It had been all she could do to stop herself shouting it out loud. That scared her. However, if she wanted to talk to him, she'd have to leave her bedroom. She sucked in a deep breath, let it out slowly and turned around.

Walking out of her bedroom, she heard movement in her studio. The one room she didn't want him anywhere near. Her heart racing, she made her way down the hall, stopping in her studio doorway. Jack was standing in front of the painting she was currently working on, his back to her.

"It's not finished yet," she said quickly.

He turned to face her, doing a double-take to see her standing.

"Sorry, I didn't mean to poke around. I was just curious."

"It's fine," she lied.

He nodded graciously, turning his attention from the unfinished canvas in front of him to the stack of finished paintings that leant against the studio walls. The tension grew. It seemed as if he was inside her head, poking through her most intimate thoughts. She felt sick, watching as he ran a finger over one of the canvases.

"These are amazing," he murmured.

"Thanks."

He moved slowly along the stacks of finished pieces, stopping and easing a canvas aside so he could access the one hidden behind. It was hidden for a reason. He stared at the painting for several moments as she frantically tried to stem the rising flood of panic that threatened to choke her. She didn't dare take her eyes off him. She didn't need to look at the painting to know what he was seeing.

The background was midnight blue. A deep red torso floated in the foreground, the limbs feathered away to mere wisps, a mass of dark, tangled hair suspended in mid-air. The face was featureless except for black eyes staring out from hollow sockets. There was a ragged hole in the chest where the heart should be, and the chest cavity was exposed and bleeding a deeper red, dripping down the torso to pool at the bottom of the canvas.

The empty eyes captivated her as much now as they did then, transporting her back in time.

She spent weeks creating the haunting image. It was a dark time. Nightmares plagued her. She couldn't eat. The pain in her back seemed constant and frequently overwhelmed her. She didn't leave the house for days on end. She couldn't see a way out of the darkness.

So, she painted. She worked relentlessly until she thought she had exorcised the demons from her mind. But the painting had not had the cleansing effect she had hoped it would.

She was still in two minds about exhibiting it. Her desire to exhibit the entire 'Evolution' series meant that she had to but she wasn't sure she was brave enough to allow the world to see it just yet. Seeing Jack looking at it now reinforced that fear. She felt violated.

Don't. Please don't.

But he asked anyway.

"What is it?"

The silence that followed soaked up his words. Taking several moments to gather her frayed emotions, she smiled tightly.

"Self portrait of the artist?"

The silence grew heavier and his eyes never left hers. She couldn't help but wonder. Did he know? Could he see it?

She had to get out. Turning away from him, she moved toward the kitchen.

"I wasn't much fun to be around for a while there," she said over her shoulder, relieved to hear him following her across the hall. "Ready for that coffee?"

"Sure."

She positioned herself between the table and the countertop, setting the coffee pot and two mugs on the table. Jack took a seat opposite her as she rested her crutches against the table, lowering herself into a chair. She was grateful when he began to pour the coffee, afraid that her trembling hands would betray her.

"You didn't have to ditch the wheelchair for my benefit," he said, handing her a mug of steaming coffee.

She took the coffee mug from him, her fingertips brushing against his.

"I didn't do it for you, I did it for me," she said.

His eyes reached down into her soul, threatening to expose her.

"Can I ask you something?"

Her heart pounded so hard she thought it might leap out of her chest.

"Sure."

"I've been wondering. What changed? I thought the damage was irreparable - permanent. And yet, here you are, walking. How?"

"The damage *is* irreparable," she said, desperate to be clear even though it hurt more than she thought it would. "And it *is* permanent. A couple of years ago, I learnt how to walk wearing braces. It gave me back some of the freedom that I lost. It's not easy but it's worth it. I try to split my time between braces and chair now, depending on what I need to do. Long distances are easier with my chair, accessibility is better with my braces."

"I don't understand," he said. "I'm sorry, you'll have to - I mean, how is that even possible?"

She shrugged, downplaying everything because it was easier for both of them if she glossed over the details.

"It's a technique I learnt," she said. "I compensate. To an extent, I can still control the way my legs respond even if they aren't getting the messages from my brain. Braces keep my legs straight so I can stand. By using the muscles in my hips, my back and my abs, I can raise my hip. My leg follows and the rest is just forward momentum. It has its challenges because I have to see what my legs are doing in order to direct them but it's a small price to pay."

She was used to seeing pity, nervousness and even condescension in the faces of strangers but she wasn't used to seeing this bone-deep sadness, not from Jack. She wanted so badly for him to see how well she was coping, how together she was but that wasn't the vibe she was getting from him at all. He looked broken and she felt responsible for that. She had failed. He could see the truth despite the smoke-screen she put up for everyone else. Because this was Jack and he knew her better than she knew herself.

"I had no idea," he mumbled. "So, you can't feel anything, at all?"

She lowered her gaze to stare at the mug in her hands.

"Below my hips, everything is pretty much numb. The best way I can explain it is that my legs feel like they're packed in ice. They're not cold, just kind of… disconnected from the rest of me, if that makes any sense. Sometimes I get a bit of nerve pain and they tingle, sort of like a bad case of pins and needles."

Almost like they're waking up but they never do.

"Nerve pain? That sounds like it hurts?"

"Sometimes," she mumbled.

Why did he have to ask all this? Desperate to turn the conversation around, she glanced up and tried to be positive.

"My neurologist says I'm lucky, overall. I don't have any muscle spasms, just a bit of back pain sometimes. Callum helps me with massage and exercise, and I swim. That helps."

She cringed internally. A bit of back pain? Uncomfortable? Not exactly white lies, more like big black ones but worth it if she managed to minimise the impact. He was clearly having trouble processing everything so she waited, giving him time.

"I've replayed that night over and over in my head," he said, sitting back in his chair and staring blankly at the coffee mug in front of him. "I dream about it, the accident. Sometimes it feels like I can take control of what happens, like I can change things, some things. Nothing important, though. It doesn't matter how hard I try or what I do, I can never change how it ends."

She thought about the running dream. It was different all the time but the overall feeling of helplessness remained long after she woke up. Was it the same for him?

"I think about what I could've done differently, what might've happened if I'd done this instead of that; if Callum hadn't needed a lift and we'd taken the bike instead of my car; if we hadn't taken River Road; if we'd just been somewhere else - anywhere else - at that exact moment."

"I don't remember any of it," she shrugged helplessly, wishing she had something more encouraging to say. "I don't even remember waking up that morning. I remember the day before and I remember waking up in the hospital. The rest is just... gone."

He didn't look at her and the silence in the room was suffocating.

"Do you know what the two most dangerous words in the English language are?" she said. "What if. They can drive you mad. You can't spend your life wondering about what might've happened. It doesn't matter how much we want to change things; the fact is we can't. The only thing we have control over is the present and the future. The past is gone, over. We have to move forward. We don't have a choice."

He reached across the table and laid his hand gently over hers. She fought the urge to pull away, the gesture so terrifyingly familiar that it hurt. She watched his hand on hers, afraid to look up, heart racing. He didn't speak and she couldn't find any words. He turned her hand over in his, gently running his fingertips over the calluses at the base of her fingers.

"Please don't," she said, cringing as she tried to ease her hand out of his. "I hate them."

He held on, not letting her go.

"Why do you hate them?"

"Look at them - they're ugly."

"They're not ugly," he said hoarsely. "You should be proud of them."

She glanced up and found she couldn't tear her eyes away from his, now molten pools of green. She wanted to dive in suddenly, to get away from all of this and start again.

"You should be proud of yourself," he insisted, squeezing her hand, holding her gaze. "You're incredible. So much stronger than I was - than I am."

"I didn't have a choice," she managed, feeling like a fraud and a trickster.

He had no idea what he was saying.

"There's always a choice, Ally. I should know. I was scared and I did the wrong thing. I wish I could change that, believe me," he said with quiet conviction. "I don't deserve another chance so I'm not going to ask you for one. Just know that I'm going to try and make it up to you somehow, even if it takes the rest of my life."

Goosebumps rose on her arms and she prayed silently for strength even as she felt it flowing out of her.

"I don't know what you want me to say," she whispered.

"You don't have to say anything, I just wanted you to know. I'm not walking away this time. You have my word."

Her heart believed every word. Her head wasn't quite so sure as Callum's words echoed in her ears.

He'd never believe him and he needed to, for all their sakes.

FOUR YEARS EARLIER

Jack stood outside Callum's hospital room, his shoulder aching despite the miles of tape and the sling keeping his arm immobile.

"Thank you, son. That's all we need for now. I'll let you go see your friend."

The policeman who reminded him of a younger version of his father put his notebook away and offered his hand.

"Thanks," Jack said, shaking it.

"You take care now."

"Yeah, thanks."

Jack watched him walk away, sinking back against the wall and trying to stop his head from spinning off his shoulders. He wondered if he should have taken the painkillers offered to him when they taped up his shoulder but it had felt like cheating somehow. It was hard enough to keep a thought in his head without drugs muddying the waters.

He desperately wanted to see his father one minute and was overcome with shame the next. How the hell was he going to explain this to his father, to Ally? He let out a shuddering breath and forced himself to enter Callum's room.

Callum sat on the edge of the bed, staring at the floor. His clothes were heaped in a pile beside him, the hospital gown he had argued about putting on, hanging off him loosely. He glanced up when Jack entered.

"Everything okay?" he asked.

"Fine."

"What did he want to know?"

"What the road conditions were like, how fast we were going, if I'd had anything to drink," Jack sank down carefully into the chair in the corner. "He breathalysed me."

"Makes sense."

The doctor's words hung in the air between them, heavy and oppressive and coating Jack in a thick layer of guilt he could barely breathe through.

"She's going to be fine," Callum said. "She'll get through this and she'll be okay."

Jack could feel his muscles contracting, almost turning him inside out.

"No, she's not," he said through teeth clenched so tightly his jaw hurt. "She's not gonna be fine. Weren't you listening? She's paralysed and it's my fault."

"Jesus. How many times? You didn't do this!"

"Yes, I did!"

He stood up and began to pace, his body anxiously needing to mirror the frantic activity going on inside his brain.

"She had a spinal injury and I moved her!"

"You didn't know!"

The moment of impact rushed back, with everything else that followed playing out in front of him like a movie.

"If I'd left her in her seat, if I hadn't moved her, if I'd just listened to you, she'd be fine."

"You did the right thing," Callum insisted. "The car was leaking gas. You didn't have a choice, you couldn't just leave her there."

"Oh God, she's gonna hate me. She's gonna – "

Jack froze, his knees trembling as the weight of his decision pushed down on him.

"You were trying to save her life; the car could've gone up at any time and she would've been inside it if you hadn't pulled her out!"

Jack blinked, coming back to reality with a jolt.

"But it didn't, did it? It didn't ignite. Maybe I imagined it? Maybe there was no gas, maybe it was all in my head?"

"Listen to me," Callum rasped sharply, tears gathering in his eyes. "You didn't imagine it. I smelt it too. For God's sake, this isn't helping. Remember what the doc said? When she wakes up, she's gonna need you. If she sees you like this it's just gonna freak her out. You need to get a grip, dude. I mean it."

Jack stared back at him, dumbstruck. He knew without a shadow of a doubt that he couldn't stand there in front of Ally and tell her that because of what he did, she was never going to walk again. He couldn't apologise. There were no words for what he had done. And what did it matter anyway? Words wouldn't fix it, nothing would. His whole body went numb as the realisation coursed through his veins, eating away at his insides, hollowing him out.

The door opened then and it felt like time had slowed down again. His father appeared and at the look of anguish on his face, Jack broke down.

"Son," he said simply, and then Jack was freefalling into his arms.

CHAPTER NINE

*"Not everything that is faced can be changed.
But nothing can be changed until it is faced."*
- James Arthur Baldwin

*J*ack climbed into his car and sat there, staring into the darkness.

She wants me to stay.

It only took a moment before the joy turned to anxiety. She had given him a second chance. How was he ever going to prove to her that he was worthy of it if he didn't believe he deserved it?

His phone vibrated in his pocket and he dug it out, declining the call and tossing it onto the passenger seat. It wasn't the first time Ben had tried contacting him and probably wouldn't be the last. The sooner he picked up a new phone, the better.

He turned the key and listened to the engine idling, contemplating his next move. He'd promised himself that if she gave him a second chance, Callum would be his next stop. He needed him to know that he was here to stay and that there was no point standing in his way. It would be much easier on Ally if he didn't, although how he was going to convince him of that was still a mystery.

He couldn't let her down this time. She was both a tower of intimidating strength and a pool of heart-wrenching vulnerability and the dichotomy was mesmerising. Pulling away from the curb into the darkness, he had a fair idea of the reception he would get from Callum and he hoped that some of that strength would rub off on him.

Driving through town, the roads were more or less deserted as he left the streetlights behind, detouring from the main road and onto a quiet side street. He hadn't been to Callum's house in years but he drove on autopilot, as if he were here just yesterday. He pulled over to the curb opposite the last house on the street and sat in the car, staring at it. The house was in darkness and there was no car in the driveway and no sign of the van he had put so much work into getting on the road four years earlier.

It felt as if he'd been away for a lot longer. He could tell from the way Ally talked about him that she and Callum were close. He understood why and it made sense but it still hurt. He had no right to be jealous. He walked away, Callum stayed.

If he wasn't at home it meant he'd have to go looking for him so he pulled away from the curb and headed back out to the main road. Barney's was the obvious choice. He hadn't been inside since he returned to town but he was willing to play the odds. He started to sweat. Barney's was familiar territory and he had purposefully avoided any such places since the debacle at the funeral. The curtain-twitching next door was bad enough.

---

*C*allum glanced up from the sink as the men's room door creaked open. Andy McLeish stood in the doorway, wearing a self-satisfied smirk that Callum immediately wanted to wipe off his face with his fist. Instead, he grabbed a paper towel and quickly dried his hands, tossing it into the tin bucket in the corner.

"Well, look who it is," Andy purred.

The tone of his voice made the urge to hit him double.

"What the hell do you want?" he said. "Don't you have somewhere to be?"

"Why? Am I making you nervous?"

"Nope," he mumbled, pushing past Andy irritably. "But the smell of bullshit in here is making me gag."

Andy grabbed Callum's arm as he passed, twisting it up behind his back and pushing him up against the wall. Callum's face smacked into the hardboard panelling as Andy pinned him in place, pain shooting up his arm.

"Careful," Andy breathed in his ear. "That was almost assault. Wouldn't that be a violation of your probation?"

Callum breathed heavily through his nose, his temper rising with every heartbeat. Just as he was sure he wasn't able to rein it in any longer, Andy let him go and stepped back. Slowly, Callum turned to face him, flexing his hand and ignoring the dull ache in his elbow. He glanced at Andy out of the corner of his eye and turned to head straight for the door.

"I saw her the other day, on the street. She didn't see me but I got a good look at those skinny little legs in action. I gotta say, she has a great ass - for a cripple."

Callum stopped in his tracks, one hand on the door, not daring to turn around. The hair on the back of his neck stood on end and his lungs felt like they were sitting in his throat.

"I mean, there's no doubt that the sex would still be weird but I'm willing to bet that she could do other things just as well as normal chicks - maybe even better. I mean, is it kinda like blind people having great hearing? Y'know, other senses compensating for the one that's gone?"

Callum's jaw clamped so tightly he thought his teeth were

going to crack. The thought of Andy anywhere near Ally made his skin crawl. He turned around to face him, barely able to contain his temper, clenching his fists in anticipation as they slowly circled each other. What he wouldn't give to knock that cocky smile right off his ugly face.

Andy raised his eyebrows at him and threw his hands up in mock surrender, inviting him to hit him. Callum seriously considered it for a moment. Then he realised what was happening and knew he had to get out of there. Andy had positioned himself in front of the door again, smiling.

"Get out of my way," he hissed, elbowing him aside and shoving the men's room door open so hard it rebounded off the wall.

He stopped in his tracks as the door swung back behind him. Jack stood at the bar, beer untouched in front of him.

"Hey!" Andy yelled, addressing Harry, the bartender. "You can't do that - that was assault! Did you see that?"

"See what?" Harry turned his back and ambled down to the other end of the bar. Callum couldn't help but smirk. Harry, in his usual straightforward way, was letting Andy know exactly what he thought of him.

"He pushed me!"

Callum ignored him as he walked towards the bar stool he had vacated minutes earlier, reaching for his jacket.

Jack nodded at the half-finished beer on the bar in front of Callum.

"I've never known you to walk away from a beer."

"Yeah well, times change."

"Hey!" Andy called. "Ferguson! We're not done yet!"

Callum could feel the anger welling up inside him. He pushed open the door out into the street and fished his car keys out of his pocket.

"Ferguson!"

He heard the door creak open again behind him, Andy's voice

hanging in the cool night air. Sighing, he stopped. Clearly, this wasn't going to just go away.

"What do you want?" he demanded, turning to face him.

Andy smiled, happy to have his full attention again. The street was deserted. No witnesses. Could he risk it? It'd certainly be worth it.

"Look, I can see why you're sweet on her. I mean, she's pretty, and with her legs being all screwed up like that, she's bound to be grateful for the attention. But if you don't make a move soon, I'm gonna beat you to it and you'll have no one to blame but yourself."

"I'm not gonna tell you again. Stay away from her."

"Or what?"

Callum's fists clenched at his side.

"You don't want to know."

"Sounds like a threat to me," Andy chuckled.

"Whatever, man," Callum turned his back on him again. Andy's hand on his shoulder immediately sent his blood pressure soaring but before he could react, Andy had spun him around to face him.

"I'm not done with you, Ferguson."

"Back off!" Callum growled, shrugging his hand off him and taking a step closer in one fluid movement. "If you ever touch me again, I'm not going to be responsible for what happens to you, understand? I *will* do jail time for what I do to you and it'll be freakin' worth it, got that?"

He stared into Andy's face a moment longer, mentally tying his fists to his sides so they wouldn't reflexively jab up and under Andy's chin. Andy stared right back at him, not moving a muscle.

"I don't know how we got off to such a bad start," Andy said evenly. "We got a lot in common. I mean, just look at her - we're obviously both into the kinky shit. Now, I can't speak for you, but I would definitely consider tapping that once, at least. Call it curiosity or whatever but I'd go there. I mean, can she even feel anything down there? Cos if not, maybe foreplay isn't really necessary y'know? Or maybe that's out of the question completely. Could be that she's more of a giver than a taker, if you catch my –"

Suddenly, Andy was careening away from him. Jack bulldozed him across the pavement, turning and slamming him up against the nearest wall, face-first. Callum, his brain struggling to make sense of what just happened, could only stand and watch as Jack leaned in close to Andy, whispering something. Then he spun him around to face him, punching him so hard that Andy's head rebounded off the wall with a sickening crack.

Callum stood, frozen, as the scene unfolded before him. If he didn't know better, he would have sworn that wasn't Jack but someone else. As long as he had known him, Jack had never been a fighter. Jack was the voice of reason, Callum was the one with the temper. Watching him now, though, Callum could see that something had changed.

"That's assault!" Andy gasped, blood pouring out of his nose and dripping off his chin. "You're gonna be sorry you did that, just like he was!"

Jack didn't miss a beat. He punched Andy again, sending him toppling sideways. He reached down to haul him to his feet before driving a hammer punch into his ribs, doubling Andy in two.

Callum tried to reconcile the Jack that stood over Andy now with the friend he once knew. The two seemed worlds apart. As teenagers, they had brawled once, and it had been while Jack's mother was going through chemo. Jack hadn't had the skill or experience that Callum had and it was over with one punch. Callum had put it down to stress and they never spoke of it again.

But this was different. He hadn't had time to think about it at the funeral, but watching Jack now gave him chills. He fought like a pro. He knew where to hit, when to hit and when to dodge.

His body moved differently. He seemed calm and calculating, even when he delivered a blow. It was chilling.

Jack hauled Andy to his feet and pushed him out into the street. Andy staggered, hunched over with his arm held close to his ribs. He glanced up at Callum briefly, blood pouring from his nose, dark in the streetlight, before stumbling down the street towards his car.

"Why'd you do that?" Callum asked.

"He deserved it."

Jack cradled the knuckles of one hand in the palm of the other. Callum tried to read him but came up empty.

"I heard what he said, about Ally," Jack added. "He's an asshole, nailed to a pair of feet."

It was one of Tom's expressions and they both knew it.

"I don't know about you," Jack said. "But I could do with a drink."

Callum nodded slowly, the blood still rushing in his ears. If he didn't know better, he would have sworn it was nerves. He had no idea what had happened to Jack in the last four years, but the guy standing in front of him wasn't the Jack he thought he knew. This guy could hold his own in a fight. This guy had an almost dangerous air about him, hidden right beneath the surface. This guy had some explaining to do.

"Yeah," he said. "I could do with a drink right now myself."

***

*J*ack sat in a booth inside Barney's, rubbing his aching knuckles. Callum waited at the bar while Harry poured their drinks. The place was almost empty, except for a guy Jack thought he recognised propping up the bar and a couple of guys he didn't know playing pool. One of them laughed loudly and Jack cringed as the sound echoed through the room. He and Callum used to spend hours playing pool, just like them. Life seemed to be split into two distinct chapters: before the accident, and after. It seemed like it was a defining moment, for all of them. After that, everything changed.

Callum walked towards him with two beers in one hand and two shot glasses in the other. He set them down on the table and sat down opposite him. Without a word, both men picked up the shot glasses and downed them in a single gulp. Jack glanced up at Callum as the fiery liquid burnt its way down his throat, wondering what was supposed to happen next.

He had come in with a plan but the fight had turned everything upside down and he wasn't sure what to do now. He rolled the empty shot glass between his palms on the table.

"Who was that guy?" he asked.

"Andy McLeish. Works at the mill."

"He's got a mouth on him," Jack set the shot glass aside and picked up his beer instead, taking a quick swig.

"He has."

An ice pack appeared on the table in front of him and Jack glanced up to see Harry walking back towards the bar.

"Thanks," he called after him, picking it up and easing it onto his knuckles with a wince. "What did he mean? Something about me being sorry, like you were?"

"That's part of his *charm*," Callum said sarcastically, taking a mouthful of beer and setting the bottle down on the table again. "If being a dickhead was an Olympic sport, he'd be a gold medallist several times over. He said something about Ally a while ago and I pretty much reacted the same way you just did. He pressed charges, I ended up in court. I'm on probation and he knows it. It was worth it, though."

"Probation?"

"Good behaviour bond. And some anger management bullshit."

"Wow."

Jack couldn't help but smile.

"Yeah," Callum took a hurried swallow from his beer bottle. "So enough about that. I thought you'd be long gone by now. Why are you still here?"

Jack's smile faded.

"I heard what you said the other night," he said. "And I get it. I messed up and there's no changing that. But I meant what I said. I'm not going anywhere and if that means you want to take a swing at me again, fine. Go for it, I deserve it, and a hell of a lot more besides. Shit, if it'll make you feel better, beat me to a pulp. I won't stop you." Callum raised his eyebrows, opening his mouth to interrupt. Jack beat him to it. "But we're still gonna have to talk about this when you're done."

Callum closed his mouth, surveying him from across the table.

"What the hell happened to you?" he asked. "Where'd you go?"

Jack was prepared for animosity, reflexive anger, wisecracks and whole lot more besides. He wasn't prepared for sincerity.

"What do you mean?" he asked, buying time to think.

"I mean, that - outside, with Andy - where the hell did that come from? Where'd you learn to fight like that? Where have you been?"

"Didn't Dad tell you?"

"I stopped asking. He acted like you were in Witness Protection."

That sounded like his dad. Would it always feel like this when someone mentioned him? Like a little piece of his heart was being ripped out? He chose to ignore the last part of Callum's question, instead concentrating on the first part.

"All over," he said, discarding the ice pack. "I moved around, went where the work was."

He could feel the questions building. He knew it wasn't enough, that he owed him more of an explanation, but it felt like it was too soon to be talking about any of this. He didn't need

Callum judging him any more than he already was, especially when the full story was nothing to be proud of.

"Okay," Callum's eyes narrowed. "Well, if those questions are too hard, let's start with something easy. What are you doing here, tonight? Looking for me or just felt like getting out and about for old times' sake?"

"I've been talking to Ally."

He steeled himself, but Callum's expression remained neutral. "Really."

"Will you just hear me out?"

Callum's response was to take a swig of beer. Jack took this as a sign of acquiescence so he barrelled ahead before he lost his nerve completely.

"Something Ally said to me tonight really struck a chord. She said the only thing we can control is the present and the future. She's right - the past is gone, nothing I can do will change what I did. I'm not gonna sit here and beg you for forgiveness either, because I don't deserve that. I missed my chance to make things up to Dad and that's something I'm gonna have to live with but I sure as hell don't want to make that mistake with Ally, or with you."

Callum remained unusually quiet and still. He stared at Jack across the table for several long moments, during which time Jack tried to prepare himself for what was to come next.

"What do you want, exactly?" Callum asked finally.

"You gave me plenty to think about the last time we talked and I finally realised something. It's not really up to me to decide if I should stay or go. It should be her choice. So, I asked her. I told her I'd leave if she wanted me to. She asked me to stay."

The muscle in Callum's jaw ticked ominously but he didn't speak.

"So, I'm not going anywhere this time. I know you probably don't believe me but it's the truth. As for what I want, I guess I want to not have to fight you on this. I want to try and make up for what I did then by being here now. I want to make a difference, here and now and as long as she'll let me."

His breath caught in his throat, his heart racing a million miles an hour.

Callum stared at him from across the table.

"Well?" Jack urged, desperate to know where he stood.

"You want to make a difference?"

Jack nodded, a sense of dread crawling up his spine.

"You could've made a difference if you'd been there when she woke up, after the accident," Callum said, his blue eyes blazing. "Maybe if you'd been the one to tell her that the reason she couldn't feel her legs wasn't because of the medication, but because her back was broken, that would've made a difference. You could've been there with her when she was in rehab for all those weeks, when she just wanted to give up - you could've made a difference then. You know what? I can think of at least a hundred times over the past four years when you could've made a difference, Jack, but where were you then? Because you sure as hell weren't here."

Jack felt sick to his stomach as Callum continued, quietly but deliberately.

"And what about Tom? Maybe he'd never have had to defend your actions to his friends if you hadn't left like that. Maybe he wouldn't have had to step up and make these decisions with Ally because you weren't here to do it, maybe his life would've been a little bit easier if you'd been around to help."

Jack felt like getting up and walking away, the truth cutting far deeper than he imagined it would. Yet all he could do was sit there as Callum stared at him across the table.

"And what about me, while we're on the subject? Where the hell were you when I needed you? You just walked away and you left me with all this shit and you didn't even have the guts to talk to me. Did you ever think about maybe just picking up the damn phone? You brushed me off like I was something stuck to the bottom of your shoe. All I could do was stand by and watch Ally falling apart and there wasn't a single damn thing I could do about it!"

Callum choked on his words and had to stop for a moment, taking a swig from his beer bottle with a trembling hand. Jack winced as he slammed it back down on the table.

"So, do I think you can make a difference here, now? No, I don't. I think it's too late for that. We've adjusted, we're handling it. We don't need you. God knows what it is you think you can do to change anything, but go ahead, knock yourself out." Callum made a sweeping gesture with his hand. "The floor is yours."

Jack stared at him, dumbfounded.

"One more thing, and I want an honest answer - no bullshit," Callum continued, sitting forward. "Why'd you leave?"

Stunned, the answer came directly from his heart.

"I was scared."

Callum nodded, staring at Jack's beer bottle for a moment. Then he lifted his gaze to stare directly into Jack's soul.

"You still scared?"

"Terrified."

"Yet you say you're gonna stick around. How do you know?" he prodded. "How do you know you're not just gonna bail again? Tomorrow, or next week, or next month?"

"I won't."

The words squeezed out from behind clenched teeth, his jaw locked up to try and retain some semblance of control over his emotions.

"Not exactly an Oscar-winning performance."

Callum took a long pull on the remainder of his beer and stood up, grabbing his jacket from the seat. Jack stared up at him in surprise, watching as he walked out of the bar, the door swinging closed behind him.

Jack stared at the empty seat across from him for several moments. Then he abandoned his beer and raced after him.

CHAPTER TEN

"There is a space between man's imagination and man's attainment that may only be traversed by his longing."
- Khalil Gibran

FOUR YEARS EARLIER

*N*one of it seemed real. He was an intruder, trespassing in another world, stuck in some alternate reality. Back in the real world, he had already dropped Callum off at his place and was down at the river, proposing to Ally. He desperately wanted to get back there but he was trapped. They all were.

The ICU was busy. A doctor and nurse, heads bent over a clipboard, spoke in conversational tones at the entrance to one cubicle. Another nurse consulted a chart at the foot of the bed next door. She looked up and smiled encouragingly at him as they passed. He felt like screaming. Ally's life was being ripped apart. There was nothing to smile about.

The nurse who had ushered them up to the ICU disappeared into a cubicle, Callum close behind. Jack watched in silence as the loose, hospi-

tal-issue, open-backed gown that Callum wore over the blue, hospital-issue pants ("I'm not flashing my ass to the entire hospital") vanished.

Guilt ate away at his insides. The only positive he could find right at this moment was that Ally was unconscious. She didn't know yet. When she woke up everything would change. For the second time tonight, he wished he didn't have to be there for that. He didn't want to see the look of realisation when she finally understood what had happened.

"Jack? Are you with us, son?"

His father gently squeezed his good arm. He took a few hesitant steps into the cubicle where Ally lay, acutely aware of his father right beside him. Strangely, it did nothing to comfort him. The crushing weight of guilt bore down on him instead.

She lay on her back, dark hair pooling beside her. A rigid white plastic collar encircled her neck and her ghostly complexion blended into the white sheets. Her entire body was bathed in an ethereal light cast by the fluorescent bulb on the wall above her head. It was as if the world had tilted sideways. One minute, everything was perfect, the next he was trapped in this nightmare. In between was a split-second decision he would regret for the rest of his life.

The nurse began talking, explaining to them what all the tubes and machines were for, but Jack couldn't concentrate on anything she said. His attention was focused on Ally, lying there, so still, so pale. He willed her to understand how sorry he was. His father squeezed his arm again, murmuring something that he couldn't hear for the buzzing in his head. Callum approached the bed and reached out to take Ally's hand, holding it for a moment before turning to him, tears glistening in his eyes. Jack looked away, guilt wrenching at his insides.

"Just hold her hand, Jack. Let her know you're here," his father said gently.

Tears blinded him. A hand on his back urged him forward and he wanted to shrug it off and run but he couldn't. Callum shuffled out of his way and a look of understanding passed between them.

Shock. Despair. Terror.

Jack picked up Ally's hand, her fingers cool and smooth. She felt so fragile. This wasn't happening. It couldn't be. Things like this happened to other people, not to them. He laid her hand down on the bed again, tears rolling down his cheeks. He felt like he was hyperventilating and he fought to control his breathing, to slow it down so the world didn't feel like it was closing in on him.

"Hey, it's okay. Come on, take it easy," his father whispered.

Jack turned toward him, silently willing him to help. Just like he had when his mother was dying. And now, as then, he realised there was no way out of this. It was happening. The agony and heartache of this night was already etched into the lines of his father's face.

He turned his back on everything, trying to put the nightmare behind him, rounding the corner of the cubicle and out into the main floor of the ICU. He only made it a few steps before his knees buckled and he hit the floor heavily. Balancing on his knees and his one good hand, he stared blankly at the linoleum. Callum's voice rang in the background, his vision swam, his shoulder burned hot. He found himself wanting to just lay down right there on the floor, not caring what happened next. What did it matter, anyway? Life as they knew it was over.

Instead, he was hoisted physically upwards. His vision slowly cleared and he blinked, lifting his head. He sat in a plastic chair, a nurse leaning over him. He heard the words "panic attack" and from somewhere deep inside, he agreed. He was panicked. He was absolutely terrified.

Something bright shone in his eyes and he swatted it away. Someone asked if he wanted some water and he nodded. Looking over the nurse's shoulder, he saw his father staring at him, his face twisted into an anxious frown.

"I'll get you some water. You just wait right here, okay?" he ordered gruffly.

The nurse left him a few moments later and he glanced over at Callum, pale and stoic in the chair opposite him.

"Sure, you're alright?" Callum asked.

Jack began to nod, then thought better of it, his head still pounding.
"I'm fine."

"You passed out."

Jack stared back at him, trying to breathe normally. His head swam.
Callum leaned forward, the hospital gown stretched taut over his knees.

"It's not your fault," he said. "You didn't do anything wrong."

"How the hell am I gonna tell her?"

"You tell her what she needs to know. That's it. No guilt tripping,
Jack - I mean it. Stick to the facts."

"The fact is I did this to her," he whispered.

"Hey, we talked about this. Don't complicate it, don't make it harder
than it already is," Callum frowned. "We all have to be strong for her.
She's going to need us - especially you - when she wakes up."

Jack shook his head again, his heart pounding.

"I can't. I can't do it... "

"You have to," Callum said simply. "You can't let this shit take over,
dude. Just breathe - you need to breathe."

The aches and pains from earlier in the night seemed to vanish and
Jack felt as if he floated far above himself, watching from a distance.
Just hours ago, the future had stretched in front of him, an engagement
ring tucked safely in the pocket of his jeans.

Now there was nothing.

---

*C*allum was halfway to his car by the time Jack caught up with him.

"Hey!" he called out.

Callum turned around to face him as he fumbled with his keys.

"Look," he sighed. "Congratulations, you finally grew some balls. But let's just get one thing straight here. You make her a promise like that, you better keep it. If you disappear again I will personally hunt you down and kill you. Understand?"

Jack nodded, holding his ground as Callum eyeballed him.

"I understand."

"Good," Callum said. "Get in the car."

Obediently, Jack did as he was told. The silence in the car was deafening and Callum didn't seem in any hurry to break it. They watched the guy who was propping up the bar walk out of Barney's and make his way up the street, staggering slightly. The temperature had dropped over the past hour and the light mist that had settled over the town gave the streetlights an eerie glow.

"I hated you for leaving," Callum said into the heavy silence. "I mean, I knew you felt responsible for what happened to her but I never thought you'd just leave her like that. You were going to propose, Jack. What the hell were you thinking?"

Jack stared at his hands, clenched into fists on his thighs. He thought back to that night like he had hundreds of times.

"I wasn't - thinking, that is. I was just scared. I didn't want her to push me away so I left before she could."

"That's a really shitty excuse."

"I know it's shitty, but it's not an excuse. It's the truth. I was scared. I didn't know what else to do."

"We were all scared," Callum said. "Do you think it was easy, watching her try to deal with this?"

"Do you think it was easy walking away?" Jack countered, turning towards him.

"Don't you dare do that, no one made you leave, that was your choice!"

There was no arguing with that.

"I know that saying I'm sorry doesn't fix anything, but I am. I really am."

Silence settled over them once again and all Jack could hear was the pounding of his heart in his ears.

"Surgery seemed to take forever," Callum said finally, almost to himself. "And that whole time I kept hoping that somehow they'd gotten it all wrong, that they'd come out of the operating room and say whoops, sorry, made a mistake, she's gonna be fine."

Jack tried to breathe but if felt like his chest was in a vice.

"The next few days, the meds were pretty strong. She only came round for a few minutes at a time, they made her really groggy. Every time she opened her eyes, she asked for you. We just kept saying you were on your way. Luckily, she couldn't stay awake long enough to question it."

"I'm sorry," Jack murmured, knowing full well that it wasn't enough.

Ignoring him, Callum continued.

"Finally, we had to tell her what happened. We couldn't wait for you anymore, she was getting agitated, anxious. It was making things worse. That was one of the hardest things I've ever had to do. If Tom hadn't been there with me, I don't know if I could've done it. For a long time afterwards, I felt like I'd stolen something from her."

"How did she take it?" Jack asked, not sure he wanted to know the answer.

Callum seemed lost, staring out the windshield.

"She cried."

Jack's head bowed low. His heart felt like it was being shredded.

"I think deep down, on some level, she might have known," Callum reflected quietly. "She said she couldn't feel her legs. We kept blaming it on the meds, stalling until we could find you, but the doc said we needed to tell her. The sooner she knew, the sooner she could start to accept it. She was so scared and there was nothing I could do," he paused, swallowing noisily. "All through rehab, even months later, she still thought you'd come home. She was fighting so hard to be independent because she didn't want you to be scared off again when you came home. Did Tom tell you that?"

"No," he whispered. "He didn't."

Callum huffed out a breath, shaking his head in disbelief.

"It wasn't his fault," Jack said. "I told him not to. It was... it hurt too much."

"So, you just walked away and didn't want to know anymore, is that it? Fresh slate? Never gave us a second thought?"

Jack tried to think of words that would explain what the last four years had been like but everything sounded trite by comparison. It didn't matter what he had been through, only what he had put everyone else through by leaving.

"It wasn't like that," he said finally.

"Then what was it like?"

"I'm not going to make excuses for what I did. There's nothing I can say that's gonna make it easier for you to understand. But I didn't just walk away and forget about you all either, trust me."

"Where'd you learn to fight like that?" Callum asked abruptly.

"I've done a lot of things I'm not proud of. Leaving here that night isn't exactly the end of that list."

"Jesus," Callum huffed "Would a straight answer kill you?"

"Nutshell? I hung out in shitty bars with shittier people."

"That's it? That's all you got?"

"For now, yeah."

He prayed that Callum would leave it at that. He didn't want to have to lie to him but he wasn't ready to share the truth yet either. Jack cleared his throat and glanced out of the windshield again. The guys he had seen at the pool table were coming out of Barney's together, laughing as they made their way down the street. Jealousy pulled at his gut.

"That used to be us, once upon a time," he said.

"Feels like a hundred years ago."

Silence buzzed around them again.

"Do you still love her?"

Jack didn't have to think about his reply.

"I never stopped."

"What if she doesn't feel the same?"

"Doesn't matter. I'm not going anywhere."

"What if she's with someone else?"

Jack glanced over at him.

"Is she with someone else?" he asked.

The thought had never even crossed his mind. Callum regarded him sombrely for a moment before finally shaking his head.

"No. But what if she was?"

"Then I'd deal with it. It wouldn't make me take off again, if that's what you're asking."

"You sound pretty sure of yourself."

"First you tell me I'm not convincing anyone, now you say I'm too cocky?" Jack snapped. "Make up your damn mind."

Callum seemed about to say something, then changed his mind, frowning as he went back to staring out the windshield.

"So, what now?" he asked, tapping his fingers against the steering wheel.

"I don't know. One day at a time, I guess."

Jack turned his attention back to the misty street. This next part was going to hurt but it had to be said.

"I can see how close you two are," he said. "And I just want you to know that I'm grateful that you were there for her."

"I did it for her, not for you."

"I know."

"Tom was there for her just as much as I was. He should've gotten this speech, too."

"I know he should've."

A knife twisted in his gut as he thought about all the things he never got to say. He saw himself sitting in his car outside the cemetery gates earlier, afraid to go in.

"I think we're done here," Callum said, jolting him out of his guilt-trip.

"Yeah," he murmured, fumbling with the door handle. "I should go. I guess I'll see you around."

"I guess so."

Jack climbed out of the car, bone-weary suddenly. He watched Callum's car disappear down the misty street until all that were left were red tail-lights, shining like devil's eyes in the dark. He stared down at his bruised knuckles and flexed his fist a few times, remembering Andy McLeish's words and the anger that had sprung up from deep inside when he heard them. Glancing over at Barney's, the neon sign glowing in the eerie mist, he couldn't help but think of simpler times.

*J*ack had suggested they meet for a drink and before she knew what happening, Ally was agreeing. The anxiety set in almost immediately. She hadn't been to Barney's on a weekend in over a year. Last time had been a disaster. A crowded bar was no place for someone with her mobility issues.

You're in control, remember? You can do this.

She turned to take stock of herself in the full-length mirror. Wearing her favourite jeans and a simple long-sleeved black cashmere top, she was going for an understated look. How she felt was under-prepared.

She couldn't help but think about what had happened in the diner. The whispering, the gossiping, the stares. Was Jack ready for that? Was she? She tried to push the doubts aside as she slipped one arm out of the cuff of her crutch and pulled an earring free from her hair.

A knock on the door sent her pounding heart into overdrive. She was starting to wish she hadn't sent Maggie home.

"I'm just a phone call away," Maggie had said.

And she was. Which might be a good thing, depending on what happened tonight.

"I'll just be a minute!" she called, retrieving her jacket from the bed and slipping it on. She made her way to the front door, pausing to take a deep breath before opening it. Jack stood on her porch wearing his black leather jacket, a khaki shirt and jeans. He looked as nervous as she felt and it was strangely comforting.

"Hi," he smiled tentatively.

All the trepidation from a few minutes ago melted away and for a brief moment in time, the last four years seemed to fade into the background.

In spite of herself, she smiled back.

CHAPTER ELEVEN

"Out of suffering have emerged the strongest souls;
the most massive characters are seared with scars."
- Khalil Gibran

*J*ack was amazed at how busy Barney's was for a
Friday night. The only park they could find was
down a side-street. He worried that it was too far
away from the bar but Ally insisted it was fine. By the time he got
out of the car and walked around to open her door, she was
already lifting her legs out of the car. Her crutches leant against
the inside of the door and in his haste to help, he pulled the door
open wider for her, sending them crashing to the ground.

"Shit, I'm sorry," he mumbled, hastily gathering them up and
handing them to her.

"It's okay, they're not made of glass."

She didn't seem fazed but he felt like an idiot just the
same. He retreated to a safe distance, holding the door as she
leaned the crutches against them again, moving herself

forward and preparing to stand. Using the car door and the back of her seat to hoist herself upright, she checked the locks on her braces through her jeans. Shuffling until she got her balance, she reached for her crutches, sliding her arms into the cuffs. Despite the intense concentration on her face, she didn't even break a sweat. Once again, his admiration ran deep.

He fell in step with her as they made their way up the sidewalk towards the corner. It was a far cry from the way they used to walk together. He pushed his hands deep into his pockets to avoid reaching for her hand.

Barney's was noisy, crowded and fairly well-lit. A loud group of revellers jostled them as they made their way through the door and into the bar. He grabbed Ally's arm automatically, stepping in closer to her. This was exactly the opposite of what he expected and his heart sank.

"Sorry," he said, raising his voice to be heard above the general din. "I had no idea it was gonna be like this."

"It's fine, don't worry about it," Ally smiled tightly. "Let's see if we can find a table."

"I was here the other night and it was pretty much dead. Is it always like this on a Friday?" he asked, leaning closer to her in order to be heard.

"I guess so. I haven't been here on a Friday night in a long time, too crowded for me."

Jack took her arm again, careful not to interfere with her balance. "You should have said something. We could have gone somewhere else instead."

"There really isn't anywhere else these days, that's the problem. Harry kind of has the monopoly."

"Just between you and me, I'd have happily stayed home and had a drink there," he admitted, wishing they had.

"We're here now, I guess we might as well make the best of it," she said, inclining her head towards the rear of the room. "Hey, look. I think that booth is clearing out up the back. Maybe we can grab that?"

"Looks like a good bet," he said, following her gaze.

He kept his eye on the group of people who were exiting the booth, deep in conversation over the music blaring out from the jukebox. Ally began navigating slowly across the room towards them and he fell in behind her, watching nervously. She seemed confident enough but it wasn't her he worried about, it was everyone else. Half the bar was intoxicated, and as a result, completely self-absorbed. As if to illustrate his fears, she narrowly avoided being knocked over by a guy in a Metallica t-shirt and shaggy hair. He slurred an apology as he stared at her with open curiosity. With one eye on the table and one on Ally, Jack made a quick judgment call, recklessly abandoning chivalry to walk ahead of her. With one arm held out protectively behind him, they moved slowly through the crowd towards the corner.

They finally got to the booth as the last of the table-stragglers was leaving. He waited while she eased herself in, sliding in opposite her. She quickly stowed her crutches beneath the table and away from the masses, and then it was just the two of them, smiling nervously at each other over the table.

"That wasn't so bad," he quipped, trying to lighten the mood. "Next stop: Everest."

Her smile became more genuine and the trepidation melted away a little.

"Right," he stood up again and dug out his wallet from the depths of his pocket. "First things first: beer. I'll be right back."

He fought his way through the crowd to the bar and waited impatiently to be served. He glanced back at her a few times, but she seemed engrossed in people-watching. Someone jostled him, apologising loudly. He brushed it off, moving closer to the bar.

"Jack!"

The throngs of people around that end of the bar seemed to hush and he turned around slowly.

"I thought that was you. Heard you were back in town."

Brown eyes narrowed slightly as a guy he went to school with made his way through the crowd towards him.

"Dave." He greeted him formally, offering his hand. They had never been particularly close and he was wary now. It couldn't hurt to be polite. "It's been a long time."

Dave reached out to shake it.

"Sorry to hear about your Dad."

"Thanks."

With a nod of his head, Dave indicated the booth where Ally sat.

"Never thought I'd see the day you two were back in here, together. Almost like old times huh?"

"I guess so," Jack said, uncomfortable with the comparison.

"So, what the hell happened to you? We thought you were dead, you just dropped off the face of the earth."

Jack smiled tightly. Polite conversation was one thing, but the answers to questions like this weren't something he could just whip out of thin air in the middle of a crowded bar.

"Yeah. I guess it might've seemed that way."

He kept an eye on the bar behind him, searching for an excuse to order their drinks and escape the scrutiny.

"It did seem that way," Dave insisted, his gaze levelling uncomfortably on him. "I can't believe she's even giving you the time of day after you disappeared like that. If it were me, I sure as hell wouldn't."

"Correct me if I'm wrong, but none of this is any of your business, is it?" Jack silently dared him to say more. He pushed his wallet back into his pocket, preparing to defend himself physically, if it came to that.

"Dave!" Harry barked from behind the bar. "Back off. I don't want any trouble in here tonight - I'm getting too old for this shit. Jack, what are you having?"

"Beer," Jack answered without taking his eyes off Dave. "Two."

Dave glanced back at Harry, stony-faced.

"Fair enough," he said. "I'm not looking for any trouble. Just had to say my two cents worth."

"Well, you've said it. Now go bother someone else," Harry grumbled, pulling out two beers and popping the tops off them as he shot Dave a withering frown.

"I'm only saying what everyone else is thinking," Dave insisted.

Jack kept an eye on him as he dug into his pocket again and withdrew his wallet, trying desperately to stop his hands from trembling. Adrenaline raced through his system as he handed cash over the bar and took the bottles from Harry.

"Thanks," he mumbled.

Harry leaned over the bar and pushed the cash back in Jack's direction.

"Put your money away, these are on the house. Callum told me what you did to McLeish. Welcome home."

"Thanks," Jack nodded, bewildered, as he slipped the cash back into his pocket.

Harry moved on to take the next order and Jack turned to find Dave had vanished. Making his way back through the crowd to Ally, he set the beers down on the table between them.

"Are you okay?" she asked.

"I'm fine. Why?"

"I saw you talking to Dave."

He took a sip of beer and tried to shrug off the whole experience.

"He was telling me how sorry he was to hear about Dad."

"Was that all?" she asked. "I saw your face. It didn't look like he was just passing on his condolences."

"You know Dave," Jack smiled tightly. "He never knows when to keep his mouth shut."

Ally looked down at the beer bottle in front of her and dragged it closer, picking at the label absentmindedly.

"Hey," he leaned forward. "It's fine, don't worry. I won't self-combust if someone looks at me sideways."

She glanced up, concern furrowing her brow as her eyes flitted over the healing cuts and bruises on his face.

"It's not the fact that they're looking at you sideways that bothers me."

He shrugged casually, trying to set her mind at ease.

"You're acting like you're not surprised by any of this," she said.

"I'm not. Why would I be? I'm the villain here. I deserve it."

"I wish you wouldn't say that."

"Say what?"

"You're not a villain, you're a human being. You made a mistake, that's all. You're not the only one who's ever made a mistake. The important thing is that you're here now, and you're trying to make up for it. What you deserve is a break - from Dave, from Callum, and from yourself."

He gripped the beer bottle in his hand so tightly, he thought he might crush it.

"Point taken," he said, taking a quick sip to hide his discomfort.

He stared out over the crowded bar. Did she have any idea what she was asking him to do? She made it sound easy, like forgiving himself was just a check-box on a shopping list. Make a mistake: check. Get over it: check.

Ally placed her hand over his and he turned back to her. She was staring at him so intently, he almost forgot to breathe.

"Stop beating yourself up," she said, loud enough so he could hear above the noise. "Everyone makes mistakes. The key is learning what not to do next time, then moving on. You can't wallow. It'll kill you - trust me, I know."

"I wish it was that simple," he said, before he had time to engage his brain.

"It is. You just have to try harder."

147

She released his hand and picked up her beer as a million questions raced around inside his head.

"A toast," she said, raising her bottle before he could ask any of them. "To Tom."

He lifted his bottle to gently clink it against hers.

"To Dad."

They both took a sip and his peripheral vision seemed to return in a rush. The music seemed louder, he could make out snippets of conversations going on around them and he almost felt like he was trapped in some kind of time warp. Sitting across from her like this, it was as if the last four years had never happened.

THREE YEARS EARLIER

Ally sat on the floor of her studio, surrounded by tubes of paint, dirty brushes and cloths and a finished canvas that scared the hell out of her. The hollow eyes in the painting seemed to follow her. A chill worked its way up her spine, from the point of injury, where sensation below ceased, right up to the base of her skull before exploding into her head.

I can't do this.

The phrase echoed relentlessly.

I can't do this. I can't do this. I can't do this.

The canvas blurred in front of her and she blinked, hurriedly stemming the flow of tears while she still could.

The twelve-month check-up with her neurologist had arrived like a storm-front, dark and foreboding. Now that it was over she felt empty. The hope she had been hanging onto and the fear she had been desperately trying to keep at bay, had simultaneously deserted her and slammed into her, leaving her reeling.

She couldn't remember the last time she ate. Going to bed had seemed a fruitless exercise so she hadn't, choosing to paint instead. She had stopped answering the phone. All that mattered was getting this pain out of her head and onto canvas before it drove her mad.

For the first time since the accident, there was nothing. Nothing to fight for, nothing to aim for, nothing to cling to. Just a big, black hole of nothing that was consuming her, piece by piece.

She didn't know how long she had been sitting there. She glanced up towards the window and saw the soft light of a new day filtering into the room. She felt similar to the way she had when she woke up in the hospital, after the accident; detached, not fully aware, reality constantly slipping through her fingers like grains of sand.

The past twelve months seemed to have passed in a blur yet the rest of her life stretched out in front of her, a yawning chasm of uncertainty. She glanced down at her legs; knees bent, feet pulled in close on the floor in front of her. She hardly recognised them anymore. The muscles had atrophied, just like she had been warned they would, despite the regular range-of-motion exercises Callum put her body through and the massage and stretches she performed on a daily basis.

Her conscience pricked slightly at the thought of Callum. The one thing she knew with absolute certainty was that she could never have gotten to this point without him. Yet as hard as he tried, it wasn't enough.

I can't do this. I can't do this. I can't do this.

On the brink of exhaustion, her mind wandered to Jack. She didn't talk about him anymore because it just seemed to upset everyone but she hadn't been able to banish him from her mind. He remained there, perched on the edge of her consciousness, messing with her peace of mind. The unanswered questions taunted her as much as the random pain in her back and the frequent nightmares.

A phone rang somewhere inside the house. She didn't even flinch when she heard it this time. It had rung several times yesterday, or was it this morning? She heard her own voice on the answer-phone message, followed by Tom's. She picked up on the worry in his tone, even if she couldn't quite make out the words. She couldn't afford to let the guilt seep in any further than skin deep.

She looked around for the wheelchair she had abandoned at some stage during the night. In a desperate frenzy, driven to the point of madness as she had tried to exorcise the demons in her head, she had climbed down onto the floor, dragging the canvas with her so she could access it more easily.

That was the thing about her wheelchair; it got in the way. It was as if no one saw her *anymore. It didn't matter what clothes she wore, what she did with her hair, whether or not she wore make-up - they didn't see any of that. She had ceased to exist. Sometime over the past year, her old self had quietly slipped away, leaving behind a shell, and an incomplete one at that.*

She had fallen through the stages of grief the same way you fell in a dream. Slowly, desperately clawing at your surroundings as you tried to stop the descent. First came the denial, then the anger, the bargaining and the depression. When everything else had gone - when the acceptance should have come but didn't - the hope was all that remained. And now that was gone, too.

Overwhelmed by a sense of finality that numbed her emotions, she balanced with one palm flat against the floor, reaching over for her chair with the other. Dragging it closer to her, the wheels squeaked gently against the floorboards. She transferred up into the chair and sat there, watching her bare feet resting on the floor.

She thought about what she was about to do. Her stomach contracted, as if her body was trying to protect itself somehow, one last-ditch attempt to change her mind. Sweeping the guilt aside, she lifted her legs up and nestled her feet into the footrest.

Screw everyone else. It was her life, after all. She was tired of putting on a brave face, tired of being conscious of everyone else's feelings, tired of putting them before her own. She had been selfless for long enough. Now it was her turn.

She released the brake, glancing down at the canvas staring up at her from the floor. For the first time, she saw it for what it really was.

A reflection of her soul.

*R*eminiscing with Ally, Jack felt as if she had reopened the book of his life and only good memories came pouring out, washing away the pain, if only temporarily.

These past few years, because everything seemed to hurt so much, he had shut out memories like these, only allowing himself to wallow occasionally, the pain of what he had lost too great. Now, buffeted by Ally's smiling face across the table from him, he felt as if a little piece of him had been regained. A sense of fullness and warmth enveloped him as he pushed all the negative, self-loathing thoughts aside and concentrated on living in the moment.

He excused himself to get another round and she handed her empty bottle to him, their fingertips touching. Goosebumps crawled up his arm and he smiled down at her. She smiled back shyly and he almost floated to the bar.

Leaning against it, he pushed the empties across and waited his turn. This time, he didn't really care that at least half a dozen pairs of eyes were trained on him. Dave was nowhere to be seen. Curious stares didn't even register. He glanced over towards Ally but her attention was focused on something across the room. His inner smile faded when he realised she was watching the dance-floor. Several couples and a few large groups were dancing, along with one guy who looked like he had already had more than his fair share tonight.

"Same again?" Harry asked.

Jack nodded and turned back to the bar. He watched Harry dispose of the empty bottles and grab another two beers. Money changed hands.

"Thanks," Jack said, taking the bottles as Harry moved further down the bar to serve other patrons.

Ally was still enthralled by the dance-floor. He stood at the bar, watching her. What must it be like for her, knowing she couldn't get up there with them? He remembered a time when she used to kick her shoes off and climb up on the table with Maggie and Jane, the three of them shaking their booties till someone dragged them down again. He remembered being that someone on more than one occasion, throwing her over his shoulder amid much laughter. The sadness, the intense longing he saw even from this distance, shredded his insides. Slowly, he made his way back to her through the crowd.

She glanced up as he put the bottles down on the table between them and slid into the booth.

"You looked miles away, just then," he said before he could stop himself.

"Did I?"

She smiled, but he could tell she wasn't really there. He felt as if he had interrupted something. He turned his attention back to the dance-floor, mostly to give her some time to compose herself. The drunken guy he had spotted earlier threw himself into a group of revellers before being promptly shoved aside. He lost his balance and careened into a table, sending the occupants scattering.

He smiled and turned back to Ally.

"I think someone's night is about to come to an abrupt end."

She nodded, the tight smile still in place.

"Are you okay?" he asked cautiously, fully aware of the tightrope he was walking.

She didn't answer immediately, taking a slow sip from the bottle in front of her.

"Yeah, I'm fine. There are just times when I…"

She glanced towards the dance-floor, frowning as if she was making a decision that might change the course of history. He waited patiently but it became clear she wasn't going to continue.

"Do you miss it?"

Idiot!

Why couldn't he manage the simple task of keeping his foot out of his mouth?

"I miss a lot of things."

The answer may have been casual but one look at her face and he could see the truth. He kicked himself mentally again. He didn't know if she meant for him to see that pain but he had. Now he felt like an intruder, a voyeur. Worse still, he couldn't pretend he hadn't seen it.

"No one's ever come straight out and asked me that before," she said.

"Probably because it's a stupid question. I'm sorry, I didn't – "

"Don't ruin the moment by apologising," she said, and he had to lean closer to hear her over the music. "It's kind of refreshing, to be honest. No dancing around the subject - excuse the pun. But the night is young and we've got a million other things we could talk about so let's talk about something else, okay?"

She forced a smile and he sat back in the booth, curious but not willing to push it. She was right, they had time and it didn't feel right talking about it here. He racked his brains for another topic instead. Something safer, this time.

"Okay. Well, why don't you tell me about this exhibition of yours?"

"How did you know about that?"

"Dad's got a couple of newspaper articles on his fridge. It sounds like it's kind of a big deal, you must be thrilled."

"Yeah, I am."

She picked up her beer and drank slowly, avoiding eye contact.

"I'm happy for you. You deserve this," he said, beginning to think he'd hit another raw nerve.

"You think so?"

"Don't you?"

"I don't know," she shrugged. "Yeah, sometimes. And sometimes I just feel like a giant fraud. I keep thinking I'm going to get found out."

"What do you mean?"

She picked at the label on the bottle before taking another long drink.

"Do you ever feel like you're stuck in someone else's life?" she said finally, setting the bottle down again and looking over at him. "Like this isn't where you're meant to be, or who you're meant to be... or whatever? Like you got lost somehow and you just ended up here and it doesn't matter how hard you try to be somewhere else - to be someone else - you can't seem to escape?"

Her eyes pierced his soul, intent on uncovering his deepest, darkest secrets. He found himself unable to look away.

"Never mind," she smiled thinly, shaking her head. "I'm sorry, I'm rambling. Just ignore me."

He debated whether or not to answer her or let it lie. He decided on the former.

"No, I get it. I feel that way too sometimes."

"You do? What do you think it means?"

"I don't know. I was hoping you'd be able to enlighten me."

"You're asking me for insight?" she smiled.

"You're the artist. I thought it might be a question of perspective or something."

"Sounds like a cop-out to me," she said, eyes twinkling. "Anyway, something tells me I'm not nearly drunk enough for this conversation."

"Speaking of which," he indicated her bottle. "Drink up. You're lagging."

"You trying to get me drunk?"

"Maybe. Is it working?"

"Maybe," she grinned. "But the joke's gonna be on you when you have to carry me out of here."

"Wouldn't be the first time, would it?"

Her grin widened as she shook her head, scanning the room.

"I'd forgotten how busy it gets in here on Fridays," she said.

"I was meaning to ask you about that. No more Friday night debriefs?"

"We haven't done that in a long time."

"Really?"

The Friday night debrief had been a long-standing ritual. They would all meet at Barney's after work on Friday and generally stay until closing. It was a gateway into the weekend.

"I think that was my fault," Ally said, the smile fading. "I told them they could come without me, I didn't need to be there, and I didn't mind. But they wouldn't."

"Because it's so busy?" he asked, reading between the lines.

She shrugged, as if it was a foregone conclusion.

The bar was getting noisier. Jack watched as a large group burst through the main door. He glanced over at Harry, who was also watching them, his expression dark. The group elbowed their way to the bar, amid protests from other patrons who were unimpressed with their behaviour. It was apparent they had had a copious amount of alcohol already.

"Shit," Ally mumbled, also watching the group.

Jack spotted Andy McLeish, holding court at the centre of the bar, laughing raucously. Jack's blood began to boil just watching him. He turned back to Ally, who was trying her best to look inconspicuous. She was clearly nervous, and from what Callum had told him and what he had observed himself the other night, he could understand why.

"I met him the other night," he said, nodding in McLeish's direction.

"You what?"

"Sunday night, after I left you, I went to talk to Callum, I found him here. Along with Mr. Personality over there."

"What happened? He and Callum didn't – "

"He was just shooting his mouth off. Nothing happened," he lied.

"Thank God. You need to keep away from him, Jack. He's pure evil, and he's got just enough between his ears to bring a whole lot of trouble down on you just as soon as look at you."

"Yeah, Callum told me about that."

Ally looked more and more uncomfortable by the second.

"Come on, let's get out of here," he said.

Ally didn't waste any time arguing. She grabbed her crutches from under the table and shuffled sideways in her seat. Straightening her legs, she used the table and the back of the booth to hoist herself up.

He noticed that several pairs of eyes were on her but she was too preoccupied to notice. He moved in front of her, shielding her from prying eyes, his protective instinct in overdrive. Shifting her weight, she reached over for her crutches.

"Okay, let's go," she said, looking over his shoulder, nervously judging the crowd of people between them and the door.

"I'll take it slow," he said.

He shot a glance towards Andy and his entourage as they made their way towards the door but thankfully they appeared to slip away unnoticed. Heading slowly through the throng, he kept one eye on Ally and the other on the door. Finally, they were making their way out onto the street and into the cool night air.

They trudged away from the bar in silence. He tried to think of something to say to lighten the mood but nothing came. As they rounded the corner onto the side street and his car, she suddenly stumbled. He moved quickly to catch her before she fell, grabbing her around the hips.

"Steady," he said, still holding her as she hurried to right herself. "Are you okay?"

"I'm fine," she snapped.

Reluctantly, he let her go, afraid he had grabbed her too hard.

"I'm sorry, that was just instinct. Did I hurt you?"

"Just my pride," she said, clearing her throat. "But I'm sure I'll live. The lighting out here is crap. Makes it kinda hard to see what I'm doing."

He remembered what she'd said about having to see her legs to control them.

"How about I bring the car closer?"

"Thanks. That'd be great."

"No problem. You going to be okay here for a minute?"

"I'm fine as long as I don't try to walk," she smiled tightly. "How's that for irony?"

He gave her arm a gentle squeeze.

"I'll be right back."

"And I'll be right here."

Her tone reeked of frustration. He headed for his car at a brisk walk, heart pounding. This was not how he was hoping the night would end. It was all he could do to stop himself from running back to her but he forced himself to jog the last few steps to his car instead. He drove back up the street, double-parking and leaving the engine idling as he jumped out and made his way over to her.

"Your carriage awaits," he bowed slightly.

She flashed him an anxious smile before slowly making her way towards his car. He hovered behind, just in case, but she managed to get herself between the parked cars safely. Waiting while she eased herself in, he closed the door behind her and made his way around to the driver's side.

He could not have foreseen any of this. This is what it was like for her, all the time? Something stupid like bad lighting becoming less of an inconvenience and more of a real safety issue? The simplest things turning into one hurdle after another? The guilt that he had successfully managed to push to the edge of his subconscious over the past couple of hours seeped in again.

As he pulled out onto the street, the tension in the air was palpable. Ally seemed closed off, staring out the side window. The easy companionship they had shared earlier had disappeared. The lights from the car behind them reflected off his rear-view mirror and he squinted, tilting it slightly. He took the next corner slowly and the car behind did the same. He frowned, suddenly feeling claustrophobic.

"I'm sorry," Ally said.

"What do you have to be sorry for?"

"This wasn't exactly what I was hoping for tonight," she mumbled, echoing his sentiments.

"Me neither. But the night's still young, right?"

She didn't answer and all too soon they were turning into her street and he was afraid the night really was over. He slowed down as he approached her house, pulling into her driveway and setting off the security light. The car was bathed in the eerie glow as he cut the engine and the silence deepened. He glanced over at her but she was staring at her hands, wrapped around her crutches.

"Can I ask you something?" she asked.

"Sure."

"Does driving make you nervous? I mean, since the accident. Was it easy, to just get back behind the wheel again?"

He didn't answer straight away.

"It wasn't easy," he said finally. "It took a while to get my confidence back. I'm definitely a more cautious driver now, that's for sure."

She nodded but didn't elaborate. Why did she want to know that?

"How about you?" he asked. It was a risky move. "You drive, don't you? Does it make you nervous?"

She shrugged, still studying her hands.

"This hole in my memory where the accident should be, it kinda comes in handy sometimes. I'm not a nervous driver or passenger or anything like that but learning how to drive with hand controls took some getting used to."

She fidgeted with her crutches and he got the feeling she was building up to something.

"I had an accident about a month after I started driving again," she said finally. "It wasn't anything serious, just something stupid, really."

"What do you mean by stupid? What happened?"

"I was still having trouble with my balance and my seatbelt wasn't pulled tight enough. I took a sharp turn a little too fast, I think, and I fell sideways, ran off the road."

"Oh shit."

"I wasn't hurt or anything," she said quickly. "I just felt like such an idiot."

He could imagine how daunting it must have been at the time, despite her bravado.

"You're the only person I've ever told about that - the truth, that is."

"Really?"

"I told Tom and Callum that I just lost my concentration for a minute. There was no way I was going to tell them what really happened, I was too embarrassed. It was a rookie mistake, one of those 'live and learn' moments."

She turned her grandmother's ring around and around on her finger, staring at her darkened house through the windshield.

"I have these dreams," she said, her voice little more than a whisper. "About running - jogging, really. Y'know, like I used to. In my dreams, I'm always either walking or running. I've never dreamt that I'm paralysed, ever – not once. I never see my wheelchair in my dreams, or my braces. Sometimes, when I'm running, there's this little alarm bell inside my head that tries to tell me something's wrong but I just ignore it. It bothers me sometimes. I wonder if that means I'm still in some kind of denial about what happened."

Jack watched the emotions play over her face.

"Maybe you don't see yourself that way because that's not

who you are, it's just something that happened to you," he said gently.

She seemed to digest this information, casting a brief glance at him, complete with tight smile. Then she retreated back into herself, turning her attention to what lay beyond the windshield.

"Jogging's not the only thing I miss," she said, almost to herself. "Dancing. Walking on cool grass on a hot day. Flowing dresses. Pretty shoes. Silly things, really. None of the things I thought I'd miss."

Jack reached for her hand, holding on tight. He tried to conjure up some sage words of comfort but they refused to come. Eventually, she turned to him and smiled through the tears that had gathered in her eyes.

"I'm sorry," she said. "I didn't mean to blurt out all this stuff."

He squeezed her hand.

"It's fine, don't worry about it."

"You should feel honoured. I don't babble my secrets to just anyone."

"It's okay," he murmured, reaching up to brush a stray tear from her cheek. "Your secrets are safe with me."

A breathless mixture of fear and longing danced within her eyes.

"Do you want to come inside?" she asked tentatively. "Maybe we can order pizza or something?"

"I'd really like that."

CHAPTER TWELVE

"If you get a chance, take it. If it changes your life, let it."
- Harvey MacKay

he evening was the definition of surreal. Barney's, pizza, beer, familiar music, easy conversation. All of it combined to create a warm glow that wrapped around Ally like a blanket, cocooning her from anything that might hurt her. She had found herself saying things to Jack that she never would have said had she been stone cold sober. To her surprise, he hadn't backed away in fear or run in the opposite direction. In fact, as he tucked into another slice of pizza in her living room, he was the most relaxed she'd seen him since his return home.

Music filled the room, Adam Duritz's sultry voice swirling around them as he sang about the price of a memory being the sorrow it brings. Very fitting, she thought, taking another sip of her beer.

"You know, every time I hear this song I think of that night," she said.

It took him a moment, but he smiled over at her as the fog lifted.

"I remember. Best road-tripping song ever."

"And best get-you-in-the-mood-for-a-night-on-the-town song ever. And best Sunday-morning-lazy-breakfast song ever," she said. "It's also a pretty good hiding-from-the-world song, too."

Where the hell had that come from? His smile faded but he nodded in agreement. Maybe she was more smashed than she thought. She vowed to keep her mouth shut from now on, just in case.

She ate the last of her pizza, washing it down with more beer, just as a new song filled the room. This one had altogether too many memories attached to it and she began to wonder if she should switch off the music altogether. In the meantime, Eddie Vedder growled sensuously about five horizons revolving around her soul.

"I should've known this song would be on there somewhere," he said.

She smiled, trying to ignore the butterflies in her stomach. Vedder's voice surrounded her with memories. Jack picked up his beer and took a sip, placing it back on the table. Then he stood up and walked around to stand in front of her, holding his hand out.

"C'mon," he prompted gently. "Dance with me."

She stared up at him, the last vestiges of a smile disappearing from her face.

"What?"

"You heard me. Dance with me - right here, right now."

She searched his expression for some sign that he was just kidding around but she didn't find any.

"What are you talking about?" she said, waving his hand away.

"We can do this, I've been thinking about it since Barney's."

She shook her head, about to tell him that he was crazy, her heart threatening to jump into her throat.

"Come on," he pleaded, reaching down to take her hand in his. "Trust me. Please?"

His gaze enveloped her, drawing her in and wrapping her in a thick, warm cloak of reassurance until she was nodding up at him.

"You just need to stand up," he said, releasing her hand. "I'll do the rest."

A lump the size of Texas seemed to be stuck in her throat but somehow, she managed to get her trembling hands to co-operate. Taking more care than usual, she used the table and the back of her chair to hoist herself upright then leaned down to check the lock on each brace. Standing there, leaning on them for support, she had never been more frightened.

"You know that I can't – "

"Don't worry," he assured her, stepping in closer to settle his hands on her waist.

"Put your arms around my neck. It's okay, I've got you."

She did as she was told, holding on tight as her weight shifted towards him and he stepped in even closer. His cologne wafted over her and she squeezed her eyes shut, trying not to think about falling.

"Can you loosen that grip a little? I'm not going to be able to do this if I can't breathe," he joked, his voice in her ear giving her goose bumps. "I'm not going to let you fall, I promise. I just need a little wiggle room."

"Wiggle room?" her eyes flew open.

"Just trust me."

She relaxed her grip as he jostled her a little.

"What are you doing?"

"I'm just going to lift you up a bit."

His arms wrapped even tighter around her waist.

"Why?" she demanded, breathless with the combination of being this close to Jack and of what he was suggesting. She tried to resist the urge to hold on to him even tighter still.

"Did you ever dance with your Dad like this when you were a kid, standing on his feet?" he asked, as she felt him lift her.

"Is that what you're doing?"

"Yeah," he huffed, her weight shifting again. "There, that's it."

"That's what?" she demanded, afraid to move.

"Just relax."

"I'm relaxed, what makes you think I'm not relaxed?"

He chuckled and the sound filled her with joy, despite her precarious position. Suddenly, she realised something.

"Jack, where are your hands?"

"I'm holding your… jeans."

She cringed.

"You're holding my ass, aren't you."

"Yeah," he chuckled again.

She didn't know whether to laugh or cry.

"You better watch it, mister," she managed. "No funny business."

"Best behaviour, ma'am. I promise."

The smile in his voice was obvious. When he spoke again a moment later though, he was deadly serious.

"I've got your feet on top of mine now, so we can dance like this as long as you want to."

They began to sway from side to side. Now that the blood had stopped rushing to her head, she could hear the music again. She tried to concentrate on that, rather than the fact that she was in such close proximity to Jack and she was actually dancing.

"Is this alright? You're pretty quiet."

She nodded into his neck but couldn't bring herself to speak. He rubbed her back gently with one hand, sending shivers through her. Slowly, she gave herself over to the movement, relishing the way her body moved with his.

As the song ended and another began, the tears came, silently sliding down her cheeks and burying themselves in his shirt. She felt like she was floating and Jack was her anchor, solid and safe and here. She wished the moment would last forever.

He was holding her in his arms again, where she felt so warm and safe and comfortable that it scared her. With an aching heart, she pushed aside the reflection with a sigh that emerged as more of a choking sound.

"Are you okay?" Jack asked gently and they stopped moving, his hand motionless on her back.

She nodded into his neck, afraid to speak in case her voice betrayed her.

"The last time we did this was at the Pearl Jam concert," he said, as the swaying began again, slow and rhythmic.

He pulled her closer, his hand strong and firm against her back.

"We were queuing to get into the venue and the support band came on. We danced while we were waiting, in front of everyone." She heard the smile in his voice. "It was your idea, as I remember it - you didn't exactly give me much of a choice."

The usual black void engulfed her as she thought about the night of the accident. He might as well have been talking about someone else. She was almost jealous of her other self from that night, dancing with Jack, having a great time.

The music faded as the song came to an end and they stopped moving. She stood with her arms around his neck, the rhythmic beating of his heart almost mesmerising.

"Are you ready for a break?" he asked, gently brushing her hair away from her shoulder.

"Just one more?" she whispered, not ready to let go of the moment just yet.

"You're the boss."

They began to sway in time to the music again and she closed her eyes. She let the music in properly this time and it took her back to places she hadn't been in a long time. Memories flooded through her. Jack's shirt felt damp beneath her cheek and she sniffed, opening her eyes and blinking in the dull light of her living room.

"Hey, hey," Jack soothed, smoothing her hair away from her face as she pulled away from him. "What's wrong?"

"I think I need to sit down," she whispered, light-headed suddenly.

"Okay, sure, just a second here." He manoeuvred them both towards the couch and turned around so her back was facing it. "I'm just going to lower you down here, just hold on to my - yeah, that's it. Okay, there you go, no problem," he said gently, easing her onto the couch.

She sniffed again, wiping her eyes with trembling fingers.

"You okay?" he asked nervously, sitting on the edge of the couch beside her. "Did I say something wrong?"

"No," she mumbled vaguely. "I just felt a little dizzy, but I'm fine now."

"You look kinda pale. I'll get you some water."

She didn't bother arguing and watched as he disappeared into the kitchen. Unlocking her braces with trembling fingers, she eased herself back into the couch as he came back to sit beside her again, glass of water in hand.

"Here. Maybe you should drink this," he suggested, and she took the proffered glass, taking a small sip.

"Thanks. I just… I think it was just the… everything."

She rested the glass on her thigh, watching it closely, as if it might provide all the answers to the questions in her head.

"Ah yes, the everything. That'd certainly do it," he said, and she glanced up to find him smiling at her.

She felt the tears coming again as she looked at him, staring back at her with a tender, slightly bemused, expression. She blamed her low alcohol tolerance but she knew that it wasn't solely to blame. She fought through the haze of emotions and chemicals, frantically trying to rebuild the carefully-constructed wall that held her fragile soul safe. She felt the wall crumbling but she was determined not to give up the cause yet, so used to protecting everyone from the mess inside her head that it was second nature now. So why was she telling Jack things she had never told anyone else?

"You scare me," she whispered, alcohol connecting the direct line between her brain and her mouth. She took a quick sip of water and her hand shook so much, she almost dropped the glass. "This - us - tonight... all of it. Dancing, talking - secrets - so many things. And feelings - the way you make me feel... it's all so... it's like you never left, only you did leave, and it's all so different now."

Jack's face, so worried just moments ago, relaxed.

"It's kind of overwhelming," he said gently. "Is that what you mean?"

"Yes!" she nodded vehemently. "That's what I mean! Isn't that what I said?"

"Kind of, yeah," he smiled, taking the glass of water from her and setting it down on the side table.

She groaned, leaning forward and covering her face with her hands.

"I'm drunk, you've gotten me drunk. I hope you're happy."

He laughed softly, rubbing her back.

"Yes, you are. But it's okay, you're safe."

Her hands fell into her lap and she looked up at him, intent on saying something important. But whatever it was mysteriously disappeared and she just stared at him. He smiled at her, so tenderly she forgot where she was. She wanted to surrender to him, right here, right now.

She leaned unconsciously towards him and his smile faded. His eyes lingered on her lips for a nano-second, sending a shiver of anticipation through her. She waited impatiently as he searched the depths of her soul until his lips were on hers, warm and soft and tasting vaguely of beer. She closed her eyes as his fingertips caressed her cheek, the nerve-endings coming alive with his touch.

Just as she felt herself giving in to him completely, he pulled away. She stared at him breathlessly for several moments, her mind struggling to ascertain fact from fiction.

"Am I dreaming?" she whispered, her head spinning.

Jack's thumb caressed her jaw.

"Nope. Not dreaming."

His hand slipped from her cheek and he looked nervous, leaning away from her as if wanting to put some distance between them.

"I'm sorry," he mumbled. "I didn't mean to do that... I shouldn't have done that."

"It's okay. I wanted you to."

He glanced at her anxiously.

"I think that maybe..."

She smiled, her inhibitions leaving in an all-out stampede. Whatever he was about to say vanished into the ether and he smiled back at her, amused.

"I think that maybe we need some coffee. You definitely do."

She shrugged, still tasting his lips on hers and feeling like her grip on reality was slipping a little. For a change though, it didn't worry her. In fact, she liked it.

---

*J*ack waited impatiently for the coffee to brew. He glanced through the kitchen door at Ally, who was still sitting on the couch, getting comfortable.

Why did I do that, why did I kiss her? What was I thinking?

He had taken advantage of her, which only served to make him feel like more of a fraud. He had to tell her. Only now, there was so much more at stake, which made everything harder. God, how he wished his father were here. He would know what to do.

The coffee finished brewing and as he poured, his phone began vibrating. He frowned, digging it out of his pocket and staring at the screen for a second before declining the call. He promised himself he'd get a new phone first thing tomorrow morning.

He picked up both cups of coffee and made his way back to the living room.

"Here we go. Nice and strong, just what – "

Ally was fast asleep, slumped back into the couch, her head resting against the over-stuffed cushion behind her.

"Excellent timing," he murmured.

He put the coffee cups back on the kitchen counter. Walking over to sit down on the couch beside her, he picked up her hand and gave it a gentle squeeze.

"Ally? Hey, time to wake up."

She didn't even stir. He looked down at her hand in his and had a flashback from the night of the accident, holding her hand as she lay in the ICU. Small and pale, it had scared him then. He turned her hand over, gently touching the callouses at the base of her fingers. She was stronger than he had given her credit for.

Glancing towards her bedroom, he debated his next move. He couldn't just leave her on the couch and go home. He stood up, gathering her carefully into his arms.

"Come on," he murmured. "Time to sleep it off somewhere a little more comfortable."

Walking towards her bedroom, he was acutely aware of how much she had changed. Her small frame was divided into two very distinct parts; the strong shoulders he cradled in one arm and the slight legs draped over the other. Her braces dug into his arms, her head lolling against his chest. It wasn't only her body that had changed, though. With the brief insight into her life over the past day or two, he had seen glimpses of inner fortitude that left him awestruck. In return, he'd given her nothing. No insight, no details, no explanation beyond a heartfelt yet underwhelming apology.

That was one of the reasons he wanted to dance with her. He wanted to give her something back, something to help make up for everything he'd taken from her or was hiding from her. The way she'd held onto him, the weight of her body on his, the feeling of having her in his arms again; all of it had awakened something inside of him.

Hope.

He carefully pushed her bedroom door open wider with his foot. Sidestepping the wheelchair next to her bed, he set her down on top of the covers. She stirred and he knelt beside the bed, waiting to see if she would wake.

"Dreamt I was dancing," she smiled sleepily, eyes still closed.

His heart melted.

"It wasn't a dream. You *were* dancing."

"I like dreams like that, better than the other ones," she murmured into the pillow.

He brushed her hair tenderly away from her face.

"What other ones?"

She didn't answer and after a few moments her breathing became heavier. Maybe it was better he didn't know. He sat there for a few minutes, watching her. She had said something about secrets earlier and he wondered what she meant. Her secrets or his? He thought about everything he had put himself through over the past four years. How much of that did he actually want to share with her? What would she think of him if he told her he'd been fighting strangers for money? No. That part of his life was over. Knowing how he had spent the past year would only hurt her. This was a fresh start. And as for the other secret, the one that had driven him away from her in the first place, he promised himself he would tell her when the time was right.

He pulled the covers from the other side of the bed over her and stood up. Stepping back, he almost tripped on her wheelchair, reaching out to stop himself from falling. He waited to see if she would stir but she remained blissfully unaware.

He let go of the wheelchair then frowned, reaching out for it again. He pushed it backwards and forwards a few times. Leaning to the side, he inspected it closely. The seat back was much lower than he thought it would be and there was a deep foam cushion on the seat but no sides, no arm rests. Now curious, he sat down in it, a quick glance assuring him that she was still sound asleep. Hesitantly, he put his feet on the foot-rest and grabbed the push rims, propelling himself forward and then backwards. He pulled on one rim, turning, but not in the direction he had thought. After turning himself around in circles a couple of times, he was hit by an overwhelming sense of shame.

This wasn't a toy.

He stood up and walked to the door, pausing for one final check to satisfy himself that she was sleeping soundly.

He sank into the couch in the living room with a heavy sigh. Part of their conversation in the bar earlier that evening came back to him.

"You can't wallow. It'll kill you - trust me, I know."

Leaning back into the couch, he stared at the ceiling. What would it feel like to not be able to stand up and walk away from that wheelchair like he had just done?

His heart hurt just thinking about it. Exhausted, he closed his eyes.

THREE YEARS EARLIER

"Have you talked to her?" Callum asked, pacing across his kitchen, phone clamped to his ear. "I can't get her on the phone, landline or cell."

Tom sighed and he imagined him taking off his glasses and running a hand down his face as he had seen him do so often.

"No. I've been calling too - no answer. I went over there yesterday and her car was there but she didn't answer the door. I thought she might be sleeping so I didn't push it."

"Something's wrong, I can feel it. I was over there on the weekend and she was really weird. She said she'd been working on something new but she wouldn't let me see it. I waited till she was in the bathroom then I went in there to check it out. It's... it's really dark, Tom. And I mean really dark. I've never seen her paint anything like that before, it was like something out of a horror show. The studio itself was a disaster area, which is another problem entirely. This mood or whatever that she's in, it's getting worse and I've got a bad feeling."

"I'd be lying if I said it didn't worry me. I'm just hoping that it's temporary - you know how she gets sometimes. Maybe it's just taking a bit longer for her to work it out of her system this time."

"It's been weeks. I knew the anniversary would be tough but she seemed okay, y'know? But she's not okay now. Something's wrong she just won't tell me what."

"Do you think it's got something to do with the appointment with Pavlovic? What happened on Monday, at the check-up?"

"What check-up?" Callum frowned. "She hasn't had it yet, she's still waiting on the appointment coming through."

"Well when we had coffee last week, she said the appointment came through and it was for Monday."

"Monday this week? Are you sure? That doesn't make any sense. Why the hell didn't she tell me?"

"The more pressing question is why did she lie to me about it?"

"What?"

"I asked her if she wanted me to go with her but she told me there was no need because you were taking her."

"What the hell is going on?"

"Damned if I know but I don't like the sound of this. I'll meet you over there, and I'll bring the spare key in case she doesn't answer the door again. Maybe between the two of us, we can get the truth out of her."

"See you there."

Callum shoved his cell phone in his jacket pocket, snatched his car keys from the counter top and headed for the door.

Ally dreaded the appointments with her neurologist, that's why he went with her for moral support. She said it was like sitting an exam she hadn't studied for. Her behaviour over the past few weeks made more sense now. She had been withdrawn recently. When he saw her on the weekend, her emotions seemed to see-saw from one extreme to the other. One minute it was like she was going to burst into tears, the next she was smiling and fobbing him off. He slammed his palm against the steering wheel. He should have known something was wrong.

The drive to Ally's house took a lot less than the ten minutes it should have. Approaching her house, Tom's car was nowhere in sight. He pulled into her driveway and parked behind her car, jumping out as soon as he cut the engine. He gave her car a cursory glance as he jogged up to the front door, taking the steps in two long strides. Pounding on her door, he called out her name but there was no response.

"Ally!" he tried again, pounding harder. "Ally, if you're in there, open the door!"

He stopped to listen, his ears straining for any kind of sound within. He thought he could hear music but he wasn't sure. He pounded again, more desperately.

"Ally! You open this damn door, you hear me? I'm not kidding!"

Nothing.

"If you don't open this door, I'm going to break it down, I swear to God!"

Silence.

Anxiety grabbed him by the throat and he pounded on the door even harder. Frustrated at the lack of response, he started to think outside the square. He peered through the window into the living room but could see nothing. He tried to budge it but it was locked tight. Tom was taking far too long.

He struggled out of his jacket, wrapping it tightly around his fist.

Angling his body away, he punched through the living room window, stepping back to avoid the falling glass.

"Ally!" he called through the window, clearing a space to climb through.

There was no response. He climbed in and the first thing that hit him was the smell; paint. Pearl Jam was playing on her iPod, which was docked in the living room, but she was nowhere to be seen. He strode through the house, calling out to her as he headed for the studio. The room was a mess and in the middle of it all a canvas lay on the floor, surrounded by tubes of paint - some open, which accounted for the smell - along with brushes and rags. It was the same horrific painting she'd been hiding from him.

"Ally!"

He headed to her bedroom next, pushing the door open, anxiety forcing every other emotion aside. The curtains were still drawn and she was lying on her bed, fully-clothed, her wheelchair beside her. Everything looked normal. Why did she have music playing in the living room if she was in bed? And why hadn't she woken up when he pounded on the door? Or smashed the window? Or called her name?

"Ally?"

He squinted into the gloom, walking over to take a closer look. The bed was littered with photographs. An empty bottle of pills, cap off, lay on the bed beside her.

His heart stopped. For a moment, time seemed to stand still. He scrambled over the bed on his knees towards her.

"Ally! Wake up!"

He grabbed her shoulders and shook her but she didn't respond. His hands trembled uncontrollably, adrenaline coursing through his body as he checked her neck. Her pulse throbbed lethargically beneath his fingers.

"Oh Jesus... what have you done?" he breathed.

"Callum?"

"Tom! In here!" he shouted, his voice breaking as he fought the rising panic.

He pulled Ally into his arms, rocking backwards and forwards.
"What the hell?"
Still cradling Ally, he looked up to see Tom in the doorway.
"Help me!"
The look of horror on Tom's face as he spied the empty bottle of pills on the bed mirrored his own.
"Oh my God."

---

*J*ack woke up slowly, stretching. He squinted, hauling himself upright as he tried to get his bearings. Apparently, he had slept on Ally's couch and it was surprisingly comfortable. For the first time in a long time, he'd slept right through the night without waking.

A crash rang out in the silence.

Ally.

Jumping up from the couch, he ran across the hall and burst through her bedroom door. She was sitting on the floor by her bed, wearing the same black top from last night, and her underwear. She stared up at him in shock but she wasn't the only one startled.

From the waist up, she looked more or less the same. From the waist down however, it was a very different story. Her legs were pale and thin, the lack of muscle tone made more pronounced by prominent knees.

"Get out!" she cried, eyes wild as she leaned forward, effectively bending herself in half to preserve her modesty. "Get out of here!"

Startled and speechless, Jack could only oblige, backing towards the door.

"I'm sorry," he mumbled nervously, pulling the door closed behind him.

Standing in the hall, unsure of what he should do next, he

heard her utter a string of curses. Tentatively, he addressed the closed door.

"Ally?"

"What the hell are you still doing here?" she demanded.

"I uh, I fell asleep on your couch last night. I heard a crash, or something. Are you okay?"

"I'm fine!"

He leaned his shoulder against the door.

"I'm sorry. I thought you were in trouble - I thought you needed help."

"I don't need your help!"

"Okay," he winced. "I'm sorry - my mistake."

There was a heavy silence before she spoke again.

"What happened last night?"

"What do you mean?"

"I mean, where the hell are my crutches and why is my chair on the other side of the room!"

He'd messed up. Again. He could've kicked himself.

"Shit. I'm sorry, that was my fault. I moved your chair out of the way when I carried you to bed last night and your crutches are still in the living room. It didn't even cross my mind to bring them through. I'm sorry. Do you want them? I can bring them – "

"No!"

He searched for something to say but she beat him to it.

"Did you say you carried me to bed?"

"Well, yeah," he stared at the ceiling, mentally crossing his fingers. "You fell asleep while I was making coffee. I couldn't just leave you on the couch all night."

"God, I must've been drunk," she mumbled, so quietly he could barely hear her.

He heard movement from within and he waited anxiously. After a few minutes, the door opened. She sat in her chair with what looked like a robe strewn over her legs. She didn't look at him, moving past him up the hallway without a word and disappearing into the bathroom.

He breathed out heavily and ran his hand through his hair. The sight of her bare legs had rattled him, there was no denying it. Even though her gait was awkward and exaggerated, she looked more or less solid and stable when she was walking. But glimpsing behind the curtain, the truth was something very different. Worse still, he hadn't been able to hide his shocked reaction from her. No wonder she had withdrawn from him.

He retreated into the living room, wondering what to do next. He couldn't just leave, that felt wrong. It would be like running away and he had promised himself he wouldn't do that again.

So, he set about making coffee in her kitchen for the second time in as many days.

THREE YEARS EARLIER

Callum and Tom sat in stony-faced silence in the hospital waiting room. Callum stood up and started pacing the length of the room, stretching his arms above his head. The familiarity of the past hour or so was grinding down his last nerve.

"Sit down. Please?"

Callum frowned at Tom, shaking his head. Sitting down was worse than pacing. At least when he was pacing, he felt like he was doing something, even if it was nothing helpful. Nothing he did seemed to be helpful lately.

He stopped at the end of the room and leaned on the windowsill, staring down at the parking lot. He was thankful Maggie and Jane were getting coffee. He didn't think he could keep up the pretence of being in control for much longer.

After everything Ally had been through, why would she do some-

thing like this now? Why give up after she had fought so hard to get her life back? What in the hell would make her want to throw it all away?

He straightened up and shoved his hands into the pockets of his jeans. His entire body felt like an over-coiled spring. He tried to relax his shoulders and turned to resume his pacing across the room.

"Callum – "

"Don't tell me to calm down and don't tell me to sit," he snapped, with more force than he meant.

Tom wisely backed down. Callum strode past him again and leaned with his back against the wall at the opposite end of the room, staring at the floor.

Whatever it was that he'd missed, it was big. Big enough that Ally didn't feel she could talk to him about it. He had failed her. She needed Jack, not him. His heart sank as the truth seeped in. It didn't matter what he did, he wasn't Jack.

He stood up and crossed the room to stand in front of Tom.

"Call him – now," he said. "Tell him."

Tom stood up slowly.

"No."

"Tell him he needs to get his ass back here, pronto." When Tom opened his mouth to object, he cut him off. "I mean it. This has gone on long enough. He needs to come home. She needs him," he said, pointing desperately towards the ER treatment room where Ally was currently having her stomach pumped.

"And you think that telling him what happened would help?"

"Yes!" he cried, his emotions bubbling to the surface. "I don't know why the hell she did this, but if Jack were here it wouldn't have happened - he wouldn't have let it happen!"

Tom sighed and put a comforting hand on Callum's shoulder. He shrugged it off irritably and backed up, sinking into a plastic chair opposite him, exhausted suddenly.

"He'd have stopped it, he'd have seen it. I didn't. I missed it. I missed it and she nearly – "

He shook his head, staring down at the linoleum beneath his feet. Tom sat down beside him.

"It wasn't your fault," Tom said. "I missed it too. And telling Jack now wouldn't make any difference. It wouldn't change anything."

"I don't care. He needs to be here - she needs him. It's time he grew up and came home."

Tom was silent for a moment, then he put his hand on Callum's shoulder and squeezed.

"Don't you think that if I could bring him home, I would've done it by now? I don't even know where the hell he is."

---

*J*ack sipped a steaming cup of coffee, staring over the table at the empty space across from him. Ally had yet to come out of her bedroom and he was beginning to wonder if she was waiting for him to leave.

His jaw set. It was no use asking him to stay if she was just going to hide from him. All in, all the time, no matter what. He finally heard her bedroom door open and a few moments later she appeared in the kitchen doorway. He tried to smile casually, although he felt anything but relaxed.

"I made coffee - strong coffee. Want some?"

She nodded, rolling into the room while he got up to pour her a cup.

"Here you go," he said, setting down the cup on the table across from him.

"Thanks."

She placed a bottle of aspirin on the table between them.

"How's your head?" he asked.

"I'll live," she said, rubbing her temples. "I had all these weird dreams last night. Crazy stuff. Must've been the beer. I dreamt I was dancing."

"That wasn't a dream."

"It wasn't?" she asked, looking at him properly for the first time.

"Nope."

He took a gulp of coffee that sounded way too loud in the quiet room.

"I don't usually drink these days," she said after a few moments. "It all happened so fast. One minute I had a little buzz on, the next..."

He smiled, grateful she was at least talking to him.

"But you remember dancing?"

"Yeah. I wish I remembered more of that, to be honest."

"Well, we're just gonna have to do it again when we're sober."

She blushed but didn't comment. He wondered if she remembered the kiss they shared but he didn't want to risk asking. She took a sip of her coffee before setting the cup down in front of her and looking over at him.

"I'm sorry I bit your head off before."

"I'm the one who should apologise. I'm sorry I burst in on you like that. I wasn't thinking straight, I just heard a crash and I panicked."

"I knocked some stuff off my bedside table when I got out of bed. It's not as easy as it used to be."

She glanced down at her coffee cup again, avoiding eye contact the way she seemed to do when she was embarrassed or hurting. He wanted to somehow ease the discomfort but he didn't know how and he hated himself for it. He shouldn't have touched her wheelchair last night. He should've thought about bringing her crutches through. He should've known.

"Please don't move stuff around," she said quietly, as if reading his mind. "Everything's where it is for a reason."

"I'm really sorry, I guess I'm still learning. I won't do it again, I promise."

She looked almost as embarrassed as he felt.

"I've never had to ask that before," she said, glancing over at him tentatively. "This is all kinda new to me, too. I guess we're both still learning."

"I guess so," he smiled, relief pouring out of him. "Hey, can I ask you something?"

Her expression was guarded, as if she was keeping him at arm's length, protecting herself. He hated that, too.

"Can I use your shower?"

Her relief was painfully obvious.

"Absolutely."

CHAPTER THIRTEEN

"After climbing a great hill, one only finds
that there are many more hills to climb."
- Nelson Mandela

*C*allum strode up Ally's front path with two cups of takeaway coffee, as per their Saturday morning tradition. He wondered what kind of mood he would find Ally in this particular Saturday morning. She and Jack had gone to Barney's, on a Friday night, together. Ally hated going to Barney's on a Friday night and he couldn't blame her. Was she trying to prove to Jack that nothing had changed? If she was, she was playing a dangerous game and Jack was in for a rude awakening.

He was stuck between a rock and a hard place. It looked like they were both withholding cards from each other and he was the only one who could see both their hands. The kicker was, he had no choice but to keep his mouth shut if he was to be of any help to Ally.

As soon as she opened the door he could tell something was up.

"Morning," he said, holding the coffee up as she moved aside to let him in.

"Hey. Thank God. I could do with the good stuff."

She closed the door behind him and he turned around, checking her out more closely. She looked paler than usual and that smile wasn't fooling anyone.

"Really? What's up?"

"I had a few beers last night. I haven't done that for so long, I forgot how it made me feel. And this morning, I remembered."

"Ah yes. The mighty hangover. I'm familiar."

"Exactly. My head hurts and I feel like crap. Do we have to do the exercise thing today?"

"Define 'crap' for me."

She shook her head dismissively.

"Just your general run-of-the-mill hangover."

"Are you sure it's not – "

"Yes, I'm sure," she snapped. "I'm not running a temp and I don't have any other symptoms so you can stand down, doc."

"Okay, chill. Just checking."

"Sorry," she mumbled, rolling past him as she headed towards the living room. "Like I said, not feeling that great. Hangovers suck."

He followed her through and set her coffee down on the table, sinking into the couch.

"No arguments there. So, speaking of last night, how'd it go?"

"Fine," she said, taking a sip of her coffee.

"Just fine?"

"It was fine. It was okay."

"Must've been more than okay if you had a few beers, or was that Dutch courage?"

"Something like that."

Not a lot in the way of details were forthcoming. She took

another sip of her coffee. He wanted to shake her until she told him everything, but she looked so fragile that he took pity on her.

"I can come back tonight if you want. Maybe you'll be feeling better then and we can exercise then."

"That'd be great. Thanks."

She seemed distracted.

"You can talk to me about last night if you want," he offered. "I'm not gonna do anything stupid, I promise."

She fiddled with the lid on her coffee cup, frowning at it.

"Thanks, but it's fine. I wouldn't know where to start, anyway."

"Come on - talk to me. What happened?"

She hung her head. Something was definitely up. His imagination began to run wild.

"What did he do?" he demanded.

"What? Nothing, he didn't do anything."

"I swear to God, I'll knock him straight into next week, if he so much as – "

"Oh, for God's sake, it's not his fault, it's mine!"

"What do you mean by that?"

"I don't know if I can do this," she mumbled, putting her coffee cup back on the table in front of her.

"Do what?"

She stared at her hands in her lap, her fingers finding her grandmother's ring and twirling it over and over until he had to fight the urge to lean over and physically stop her.

"Be near him," she said finally. "Talk to him. Every time I look at him, I can see both of him."

"Both of him?"

She shrugged, hair falling forward to partially obscure her face.

"Who he was before, and who he is now."

Finally, Callum understood what she was trying to say. He'd seen it too.

"He's changed."

"So have I," she said quietly.

THREE YEARS EARLIER

"So, what happens now?" Tom asked.

The doctor looked up from the chart in his hand and pushed his glasses further up his nose. "We'll keep her in for a couple of days, for observation. Someone from the psych team will assess her tomorrow then contact you to talk things over and explain what happens next."

"Is she awake now? Can we see her?" Maggie asked.

"Yes, she's awake, and you can see her. She's likely to be a little uncomfortable, though. She might also be withdrawn - possibly angry, maybe even embarrassed, just so you know what to expect, potentially."

Callum nodded, taking a deep breath and letting it out slowly.

"Thank you," Tom said quietly, and he and Callum exchanged a wary glance.

"Keep the visit short," the doctor cautioned. "She's been through an ordeal, she needs to rest. Save the questions until later, when she's feeling stronger. Perhaps just two visitors for now?"

Maggie enveloped Tom in a hug.

"You and Callum should go to her. Tell her I love her and I'm thinking of her and I'll see her tomorrow."

Callum nodded at Tom over her shoulder. Maggie pulled away, wiping her eyes.

"We won't be long," Tom said, squeezing her shoulder. "Wait here, okay? I'll take you home. I don't want you driving, not like this."

Jane slipped her arm around Callum's waist, leaning her head on his shoulder. He pulled her into a hug, holding her close.

"Give her that, from me," she said, releasing him and forcing a smile. "I will."

Tom and Callum followed the doctor down the hallway. Callum's heart pounded. He had no idea what to say to her. Staring at her from the doorway, the hospital bed seemed to swallow her up and he was immediately reminded of the aftermath of the accident, a little over twelve months earlier. This time though, Ally was awake and staring out the window of the small room. She made no indication of having heard them enter.

Exchanging a worried glance with Tom, he settled himself into the chair beside her bed with Tom standing beside him.

"Hey," he said quietly.

She looked so sad. Was she sad she tried to end it, or sad she failed?

"How're you feeling?"

He reached out for her hand and enclosed it in his own. She didn't respond.

"You scared the shit out of me," he whispered.

He remembered what the doctor said as he studied her. She didn't look embarrassed or angry. She looked empty.

"Maggie and Jane are here. They send their love."

She continued to stare out the window as Tom laid a hand on his shoulder. He glanced up at him but Tom's attention was firmly fixed on Ally.

"Hey honey. Just relax, okay? You need to get your strength back."

The love and helplessness reflected in Tom's voice had Callum swallowing back tears. He felt as if wherever it was she had gone, she wasn't coming back to them anytime soon.

"She needs her rest and the doc said we shouldn't stay long," Tom said. "Maybe we should come back later."

"I think I'll stay for a while longer."

There was no way he was leaving her alone, not after what just happened. He had screwed up once already. He wasn't going to do it again.

"I'll collect some of her things from the house and be back here in an hour or so. I'll bring you something to eat."

"I'm not hungry."

"I didn't ask if you were hungry."

"Fine," Callum sighed. "And bring her chair, will you? These hospital ones are so bulky."

"I will." He reached over Callum and rubbed Ally's arm awkwardly. "I'll be back soon, honey. Okay?"

Ally made no indication she had heard him. As Tom backed slowly towards the door, Callum tried to give him a comforting smile that fell woefully short of the mark.

Turning back to Ally, he noticed her reflection in the window-pane. She wore a vacant expression that he had never seen before. It was as if her essence, her soul, had been scraped away and all that was left was a shell, brittle and fragile. He squeezed her hand gently, afraid of hurting her.

"It's going to be alright," he said, trying his best to convince both of them. "I'm not going anywhere."

His words hung in the air between them for a while longer before the silence swallowed them up.

---

*J*ack took his new cell phone out and tossed the box aside. Inserting the battery, he plugged it into the charger and scrolled through the options, familiarising himself. One phone seemed much the same as another and it wasn't the first time he had discarded a perfectly good cell phone in order to wipe the slate clean. Pausing for a moment, he went into the contacts function and added Callum's number from his old phone, just in case. A moment later, he added Ally's.

He picked up his old phone again and scrolled through the contacts list, pausing on his father's name. His heart seized as he stared at it. He would give anything to be able to tap that call button and hear his familiar voice on the other end.

Turning the phone over, he pulled out the SIM card and threw both phone and card into the garbage. No more missed calls from Ben. No more threatening voicemail messages. No more looking over his shoulder.

Once again, he was walking away from his old life.

---

*A*lly was pulling the yoga mat out of the hall cupboard when she heard a knock at the door. Callum was early, not that it mattered. She deposited the yoga mat on her lap and headed down the hall to answer the door. Much to her surprise it was Jack, not Callum, who stood on her doorstep.

"Hi," he smiled.

"Hi yourself."

He waggled a DVD in one hand and a bag of popcorn in the other. "I hope I'm not being too presumptuous?"

Despite her best efforts, she couldn't deny the wave of happiness that overcame her. All her misgivings from earlier seemed to vanish and she smiled back at him shyly.

"Not at all. Come in."

"You sure I'm not interrupting anything?" he asked, indicating the yoga mat still on her lap.

Suddenly she remembered Callum. Anxiety destroyed the euphoria she had felt just moments before.

"No, nothing," she lied, dropping the mat on the floor beside her with a tight smile. "Let's go through to the living room. What's the DVD?"

"An old fave," he smiled.

"Sounds good. Make yourself at home, okay? I just have a quick phone call to make."

She ushered him through to the living room, grabbing the phone on the way and disappearing into the kitchen with it. She kept one eye on him as she wheeled further into the kitchen, dialling Callum's number with trembling fingers. The phone only rang twice before he answered.

"Hey, I just pulled up outside your house. Meet you at the door."

"No, wait!" she hissed, heart racing. "Jack's here!"

"I know, I'm looking at his car."

"So, can we put a pin in this tonight? Please?"

She heard him sigh and she glanced towards the living room.

"Come on, it's only twenty minutes. Surely whatever you're doing can wait that long?"

He didn't sound happy.

"Please don't do this to me," she begged.

"I don't have to tell you how important this is."

"Callum!"

In response, she heard a click, then a knock at the door.

Damn it! She was not ready to give up yet. Gritting her teeth, she called out to Jack.

"It's okay, I got it!"

Speeding down the hallway, she reached up to yank open the door, ready with another tactic.

"Forget it," Callum announced as soon as she opened the door. "Whatever you were going to say, just forget it. It's twenty minutes. Deal with it."

"No," she glared up at him. "I told you I can't, not tonight!"

Callum winked at her.

"As the actress said to the bishop."

"I'm not kidding!" she hissed. "We're watching a movie!"

"Hey."

They both turned to see Jack standing in the living room doorway.

"Hey," Callum said evenly. "I hear you're watching a movie."

"Something like that. Join us, if you want?" Jack offered.

Ally glared up at him and he turned his attention back to Jack.

"What's the movie?"

"Armageddon."

"That's a blast from the past," Callum said. "I'll give it some thought. I'm actually here to see Ally, we have something we need to do. Pass that mat over, will you?"

Jack picked up the yoga mat off the floor and offered it to him.

"Thanks." Callum walked over to Ally's bedroom door. "We'll be about twenty minutes or so. You don't mind waiting, do you?"

Jack shook his head as Ally flashed him an apologetic smile. All she could think about was punching Callum in the groin, which was conveniently at eye level.

"Won't be long. There's beer in the fridge, I think. Help yourself," Ally offered, cheeks burning as she followed Callum into her bedroom.

As soon as she had closed the door behind her, she whirled on Callum.

"What the hell do you think you're doing?"

"Settle down. You heard him, he doesn't mind."

"Are you even listening to me?"

Callum sighed dramatically and sat down on the edge of her bed.

"Okay then, out with it. What's this all about? Is it because he's here?"

"Of course it is!" she blurted out, wishing immediately she could take it back.

"Why?"

Her blood pressure soared as she tried to control her racing heart. The thought of Jack walking in on them made her break out in a cold sweat.

"You know why!"

"Okay, listen," he soothed. "You know this is important. Just because he's here, you want to start letting this stuff slide? For how long, Ally? How long do you want to hide this from him? Because if he's going to stick around like he says he is, that's gonna get pretty damn awkward, pretty damn quick."

He knew her too well, which was more irritating than usual

right now. Of course she wanted to hide it from Jack, why wouldn't she? How could she convince Jack that she was in control if he saw her like this? And why the hell was Callum being so reasonable about it? That was her domain, damn it.

"The clock's ticking," Callum said, laying out the yoga mat on the floor.

She wished she could stand up and knock him out cold. Instead, she threw him a withering look and hoped he could read her mind.

*J*ack squirmed on the couch, trying to get more comfortable. He shot a glance at Ally, sitting on the other end of the couch. To all intents and purposes, she looked engrossed in the movie, but he suspected otherwise.

He turned back to the TV but the uneasiness in the air was impossible to ignore. They both liked this movie, that's why he had chosen it. She had seemed happy enough to see him when he arrived but as soon as Callum had shown up, things had gotten weird. First there was the hold-up while they did whatever it was they were doing in her bedroom - he assumed some kind of workout or massage or something, judging by the yoga mat - and then Callum had left without saying goodbye straight afterwards. Ally had been withdrawn and moody ever since.

"Can I get you another drink?" he asked, trying to ease the ever-growing silence between them.

"No thanks."

He took his time in the kitchen, grabbing another beer out of the fridge. He took a quick gulp, peering back out into the living room again. She had been sitting in the same position for over forty minutes, her elbow propped up on the arm of the sofa, head resting in her hand. She looked miserable. Maybe he needed to clear the air? If something was wrong, he would much rather know about it and try to deal with it. Pretending it wasn't happening clearly wasn't working, for either of them.

He walked in and sat down on the couch again. Reaching over for the remote, he switched off the TV.

She frowned over at him.

"What are you doing?"

"Just hear me out. I can go if you want. I didn't mean to just barge in here and make things all weird again."

She regarded him cautiously.

"You don't have to go. And you didn't barge in, either."

He immediately picked up on what she didn't say.

"But things are weird, aren't they?"

"I'm sorry," she sighed. "I'm not very good company tonight, am I?"

"If I'm over-stepping the mark, I'm the one who needs to apologise," he said gently, "But has this got anything to do with Callum? Because everything seemed fine before he arrived. Did he say something? I thought we'd sorted that out, but if – "

"No, it's not that," she said. "I think I'm just tired. Between the late night last night and feeling like crap today, I guess it's taken more out of me than I thought. I don't normally drink that much these days, and - anyway, I'm sorry."

"I can understand that," he said, attempting a smile. "And I'm guessing by the yoga mat, you had some kind of exercise thing earlier? Hangovers and exercise don't usually mix well."

Something in her expression told him he had just made a huge mistake. His heart sank.

"I think we should do this another time," she snapped, reaching around the side of the couch to pull her wheelchair over.

He should just collect his DVD and get the hell out of here before he made things worse but he was reluctant to just leave things like this. She transferred over to her wheelchair, and he couldn't help but admire her technique. She handled it the same way she seemed to handle everything else, with confidence and grace.

"I'm sorry I'm being such a bitch, I'm just tired," she said. "I'm busy tomorrow night, but why don't we try this again on Monday night? I'll try not to be such a pain in the ass, I promise."

"Okay, and you're not being a bitch," he said, forcing a smile.

"Yeah, I am," she said wearily. "But to be totally honest, I'm just too exhausted to care."

He took the hint and got up to retrieve the DVD from the player and pop it back into the cover.

"Well, I'll get going then. I hope you get some sleep and feel better tomorrow."

Throughout the drive home, and long afterwards, the one thing he couldn't quite reconcile was what had made her snap at him like that. He had said something about hangovers and exercise. What was he missing?

CHAPTER FOURTEEN

"Sometimes, you find yourself in the middle of nowhere.
And sometimes, in the middle of nowhere,
you find yourself."
- Unknown

*M*aggie slid the phone back into her pocket and whistled under her breath.

"She sounds really tired - and really pissed at you. Apparently, you ruined her night."

Callum shrugged, trying to feign an indifference he didn't feel.

"She'll get over it."

"Why'd you do that? You know she likes to keep that stuff private."

Callum searched for an answer. The one that came to him was not the one he spoke out loud, though.

"Because it's important and she knows that."

"Well, yeah, she does. But Jack was there. It couldn't have

waited?"

Callum shot a sideways glance at her, frowning.

"So just because Jack was there, she should let this stuff slide?"

"No. I guess not. But you could've been a bit more delicate about it."

"Shockingly, delicate isn't really my forte."

Maggie nodded in agreement.

"She's putting on a show for him," he said. "Trying to pretend like everything's fine, that it's exactly the way it used to be. It's about time she was honest with him. He needs to know the truth. Besides, we had a deal. I didn't think she'd go all psycho about it."

"I can't blame her for wanting him to see her through rose-tinted glasses for just a little bit longer. I think that's natural."

"It's dangerous, is what it is."

"What do you mean by that?"

"What happens when he finds out about all this stuff, the stuff she wants to keep hidden from him? How do you think he'll react then? That's a lot of shit to dump on someone who carries the kind of guilt that Jack does."

"So, you still think he's gonna take off, at some point?"

He thought about the conversation he had with Jack in the car outside Barney's.

"I think it's still on the table, yeah."

"So, you're trying to protect her?"

"Obviously," he said, glaring at her.

She sat back in her chair, sighing.

"She was so nervous on Friday night. I guess it was like a first date all over again."

"We talked about that this morning when I went over there. I don't know what happened because she didn't exactly say, but she seemed pretty shaken up."

"Even more reason not to push her into anything tonight, but I guess it's too late for that now."

Callum sat back in his chair and rolled his eyes.

"Okay, okay."

"So, any idea how you're gonna work your way out of the doghouse this time?"

"Yeah," he sighed. "Thought I'd give her a little space and see what happens."

"Probably a good idea."

"I'll see her at the pool tomorrow night anyway. Hopefully she's talking to me again by then." He checked his watch. "Look, I gotta get going. I've got some stuff I need to do."

As he walked out towards his car, he would've given everything he owned to have been able to drive over to Tom's house, drag Jack out, throw him into his car and follow him to make sure he left town - for good this time.

---

*A*lly glanced over the table at Jack, who was immersed in the menu. The diner was busy for a Monday. As seemed to be her usual state around Jack lately, she was filled with a heady mix of excitement and anxiety.

A distinct murmur had gone through the diner when they arrived together. She wasn't sure whether Jack noticed it too but she was grateful he chose a corner booth. She sat up straight and tried to block them out. People would get used to seeing them together. She tried not to let it bother her as she perused the menu.

"BLT," she said finally, folding the menu and laying it on the table beside her.

"That's my line," he smiled. "I thought you'd be all over the cheeseburger and fries, with extra cheese."

"Not so much into the greasy stuff these days," she shrugged.

A healthy diet was better for her system than a diet of grease and junk food but he didn't need to know any of that.

The waitress came to take their order and they chatted easily while they waited for their meals to arrive. It was over coffee afterwards that she overheard something from a nearby table.

Tom's name, and Jack's, and something she wished she hadn't heard.

She could tell from the pained look on his face that Jack had heard it too. She'd been the subject of enough gossip and sideways glances over the past four years to not feel some kind of empathy for Jack. The gossipers themselves seemed oblivious to the fact that they had been talking loud enough for half the diner to hear them.

"Ignore them," she said firmly, catching Jack's attention and holding it. "You know what it's like around here, it's a full-time occupation for some people. Don't let it get to you. They'll move onto something else soon enough."

He smiled tightly but she could see it had hit a nerve. Better they got out of here and left the busy-bodies to it.

"Come on, let's go," she said, pushing her empty coffee cup away and slipping her jacket on. "It's too nice outside to spend any more time in here listening to that crap."

Jack quickly signalled the waitress for the bill.

"You're right. About that, and about the weather."

The waitress dropped the bill off and Jack pulled out some cash from his wallet as Ally pulled herself upright, taking up her crutches.

"Hey," he said, as they made their way through the crowded diner to the door. "How about a walk through the park?"

---

*C*allum was sitting on the vinyl-covered bench that ran along the wall of the Chinese restaurant, waiting for his takeout order, when Jack came in. They couldn't help but see each other, given they were the only two patrons in the near-empty foyer.

"Hey," Jack said, nodding to him.

"Hey."

Jack's order was ready and he picked it up, paid and left without another word. Callum breathed out as the door banged shut behind him. It would take a while to get used to the fact that they could bump into each other at any time. Callum's plans for the evening included Chinese takeout, a few beers and a Bourne movie marathon with Maggie. Jane had cancelled in favour of an early night and apparently Ally had other plans. It didn't take a psychic to figure out who with.

When Callum left the restaurant a few minutes later with his order, Jack was leaning against his car waiting for him. He stood up as Callum came closer.

"Hey," he said. "I was wondering if I could ask you something."

Callum was immediately on alert. His first instinct was to tell him to get lost but curiosity got the better of him.

"What's up?"

"That's actually what I wanted to ask you about."

"If you want something, you're gonna have to stop talking in riddles," he said irritably. "It's been a long day."

"Saturday night," Jack said, squaring his shoulders. "What happened between you and Ally?"

"What do you mean, what happened between us?"

"Well, she seemed fine before you showed up, then after you left things got kinda weird."

"Define weird."

"She was really withdrawn, kinda moody. She said she was tired but I don't know."

He scratched his head then ran a hand through his hair, clearly confused. It gave Callum a perverse sense of satisfaction to see it.

Good. Let him see how hard this is.

"I think it was something I said, or did," Jack continued. "I don't know. She wouldn't say exactly. I left not long after because she said she was tired."

Ally hadn't said anything to him at the pool last night. She had been quieter than usual but he put that down to the fact that she was still pissed off at him for barging in the night before.

"It probably wasn't anything you did," Callum said, knowing full well it wasn't. "She probably wants you to think she's the Eveready bunny when the truth is she doesn't have the energy levels she used to. She gets tired easily and then she gets pissy, not that you'll catch her admitting it, especially not to strangers."

Jack smarted, just as Callum hoped he would.

"Like I said, she seemed fine before you arrived," Jack retaliated. "What did you guys do anyway, some kind of exercise thing? She got a little frosty when I mentioned it."

"Not surprising."

"Meaning what, exactly?"

"You really need to ask her."

"I did."

"Sorry, can't help you, then." He walked around to get into his car. "Enjoy your night."

*J*ack grabbed them both a drink and made his way back to the living room. Ally had settled herself in one of the armchairs and was stretching carefully from side to side. She stopped when she realised he was watching her.

"Sorry. Just a bit stiff. It's been a while since I've been for a long walk like that."

He had noticed her stretching over dinner, too. Callum's words came back to him. Was she trying to impress him by keeping up with him? He didn't want to push it tonight if she was tired. It hadn't worked out so well the other night and he wanted to avoid a repeat performance.

"No, I'm sorry," he said, handing over her glass. "We could've done something else after lunch, we didn't have to go for a walk. I'm kinda new at this. You'll need to remind me when I suggest something stupid like that again."

She reached for the glass and their fingers brushed against each other. She stared up at him with a strange expression.

"What?" he asked, afraid he'd said something else idiotic.

"Remind you?" she smiled tentatively. "That's funny. I've never had to remind anyone before. It's usually the opposite."

Another glimpse behind the curtain. Like when he saw her sitting on her bedroom floor, and the other night at Barney's, and whatever the exercise thing was she was so touchy about.

"Anyway, it's fine," she said. "If I wasn't up to it, I would've said something. It was fun, I enjoyed it."

"Good," he smiled, heart soaring. "Me too."

She smiled back. The evening was turning out better than he'd hoped. He put his drink down on the coffee table and grabbed the DVD. He'd chosen a new release this time, reasoning that it might be better to watch something that didn't have so many memories attached to it.

"I ran into Callum when I was picking up dinner," he said, popping open the DVD cover and inserting the disc into the player.

"You did?" He caught the hint of anxiety in her voice, even though he was sure she had meant to hide it. "Everything okay between you two?"

"Getting there," he lied.

The truth was that he had no idea but the last thing she needed to worry about was him and Callum. He sank into the couch, on the side closest to her armchair. Was she deliberately trying to put some distance between them by sitting separately or was that just a practical decision? She had relied heavily on the arms of the chair to sit down, now that she was wearing her braces. In any case, it was probably wise to keep a safe distance, at least for now.

They settled in to watch the movie and once again, he was sucked into some kind of surreal vortex. He was sitting in her living room, watching a movie with her. The memories seemed to mingle with the present until he wasn't sure which was which. He saw the two of them, stretched out on this very couch, Ally in his arms, watching a movie. He saw them at his place, his dad in his armchair, he and Ally sitting on the floor, their backs up against the couch, his arm around her.

His heart felt like something was tugging on it, pulling it down into his chest cavity. He missed his father so much. God, he hoped he was watching.

She giggled, immersed in the movie, completely oblivious. He turned to her, watching her for a few moments, storing away the image of her happy and smiling. It was a habit he had a hard time breaking; storing up memories of the good times for when the bad times hit.

When the credits rolled, she stretched and he grabbed the remote to switch off the DVD.

"Your choice in movies has certainly improved," she said. "I really liked that one."

"Ah, there it is," he smiled. "I was waiting for that crack. I can't say I've watched a lot of movies lately so it was more of a coin toss, really."

Talking about his other life made him feel uncomfortable. She might ask questions and he didn't have any answers for her yet. She was stretching again, slowly, side to side.

"You sure you're okay?"

"I'm good, just stiff. I'll be fine tomorrow."

"If you're getting tired, I can get going."

"I'm not tired."

She may as well have come out and said it: stay a little longer.

"Good," he smiled. "Me neither."

Getting up to put the DVD player back into its case, he spied her iPod and picked it up.

"Music?" he asked over his shoulder.

"Sure, why not. You choose, seeing as you had so much success with the movie."

He scrolled through the options, settling on something he knew they would both like. He slotted it into the dock and music filled the room. He saw her approving smile as she rolled her shoulders again.

"Excellent choice," she said. "You're good at this."

"Y'know what else I'm good at? Neck rubs. Why don't you let me see if I can loosen up some of that stiffness?"

He didn't tell her that he'd been on the receiving end of a few massages in the course of recovering from a fight, or that he knew how much it had really helped.

"It's actually more my shoulders than my neck," she said carefully. "But thanks anyway."

He wasn't going to be put off that easily.

"Neck, shoulders - same principal, right?"

"I guess – "

"Exactly. I'll give it a try and if it doesn't help, I'll give up, I promise. Deal?" he said, rubbing his hands together as he perched on the arm of the chair beside her, giving her little choice. "No charge for this one by the way. First one's always free."

"Really?" she smiled up at him, eyes shining. "Well in that case, deal. I love a bargain."

"Excellent. Assume the position please ma'am."

"What?"

He pushed her head gently forward, chuckling.

"Oh," she giggled. "Right. Okay, game on."

She bowed her head and he tenderly swept her hair aside, pushing the silky tendrils forward over her shoulder. He stared at the naked base of her neck for a moment, a thrill of anticipation buzzing through him. Trying to focus, he laid his hands on her shoulders and began to knead the muscles, not really paying attention to anything at first, except the fact that he had his hands on her bare skin and it was driving him wild to be this close to her.

They lapsed into silence as the music filled up the room around them. Realising he was holding his breath, he concentrated on breathing normally. Slowly, he kneaded deeper into the knotted muscles beneath his fingertips, tight and solid.

A little moan escaped from her.

"God, that feels good."

He smiled, slowly increasing the pressure.

"You've got a bunch of rocks between your shoulder blades," he said, digging deeper.

"Don't forget the metal rods in my spine."

Her tone was conversational but the effect on Jack was like a sledge-hammer to the chest. He'd forgotten about the surgery, pushed to the back of his mind over the years. Suddenly he was afraid of hurting her.

"Don't go easy on me," she said, noticing immediately. "I won't break, I promise."

"Okay," he said, daring to increase the pressure again as his fingers worked into the muscles.

"That's good," she breathed, her head bowing lower. "Really good."

He concentrated on keeping his fingers working at the same speed. Since the kiss the other night, they had barely touched and he pushed aside everything else to savour the moment. She smelled so good it was all he could do not to lean forward and inhale her.

"You said the other day that Callum helps with massage and stuff," he said, anxious to keep the conversation flowing. "Is this the kind of thing you meant?"

She stiffened beneath his touch and he eased up on the pressure a little, afraid he was being too rough.

"Yeah, pretty much."

Gone was the conversational tone. He should've taken it for the warning it was but he forged ahead.

"So that's what you guys were doing the other night, with the yoga mat?"

He knew immediately that he'd gone too far. It was as if the temperature in the room had dropped by several degrees in a single heartbeat.

"That's much better," she said tersely, leaning away from him. "Thanks for your help."

His hands fell away and the connection they shared disappeared. The remorse was immediate.

Shit.

"I'm sorry," he said, desperate to explain. "I don't mean to pry. I've just been wondering, that's all."

She froze, her back to him. The song that had been playing ended and the resulting silence was deafening. He tried again.

"I asked Callum about it but he said I should ask you, so that's what I'm doing."

"Oh really?" she glared up at him over her shoulder. "He said that? I should've seen that coming."

She leaned forward, preparing to stand, as he searched for something to say to make things okay between them again.

"I'm sorry," he said again, as she practically forced him out of the way, turning to push herself upwards and lock her braces through her jeans.

"It's fine. Forget it." She slid her arms into the cuffs of her crutches, refusing to look at him. "I think you should go."

"What?"

She turned away from him and he reached out to touch her shoulder.

"Ally, please. I'm completely in the dark here, I don't even know what I said wrong."

He could feel her trembling beneath his hand and he squeezed her shoulder gently, trying to keep some semblance of calm in his voice.

"I don't want to get caught up in the middle of this thing between you two," she said tightly.

"What?"

"You and Callum!"

"What thing? Look, I don't know what you think is going on here but he said I should ask you about this and I agree with him. What's the big deal? Come on, whatever it is, can we just talk about it and get it over with? Because it feels like things are getting a little out of control here, don't you think?"

His mind went completely blank as she turned to face him, her eyes burning with open hostility.

"He thinks he's being clever," she said icily. "He knows I don't want to talk about this and he knows you're desperate enough to do anything so he's pushing me from one angle and pulling you from another!"

"This isn't some kind of game, Ally. I just want you to talk to me, that's all, it's no big conspiracy, nothing sinister."

"He's playing you!"

"I don't think he is," he said carefully, trying to keep calm in the face of her anger. "I know there's a lot of stuff I don't know but I thought that maybe if I asked you when I'm not sure, we can shorten that list a little bit, y'know?"

"Why are you making a big deal out of this?"

"I'm not making a big deal out of anything. I'm just asking a question, that's all."

"So, go ahead then, ask it!"

"Alright. What's the deal with the yoga mat? Is it a massage thing? Or an exercise thing? Or something else? Because I gotta say, my imagination is running wild right now."

She narrowed her eyes at him and a chill crawled up the back of his neck.

"How about I tell you all about that once you tell me where the hell you've been for the past four years?"

He stared at her, words escaping him. What the hell just happened? The mood had changed so fast, his head swam. She was almost in the hallway before he finally came around.

"Look, I'm sorry – " he tried.

She paused in the doorway, her back to him.

"No more apologies, Jack," she said over her shoulder. "I want answers and if you can't give them to me, we have nothing else to talk about."

Dumbfounded, all he could do was watch as she disappeared.

CHAPTER FIFTEEN

"What is important is not what happens to us,
but how we respond to what happens to us."
- Jean-Paul Sartre

*J*ack sat in his car, his heart pounding while inside his head, Ally raged on. He stared at the shadows of the mature trees that surrounded the cemetery gates in the moonlight. Even in the midst of all this turmoil, his gut instinct was to seek out his father.

Digging his new cell phone out of his pocket, he paused momentarily before hitting the contacts button. Callum picked up on the second ring.

"What the hell are you up to?" Jack demanded.

"Jack?"

"You knew damn well what you were doing, didn't you? She's right - you were just playing me!"

"Whoa, hang on, what the – "

"Is this your way of getting back at me? You satisfied now?"

"Just calm the hell down, will you? What happened?"

"Don't play dumb, Callum. She threw me out, which is exactly what you wanted!"

"What?"

"Do you think this is some kind of game?"

"Just calm down! Where are you? Are you at home?"

Jack huffed out a ragged breath and looked around. The leafy trees and well-kept gardens surrounding the cemetery spread out in the darkness before him.

"No."

"Meet me at Barney's in twenty minutes."

"Why?"

"Just meet me there. No games, no bullshit. I promise."

Jack took a deep breath, letting it out slowly.

"Fine."

He threw the phone onto the passenger seat in disgust. The spark of hope that had been glowing inside him over the past few days sputtered and died. Who did he think he was kidding?

Callum sat in his car outside Barney's. He tried Ally again but she didn't pick up and he hung up halfway through her voicemail message with a frustrated sigh. All he seemed to do lately was push her away. A little voice inside his head said he had it all wrong. All *she* seemed to do lately was push *him* away. Ever since Jack got home.

He shoved his cell phone back into his pocket, climbed out of his car and headed inside. Entering the gloomy bar at this time of night, he took a few moments to spot Jack in a booth in the corner. He detoured to order a drink first and Harry nodded in Jack's direction, as if warning him.

"What's his poison?" Callum asked.

"Whisky. Neat."

Callum groaned quietly, shaking his head.

"Better give me two more."

Jack glanced up as he slid into the seat opposite him, setting both glasses down and sliding one over the table towards him.

"I've already got one."

"Got a feeling you might need another."

Jack eyeballed him, his expression unreadable.

"What's this all about?" he said. "What do you want? Because I'm in no mood for games. Whatever you want, you can have it. You win, okay? I don't belong here - I get it. Believe me, I get it. So if you're about to launch into another speech, save your breath."

He shook his head and took a swig of whisky.

"What happened?" Callum asked, although he had a fair idea by now.

"I told you," Jack said, staring into the glass in front of him. "She threw me out."

"I thought she might try something like that."

"Congratulations. You win."

"It's not a game, Jack. Far from it."

"Then why do I feel like a pinball? What's going on here? Because I honestly have no clue."

"There's no single answer to that question," Callum sighed, running a hand down his face.

"Jesus, you're as bad as she is. It's like talking to a revolving door."

Jack downed the last of his whisky and slammed the glass down on the table.

"You thought she was complicated before? Buckle up dude, you ain't seen nothin' yet," Callum said.

"Meaning what, exactly?"

He had to make his point and make it quickly because he could see Jack was teetering on the brink.

"Reading between the lines? She doesn't want you to know

anything that might make you disappear again. And that means that her injury, and anything to do with it, is off limits."

Jack stared at him for a few moments, and he could see the cogs turning in his brain.

"She doesn't trust me," Jack said simply.

"It's a hell of a lot to ask, you have to admit."

"But, I'm not gonna just - I mean, I want to stay, I told her that - I asked her what she wanted, and she said – "

"Put yourself in her place. Is it any wonder? You're not so special, by the way - she's been doing this for years. She changes the subject a *lot*. Anytime the conversation gets too raw, she backs off. It's always 'never mind', or 'it doesn't matter', or 'let's talk about something else'."

Callum saw recognition in Jack's eyes and he nodded across the table at him.

"You've seen it too, haven't you?"

"Yeah."

"It's a diversionary tactic."

"Why?"

Callum shrugged again, taking a sip of his whisky and waiting as it burned a trail down his throat.

"Best I can figure is she's trying to protect us."

"From what?" Jack frowned.

"From whatever's going on in her head."

They eyeballed each other across the table for several moments and Callum tried to block out the memories of their relationship prior to the accident. He tried to concentrate on seeing Jack as a stranger sitting across from him but the vision wouldn't stick. He kept seeing his friend, Jack - and more disturbingly, he kept seeing Jack and Ally together, before their world turned upside down. They were in love. They were going to get married and have a house full of kids.

Suddenly, the last four years fell away and some of the anger and resentment fell away with it, right along with the idea that he and Ally ever really had a chance together. She had been right all along. It would never have worked between them. Jack was the one she was always meant to be with. That was why he was here now. That was why she wanted him to stay.

Oblivious, Jack's gaze was fixed on the glass in front of him. He looked helpless, hopeless. It was the first time Callum had seen that look from the other side. No wonder Tom had taken him under his wing. A look like that was hard to ignore.

"If you knew she was gonna do this," Jack mumbled, "Why'd you make me push her into talking about it?"

It was a valid question and Callum took a moment to think about how best to answer it.

"Honestly? I guess I was testing her. I figured if she could talk to you about it then she was ready for whatever this is between the two of you. On some level, I thought since it was you asking, she might open up."

Jack seemed to deflate in front of him.

"Guess you were wrong, then," he said. "She's not talking to me about it. Jesus, I don't even know what to say to her half the time. I don't have a clue what I'm doing. I'm just an idiot, saying the wrong thing and doing the wrong thing and pissing her off."

Callum thought of all the times over the past few years when he felt inadequate.

"She's stubborn," he said. "And tough as hell. You two have that in common."

Jack looked dubious.

"You came back here didn't you?" he insisted. "And you're still here, despite everything. She's pushing you away because she doesn't want you to see what she thinks are her weaknesses. Secrets - another thing you two have in common."

Jack opened his mouth but Callum cut him off.

"That's something you have to work out between you, somehow. This is about her, and about you not giving up on her. She doesn't deserve that, not after everything she's been through.

Despite what she says or does, you need to keep that promise you made her. You need to stay."

Jack shot him a look of total disbelief.

"You've changed your tune."

Callum took a good long swallow of whisky and set the glass back on the table slowly.

"I know that, believe me. But I'm not an idiot. I can see what's happening here, to her, to you."

He looked over at Jack, his heart ripping open in the wake of the truth that tumbled out of his mouth.

"She needs you. If she tries to tell you otherwise, she's lying - I know it and she knows it. Tom knew it too, that's why he never gave up on you coming home."

He could see the effect his words were having on Jack. He swallowed his pride and continued.

"She's pushing you away because she knows that sooner rather than later, she's gonna have to start letting you in and it's scaring her to death. You hold all the power here. You can walk away, or you can pick her up and never let her go. Do you understand what I'm saying? Do you get how serious this is?"

Jack nodded dumbly.

"So, don't you dare go anywhere."

Finally, Jack found his voice.

"I made her a promise."

Callum glared at him over the table, willing his voice not to break.

"And you damn well better keep it."

The next morning, Ally sat in her studio, staring at the unfinished painting on the easel in front of her. Her head pounded and even though she knew she should eat something, her stomach churned so much she felt queasy just thinking about food.

She didn't know how long she'd been sitting there but it felt like a while. She braced her hands on the wheels and rims of her chair and straightened her elbows, pushing herself upwards to temporarily relieve the pressure on her backside. Holding the position for several seconds, she eventually let gravity win and lowered herself back onto the chair, her shoulders burning. Maybe a workout would take her mind off things? Who was she kidding? She had no energy to eat, never mind work out.

Sullenly, she went back to staring at the canvas. It was supposed to be the final piece in her 'Evolution' series, the piece that signified her return from the abyss, but deep down she still felt in limbo. Jack coming home had highlighted that. She had thought that she'd accepted the accident and how it had changed her life but Jack was such a huge part of that equation and she still had so many unanswered questions.

The anger she had wanted to unleash on Callum earlier had faded. In its wake was a morbid acceptance. All Jack had done was ask a question and she was unable to answer it without lashing out. None of that was Callum's fault. It was hers. The weakness was hers.

Frustration and embarrassment mingled with the overriding fear that he might not be able to handle it, handle *her*. How could she be honest with him when she didn't trust his reaction? And why should he be honest with her in return? Honesty was a two-way street and she was throwing up road-blocks and detours. Her heart felt physically heavy, as if it might fall out of her body altogether and smash into a million pieces on the floor right in front of her.

The phone rang again. Irritated, she turned slowly and wheeled over to the studio door, pushing it shut. Silence engulfed her and she turned, rolling toward her iPod on the workbench. She scrolled through until she found what she was looking for –

Pearl Jam's *Ten* – and slotted it into the dock, turning the volume up to the max. Something had to drown out the voices in her head. The opening bars of *Once* filled the space around her and she closed her eyes, trying to give herself over to the music. She rocked backwards and forwards slightly in her chair as the music took her away from her thoughts, then turned around in circles as the first verse slammed into her senses.

Rocking harder, she turned in the other direction and pushed herself backwards, hanging on to the fantasy of being somewhere, anywhere, but here. She crashed into something and her eyes flew open as she saw the unfinished canvas land face up on the ground. She stared at it for a moment. Frowning, she rolled forward for a closer inspection. Anger building out of nowhere, she tilted her chair backwards and slammed her front castors down on top of it. The music masked the sound but she stared down at the ripped canvas with a sense of satisfaction.

Tilting her chair to remove the castors from inside the frame, she spun in a half-circle and clumsily knocked the easel to the ground. She watched it fall with a muffled sense of detachment. Curiously, she rolled over to the workbench and swiped her arm across its surface, sending tubes of paint, brushes, bottles and supplies flying to the ground. Again, no sound except the chorus of the song blaring through the room.

*J*ack stared at the phone he had slammed down on the mantelpiece earlier. He itched to pick it up and hit the redial button. Ally didn't want to talk to him. He understood that but he couldn't let it go.

She deserved to know everything that had happened, from the night of the accident to now. God knew, she had every right to ask. He owed her that and so much more. He sank down into the couch.

"You want to know where I've been?" he mumbled. "Well, here it is: I've been everywhere but here. I've been hiding because I hate myself for what I've done to you and I can't fix it or forget it."

Saying it in an empty room was one thing. Saying it to her was something else entirely.

A knock at the door startled him and he practically ran to the door, hoping it was Ally. Instead, Maggie stood on the doorstep.

"Hi," she said.

He couldn't help but feel disappointed.

"Hey."

"I need a favour. Your Dad had a key to Ally's place. Can I have it?"

Something was up. She was even more frosty than usual.

"Why? What's going on?"

"I just need it."

"I get that, but why?"

"Quit being an asshole, Jack," she snapped. "Can I have the key or not? I haven't got time for this."

That wasn't just disdain. It was fear. What was she so afraid of?

He turned and Maggie followed him down the hall to the kitchen, waiting as he sorted through the keys that hung on a series of hooks next to the door. Finding one with Ally's name on it, he grabbed it and she reached out to take it from him.

"Not unless you tell me why you need it," he said, shoving it into his pocket with a frown.

"You're... infuriating," she seethed, anger surpassing the fear.

"Start talking."

"She's locked us out," she spat. "Not answering the door, not picking up the phone. We just want to check on her."

"We had a fight last night," he said, scratching his head absentmindedly. "Maybe she just needs some time out?"

"Right. Time out, with the music blaring so loud I'm surprised the neighbours haven't complained."

Ally's penchant for drowning out the world when she was upset came flooding back. Was this because of what happened between them last night?

"Y'know what?" she said, turning on her heel. "Keep the key. We'll find another way."

He stared after her, some of her fear rubbing off on him. What the hell was going on?

"I'll cut you a deal," he called. "I'll bring it with me."

She stopped dead, whirling around to face him down the length of the hall.

"If you – "

"If I what?"

She glared at him but her mouth remained a thin, tight line.

"I'm coming with you," he said, walking towards her. "Like it or not."

THREE YEARS EARLIER

Callum stood in Ally's kitchen, wrestling with his instincts. Over-sleeping was one of the danger signs they had been warned to look out for. She usually got up around six, six-thirty. It was now well after eight.

She'd been discharged two weeks earlier and he'd been sleeping on her couch ever since. After what happened, there was no way he was letting her out of his sight. She hadn't even argued about it. In fact, she hadn't said much at all. She had withdrawn into herself, blocking everyone out, including him. They hoped that her new therapist would be able to help. Dr Saunders came highly recommended but he was getting impatient. The voice of reason, Tom reminded him that it had taken her twelve months to reach this low, she wasn't going to just bounce back within a few weeks.

Steeling himself, he picked up the cup of coffee he had prepared for her and walked along the hall to her bedroom.

"Hey, you awake?" he called through the closed door, straining to hear sounds of movement from within.

He opened the door and peered around the corner, fighting the irrational fear that he'd find her lying there beside an empty bottle of pills again. He'd taken precautions against that already, he reminded himself. She lay on her side, facing away from him. He pulled the curtains back and mid-morning sunshine flooded the room.

"Pills," she croaked, voice laced with pain.

He covered the distance between the window and her bed in seconds, practically dropping the coffee cup on the bedside table. She stared up at him, pale and miserable, sweat glistening on her brow.

"Jesus," he breathed. "Why didn't you call me? I'll be right back."

He ran out of the bedroom and across the hall to the living room, reaching up onto the top shelf of the bookcase on his tiptoes and grabbing the bottle of painkillers. Sprinting back to her room, he fell to his knees beside her bed, fumbling over the lid of the bottle as he elbowed her wheelchair aside.

"One or two?"

"Two," she said, squeezing out the word between clenched teeth.

He tipped two pills out into his palm and grabbed the small bottle of water on the bedside table, opening it and discarding the lid. She grimaced, reaching with trembling fingers to take the pills from him, slipping them on her tongue slowly and taking a sip of water as some overflowed, spilling onto the pillow.

She closed her eyes and he sank back on his heels, anxious for the medication to take effect. He smoothed her hair away from her clammy forehead, cursing under his breath.

"I'm sorry," he said, as she took shallow breaths. "I thought you'd just overslept."

She opened her eyes and he could see the pain embedded within them.

"Just hang in there. The meds will kick in soon."

He squirmed into a more comfortable position on the floor beside her bed as the minutes ticked by slowly. She lay perfectly still in the quiet room, eyes closed. The grandfather clock chimed in the hall.

Finally, the pain eased and he helped her sit up, carefully lifting her legs over the side of the bed so that she didn't have to. She inhaled sharply, eyes squeezing shut again.

"Too soon?" he winced. "Take a few more minutes."

She held onto the mattress, breathing out through her teeth, before opening her eyes again.

"It's better when I'm up," she said.

She knew better than anyone so he didn't argue.

"We're gonna have to rig up some kind of system so this doesn't happen again," he said, crouching on the floor beside the bed.

"Give me back my meds and it won't."

"I can't do that, not yet."

Her fingers dug into the mattress.

"I'm not a child. I don't need babysitting."

Callum was so scared of saying the wrong thing, he took a moment to formulate a reply.

"I'm sorry if it feels shitty right now," he said gently. "I really am. But it's for the best. We're just worried, that's all."

She didn't react and he wondered if that was all she was going to say on the matter. It was more than she'd said for days.

"I'm gonna take a shower," she said. "The warm water helps."

"Do you need a hand to transfer?"

He pulled her wheelchair closer to the bed.

"I can do it."

She took hold of the chair and repositioned it, applying the brake. Slowly, she transferred her pain-wracked body into it and made her way to the bathroom.

Sighing, Callum ran a hand down his face. He couldn't take much more of this. She was a thousand times worse than after the accident. Back then, at least she was trying to put on a brave face, even if he could see right through it. Now it was like she'd given up. Where the hell was Jack? Why wasn't he here for this?

He pushed down the anger and the bitterness and the fear and headed for the kitchen to put on a fresh pot of coffee.

When she appeared in the kitchen some time later, he had prepared a light breakfast. He got the feeling that if he didn't insist she eat, she wouldn't bother.

"How do you feel now? Did the shower help?"

"Yeah, a bit."

As she reached for the coffee, he noticed she still moved gingerly. She sipped her coffee in silence but didn't touch the toast or eggs.

"You should eat something," he said.

"I'm not hungry."

She stared at her hands, wrapped around the coffee cup in front of her. She looked so fragile, he didn't want to push it.

"I'm sorry," she said quietly.

"What for?"

"For what happened that day."

His heart stopped as her words sank in. After spending the past two weeks wishing she would open up to him, he wasn't sure he was ready to hear it now.

"Does this have anything to do with the appointment with Pavlovic?" he asked tentatively.

Ally nodded and he saw the façade starting to crack.

"What happened?"

She looked over at him through tear-filled eyes.

"It's okay," he whispered. "Whatever it is, it's okay. Just tell me."

The heartbreak was written all over her face as she shook her head.

"It's not okay."

He could see the struggle within her, the battle for control over her emotions and the inner strength that made her hold on when she so obviously wanted to let go.

"He said that this was it," she murmured. "It's been a year and whatever recovery I'm going to have, I've had it. In his words, it's highly unlikely there will be any further nerve regeneration now. My window's closed. This is it for me."

Her words stung. He knew how much she'd been holding on to the hope that somehow, she would be in the five percent, that the nerves would regenerate, even a little. He imagined he saw the last ray of hope die in her eyes, sinking into the abyss without a trace. It wasn't fair. She'd fought so hard. She deserved a miracle.

He stood up and walked around the table, kneeling down beside her to gently pull her into his arms. Not for the first time, he found himself wishing that they could trade places. If he could have taken some of the heartache away, he would have.

"I'm sorry," he whispered.

Two words, woefully inadequate.

She grabbed a handful of his shirt and pulled him closer, shuddering sobs wracking her body with such intensity that he winced. There was nothing he could say that would ease this pain. He felt just as helpless as he had barely an hour ago, watching and waiting for the pain medication to take effect. Only there was no medication to take away this pain.

"You're stronger than you think," he said into her hair. "I promise you that."

The sobbing continued but silently now, as if the pain inside was so great it had sucked up every last breath. Finally, she spoke, sounding so vulnerable it made his chest hurt

"I thought if I got better, if I... then he'd come back. If he left because of me, because he was scared to see me like this, then maybe I could show him that it wasn't... that I wasn't..."

This was what she'd been keeping hidden all this time? This was what she thought?

He smoothed her hair down, feeling completely helpless. Too late, he realised that his wish to take some of her pain away had been granted and he felt the weight of her sorrow bearing down on him now, crushing him.

"Listen to me," he said, with as much conviction as he could muster. "It doesn't matter if Jack's here or not. You can do this. You're not alone. Do you hear me?"

She didn't answer and he didn't know what else to say that would convince her. Her heart was broken, her body too. It had to hurt beyond anything he had ever encountered but he couldn't just let her give up. She had more fight in her than anyone he'd ever known. If anyone could overcome this, she could. She just had to believe it.

Carefully extricating himself from her, he ducked through to the living room, roughly wiping away the tears from his cheeks before she could see them. Pulling out the small wooden box he had replaced in the bookcase prior to her return from the hospital, he took it back into the kitchen. He knelt down beside her as she wiped her eyes. When she recognised the box in his hand, she groaned.

"I don't want to see that."

He ignored her, opening the box and pulling out a journal.

"Remember this? I want you to look at it - all of it." He put the journal on the table and pulled out a wad of photographs. "Do you see these? Do you remember when they were taken?"

She stared at the memory box in his hands. The journal, the photographs, all the mementos of her journey over the past year. The hospital, rehab and plenty of victories since, all wrapped up in one small box, heavy with triumph and courage. She had insisted on recording everything.

"You're capable of so much more than you think you are," he said, holding out the photographs to her. "You always have been. Here's the proof, Ally. Don't you get it?"

She stared at the photographs, tears sliding down her cheeks silently.

"Don't you get it?" she said, lifting her gaze to look at him. "I did all that for Jack, not for me. I don't want it anymore. I don't need it. You can burn it, burn all of it for all I care. It doesn't matter now, none of it does."

Callum shook his head, the pain in his soul burning with such intensity that he lost the power of speech for a moment. She may have *thought it was all for Jack but his perspective was very different. It wasn't for him, it was for her, to remind her of what she was capable of, of the strength that was buried deep inside her.*

"Come on Ally, you – "

"You're not listening to me!" she demanded, her voice bordering on hysterical suddenly. "It doesn't matter anymore! He's not coming back and even if he did, look at me!"

She knocked the photos out of his hand and grabbed the journal off the table, hurling it across the room.

"I am looking at you!" he roared, desperate to reach her. "And I see strength beyond anything I've ever seen in my life, courage of gigantic proportions, grace that would put Mother Teresa to shame! I know you want him to come back, I know you miss him, but he's not here - we are. We're here and we need you to fight, Ally. I need you to fight."

She stared at him in shock, red-rimmed eyes wide and desperate, tears sliding down her ruddy cheeks, whole body trembling. He barely dared to breathe, afraid to touch her, to say anything more. Then, before his eyes, the pain reached saturation point and she folded in on herself, doubling over and sobbing as though her heart was being torn out.

He pulled her close again, holding her as tight as he dared as the heartache, grief and anger seeped out of her.

CHAPTER SIXTEEN

"Our greatest glory is not in never falling,
but in rising every time we fall."
- Confucius

When Jack pulled up outside Ally's house, Maggie was already heading up the front path. Callum's car was parked in her driveway and, as he walked up towards the house, he saw the two of them, deep in conversation on her porch over the music that blared out from within.

"You don't need to be here," Callum said, holding out his hand. "It's just the key we need."

"It's a package deal," Jack said. "Besides, last night, you told me to fight and that's exactly what I'm doing."

Maggie glanced nervously from Callum to Jack.

"Not here, not now," Callum said. "You need to trust me on this. Go home."

"Sorry," Jack shook his head. "Can't do it. If I'm in, I'm in - I'm not doing this half-assed."

The muscles in Callum's jaw twitched but he kept his mouth shut, turning his back on him and thumping on the door.

"Ally! Open up or we're coming in!"

Jack shifted his weight from one foot to another as they waited for a response.

"Key?" Callum demanded, turning back to him.

Jack dug it out of his pocket and handed it over without a word, watching as Callum unlocked the front door, his heart racing.

"Ally!" Callum called, heading left into the bedroom as Maggie went right, into the living room.

Jack followed the music down to the studio at the back of the house. He pushed the door open, not bothering to knock, figuring she'd never hear it over the music anyway. The room looked like a tornado had been through it. Paint, canvases and supplies littered the floor. He scanned the room, taking a moment to spot Ally behind the door. She sat with her back to the wall, legs splayed out in front of her. Her eyes were closed and her wheelchair some distance away. She looked paler than usual, and tired. His heart sank.

Shit.

Callum pushed past him, sinking to his knees beside her and giving her a solid shake. Her eyes flew open and he shouted something at her that was lost beneath the music. Ally looked up as Maggie swooped past him, but her gaze locked onto Jack, seeing him for the first time. She didn't have time to react before Maggie enveloped her in a brief but frantic embrace. Callum yelled at her again, the exact nature of the conversation lost in the din. Ally looked just as confused as he was.

He scanned the room again, locating the source of the music and picking his way carefully over the debris-littered floor to turn it off. The air buzzed around them in the sudden silence.

"– the hell are you playing at?" Callum demanded.

"What are you doing here?" she asked, trying to wriggle feebly out of his grasp. "How'd you get in?"

"Are you okay?" Maggie's tone was gentler than Callum's.

Before she could answer, Callum grabbed her hands and forced her fingers apart, searching for something but finding nothing. Ally's expression morphed from confusion to embarrassment to fury. She snatched her hands back, shoving him backwards in the same movement.

"Get the hell off me!"

Maggie reached for her again but she pushed her hand away.

"Just calm down," Maggie soothed. "What are you doing in here? And what's with the mega-decibels? Don't you answer your phone anymore?"

Frustration written all over her rapidly reddening face, Ally pushed Maggie's hand away a second time.

"What is this, twenty questions?"

"You ignore your phone and lock yourself in here with that thing blaring," snapped Callum. "I think we've got a right to be a little concerned, don't you?"

"I'm fine!" she shouted, eyeballing him.

"Really? You look fine, sitting on the floor like this, amongst all this shit! Did you do all this?"

"It's my house, my studio, I can do what I want. I don't have to answer to you or anyone else!"

"You're right, it is, and I don't give a shit what you do in here, but why didn't you answer your phone, or the door? Being pig-headed is one thing, but this is just plain selfish!"

She pushed him away irritably.

"Get out of here, I'm fine! I don't need the third degree, especially not from you!"

"Oh, okay, I get it. You're pissed off at me, is that it? Is that what all this is about?"

"I'm not pissed off at anybody! I just wanted to be by myself for a while but apparently that's too much to ask! You don't need to run over here every time I miss a call!"

"Check your damn messages, it wasn't just one phone call you missed! Jesus Ally, do you even know how freaked out we were, or do you just not give a damn?"

Her face reddened.

"It's been a rough week, with Tom, and all this other stuff happening," Callum shot a quick glance over his shoulder at Jack. "I know things have been kinda crazy, but you can't do this, you can't ignore the phone and ignore us and expect us not to worry! We had a deal, remember?"

"I'm fine - you can see I'm fine!"

They glared at each other in silence for a few moments before Maggie intervened.

"We're sorry. We were worried, that's all."

"How did you even get in here?" Ally ignored her, directing her question at Callum, who appeared to be taking the brunt of her anger.

Jack cleared his throat self-consciously.

"Dad had a spare key."

"You wouldn't answer your phone, or your door. If you want to blame anyone, blame me, it was my idea," Callum snapped.

She glared at him.

"Bring me my chair."

"There's broken glass everywhere," he warned, standing up and picking his way over the debris to her wheelchair. "And paint, and whatever the hell the rest of this crap is. I'll give you a hand."

"I don't need your help."

Jack cringed at her tone.

"Right. Would you rather pick up an infected cut instead?"

She glowered up at him but he swooped in to pick her up off the floor anyway. Jack was impressed. Had she looked at him like that, he wasn't sure he would have had the guts to go anywhere near her.

Maggie tilted her wheelchair back and guided it carefully through the room and out into the hallway. Jack followed her, standing in the kitchen doorway, his head spinning.

Callum expertly deposited Ally into the waiting chair, one of her shoes falling off in the process. He picked it up and she snatched it off him, dropping it in her lap and immediately heading away from them down the hallway.

"You're welcome!" Callum called after her.

She whirled around to face them, blushing furiously.

"Thanks for completely over-reacting and treating me like a five-year-old, really appreciate it."

"Oh, for God's sake, just calm down, alright?"

"Don't tell me to calm down!" she yelled. "This is my house! Sideshow's over - now you can all get the hell out!"

"Yeah, that's not gonna happen until you un-bunch your panties," he shot back. "I'm gonna brew some coffee. Maybe when you've stopped hulking out, you can come into the kitchen and join us and we can talk about this like the civilised people we're supposed to be."

She glared at him, then turned around and disappeared into her bedroom, slamming the door shut behind her.

Callum breathed out a frustrated sigh and leaned back against the wall as Maggie stared after her. Jack barely dared to breathe. Somehow, he had managed to blend into the background. They stood in silence for several moments before Callum pushed himself upright.

"Well, like she said, show's over." He addressed Jack pointedly. "You can go home now."

Jack shook his head.

"I'm staying."

"He's right," Maggie said. "You should probably go home. We'll stay for a while longer, just in case."

"That's what I want to talk to you about," he said quietly. "In case of what?"

Maggie shared a guarded look with Callum.

"I'm not leaving until someone tells me, so you can count me in for that coffee."

"You're better off not knowing," Callum said. "In fact, I can pretty much guarantee that if we did tell you, you'd wish we hadn't. You should go home, Jack - I'm serious."

Jack nodded, his stomach churning.

"Yeah, well, so am I."

$\mathcal{A}$lly hadn't come out of her room and Callum and Maggie were in the kitchen, making coffee. They spoke in hushed tones and Jack couldn't make out what they were saying. He supposed he should go in there but he stood in the hallway, reluctant to move. If what Callum said was true, he wasn't going to like what he was about to hear and if he was honest with himself, he was scared.

Cupboard doors opened and closed and he heard footsteps, followed by the sound of the TV being switched on. He stood for a moment, debating his options, before walking down the hall to Ally's door, knocking softly. There was no answer but he took a chance and pushed it open anyway, peering around the corner. She sat on the edge of her bed, frowning at him. He took the bull by the horns, remembering his chat with Callum the night before. Somehow, it had seemed much less frightening then. Now, faced with her obvious anxiety, doubt began to creep in.

Aware that he was standing there, staring at her, he cleared his throat quietly.

"Hi. Can I come in?"

She shrugged sharply, indicating she didn't care one way or

the other, although her body language suggested otherwise. Easing the door closed behind him, he stood awkwardly, waiting.

"Where are they?" she asked, fear lurking beneath her words.

"In the kitchen."

Taking a shuddering breath, her gaze sank to the floor.

"Why are you still here?"

He slipped his hands into his pockets.

"I was hoping we could talk - y'know, without all the yelling."

She didn't respond, even though he waited for longer than was comfortable.

"Can I sit down?"

She shrugged again and he walked over to her, sidestepping her wheelchair and sitting down on the bed beside her. He braced his hands on his thighs, stealing a sideways glance at her.

"Are you alright?" he asked carefully. "That was pretty intense."

"I'm fine."

Clearly a knee-jerk reaction because she sounded far from it. He noticed she had replaced the shoe that had fallen off earlier and he stared at her feet. Her shoes were flat, black and leather with thin straps that fit over the tops of her feet. The leather looked soft, giving him the impression of ballet slippers. The sort of shoe she used to hate. She preferred boots in the winter, her favourites being a purple leather pair with a two-inch heel that made them almost the same height. In summer she favoured strappy sandals with heels in bright colours, the brighter the better.

Swallowing down the observation, he tried again.

"I don't know what just happened here," he said, turning his attention from her shoes to her face. "But it feels like I'm missing something important. Do you want to tell me what it is? Because I gotta say, Callum's threatening to fill me in and I'd much rather hear it from you."

She stared at the floor. As the seconds ticked by, he tried to imagine what the big revelation might be.

"Can we talk about this another time?" she said finally. "I don't know if I can do this right now."

He fought the temptation to yield, given she was obviously upset, but it seemed that this was some kind of defining moment. Callum was right - she was scared of letting him in. He had to find a way to show her that it was okay, whatever 'it' was.

"Talk to me," he murmured, reaching over to enclose her hand in his. "Please?"

She was trembling and he ran his fingers over the callouses on her hand gently. So strong yet so vulnerable. Tears slid down her cheeks, tearing at his heart. It wasn't a physical pain but an emotional one, a pain that settled in your soul and left scars. He knew because he had seen that look before, in the mirror. No one should feel pain like that. He wanted to hold her in his arms and never let her go.

"I did something," she whimpered. "Something I really regret now."

He nodded, trying hard to keep his expression neutral when his heart told him that anything that had hurt her this much was going to hurt him even more.

***

Maggie stopped halfway down the hallway, straining to hear.

"What's going on?" Callum murmured as she frantically waved a hand behind her, urging him to be quiet.

They both stood motionless. After a few moments, she shrugged and tip-toed back to the kitchen, pushing him through the door on her way past.

"Well?" he asked, as she picked up her cup of coffee off the kitchen table.

"Can't hear a thing."

He took a step backwards and glanced down the hall towards Ally's room.

"Do you think she's telling him what happened?"

"Get in here!" she hissed.

Reluctantly, he did as he was asked, sitting down at the table again. He picked up his coffee cup and took a sip.

"I feel like we should be doing something," Maggie said, chewing on her bottom lip. "Don't you feel like we should be doing something?"

"Like what?"

"I don't know."

He set his coffee cup down on the table in front of him and stared at it.

---

*J*ack felt like the floor had opened up beneath him and he was spiralling down into the bowels of hell.

Ally's voice came at him as if via a tunnel, the words whooshing past him as he plummeted.

He couldn't let go of her hand, couldn't look away from the haunting eyes, the tear-stained face.

Goosebumps broke out all over his body as he began to understand the gravity of what she was saying.

The scars on his soul deepened, swelling and rising and splitting open once more.

When she had finished speaking, her silent plea for understanding was as clear as any words she spoke aloud.

In return, he had no words for her. Nothing he could say would make any of this go away.

Instead, he leaned in closer, pulling her to him, holding her close to his heart in a

desperate attempt to save them both.

*C*allum picked up the broken glass littering Ally's studio, depositing it into a small cardboard box he found under the workbench. He glanced over at Maggie, who was picking up paint tubes and brushes on the other side of the room.

"Shit - holy freakin' shit," she mumbled under her breath. "Look at this."

Callum sat back on his haunches as she lifted up a canvas, ripped in several places. She tilted it for him to see and he sighed heavily, blowing out air through his teeth.

"Is that...?"

"Yeah, it is."

They both stared at the painting Ally had been working on for weeks, the final one for the exhibition. Maggie shook her head and fingered the ripped canvas gingerly.

"It's trashed," she said. "There's no way to repair this."

Callum shrugged helplessly. Was this some kind of a statement on Ally's part, or just a tantrum that had gotten out of control? Either way, the painting was history.

A door opened and they heard footsteps down the hallway followed by the back door opening and closing. They both sprang to their feet and made a beeline for it. Through the glass, they saw Jack standing in the back yard with his back to them, his fingers laced behind his neck.

"See if she's alright," Callum said. "I'll go talk to him."

Maggie threw one last anxious glance at Jack before heading down the hall. He took a deep breath, opened the back door and walked out onto the ramp. He stood for a few moments, waiting for Jack to turn and acknowledge him. When he didn't, he cleared his throat.

No response.

He tried to put himself in Jack's shoes, which only increased his anxiety. Despite the obvious differences in him, he knew Jack well enough to understand that this would hit him hard. His presence here was tenuous, even though he claimed otherwise. How would he react? Ally needed him now more than ever but his past record when it came to reliability wasn't exactly stellar.

He slid his hands into his pockets as he walked down the ramp towards him.

"Hey, you okay?"

He waited several moments for an answer.

"Not really, no."

"She told you, then."

"Yeah, she told me."

They stood in silence. A cool breeze sent a chill down Callum's neck. Jack's hands fell to his side as he finally turned to face him. The look on his face took Callum's breath away. Tears rolled down his cheeks and he swiped the back of his hand under his nose roughly.

"Why didn't he tell me?"

Callum shook his head, speechless.

Suddenly, Jack had him by the shirt, propelling him over the lawn and slamming him up against the side of the house, knocking the breath out of him.

"Why didn't you tell me?" Jack hissed, face contorted into a heartbreaking combination of rage and fear. "Why didn't *someone* tell me?"

Callum gasped, winded. Jack's face was inches from his and he was scared. He blinked rapidly, pushing at Jack to get him to back off. Jack drew back his fist and Callum squeezed his eyes shut, bracing for the impact. When it didn't come, he opened them warily and Jack aimed his palm into the wall next to him instead, missing his head by a fraction of an inch.

Jack released him, stumbling away as Callum slid to the ground, gasping for air.

"I wanted to tell you," he heaved, his throat burning. "I wanted Tom to tell you, but he wouldn't."

Jack turned to face him, scepticism written all over his face. "Bullshit!"

Callum shook his head, pain shooting up his neck.

"It's true! He said it wouldn't do any good, it wouldn't change anything."

Jack huffed out a sarcastic laugh, still pacing up and down, shaking his hand out.

"Would you have come back if you'd known?" Callum demanded. "Honestly?"

Jack glared at him helplessly, then turned away.

"Come on - would you?"

"I don't know," Jack mumbled, standing with his back to him, inspecting his hand.

"Then don't go blaming anybody."

Callum pushed himself away from the house and onto his feet.

"You weren't here, you didn't know. That was three years ago and she's still here and she's doing fine. Well, she was, until you came back."

Jack turned back to him, eyes narrowing dangerously.

"What are you saying?"

"I'm saying be careful. If you need some time to think about this, fine, take it, but make it quick."

"Time to think about what?" Realisation dawned. "For Christ's sake, I don't need any time to think about anything!"

"You sure about that?"

"Am I pissed off that nobody told me about this? Damn straight. Does it hurt? More than you'll ever know." His voice caught in his throat and he took a moment to gather himself together. "But does it make me want to get the hell out of Dodge? No way. I'm here and I'm staying and I'm starting to wonder how many times I have to tell you people that before you get it!"

"You – "

"Yeah, I know - shitty track record! But if you thought this was gonna change things, you're dead wrong."

Callum fidgeted uncomfortably and Jack honed in.

"You did, didn't you? You thought that once I knew about this, I'd take off again!"

Callum didn't bother denying it.

"Why the hell did you give me that pep talk last night if you felt that way?" Jack demanded.

"Jesus, get over yourself!" Callum exploded. "That wasn't a pep talk! It's not about you - none of this is about you! Don't you see what you're dealing with here? You can't just pick and choose what you can and can't handle! It's a package deal - all or nothing, those are your options!"

Jack breathed heavily through his nose, his jaw clenched tight. The breeze gently rustled the leaves above them.

"You have to decide," Callum continued, calming himself. "Because if you leave, what happens to her? What happens if there aren't any more pieces to pick up? I don't know who the hell you are anymore dude, but I know her and I know she deserves a hell of a lot better than this. I can't just walk away and leave you to it, hoping like hell that you're gonna do the right thing by her. She's - *we've* - been through too much for that and the truth of it is, I just plain don't trust you."

"I know that, that's why I'm here, busting my ass to try and prove to you that you can!" Jack insisted. "And I don't expect you to walk away, either. She needs you, even I can see that."

Callum shook his head, his cheeks burning. Strangely, hearing Jack say it did nothing to comfort him. He didn't want Ally to need him. He wanted her to want him. Even as the thought crossed his mind, he knew it was impossible - now, more than ever.

The back door opened and Maggie stood in the doorway.

"Ally's freshening up, she'll be out in a minute. I made coffee for anyone who wants it," she said uncertainly, her gaze flitting between them before finally settling on Jack. "You staying or going?"

Jack drew himself up straighter.

"Staying."

*A*lly wanted nothing more than to lie back, pull the covers up over her head and stay there forever but humiliation and regret clawed at her insides and she was frozen.

She was determined to make sure that Jack would only get to see her as strong, in control, whole. She hadn't counted on him getting through her defences so easily. Now that wall was crumbling so fast, she couldn't keep up the repair work.

He knew.

She closed her eyes but she couldn't block out the pain she saw in his as he relived that day with her. She would have done anything to spare him that. Shame crept through every cell in her body.

She crossed her arms around her waist, imagining she could feel his arms around her again as they had been only minutes before. When his arms were around her, she could block out the world, she could forget about everything else. It was the two of them against the world. Now she was alone again, dangling in mid-air, vulnerable.

She wanted him to stay so badly it terrified her.

After years of trying to forget what he smelled like, trying to ignore the way her body wanted to merge with his at bedtime, trying to fight off tears when she thought of his soft, warm lips searching hers, now he was all over her subconscious again.

The kiss they had shared was like the stuff of dreams, alcohol warping and magnifying some details while removing others completely. She remembered that he tasted of beer, she knew he had wanted it as much as she had and she knew that when he pulled away, she didn't want it to end. But he had pulled away, and she had been too frightened to mention it since. It seemed safer to forget it ever happened. If only she could.

She could still feel his hands on her bare skin and it had opened a portal somewhere deep inside of her. Her rampant imagination wondered about things she had been too afraid to consider for so long. Could they make love the way they used to? Would he even want to? She wouldn't blame him if he didn't. She felt nauseous just thinking about it. Would she even be able to feel anything at all? How would it work, logistically, even if by some miracle, they managed to get to that stage?

It wasn't just the sex itself, it was the minefield of emotions that went with it. Lack of sensation and mobility weren't the only stumbling blocks. She was so self-conscious, the thought of Jack seeing her naked body sent her into a blind panic. She buried her face in her hands as she remembered the sickening look on his face when he had seen her sitting, half-naked, on her bedroom floor.

The last time they had made love she had been a different person in every way.

TWO AND A HALF YEARS EARLIER

Callum sat across the table from Tom, nervously watching him browse the information pack that had arrived yesterday.

It had been almost four months since Ally's suicide attempt and it felt like they had lost her. As each day passed, the wall she built around herself seemed to get higher. The counsellor was happy with her progress, but he wasn't. Far from it, in fact. He would find his own solution. Jack may not be here, but he was.

Tom closed the glossy brochure and put it down, picking up the booklet that accompanied it.

"Well?" Callum prompted. "What do you think?"

Tom took his glasses off and exhaled slowly.

"I think it's incredible, what they're doing there. Where did you hear about this?"

"I found it online. I talked to the hospital, I made some calls. It's legit." He leaned forward. "It works, Tom, the program works. They can get her walking again."

Tom looked sceptical but Callum wasn't giving up.

"They can't repair the damage obviously," he said. "But they can get her walking with braces and crutches, full time. It's a whole new life, no more chair."

Tom glanced down at the glossy brochure in front of him and Callum followed his gaze. A man standing in braces stared back at them, as if reinforcing his words.

"This is the hope she's been looking for," Callum said. "I know it is."

Tom stared at the brochure a moment longer and sighed, putting his glasses back on.

"With all this research you've done, did you find out if her insurance will cover it?"

"That's the tricky part. But I can cover it myself, most of it anyway."

"How in the hell are you gonna do that?"

"I've got a buyer for the van. Between that and my savings, I've already got most of it. I just need to see the bank for the balance."

"A bank loan?" Tom frowned.

Callum read his mind, silently daring him to talk him out of it.

"We need living expenses for the duration, for the both of us. She's not going through this alone."

"Look, I don't think – "

"Don't say it," Callum warned, his voice trembling as he fought for control of his emotions. "Don't you dare say it. I'm doing this for one reason and one reason only; she needs it. She told me she wanted to get better, she said it was for Jack." The words stuck in his throat, as did the idea, but they were Ally's words, not his. "And then Pavlovic pulled the rug out from under her and all hell broke loose. Well this is 'getting *better', this is as good as it gets for her. The health benefits are huge and not just physically but psychologically too."*

"I can see that," Tom said, as Callum barrelled ahead.

"I'm tired of waiting for the counselling to make a difference. We're losing her Tom, we need to do something and we need to do it now, before it's too late."

"I know. Don't go to the bank for that money, let me pay for half the total," Tom insisted, taking his glasses off again and laying them down on the table in front of him. "I want to help too. That way, you're not totally tapped out and you don't have a bank loan hanging over your head."

"Wow," Callum exhaled loudly. "Wow. Okay. Thanks."

"Did you really think I'd veto this? I know she needs something and maybe this is it. Who knows, but we sure as hell have to try," Tom mumbled, leaning back in his chair and staring at the paperwork in front of him again.

"What?" Callum asked, sensing there was more.

"That's a big commitment you're making. You're putting your life on hold."

"My life's been on hold since the accident. This is as much a part of her recovery as rehab was."

"You're a good man." Emotion heavily overlaid the words. "She's lucky to have you in her corner."

"Same goes for you."

Tom picked up the brochure again, scrutinising it.

"You're right. This could change everything."

CHAPTER SEVENTEEN

*"You gain strength, courage and confidence by every experience in
which you really stop to look fear in the face. You are able to say to
yourself 'I lived through this horror.
I can take the next thing that comes along.'"*
- Eleanor Roosevelt

The pain in Jack's soul reached saturation point. Sitting
at Ally's kitchen table earlier, sharing a quiet coffee
over awkward small-talk, all he could think about was how close
he had come to losing her. He wanted to take her in his arms
again but he had the feeling that it was all too little, too late. She
couldn't even bring herself to look at him.

When she excused herself from the table, he made his escape.
He found himself driving the streets aimlessly, with no real sense
of what to do or where to go. He just wanted it all to stop.

The look of utter despair on Ally's face refused to leave him.
He recalled with vivid clarity the way she looked as she lay in the
ICU that night, the fluorescent light above her bed bathing her in

that eerie glow. It didn't feel like four years ago. It felt like it was happening right now, all over again and the pain was just as intense now as it had been then.

It was perfectly clear to him now why Callum was riding him so hard. He was right, about everything. He had a lousy track record and Ally had already fought her way back from the brink once. What was his role in her suicide attempt? She didn't spell it out for him in so many words but his mind went there anyway. Was it his fault, because he wasn't here?

He pulled in to the almost deserted parking lot outside the cemetery. He had no idea how he ended up there but he knew it made sense somehow. He was grieving for Ally and everything she'd lost, for his father, for the lost friendships and the part of himself he would never get back.

He switched off the car's ignition and a heavy silence filled the void. It cloaked him with an invisible blanket so dense he felt like he was suffocating. His lungs burned as the silence around him thickened like a living, breathing entity, growing and gnawing at him. He gripped the steering wheel tighter.

He wanted to scream. Callum's words came back to him, grabbing him by the throat. What would he have done if he had known then what was happening? Would he have come back?

The truth did so much more than just hurt. The agony gouged at him, leaving a gaping wound. Now he knew why he had stayed away so long. Torturing himself with the unknown for all this time was one thing, but hearing the reality was another matter entirely. He gripped the steering wheel until his fingers were numb. Closing his eyes, he willed the pain to stop.

Help me. Please?

He couldn't remember the last time he'd prayed.

What he did remember was attending church with his parents when he was young, sitting between them with his neatly pressed dark trousers and crisp baby blue shirt. He would sit with his father on the back doorstep on Saturday afternoon and they would polish their shoes together, him taking as much care as a child of his age could, his father overseeing his clumsy ministrations with the polish and rag. His mother fussed over his hair every Sunday, smoothing it and brushing down the stray ends and the wisps at his crown that refused to lie flat. All the while, he would grimace but not dare move. He knew this was important. Going to church on Sunday was an Event.

He would sit as still as he could on the hard wooden pew between them until he could stand it no longer. Then he would fidget until an elbow in the ribs or a sly whisper from his parents would force him to stop. He wanted to make his parents proud. It had all been so easy then.

He was seventeen when his mother died and it changed his view on everything. After she passed away, neither he nor his father could bring themselves to go to church regularly. They went at Easter and Christmas, and that was mainly out of a sense of duty.

During the last four years, he hadn't gone to church once. He thought himself beyond forgiveness, so what was the point in asking for it? If God could torture his mother the way He did, then He must surely have forsaken him.

Yet from the brief conversations he had had with Father David since his father's death, apparently he'd been attending church regularly during the past few years. Why, after all this time? Did it have anything to do with the accident, with what happened to Ally? Or was it because of Jack and what he had done? He found himself wondering if his father had been praying for him and it made the hair on the back of his neck stand on end.

All it took was one night, one moment, and the world turned upside down.

He saw himself falling to the floor outside Ally's bed in the ICU. It was happening again. His world narrowed, darkening at the edges and he knew he had to do something. He tried to slow his breathing, putting all his energy into trying to visualize how his life would be now if the accident had never happened.

Ally was painting a mural on their living room wall, perched atop a ladder, wearing a paint-splattered pair of navy blue overalls. Her long hair was caught up beneath a bright pink bandana, and she brushed wisps of it away from her face as she concentrated, painting one brush stroke at a time, slow and steady. She hummed quietly to herself as she worked, completely oblivious to the fact that he was watching her.

The walls were littered with black and white photographs, mostly ones she took while they had been travelling around the country on his bike. Memories of their life together surrounded them. Then she turned and noticed him standing there and she smiled the kind of smile that made his knees go weak. She put the paintbrush down and climbed down the ladder, talking all the while, smiling that smile.

She crossed the floor with a skip and threw herself into his arms, wrapping her own arms around him and giggling as he twirled her around, the bandana coming loose and releasing her hair, smelling of paint and vanilla.

He lay her down on the couch, covering her mouth with his and smiling to himself as he felt her body respond. She wriggled beneath him as he lay down on top of her, her legs wrapping around his waist and locking behind his back as his lips sought out her neck. Her arms snaked around his ribs as she pulled him closer, leaning into him...

A sharp rap on the window brought the fantasy crashing down. His eyes shot open and the worried face of Father David stared back at him. He spent a few moments putting things back in their rightful places; fantasy there, reality here.

The priest's mouth was moving. Jack stared at him blankly before realising that he needed to wind down his window to hear him. Feeling oddly detached, he did so.

"Jack? Are you alright?"

Jack automatically nodded, incapable of anything else.

The priest searched the interior of the car, leaning on the sill.

"Are you sure? You don't look so good."

He felt drugged, as if the emotions were there but they were just beyond his reach. He went from feeling everything just moments ago, to feeling absolutely nothing.

"I'm fine. Thanks."

The priest looked him over again, obviously not convinced.

"What are you doing out here, son?"

"I don't know."

"You look like you need some air," he mumbled, reaching in to squeeze Jack's shoulder. "Care to take a stroll with me?"

Jack found himself exiting the car on autopilot. He looked around him, dazed, unsure. The priest's hand on his shoulder again grounded him and he turned towards him.

"Come on," Father David prodded gently. "Let's go this way."

They walked in silence at first, Jack's head still foggy as they made their way into the cemetery. He stopped to wait as Father David closed the gate behind them, and they strolled up the centre path together slowly.

"You look like you could use a friendly ear, Jack."

Walking through the well-kept gardens and shady trees that overlooked the headstones, Jack waded through the words in his head. Where should he start when everything was so messed up?

"Maybe I can help?" Father David offered gently.

The idea was so ridiculous that Jack huffed out a laugh. Embarrassed, he shoved his hands into his pockets and hung his head.

"I wish it was that easy."

The priest didn't speak for a few moments and the only sound was of their footsteps. The headstones spread out either side of them like a miniature city, dotted with flowers and greenery.

"Y'know," Father David said. "Contrary to popular belief, I don't spend a lot of time at the cemetery. To my way of thinking, the dead are already being taken care of. My concern is with the living."

Jack didn't answer.

"I saw what happened at your Dad's funeral," Father David said, glancing sideways at him. "I didn't know your Dad as well as you did but I think I can safely say I knew him longer. We talked about a lot of things over that time, especially over the past couple of years. I think he would've been proud of you for coming home. It can't have been an easy thing to do."

Jack's hands clenched into fists inside his pockets.

"I'm not so sure about that," he said. "I don't feel like I've made any difference at all, coming back here."

The rhythm of their footsteps lulled him and he felt rather than saw Father David's nod of understanding.

"I'm sure you have," he said quietly. "Even if it doesn't feel that way at the moment."

Jack stared up at the path winding ahead of them and his head began to spin.

"You're only human, Jack. Mistakes are part of the package. You show me one human being who's never made a mistake in their life and I'll show you a liar. God expects us to make mistakes. And He's not the only one with the power to forgive, either. People have that power, too."

"What if you don't deserve forgiveness?"

The priest's hand on his shoulder startled him and he looked up into Father David's penetrating gaze.

"Everyone deserves forgiveness, Jack," he said firmly. "If God forgives you, you should forgive yourself."

Jack found it impossible to tear himself away.

"How do I know that God forgives me?"

"He will. You just have to ask Him."

They stopped walking and stood facing each other. Jack struggled hard to breathe normally, frustration clawing at his insides. He wanted to believe so desperately. He just wanted the pain to end.

"You can't change the past," the priest said. "But you can change the future. You're here now and that's what matters."

Ally had said something similar but rather than hearing an encouraging affirmation, it tore him apart.

"Ally tried to kill herself," he whispered hoarsely, tears spilling down his cheeks before he could stop them.

Some part of him hoped that it wasn't true, but saying it aloud made it seem so much more real. The priest's face was a picture of solemn acceptance.

"Yes, I know."

Jack stared at him in silence, hopelessness oozing out of every cell in his body.

"She was at her lowest. She was in pain," Father David said with a knowing look. "Like I said, we all make mistakes. You have to learn from them or it's a lesson you'll have to keep learning over and over again. She made up for it by not giving up, by fighting back, by choosing to be here, with us. You can choose to give in to it or you can choose to fight. Ultimately, that's what it comes down to for all of us."

Jack let his brain absorb the priest's words, fighting their way past doubt and guilt and self-condemnation. His chin trembled as he fought for control.

"I don't know what to do."

"Maybe you could try talking to her?"

Although deep down he knew the priest was right, the prospect terrified him.

"But first, perhaps there's someone else you need to talk to."

He indicated a spot just over Jack's right shoulder. As Jack turned around, he saw a grave. Covered in flowers, a simple marker at its head bore his father's name.

---

*A*lly sat at her kitchen table at 4am, listening to the wind. The huge tree in her backyard scraped against the house, the windows rattled in their frames.

She thought she had put that day behind her, accepted the past and moved on. She had forgiven herself. But how could she ever forgive herself for what she had done to Jack by sharing it with him?

She had thrust a knife into his heart and twisted it.

*J*ack walked up Ally's front path the next morning, shaking his hands out like he was approaching a bout in the ring. He breathed out through his teeth and tried to line up the words that swirled inside his head. Somehow, he had to make her understand.

He took the steps slowly and knocked on the door, shifting his weight impatiently from one foot to the other as he waited.

Finally, the door opened and Ally stood before him in jeans, a t-shirt and a multi-coloured, paint-splattered apron.

"Morning," he said tentatively.

She looked exhausted. He could relate. Sleep hadn't come easily to him last night, either.

"Hi."

She wouldn't look at him and his heart sank. He was going to have to give this everything he had.

"Can I come in?" he asked.

She took her time thinking it over and he wondered if they were going to have to have this discussion on her doorstep.

"Okay."

She moved aside and he walked past her into the hallway. Unfortunately, his thoughts didn't become any clearer inside the house than they had been outside of it. After his chance meeting with Father David yesterday and the time he had spent sitting by his father's grave, his heart and his soul in turmoil, he had hoped this would come easier.

"I want to apologise," he began. "If I was a little off yesterday,

I'm sorry. I was just blind-sided, really. I know it happened three years ago but to me it feels like it just happened yesterday. I mean, it scared me - really scared me."

She stood before him, head bowed, silent. Had he messed up the apology, too? Why wouldn't she look at him?

"Me too," she said in a small voice. "But it's over now. We don't have to talk about it anymore. It's in the past."

Not this time, babe.

He reached out to take her by the arms, squeezing gently and wishing like hell she would look at him.

"I get why you don't want to talk about it," he said, his heart racing. "But I just want you to know that you can trust me. I'm not judging you, Ally. I don't have the right to, no one does. And you don't have to protect me from anything, either. I can take it. I came back, didn't I? I'm not going anywhere, no matter what. Please don't shut me out."

He felt a shudder go through her. He waited, his heart sitting in his throat as he stroked her arms with his thumbs, afraid of hurting her. She seemed so fragile.

Finally, she lifted her head. Her beautiful eyes, more blue than green now, were brimming with tears. She nodded, setting them free.

He reached up to brush a stray wisp of hair away from her face, trying not to think about what might have happened if Callum hadn't found her in time.

"You're here," he said gently. "Nothing else matters except that. We've got a shot at something really special here; a second chance. Not everyone gets one of those."

She trembled in his arms as he pulled her close, lacing his arms around her. The need to simplify everything was overwhelming. If he held her close, it wasn't so frightening. If he held her close, he could keep her safe.

"I'm sorry I wasn't here for you the but I'm here now."

She gave herself over to him physically, wrapping her arms around his back as he buried his face into her hair.

"Thank you," she whispered into his shirt.

He smoothed her hair under his chin, her heartbeat solid and steady against his own.

CHAPTER EIGHTEEN

"Life can only be understood backwards,
but it must be lived forwards."
- Soren Kierkegaard

"I think that's it," Ally announced finally from her place on the floor, fitting the lid onto the full container of sea sponges and handing it to him as she directed him to the shelf on which they belonged. Adding the container to the many others already there, he turned to face her, running his hands along his jeans to clean them. It felt good to be involved in something as mundane as cleaning her studio with her. He looked at it as a metaphor.

Then he spied the ripped canvas leaning up against the opposite wall. Was that a metaphor too?

"What are you going to do with that?" he asked.

She stared at it for a moment.

"Trash it."

"Wasn't that the painting I saw the other day, the work in progress deal?"

The easy conversation of moments ago abruptly disintegrated.

"Yeah."

"Why didn't you just paint over it? If you didn't like it, I mean."

She shrugged again, turning her attention back to him.

"I don't know. Guess I didn't feel like starting over."

He nodded, anxious to keep the mood light.

"Temperamental artist kinda thing, was it?"

"Something like that."

She didn't elaborate and he didn't ask. She moved her legs and raised herself up until she was on her hands and knees. Fascinated, he couldn't help but stare.

"Do you need a hand?" he asked, readying himself.

"No, I'm fine."

She pushed herself up, balancing on her hands and straightening her arms and legs until he heard the locks on her braces snap into place. Bent in half, she quickly checked them by hand and grabbed her crutches, dragging them towards her and using them to push herself upright.

"I don't know how you can do that," he said, shaking his head.

She slipped her arms into the cuffs of her crutches.

"It's just balance and technique and practice. Lots of practice."

"You say that like it's nothing special but it's pretty amazing. You're pretty amazing."

She blushed, turning away from him. As she moved around her studio shifting things around and finishing up, he ached to tell her everything.

It was no use hiding. All that would do is drive a wedge between them. If she had been strong enough to make it back from the brink after her suicide attempt, he would be strong enough to tell her where he'd been these past four years.

She deserved to know all of it.

---

*A*s Callum slid a six-pack of beer over onto the passenger seat of his car the strangest feeling of déjà-vu washed over him. Four years ago, before the accident and everything went to hell, he would grab a six-pack and take it over to Jack's. After Jack disappeared and when things slowly settled into a new normal, he used to do the same thing with Tom. Now things had come full circle again.

After what had happened yesterday he was worried about Jack. He needed to find out where his head was at. It didn't take a genius to work out that he was hurting. He knew that feeling of helplessness all too well. It hollowed you out for a long time afterwards.

Pulling out of the parking lot, he wondered what Tom would've made of the situation. How would he have handled it? It was more than likely that Tom would have placed himself between the two of them. It was an uncomfortable thought. Tom would have also likely been the one they both turned to for counsel. Now it appeared they only had each other.

It's what Tom would have wanted.

He sat idling at the intersection, indicator blinking left, staring straight ahead.

It was Tom who had made these last few years bearable. He had been the one that Callum needed the most and he had selflessly given of himself for Callum's benefit - for everyone's benefit. He wasn't the only one feeling his loss. He had a feeling that Jack's address book wasn't exactly overflowing.

A car horn jolted him back to the present and he made the turn. Pulling up in front of Tom's house a short time later, he noticed two things simultaneously. One was that Jack's car wasn't there. The other was that there was a stranger peering into the living room window.

His curiosity got the better of him and he got out and headed over to check it out. Before he could get very far, the man spotted him and stepped away from the house. They were about the same height and the guy had cropped dark hair and shoulders like a professional football player. They stared at each other for a moment. Something about the guy didn't feel right.

"Can I help you?" he asked, keeping his tone conversational.

"I'm looking for a friend." Even his voice reeked of trouble. "Maybe you know him - Jack?"

"There used to be a Jack here, years ago. Haven't seen him recently, though," he lied, following his gut.

The guy nodded, but Callum had the feeling he wasn't convinced.

"Any chance he might be coming back around here anytime soon?"

Callum snorted derisively, mentally crossing his fingers that he was doing the right thing.

"Unlikely. Haven't heard from him in years."

The guy nodded and Callum got the impression he was waiting for something. He cast a quick glance over his shoulder, then up to the house.

"Hey, if you want to leave a number with me, just in case, I'll be sure to pass it on if he shows up," he offered, shrugging casually.

The man appeared to think it over, then started backing away.

"Nah, it's fine. Thanks anyway."

Callum watched him lumber across the lawn towards a car parked across the street. Someone else was in the car but he couldn't see for the late afternoon sun reflecting off the windshield. As soon as the big guy got in, it pulled out onto the street slowly and drove away.

*A*lly stretched, getting comfortable. She closed her eyes as the warm breeze rustled the branches overhead, feeling more content than she had felt in a long time. Her stomach was full and the relaxed air that had settled over them during lunch had hung around, lulling her into a contemplative mood.

She and Jack seemed to have found a middle-ground, somewhere they could talk and be themselves where it wasn't so awkward. She glanced sideways at him, sitting in the lounger next to her in her back yard. The sun filtered through the leaves above them, dappling his features. With his eyes closed like that, he looked so peaceful. He hadn't looked like that since he'd come back. Her gaze lingered, drinking him in; long legs, crossed casually at the ankles, hands laced over his abdomen, the complete absence of worry lines on his forehead, the fading bruises marring his skin. Again, it felt as if the last four years had just been some kind of nightmare, that they had never actually happened, and everything was just as it should be.

She let herself believe that for a moment, allowing the warmth to fill her heart as she let go of all the concerns that had plagued her. Without that anchor she felt so much lighter, as if she might float away. It was a comforting thought and she smiled to herself as Jack uncrossed his ankles, his eyes still closed.

She glanced down at her own legs. Out of the corner of her eye, she saw her crutches on the ground next to her chair. Suddenly the fantasy was over and reality crashed into her.

Why couldn't things have been different?

She pushed the thought aside, trying to convince herself that this was all she wanted, that being near him was enough. She should be grateful to finally have that. Glancing over at him again, she found him staring back at her curiously. Not wanting to ruin the moment, she forced a smile.

"What?" she asked.

"I don't know," he said. "You tell me?"

She shook her head and mentally wiped her mind clean, just in case her thoughts were written all over her face. With the way he was looking at her, she wondered if it was too late.

"It's nothing," she said. "I was just thinking."

"I could see that. Do you want to think out loud so I can follow along?"

The habits of the past few years were quick to make an appearance. Distraction. Sleight of hand. Re-direction. A burning question that wouldn't go away.

"Can I ask you something?" she asked finally.

"Sure."

A single word, swimming in a sea of anxiety. She picked up on it immediately, but she didn't let it stop her.

"Where have you been all this time? Where did you go?"

His jaw clenched, as if locking up the words, afraid they would leak out. Tearing his gaze away from hers, he stared at his boots. She watched his chest rising and falling with each breath. The leaves rustled overhead but it was no longer soothing. It reminded her of static electricity and it seemed to charge the air around them.

"What are you so afraid of?" she asked.

He waged a mental war with himself, so obvious she could feel it from where she sat. Part of her wanted to take it back, to reach up and grab the question out of the air between them and crush it with her bare hands. Another part of her begged patience. She needed this.

"I've done some things I'm not proud of," he said.

"You're not alone there."

He pulled his knees up, resting his elbows on them, his jaw set.

"Okay," he said finally.

She tried to prepare herself but she had no idea where to begin. He swung his legs over the side of the lounger and rested his elbows on his knees, searching the ground between them as if it contained all the answers. She felt far away from him then, as if he stood on the other side of a deep chasm, shouting across at her. Things were spinning out of control again.

Consciously, she closed the gap. She lifted her legs off the lounger and mirrored his stance, reducing the space between them to a mere couple of inches, their knees almost touching. He stared at her anxiously and she reached across to squeeze his forearm.

"Whatever's freaking you out, I can take it," she said, with more conviction than she felt. "I won't run away screaming, figuratively speaking."

A weak smile ghosted over his lips and she withdrew her hand, waiting for him to continue.

"I don't really know where to start," he shrugged. "I mean, when I left here, left you, that was the biggest mistake of my life. I just wanted to hide, from everyone. When I finally stopped running, I had almost no money. I had to work, so I grabbed the first job I could find. After that, I did whatever I could, wherever I could. Mostly construction jobs, because they were easy to get. As soon as I got enough money together, I moved on. I just kept moving, kept working."

"What about friends?"

He shook his head.

"It was easier on my own."

It sounded so far from the Jack she knew that her mind had trouble making the connection. Her heart ached for him and the loneliness she heard screaming out at her from between his words. She couldn't imagine having gone through the past four years alone.

"It wasn't exactly a rock 'n' roll lifestyle, but it was what I deserved," he continued. "If I couldn't come home, then I couldn't complain."

"You could've come home."

He shook his head, glancing up briefly before his gaze fell to his hands.

"No, I couldn't have. I didn't have the guts for one thing. For another, I didn't deserve to."

This was a million miles away from what she had imagined.

"How long are you going to punish yourself?"

He shook his head, staring at the grass between them, head bowed. A sudden cool change in the breeze sent a shiver down the back of her neck.

"You're home now, it's over. You need to let go, Jack. It's time."

He stared at the grass for several long, agonising moments. She tried to conjure up the right words to tell him that it was okay, to make him believe her, but her heart hurt so much it was difficult to think straight.

Finally, he looked up. The pain in his eyes stole her breath, the same way it had when they had talked after Tom's funeral.

"How do you do it?" he asked. "How'd you get to be this strong?"

"Me?" She nearly laughed out loud, the idea was so ludicrous. "I'm not. I mean, how could I be after what I did?"

"I'm talking about what you do every day. You really don't get it?"

"Get what?"

"You're literally a walking tower of strength. You do the impossible and you don't even seem to know you're doing it."

He reached over to take hold of her hand. Warmth spread up her arm, cloaking her entire body. It was so familiar that, coupled with the look in his eye, she had trouble convincing herself that this was real.

"Do you remember me kissing you the other night?" he asked, the tenderness in his voice unmistakable.

She wanted to dive right into those gorgeous green eyes and damn the consequences. Something stopped her though, and she managed to drag herself back from the brink.

"Yes," she whispered. "I also remember you pulling away."

"That was because I knew you'd had too much to drink and I didn't want to take advantage of the situation," he paused. "Did you think that I didn't want to kiss you?"

"I kinda thought that maybe you got carried away. That it was a mistake."

"It wasn't a mistake."

Her vision seemed to blur around the edges until all she saw was him, sitting inches from her, drawing her closer. He squeezed her hand and leaned forward as she felt herself doing the same, bracing herself on the lounger with her free hand. He reached up to cup her cheek and as their lips finally met, she closed her eyes.

It was as if the world had ceased to exist and she was falling through a hole in space and time, safe in the knowledge that she was with Jack and she was going to be alright.

*C*allum stood on Ally's front doorstep, shuffling nervously from one foot to the other. He knocked on the door again, frowning at Jack's car in the driveway. Where the hell were they? As it became clear that no one was coming to answer the door, he turned on his heel and headed around the back of the house. He tried to force down the bad feeling that rose in his gut. First the goliath mooching around Jack's place, now Ally wasn't answering the door? His brain conjured up a myriad of images, none of them pleasant.

He rounded the corner of the house and stopped dead. Jack and Ally were sitting on the yard loungers, kissing. He felt as if he'd been kicked in the stomach.

Slowly, they separated and, like a peeping tom, he watched as Jack stroked her hair. The exquisitely sweet, shy smile on her face told him more than enough.

Ally glanced his way and her smile faded. She murmured something and Jack turned his way, too. Drawing himself up straight, he walked towards them.

"Hey," Callum said, as Ally reached for her crutches.

Jack stood up, his expression just as guarded as his own.

"Hey," he said.

"I knocked a couple of times, around front."

He shoved his hands into his pockets and tried to act more relaxed than he felt.

"Sorry," Ally fumbled with her crutches as she hurried to stand. "Guess we couldn't hear you from out here."

Jack was sizing him up, one eye on Ally, the other on him. It gave him a perverse sense of satisfaction that Jack was worried. Good. He should be. Which brought him back to the main reason for his visit.

"Sorry to interrupt but I was actually looking for you," he addressed Jack. "Can we talk?"

Jack threw another sidelong glance at Ally. Although he wasn't thrilled with what he had stumbled across, Callum didn't want to cause her any more distress.

"It's okay," he winked at her, conjuring up a wry smile. "I just want to talk. Promise."

She nodded anxiously and he shifted his attention back to Jack.

"Quick word, in private?" he said.

Jack followed in silence as Ally looked on.

"I've just come from your place," he murmured, as soon as they were out of earshot. "And there was some guy snooping around outside the house."

Jack stopped still.

"What guy?"

"A big guy."

Jack reeked of anxiety, although he didn't move.

"Did you talk to him?"

Callum shrugged. "Well, I didn't know who the hell he was and he looked pretty damn suspicious to me, so yeah. I asked him what he was doing."

"And?"

"Said he was looking for you."

"Me, personally?"

"Asked for you by name," Callum said, getting slightly concerned at the tone of the conversation.

"What did you tell him?"

"I told him I hadn't seen you for years. Offered to pass on his number if you showed up but that seemed to spook him and he took off."

"Was he alone?"

"He got into a car across the street, I couldn't see the driver," he frowned. "Did I do the right thing?"

"Yeah," Jack said, shoving his hands into his pockets. "I mean, probably."

"What's going on?"

"I don't know."

"Then guess," Callum glared at him.

"Look, I don't know, okay?" Jack snapped.

"Getting sick of your damn secrets, dude," Callum shot back. "I need a straight answer for once. What the hell is going on?"

Jack scratched the back of his neck, glancing over towards the house.

It wasn't the response Callum was hoping for.

CHAPTER NINETEEN

"Friendship is like a glass ornament.
Once broken, it can rarely be put back together
exactly the same way."
- Charles Kingsley

ONE YEAR EARLIER

*T*he bar was like many others that Jack had happened on over the past three years. Dark and quiet, tucked away in a less-than-desirable part of town with a bartender who looked like he was working out his final days until retirement. His boots had stuck to the floor slightly as he made his way to a seat at the far end of the bar, away from the door. Even the bar stool itself had seen better days.

None of this made any difference, though. This was exactly the kind of establishment that Jack felt comfortable in these days, somewhere he could blend in and have a quiet drink, unnoticed.

He glanced up from his seat as the front door opened and a man in his late fifties walked in. He wore a trench coat, the likes of which Jack hadn't seen in a long time. It reminded him of something Elliot Ness might have worn; beige, with a belt and epaulettes on the shoulders. He took a seat at the opposite end of the bar and ordered a scotch, neat. He was dressed like he was someone of substance yet he looked weathered, as if he carried the weight of the world on his shoulders. Jack looked closer, taking a sip from his beer. It was the eyes. They seemed dead, cold, hopeless. Something, or someone, had stolen the light right out of them.

Jack turned his attention back to his beer. He felt a kinship with this man that had nothing to do with anything other than the fact that he could see himself in him. An invisible weight pushed down on him too, forcing him lower and lower until some mornings it took everything he had just to get out of bed.

He rolled his shoulders as if to alleviate the metaphorical weight that rested there. On this day, more than most, it was harder to ignore the demons in his head. He gently touched his shoulder, as if pressuring them into silence. He imagined he could feel the ink seeping into his bloodstream, as if the mark itself was merging with his soul and making itself one with the rest of him. He had branded himself so that he would never forget. He wanted the marks on his body to match the ones on his soul.

A guy near the back of the bar argued with his girlfriend, getting louder and more agitated as the minutes passed. The girlfriend, a pretty blonde wearing far too much makeup, locked eyes with him across the bar and Jack could see fear within them. He turned away, distracted by his own problems.

A few moments later, the guy started in again and Jack turned back to see what was going on. The blonde shook her head and tried to calm him down but he would not be placated. She got up to leave but he grabbed her, yanking her back down into the seat again. Jack could see tears in her eyes and his heart raced. He mentally sized up the guy she was with and waited. The guy was about his height, maybe a few years older, and he had clearly had too much to drink. His face was flushed and sweaty and Jack could see his girlfriend was wasting her time. He was too far gone now to be soothed. He turned back to his beer but kept an eye on them via the mirror behind the bar.

The spectacle continued. Suddenly, the girl got up and ran, stilettos echoing on the sticky wooden floor. She got as far as the front door before the guy caught up with her. He grabbed her by the arm as she reached for the door handle, roughly spinning her around to face him. He pushed her back into the wall next to the door and leant in close, hissing something that Jack couldn't hear. His moral compass screamed at him. What gave this guy the right? She stared over his shoulder at Jack, begging silently for help until he couldn't stand it any longer.

Temper rising, he got off his bar stool and marched over to them, grabbing the guy by the arm that held her and twisting it up behind his back. The guy was momentarily dumbfounded as Jack powered him through the door and out onto the street.

"Hey!" the guy slurred, struggling finally.

Jack spun him around to face him and punched him clean in the nose, just once. He went down like a lead balloon. The blonde came hurtling out of the bar and took one look at them both, then ran off down the street without a word, her coat flapping behind her.

The guy stayed down, to his credit, his hand covering his face, blood seeping through his fingers. Jack stood back and waited for him to come at him but it quickly became clear that he wasn't capable of it. Turning around, Jack jammed his aching fist into the pocket of his jacket and walked away, his head reeling. He couldn't remember the last time he had physically hit anyone.

It felt good.

"Your housekeeping's improved," Jack said, giving Callum's living room a quick once-over. "This place is positively tidy."

It had been Callum's suggestion that he crash at his place for a couple of days, just in case. The deal had been crystal clear;

answers to what was going on in return for keeping the real reason for their sleepover from Ally. Under the circumstances, a little white lie seemed to be the least of their worries. Ally thought Tom's place had a gas leak that was being investigated. What was really going on was another story entirely. Whatever it was, it was enough for Jack to accept his help with little more than a token effort at refusal. That in itself was reason enough to worry.

"Yeah well," Callum handed Jack a beer and they both sank down into opposite armchairs. "Ally can't navigate through crap all over the floor, it's dangerous."

They both took a swig of beer, silently sizing each other up.

"What happened to your van?" Jack asked, making an attempt at casual conversation. "I haven't seen it since I've been back."

Callum humoured him, for now at least.

"I sold it."

"Really?"

"I was offered a good price and I took it."

"Wow. I have to say, I never thought you'd give it up, especially after all the work you did on it."

"It was just a van. Ally wouldn't be walking now if I'd been all sentimental about it." Callum let that sink in for a few moments before elaborating. "I found the program that taught her how to walk. After what happened it was clear she needed something to focus on, something positive. Small price to pay."

"She told me about that," Jack said, clearly surprised. "But she didn't say anything about you selling the van to pay for it."

"That's because we told her Tom paid for it."

He could see the mention of Tom's name struck a nerve, although Jack took a swift drink to try and hide the fact.

"We thought she'd take it better coming from Tom but really, we each paid half. I told her that I sold the van because it wasn't practical anymore, which was true. It was too high for her to transfer in and out by herself, so I had to lift her. She never said as much but I knew she hated that. It made sense to get a car because it was more accessible."

"I didn't realise," Jack mumbled.

"Four years, dude. There was a lot you missed."

Jack blanched but he didn't comment. Instead he stared at the bottle resting on his thigh.

"Look, I'm really sorry you got caught up in this. But thanks for letting me crash here."

"Don't thank me yet," Callum leaned forward. "First, I want you to tell me what the hell's going on."

Jack nodded cautiously.

"That was the deal."

Callum placed his beer bottle on the coffee table between them and sat back in the armchair.

"So, spill the beans - and I mean the truth - all of it, no bullshit fence-sitting. I think we've gone way beyond that now."

Jack placed his bottle on the table, too. He sat forward, staring at his hands, grasped so tightly together his knuckles glowed white.

"I got involved in some stuff."

"What kind of stuff?"

Jack fidgeted, clearly uncomfortable.

"Fighting."

"What kind of fighting?" Callum hoped he wasn't going to have to draw whatever this was out of him, one painful word at a time.

"The kind where large sums of money are involved."

"Underground fighting? Like cage fighting or something?"

"Something like that."

Callum whistled softly.

"Well, that explains a lot," he said.

Jack frowned at him.

"The thing with Andy," he clarified.

"Yeah. I guess."

"I've never seen you fight like that - ever."

"Learnt a few new tricks."

"No shit," Callum eyeballed him over the coffee table as Jack massaged his knuckles absent-mindedly. "So how does the big guy I saw at your place fit into all this?"

Jack seemed to disappear into himself and Callum waited until he found his way back, curiosity giving him uncharacteristic patience.

"The night you called me, when Dad died," Jack began carefully, "I was supposed to fight this guy. Ben - my manager, agent, whatever - he had money on it. He said he was setting me up for something bigger but I had to throw this fight for it to all work out."

"I'm with you so far."

"But I didn't," Jack ran his hand through his hair. "I was distracted and I guess I got carried away. I didn't go down when I was supposed to. I took him out instead."

"Shit."

"It was stupid and I knew I'd messed up but my head was all over the place. I knew Ben would be pissed about it but I had to come back here. He's not what you call the understanding type."

"Shit."

If Jack was worried about this, it was serious. Serious enough for this guy to track him back here. Serious enough for Jack to crash at his place without putting up too much of a fight.

"I honestly didn't think he'd find me. I never would have come back here if I thought there was even a snowball's chance in hell that he could."

"Yeah," Callum ran a hand down his face, thinking. "Shit."

"You can stop saying that anytime now," Jack snapped.

"Sorry."

Jack took a deep breath and released it slowly, sinking back into the chair.

"How do you think he found you?" Callum asked.

"No idea. He only had my cell number. I'm pretty sure he didn't even know where I lived. Although he obviously knew more about me than I thought or he wouldn't be here."

"So, what makes you think it's this Ben guy anyway?"

"It won't be Ben himself, he doesn't like to get his hands dirty," he huffed. "He doesn't need to, he's got a posse at his disposal."

Callum eyeballed him from across the table. He looked exhausted and Callum couldn't help but feel for him. Putting that aside for the moment, his curiosity got the better of him.

"How in the hell did you end up in the underground boxing circuit?"

"Long story," Jack sighed wearily.

"I'm not going anywhere."

Jack reached for his beer and took a long swallow. Then he sat back and scratched his chin.

"It just kinda happened," he shrugged. "I was having a quiet drink in this bar down the street from my apartment. This asshole started pushing his girlfriend around so I took him outside and punched him in the face. I just wanted him to stop, y'know? He was drunk, she was scared, it was just wrong and no one else was doing anything about it. So I did. It felt good, felt like I'd done something right for a change."

This was not the Jack he knew. The Jack he knew didn't go around looking for an excuse to punch someone.

"So, I started working out in the gym on my way home from work, just punching the shit out of stuff, running till I could barely walk, getting everything out, all the crap that was in my head. And the more I worked out, the better I felt. Then one night I got talking to this guy who said he had a friend who was doing this thing where he was fighting for money. Asked if I was interested. I thought yeah, why not? It wasn't like I had anything to lose. So, I went along with him and I got into the ring with this other guy."

"And what happened?"

"He beat the snot out of me," Jack smiled wryly. "Took me three weeks to recover."

Callum shook his head, frowning.

"I don't get it. Why not just call it a day there and then? Why go back for more?"

"Because it felt good, it felt right, somehow. Don't ask."

"Getting the shit kicked out of you felt right?" Callum frowned.

"I told you not to ask." Jack shrugged half-heartedly. "Anyway, after a few fights, something happened - I started fighting back. Channelling my frustrations, I guess. I don't know."

He sank back into his chair again. By contrast, Callum felt like a coiled spring. When he had seen him attack Andy that night, he knew something was different about Jack but he'd had no idea how different.

"We've all done stuff we're not proud of," he said.

Jack snorted derisively.

"You sound like Ally."

"I'm guessing she doesn't know about any of this?"

"No, and she's not going to either, not if I can help it. These were my choices - more shitty ones, as it turns out, but mine just the same. I don't want her thinking that any of this has got anything to do with her."

Callum leaned forward and grabbed his beer bottle off the coffee table, taking a long pull.

"It has though - got something to do with her," he dangled the bottle between his knees. "You did all that because of what happened."

"Because of what I did," Jack insisted, steely-eyed.

Callum could see he wasn't going to get anywhere, so he changed tack.

"So, from what I saw earlier, it looks like things are getting pretty serious with you two."

He tried to keep his tone conversational as he met Jack's gaze across the table.

"It's going okay."

"Okay? Looked more than just okay."

"What's your point?" Jack's gaze was solid and steady, clearly on the defensive.

"Calm down, I'm just asking," he clarified. "Honestly."

Jack took a swig from his bottle.

"I think she trusts me a little more," he admitted after a few moments. "We can talk a bit easier. She seems more comfortable."

"And are you more comfortable?"

Jack glanced up at him sharply.

"It's not easy," Callum said. "There are a lot of changes to get used to."

Jack stood up, throwing him a sidelong glance as he walked over to the window. He checked the road outside through a slim gap in the curtains.

"I think it's gonna take some time," he said. "She still keeps a lot of stuff to herself."

"You're right there." Callum watched his back as he stood staring out into the street. "There's stuff that she won't even talk to me about and I've been here since it happened."

"That surprises me, given how close you two are."

"Yeah, well, she keeps her cards pretty close to her chest, as you'll no doubt know by now."

Jack continued to stare out the window, taking a slow pull on his beer. Callum debated whether he should say what was in his heart or not. Honesty won out.

"It's a really big deal, what's happening here with you and her."

Jack half-turned around, waiting for him to continue.

"There hasn't been anyone since you left, since the accident."

"I didn't know that," he said quietly.

Callum shrugged, unsure why he had even shared that with him. He drained the last of his beer.

"I need to get some sleep," he said. "Some of us have work in the morning."

He abandoned his empty beer bottle on the coffee table and paused in the living room doorway.

"I think maybe you should stay away from her for a couple of days," he said, turning around again. "Just until we can be sure this is all a storm in a teacup."

Jack nodded.

"I hate lying to her, but I think you're right."

More lies, even if they too were disguised as little white ones.

*S*he felt as if she were running in quicksand. Each step sucked her leg into the molten road but she fought on regardless. She couldn't give up, couldn't stop, not now. Smoke filled her lungs as the wind changed direction, blowing smoke and ash from the burning car straight into her face. People ran past, heading for the burning car on the road up ahead but even though she was surrounded by them she didn't call out for help.

She kept her eye on the car, horrified as the flames engulfed it. People pushed past her, blocking her view. Panic took hold, squeezing her chest.

She could hear Jack up ahead, screaming her name. She tried to call out to him but the smoke got caught in her throat and she choked on her words.

Ally woke up gasping for breath, her lungs burning. She was trembling all over. She knew instinctively that she had been moaning in her sleep, maybe even screaming. She whimpered, hating how pathetic she sounded. Her thighs ached and she tried to hang on to the phantom pain, even as the last threads of sensation died.

Yanking the sweat-soaked pillow out from under her head, she flung it across the room in a fit of angry frustration. Lying alone in the dark, she folded her arms over her face and cried.

---

*A*s Callum headed home after work the following day, he scanned the streets for any sign of the car he had seen outside Tom's house.

He had spent the day going over and over the conversation with Jack the night before. Putting himself in Jack's shoes the night he found out about Tom, he was on the brink of understanding. But the nagging feeling that this wasn't just going to go away refused to leave him.

He checked the rear-view mirror again. Who knew that Jack would turn out to be the one involved in an underground boxing ring? With his own history of 'misunderstandings', he was sure that even money would have been on him.

As he pulled into his driveway, the light was just beginning to fade and the streetlights hadn't yet come on. In the twilight he noticed that Jack had drawn the curtains in the living room. His car was still hidden from sight, parked around the back of the house. He wasn't taking any chances and that was worrying in itself. Just who exactly were they dealing with? He reached over for the bag of takeout he had picked up on the way home and headed into the house via the back door.

"Honey, I'm home!" he called, pocketing his keys as he closed the door after him.

Jack appeared in the doorway, bleary-eyed.

"Enjoy your nap? I got Chinese food."

"Great. I'm starving."

Jack rubbed his short brown hair roughly, making it stand on end even more. Callum grabbed a couple of forks out of the drawer and handed one to him, along with a carton of Chinese food.

"What? No chopsticks?"

"Rule number one: we don't do chopsticks in this house."

"That's right. Sorry," Jack said, a smile tugging at the corner of his mouth.

He grabbed two bottles of beer out of the fridge and handed one to Callum, who eyed it greedily.

"Jesus, I deserve that after the day I've had."

"Tough day at the office, dear?"

"Something like that. Dealing with idiots can give a man a healthy thirst."

"I called Ally earlier. She seemed a little out of sorts," Jack said, heading into the living room.

"Yeah, I stopped by to see her on my way home. Nothing out of place but she seemed a little down at the mouth. Said she was tired so I'm sure that's all it is."

He collapsed in his favourite armchair, taking a good long swallow of beer as Jack switched on the TV. The whole situation was surreal. Jack, sitting in his living room, having a beer with him. Memories tumbled over each other.

The night of the accident; Jack's new t-shirt; discussing how Jack was going to pop the question; his best man speech; Jack throwing punches at Tom's funeral; Andy McLeish going down in a screaming heap; Cage-fighting; Heavies who travelled in pairs; Jack and Ally kissing in her backyard.

How did they get from there to here?

Things would never be the way they were but perhaps, despite everything, there was something to salvage after all? He couldn't help but think that Tom would want them to try. He already knew what Ally wanted.

After dinner and a couple more beers, the conversation turned personal.

"Can I ask you something?" Jack lay stretched out on the

couch, one arm behind his head, the other holding his beer bottle.

"That's a loaded question."

"What happened between you and Jane?"

Callum shrugged. The question was a straightforward one; the answer not so much. He took a few moments to mentally toss things around.

"We realised that we weren't happy," he said at last.

"Since when?" Jack frowned. "I mean, things seemed fine before I left."

"Yes... and no. I could tell then that something was up but it just seemed easier to leave it alone and pretend everything was okay."

Jack eyed him over the top of his beer as he took another swig.

"After the accident, everything changed," Callum said, staring at a spot on the wall. "I spent a lot of time with Ally, and with Tom. Priorities shifted and we both ignored the obvious because it was easier that way."

"I had no idea," Jack said. "You never said anything. I thought you guys were solid."

Callum shrugged, peeling his gaze away from the wall as he took another sip from his bottle. "You had your own stuff going on, if I remember rightly. A little thing called a marriage proposal."

"Did you ever tell her about that? The ring, the plans - any of it?"

"Didn't seem much point afterwards."

Callum found himself thinking back to the accident for the second time that night. Apparently, Jack was doing the same.

"She really can't remember anything about that day?" Jack glanced over at him from the couch.

"Nope. I actually think it might be better this way. The doc said it was like some sort of protective amnesia. Her brain blocked it out because she probably couldn't handle it. He might be onto something there."

"Yeah, I guess so."

"She has nightmares about it, the accident," Callum said. "But they're not about what actually happened. Apparently, her brain has seen fit to fill in all these bizarre details of what might've happened but didn't. Seems like each nightmare has about five percent truth and ninety five percent weird shit."

"Jesus," Jack winced. "She told me she has dreams about running and walking but she never said anything about that."

"Can you blame her?"

"I guess not," Jack murmured. "She probably still thinks there's a chance I'm gonna take off again."

Callum took another sip of his beer, wondering if he'd said too much.

"Just give her time," he said. "You've been gone four years, remember. You've only been back a couple of weeks."

"You believe me, though, don't you?" Jack asked, glancing over at him.

Callum regarded him silently across the coffee table. Surprising even himself, he nodded.

"Yeah. I believe you."

Jack took another swig of his beer then set the bottle down to rest on his stomach.

"Well that's something, I guess."

*T*wo days had stretched into four and Jack was climbing the walls. He paced the house again, peering out of the windows more from habit than anything else. The street was quiet, as usual.

His packed bag waited by the door. Callum had been checking on his Dad's place a couple of times a day and had even had

Tom's neighbour, Mrs Watson, on the lookout. He had told her that there had been a couple of break-ins in the area and described the car he had seen, advising her that she should keep an eye out.

Callum had called her just that morning. After twenty minutes of chit-chat, she admitted that she hadn't seen or heard anything suspicious. As far as Jack was concerned, that meant the coast was clear. Without any leads he doubted Ben's envoy would still be hanging around.

After being able to pick up and take off whenever he felt like it over the past four years, the feeling of being trapped only increased with every passing hour. To make things worse, he could feel Ally's confusion every time they spoke on the phone. He hated lying to her, but he could tell she was starting to wonder why he was keeping her at arm's length. He could feel her starting to drift again. He had to do something and soon.

He heard Callum's car pull up and made his way back to the living room. The one good thing about this whole situation was that it had given him time with Callum. They had talked a lot over the past few days, tentatively getting to know each other again. It was a luxury he was never sure he deserved but was grateful for just the same.

The front door closed and Callum appeared, tossing his keys onto the coffee table. He noticed Jack's bag immediately.

"What's all this? You shipping out?"

"I just want to thank you again," he said honestly. "For everything. You didn't have to do any of this but I appreciate it."

Callum eyeballed him from across the room, his expression neutral.

"You're welcome."

"The coast looks clear so there's no reason to impose on you any longer."

"It's completely up to you. If you think it's all blown over, go for it."

"I do," Jack said. "But I need to do some damage control. Am I right in thinking that tonight is your night at the pool with Ally? Can I tag along? When I talked to her earlier, she was kinda weird, distant. I need for her to know that everything's okay."

"If it were any other night but tonight I'd say it's a great idea," Callum frowned. "But the pool is really not the place for a conversation like that. She goes to swim, it's not a social thing."

"I appreciate what you're saying but I think it's the perfect place. You said I should fight for her, right? Well, that's what I'm doing."

"Right. I said that," Callum mumbled, scratching his chin. "If it's what you really want, fine, but just remember that this was your idea not mine. Don't come crying to me because she didn't react the way you thought she would."

"Okay. Thanks."

"You're on dinner duty, then we'll call it even."

"Sounds fair," Jack smiled, clearly relieved.

"I'm going to go wash up. Kitchen's through there, in case you've forgotten," he said, pointing to it helpfully as he headed for the bathroom. "You need to borrow some trunks?"

"Yeah, I guess so."

CHAPTER TWENTY

"How few there are who have courage enough to own their faults, or resolution enough to mend them."
- Benjamin Franklin

*A*lly concentrated on stacking her clothes neatly in her bag and piling it into the locker at the pool. She didn't usually mind the smell of chlorine but tonight it made her feel nauseous.

What was up with Jack lately? Just when they had begun to make progress he backed off. Maybe Callum knew what was going on? If she could pluck up the courage, she would ask him tonight. There was a part of her that was afraid to hear what he might say. Maybe Jack knew more than he could handle? She couldn't help feeling that it was her fault for daring to hope and that hurt more than anything else.

She closed her locker and made her way out into the pool area. There was no sign of Callum and she wasn't in the mood to wait. What she needed was to get in the pool. Glancing around, she saw a few people swimming and a couple making their way back to the changing rooms. Other than that, no audience. She quickly moved the towel off her lap and laid it down on the concrete at the edge of the pool, near the steps. Transferring down onto the towel, she sat with her legs dangling in the water, reaching down to check the temperature. No one seemed to be paying her any attention so she leaned forward and allowed gravity to pull her into the water. As soon as the water swallowed her up, the rushing in her ears drowned out the voices in her head and she headed towards the swimming lane at a slow crawl.

Getting lost in the rhythm of stroke after stroke, she came up for air at the end of her second lap, breathing heavily. She held on to the edge of the pool and looked around for Callum. There were four swimmers in the lanes next to her but it was impossible to tell if Callum was one of them. Wiping the water out of her eyes, she turned to do another lap, consciously slowing her pace. Her arms pulled her through the water smoothly and she concentrated on each stroke, counting them to try and clear her head.

By the time she had reached the end of the pool, Callum was not even a consideration and she turned to complete another lap without pausing for breath. She swam several more laps, slow and steady, until she could feel the muscles in her shoulders and upper back burning. Her breath became harder and harder to regulate. The self-preservation alarm in her head began to sound and she reluctantly conceded, turning to head slowly towards the submerged concrete steps in the far corner of the pool.

Sitting on the steps, the heated water soothing her tired muscles, she watched the other swimmers as she caught her breath. Their smooth, powerful strokes cut through the water's surface and their feet kicked up trailing tufts of water. They made it look so easy, so graceful. For a moment, she was overcome with suffocating jealousy.

It's not fair.

Averting her gaze, she moved down onto the next step, watching her hands flutter in the water in front of her. No, it wasn't fair but it was life and she had made the decision to live it, no matter what.

Looking up, she saw Callum swimming towards her. Finally, a chance to get rid of some of the stuff cluttering up her head. He surfaced in front of her, treading water.

"Hey," he panted. "Were you early?"

"Yeah, I guess so."

"What's up?" he asked, wiping droplets of water away by running his hand down his face.

Damn him and his Jedi mind-reading crap. She mentally swiped the self-pity out of her brain.

"It's Jack," she said.

Callum looked over his shoulder. One of the few remaining swimmers was heading towards them slowly.

"Speak of the devil," he said. "And before you freak out, it wasn't my idea, it was his. He wouldn't take no for an answer."

Suddenly, she couldn't breathe. Voices screamed inside her head.

No. Not here. Not now. Not yet!

Callum climbed up the steps and sat down beside her.

"Don't make this into a big thing and it won't be," he warned, although she could barely hear him for the blood rushing in her ears.

Jack was almost upon them now.

"Relax," Callum urged. "He just wants to talk."

Before she had a chance to speak, Jack surfaced in front of them.

"Hey," he smiled.

The tension in the air was so thick you could have cut it with a knife. She tried to sink lower, hyper-aware of the fact that she wore a swimsuit that showed off too much of the body she wasn't ready for him to see.

"I think I'll head off. You guys have stuff to talk about," Callum said, giving her shoulder a gentle squeeze as he stood. "You can give Jack a lift home, right?"

She could only nod as Jack swam up to the wide concrete steps, climbing them to sit down beside her. He was so close that their shoulders touched and she fought the urge to shrink away from him. Could he see? She didn't dare look up, choosing to stare at her hands as they rested on her thighs, surreptitiously weighing them down as the buoyancy made them dance in the water.

"I'm sorry," Jack said.

His tone was sincere but she didn't dare look up.

"What for?" she asked instead, heart still pounding.

"I've had some stuff going on over the past few days that I needed to deal with."

She nodded, not thinking about anything other than speeding up this moment so that he would leave.

"It's fine," she said.

"No, it's not, but it was necessary." He paused a moment before continuing. "I'm having this problem."

She glanced sideways at him.

"Really?" she asked.

"Really."

The moment their eyes met, he had her. Hook, line and sinker.

"Want to know what it is?" he asked.

All she could do was nod.

"I can't think straight when I'm around you," he murmured. "And this stuff I had to deal with required a clear head."

"I thought you were avoiding me."

She tried not to sound like a whining child. It wasn't her style.

"Would I be here if I was avoiding you?"

She tried to shrug but only one shoulder responded.

"I guess not."

He smiled, the same lazy smile that used to drive her wild. This time, it made her forget where she was, even *when* she was. She felt sixteen again. Sixteen and carefree and uninhibited and wanting to be with him so badly it hurt. The feeling was just as intense as it had been all those years ago. So intense that it gave her a sense of vertigo, as if she was falling from a great height. Before she did, she summoned up all her courage and forced herself to look away.

It didn't help. He was in much better shape than she remembered. Rivulets of water slid down his bare chest and into the water, accentuating the muscle definition. Her insides felt as if they were liquefying. She longed to reach out and touch him, her heart racing at the thought.

It took her a few moments to realise that she was staring.

Afraid that her thoughts might be written all over her face, she tore herself away, but not before something caught her eye. As if it had a mind of its own, her hand drifted up to the tattoo on his shoulder. Small, black Roman numerals were embedded in his skin. Her brain deciphered the figures and her heart, racing only moments ago, shuddered to a halt.

"That's the date of the accident," she said.

As she ran her fingers gently over the ink, Callum's explanation of what happened that night rushed in on her, mingling with the images contained in a thousand twisted nightmares.

"I got it on the first anniversary."

She felt his body sigh beneath her fingertips and her hand fell away. For a moment she felt guilty, although she had no idea why. The pool disappeared and the world with it. Then it was just the two of them, sitting on the step in the warm water, staring at each other.

"Why?" she asked.

"I don't know. Maybe because I wanted there to be some physical evidence of what happened that night, like proof or something."

"Proof? Of what?"

"That I wasn't going insane, that it wasn't all in my head. Proof that it really happened. I guess I wanted something physical to show for it."

Her body began to tremble. The more she tried to control it, the more out of control she felt.

"That's crazy," she croaked, his face blurring. "All this time, I just wanted to hide the physical proof of what happened that night."

She could barely see him for the tears as he leaned over to cup her cheek in his hand. If he said anything after that, she didn't hear it. She couldn't hear anything. All she saw was a blur in front of her with Jack's green eyes staring out at her. As he drew her closer, she held her breath. She had never wanted something so desperately and yet been so frightened and confused by it at the same time.

Then his lips touched hers, softly at first, then more firmly. The confusion seemed to lift, floating away on a gentle breeze that smelled vaguely of chlorine.

He pulled away, gently running his thumb down her cheek and leaving goose bumps in its wake.

"You don't need to hide anything," he whispered.

Words disappeared. Thoughts, too.

"Do you understand me?"

She found herself nodding, wishing he would kiss her again. Somehow, when he kissed her, it was as if the years peeled back, pain and confusion vanished and it was the two of them against the world. Together they could handle anything.

"Come on," he said huskily. "Let's get out of here and go somewhere to talk."

Immediately, the surge of strength deserted her.

"Okay," she mumbled, forcing herself to look him in the eye as he withdrew his hand from her cheek. "Maybe you should wait out front for me, though. It takes me a while to get changed."

"It's okay, I'm not in any hurry. Take your time." He indicated her wheelchair with a quick glance. "Do you need a hand?"

"No, I'm fine," she insisted, her cheeks suddenly hot.

"Are you sure?"

"I'm sure."

He didn't make any effort to move even though she wished he would, just so she wouldn't have to do this in front of him. How long could she sit there before it was obvious?

"Honestly, you should probably wait in the foyer. I could be a while."

The words tripped over themselves. She knew from the look on his face that he wasn't buying it.

"What are you scared of?" he asked finally.

"Nothing. I'm not scared."

"Come on, Ally. It's me. Just tell me."

"Why can't I just meet you outside?"

She hated how desperate she sounded.

"Because I feel like whatever you're scared of is what we should do here."

The sincerity in his voice chipped away at the protective wall around her heart. She shook her head slowly, fighting against the feeling of being discovered for the fraud she felt she was.

"It's not that easy."

"Maybe it is, maybe it isn't but we'll never know until we give it a shot. How about we do this slowly, take it one day at a time?"

She tore her gaze away from those eyes and concentrated on her hands, resting on top of her thighs.

"And maybe today," he continued, "All it means is that we leave the pool together."

He squeezed her hand and she looked up, nodding.

"*S*he'll be fine. Jack was with her," Callum said, throwing Maggie a sidelong glance.

Barney's was unusually busy for a Sunday night, so the three of them were perched at the bar rather than at their usual table.

"Which is precisely where the problem lies," Jane interjected, taking a quick sip of her drink.

"What on earth possessed you to let him go with you tonight?" Maggie asked.

"He said he wanted to talk to her."

"That's some test you're putting him through," Jane said.

"It wasn't a test," he said, sucking his bottom lip through his teeth as he prepared to explain himself. "Jack and I've had a lot of time to talk about stuff these past few days. It's been... weird, but good, in a way. He says he's staying and I gotta say, the more I talk to him, the more I believe him."

"Seriously?" Jane frowned.

He stared at the ring of condensation on the bar in front of him.

"I saw them together, last Sunday afternoon. You should've been there. It was like before, like nothing had changed. She wants him to stay and he wants to stay. It's that simple."

"So, what was tonight about then?" Jane asked.

"Tonight was about getting her to realise that if she wants him here, she's gotta start trusting him."

"You think it's that easy?" Maggie prodded gently.

"I didn't say it was easy. I just think it's the only way. Too many damn secrets, those two. It's no way to live. They eat you up from the inside, out."

He took another swig of beer. He couldn't get the image of Jack and Ally kissing out of his mind. She had never looked at him the way he had seen her looking at Jack that day.

Talking with Jack, getting to know him again, he could see how torn up he was about what happened. He was the first to admit he had done the wrong thing by taking off and he was willing to be punished for it, seeking out that punishment however he could. He also seemed determined to try and make it up to Ally somehow and he didn't seem to care how long that took or what he had to do. Hadn't he given Ally the choice this time? And hadn't she asked him to stay? It must have hurt like hell to put that decision in her hands and it must have taken a leap of faith unlike anything he could even imagine for her to ask him to stay.

That was love, pure and simple, as much as it ripped his guts out to admit it.

He downed the last of his beer in one long gulp and stood up, wiping his mouth with the back of his hand.

"You're leaving?" Jane asked.

"Yeah, got stuff to do."

"What stuff? Where are you going?" Maggie looked up at him.

He pulled her into a quick hug.

"I'm going home to kick the cat," he murmured, releasing her.

"But you don't have a cat."

"Busted."

He gave them both a wry smile and made his way across the crowded room, past the jukebox and the guys playing pool, past the tables and the booths and across what passed for the dance-floor, out into the cool night air.

All he wanted was a little peace and for someone to tell him that he had done the right thing tonight. Not for the first time, he wished Tom were here.

*J*ack waited for Ally in the small lobby, reclining on one of the old 1960s armchairs; all style and no comfort. The arms were chrome tubing and the springs had seen better days. Even the upholstery was worn, faded all over and ripped in places. It reminded him of some of the apartments he'd lived in and he fidgeted, looking at his watch again. She did say she could be a while.

After his self-imposed exile of the past few days, all he wanted was to be with her. Being without her for four years, he had convinced himself he could live that way, if he needed to. But now that he was home and she was here, he knew he had been fooling himself. The shell of the man he used to be had begun to fill out again – the broken soul and the shattered heart had begun to heal and he could feel the physical change within him. He was becoming complete again, a whole person, not merely fragments of someone he used to be.

Kissing her tonight had been completely unplanned. He knew she would see his tattoo tonight but he was completely unprepared for her reaction. Her heartfelt, honest observation had awoken in him the basic need to soothe her, protect her, keep her safe. He knew he could do it, too, if only he could convince her to let him.

He had watched over his towel with mounting admiration as she pulled herself out of the pool. He didn't really know how she would manage, but she was more than capable. He was impressed with her strength and technique, managing the seemingly impossible with grace and dignity. He wasn't surprised. There seemed to be little she couldn't do.

He checked his watch again and stood up, stretching as he went to the noticeboard, gazing idly over the newsletters pinned there.

Before the accident, Ally was a dynamo, a force to be reckoned with. She was always talking, forever in motion. Now however, she was reined in somehow. Tethered, controlled. Something fundamental had changed, not physically, but mentally. He shoved his hands deep into his pockets. How did she see him now? He wasn't sure he wanted to know.

The door behind him opened and he turned to see Ally

making her way through the door towards him, now wearing dark jeans and a sweatshirt, her gym bag on her lap. He smiled and walked over to retrieve his own bag off the floor.

"Shall we go?" he pulled open the outer door for her.

She pushed herself through and out into the parking lot as he followed behind. The air was cool compared to the warmth of the pool building and he shivered involuntarily, falling in beside her.

"What do you want to do?" she asked. "Barney's is probably still open."

"I don't care. I just want to be wherever you are. I've missed you."

She glanced up at him and he could see her blushing even in the dim light of the parking lot.

"Me too," she said.

"Your place then? I'd say come over to mine but I still have to get some food in."

"Okay."

As they approached her car, two men materialised out of nowhere. One grabbed him and pushed him back against her car. A knee rammed tight against his and a forearm thrust hard up against his throat, knocking the wind out of him. Gasping, he stared desperately past the face inches from his own. The other guy stood next to Ally, arms folded across his chest. His heart sank.

"Well, hello there," growled Jimmy, his gravelly voice the result of years of smoking. "Small world isn't it?"

Jack struggled in vain. The knee rammed tighter into his, the arm across his throat pressing harder. It was difficult to breathe, much less speak.

"You're a hard man to find, Jack. You didn't really think you'd be able to hide in this little shit-hole of a town forever, did you?"

Jack's eyes were on Ally, silently begging for understanding. She stared back at him, wide-eyed, her hands gripping the rims of her chair. Jimmy stood just beside her, within striking distance.

"How'd you find me?" Jack croaked, his throat burning.

"None of your damn business." Jimmy moved to stand behind Ally, his huge hands resting on her shoulders. "Speaking of business, I'm here to collect the money you owe Ben. It's a straightforward business transaction. Ben doesn't like complications and you, my man, are a *complication*."

Jack winced as the arm against his throat pushed harder.

"How much?" he croaked.

"Ten grand."

Jack's heart tried to jump out of his throat but was blocked by the arm threatening to crush his windpipe.

"After you skipped out on him, that's how much you cost him in lost revenue."

"I don't have that kind of money."

"Well you've got forty-eight hours to get it. Ben's not a guy you want to disappoint, as you should know."

The guy holding Jack released him just long enough to drive a hammer blow into his solar plexus, doubling him over and sucking the air right out of him. The guy dragged him upright again and shoved him back against the car, making the pain worse.

Suddenly, Ally cried out, her upper body arching upwards as her eyes widened. Jimmy's hands remained on her shoulders, fingers curled into her skin, mouth curved into a cold smile.

"Get your hands off her!" Jack croaked, renewing his struggles.

Jimmy's eyes were dead and black as coal.

"Or we could come back and take this pretty little doll for a ride she'll never forget. How 'bout that for an alternative?"

Ally sat poker straight and perfectly still, barely breathing. Jack saw red. He twisted and squirmed, breathing heavily as he fought to get free and knock Jimmy clear into next week. Finally, the guy holding him tired of the game and head-butted him. Jack's vision swam as he fell forward. He kissed the concrete, loose stones digging into his face as the world around him faded.

He came to, dragged roughly upwards, aware of Ally begging desperately for them to leave him alone. He tasted blood. His head lolled forward and he fought to keep it on top of his neck.

"It's okay," he mumbled, his vision still hazy. "It's okay."

"What a hero," Jimmy sneered. "Ten grand, forty-eight hours. Got that?"

Jack tried to nod but his head felt like it was going to separate from his shoulders. He spat out a mouthful of blood directly onto the guy holding him. Taking exception, the guy swore at him and slammed his fist into Jack's face.

Jack's legs gave out and he slid down the side of the car, his ears ringing. As many times as he had fought in the ring, he couldn't ever remember getting a whipping that felt anything like this. What made it worse was the helplessness. It had always been his own body on the line, never anyone else's. Now Ally was in the firing line too and that made him feel infinitely worse.

Gasping for breath, crouching on the concrete, Jimmy grabbed a handful of his shirt, yanking him upright as Jack struggled to find his feet.

"Stop it!" Ally pleaded frantically, crying now. "Please leave him alone!"

"Aw, she's a keeper, Jack. She seems to have a thing for you," Jimmy chuckled, before turning serious once more. "We know where you live and we know where she lives so don't try anything stupid like calling the cops because we're watching you - both of you."

Jack blinked away the haze he was looking through, his heart pounding in his chest.

"Be smart about this and no one gets hurt," Jimmy said coldly. "You know me, Jack. I know you do. Don't push me."

Jack blinked, blood seeping down into his eye from the

stinging cut to his head. Jimmy scrutinised him, pushing him away and sending him stumbling backwards.

"Ten grand, forty-eight hours," Jimmy repeated. "I'll let you know where."

With one final soulless glance in Ally's direction, both men walked away. Jack teetered on his feet, searching through the haze for Ally, his head throbbing. The dim lighting in the parking lot made her look pale and small and he fought down the rising nausea.

"Are you alright?" she whimpered, chin trembling.

"Never mind me. Are you alright? Did he hurt you?"

He stumbled the few steps to her side, falling to his knees awkwardly as he grabbed her chair to keep himself from pitching forward.

Tears stained her cheeks but she shook her head.

"I'm okay. Who were those guys?"

His heart sank and he silently begged her not to do this to him now, not while his head still spun and he could barely string two thoughts together.

"Come on," she said, wiping tears from her cheeks. "Let's get out of here. I'm taking you to the hospital."

She helped him stand and he swayed beside her, grabbing onto her chair again for support.

"I don't need to see a doctor, I'll be okay," he insisted, even as his head felt like it was going to split in two.

"For once, please just do as you're told?"

He stared down at his shirt, his body aching, his head throbbing. Blood was spattered down the front of it. Too tired and too sore to argue, he followed her slowly to her car.

CHAPTER TWENTY-ONE

"You may have to fight a battle more than once to win it."
- Margaret Thatcher

*A*lly drove slowly, her shoulders burning. The thought of Jimmy's huge hands on her made her skin crawl. What the hell just happened?

She glanced briefly over at Jack but his gaze was firmly fixed on the road ahead.

It felt like something out of a movie. Heavies turn up demanding cash or else. Ten thousand dollars was a lot of money. How had he racked up that much debt? What had he done?

She stole another glance at him, her gaze lingering briefly on the blood clotting on the side of his head. Where would he find that kind of money in forty-eight hours? She replayed what she had seen and heard, trying in vain to fit the puzzle pieces together as they approached her street.

They're watching my house.

She peered at every parked car and up every side street,

slowing down to a near-crawl. Nothing looked out of place. They could be anywhere. Her skin crawled just thinking about it. Pulling into her driveway, she turned off the ignition.

"I still think you should see a doctor," she said, turning to Jack.

He sighed, deep and long, as if the weight of the world were resting on his shoulders.

"I'm fine."

She heeded the silent caution and waited. He didn't move for several moments and she shivered as the night air began to leach into the car.

"I'm sorry," he said finally, turning to her. "I never wanted you to get involved in any of this."

Angry red marks shone just above his collar and his eyes seemed hollow, somehow. He looked like a man with a death sentence hanging over his head and the analogy made her uncomfortable.

"I'll figure out a way to fix this," he promised huskily. "Please. Just trust me."

She desperately needed answers but she didn't dare ask him anything because he literally looked like he was hanging onto sanity by his fingertips.

"Let's go inside," she said.

Jack eased out of the car as she unpacked her wheelchair, reassembling it slowly, her shoulders aching.

Transferring into the chair, they made their way up to the house. Glancing behind her as she unlocked the door, she got her first decent look at his battered face in the porch light and froze, her hand on the key in the lock.

"That looks really nasty. If you won't see a doctor, you have to at least let me clean you up," she insisted. "No arguments."

He didn't seem to have any. She pushed the door open, pulling herself over the threshold. Jack made his way into the living room, a low moan escaping as he sat down on the couch.

"Don't move," she ordered, even though he didn't look capable of it.

In the bathroom, she dug the first aid kit out of the cupboard along with a clean, damp washcloth, and a towel. Piling everything onto her lap, she made her way through to the bedroom and picked up a small bottle of water and the painkillers from her bedside table, adding them to the mounting pile as she headed for the living room. Having a purpose helped to keep the fear at bay and she hung on to the mental list in her head, repeating it over and over.

First aid kit. Washcloth. Towel. Painkillers. Water.

Jack sat on the couch where she'd left him, staring at the floor. As much as she wanted to know what was going on, he looked too fragile to survive a proper conversation. She positioned herself in front of him and began to unload the contents of her lap onto the coffee table.

"Look at me," she instructed gently, her attention consumed by the angry lump on his forehead.

Doing as he was told, his eyes finally met hers and it felt like entire conversations took place without either of them uttering a word aloud. The pain she saw went deeper than physical pain, cutting to the very core of him. It was raw, as if it had been dragged to the surface kicking and screaming. She tried to concentrate on his wounds and not the look of pure desolation before her as she began dabbing gently at them.

His face contorted in pain as she wiped away the blood from his face. She gently applied antiseptic cream, working slowly and methodically.

Finally, she dried off her hands on the towel.

"Can you pass me that bottle of pills?"

Obediently, he did as he was told, unable to hide the grimace as he reached for it. Satisfied, she sat back.

"Take one of those," she said, nodding at the bottle in his hand as she handed him the bottled water to wash it down with.

"I don't need – "

"Take it anyway."

She could see him arguing the point in his head but he relented and tipped a pill out into his palm, swallowing it with a gulp of water. About to hand the bottle of pills back to her, he looked at it closely, frowning.

"These are prescription."

"It'll take the edge off."

She busied herself putting everything back into the first aid kit, folding the towel on her lap and putting it onto the coffee table, bloodied washcloth on top. Her shoulders ached but she daren't let it show.

"What are these for?" he asked, indicating the bottle of pills still in his hand.

"I told you, sometimes I have back pain."

She reached for the bottle but he held it away from her.

"Did he hurt you?" he murmured. "Let me see."

"No, I'm fine, really."

But he had already put the bottle of pills back on the table and turned towards her.

"Show me."

"Jack, I'm fine. You're the one who – "

Ignoring her, he leaned forward and reached up to gently pull her sweatshirt aside. She realised it was a waste of time trying to distract him now so she let him, a shiver running through her as his hand brushed against her neck. As he pulled the neck of her sweatshirt wider, the look on his face said it all.

"Jesus," he whispered.

She pushed his hands away.

"It's fine."

"I'm so sorry," he whispered, reaching for her hands and enclosing them in his. "I don't know what else to say. I never meant for any of this to happen."

"What did happen? I don't understand. What's going on? Who were those guys?"

He blew out a long breath through his teeth and shook his head slowly. She waited patiently, taking comfort from his hands on hers and willing him to do the same.

"I made a mistake," he said finally. "I did something stupid and then I took off. Sound familiar?"

"I still don't understand. How can you owe ten thousand dollars?"

He tried to pull away but she held fast to his hands, begging him silently for more. He sighed heavily, his body sagging.

"Boxing."

She stared at him, wide-eyed.

"Boxing? Like, fighting?"

"Yeah."

"But ten thousand dollars? I don't get it."

His eyes seemed flat suddenly, as if the light had gone out in them.

"I was fighting for this guy Ben, for money. They were running a book on us, taking bets. I wasn't supposed to win but I did. I wasn't thinking straight, it was the night that Callum called me about Dad... and I guess my mind wasn't on the fight. I knew I was in trouble but I figured I'd be safe if I left. No one knew how to find me." He let go of her hand, grimacing. "Or so I thought, anyway."

Her mind spun in circles.

"Fighting? I don't understand any of this. This is just... it's not you. Why would you do that?"

"I don't expect you to understand any of this because honestly, I don't really understand it myself," he admitted. "All I can say is that it happened and I'm sorry it did and I'm sorry you're involved in this - I really am. I thought that staying at Callum's would be safe. I thought they'd gone, but apparently I was wrong."

"What do you mean? You thought who had gone? Those guys? I thought you were staying with him because of a gas leak?"

Jack took on the look of a deer caught in the headlights.

"What's going on? How long have you known about this?"

"When Callum came over on Sunday, he said he'd been around to the house and found this guy snooping around over there. He said he was looking for me. Callum told him he didn't know where I was. That's why I went over to his place. It wasn't a gas leak Ally, and I'm sorry we lied to you. I thought it'd be best. I didn't want you to worry. I thought I was doing the right thing. I never meant for you to get involved in any of this."

She stared at him, wide-eyed. Where did it end? The lying, the secrets, the deceit - not only Jack but Callum was in on this too? It was too much. She blinked, the switch in her head shutting off while she dealt with all of this information behind closed doors.

She gathered up the first aid kit, the washcloth and the towel in silence, piling them on her lap and turning away from him. Heading for the bathroom on auto-pilot, she returned the first aid kit to its place in the cabinet and deposited the towel and washcloth into the laundry hamper in the corner. Not sure what to do next, she sat there, her back to the door. She heard him follow her, standing in the doorway behind her.

"I'm sorry."

"Stop saying that," she snapped, whirling around to face him.

"I was trying to protect you."

"Why does everyone think I need protecting?" she demanded, her eyes burning with unshed tears. "Am I so pathetic that no one thinks I can take the truth?"

He looked horrified at the prospect.

"That's not it at all!"

"Isn't it?"

"I just didn't want to get you involved in this, I didn't want you to end up getting hurt again because of me!"

Once again, the guilt he carried over the accident reared

its ugly head. When would it end? She fought back tears, determined not to give him another reason not to confide in her.

"I didn't want you to know how much I screwed up, how much of a mess I made of all this. Here I am, trying to convince you that you can trust me with anything and all I've done is make everything worse!"

"So, you just decided to keep it from me?"

"I'm not the only one keeping secrets though, am I?"

Her heart raced.

"It's not the same thing!"

"Sure it is! The thing with the yoga mat, the constantly changing the subject when things get a little close to the truth. You're shutting me out, too!"

"I'm not!"

"Yes, you are and I don't blame you, to a degree. I know my track record sucks but what do I have to do to prove to you that I want to be here, with you? That I'm not just gonna disappear again, no matter what happens?"

She couldn't think of a single thing to say to that.

"I can take it, Ally, whatever it is you think I can't handle, I can take it and much more besides. I'm not going anywhere, I want to be with you! Don't you get it? Even though I'm screwing up left and right here, I *want* to be here and I'm not gonna give up. I'm gonna fix this mess and then things are gonna have to change between us because I don't want you to keep me at arm's length anymore, okay?"

Her stomach twisted into a tight knot as she blinked up at him. Did he have any idea what he was asking her to do?

"I'll tell you anything you want to know, if you promise to do the same," he said. "But you have to promise me. Agreed?"

Her head swam. As broken and tired as he was, he practically glowed with desperation.

"Okay."

He closed the gap between them, grimacing as he knelt in front of her to take her hands.

"It's just a little blip on the radar," he said. "I'm gonna fix this. Everything's gonna be fine, you'll see."

She nodded, her hands trembling in his, her body threatening to follow suit. He pulled her into his arms and she found herself burying her head in his shoulder as she tried to shut out the idea that they were being watched.

"Stay here with me tonight?" she begged, her noble intentions disappearing in a flood of fear.

"I'm not going anywhere. I promise."

*J*ack sat in the antique chair in Ally's hallway, the grandfather clock towering above him. What the hell had he done, bringing this shit here, to her?

The quiet hum of voices in the kitchen grew louder. He should be in there going in to bat for himself but he didn't think he had it in him right now. He was letting Ally fight this battle, one that wasn't even hers to fight. What kind of man did that? What would his Dad say?

He had argued against getting Callum, Jane and Maggie involved but Ally had insisted. The more heads together, she said, the more chance they had of making sure this goes away. He should have argued harder, he should have stood up to her, but he didn't.

For the thousandth time in the past few hours, he went over his options.

He could make a break for it alone but all that would do was leave Ally vulnerable. He couldn't do that.

He could go to the cops but what if they couldn't protect her? It was clear that Ben's reach was further than he thought.

He could take Ally and go on the run but what kind of life would that be, constantly looking over their shoulders?

The only solution was to somehow come up with ten thousand dollars in forty- eight hours. He leaned forward and rested his elbows on his knees, staring at the floorboards. Every bone in his body ached but it was nothing compared to the ache in his heart.

A chair scraped against the wooden floorboards. Callum was talking about calling the cops. Before he could think of standing up and going in there, Ally answered for him, repeating what he had told her earlier.

"Okay," Jane said after a few moments. "Then let's talk about the money."

Jack rested his head in his palms, his head throbbing.

The money. What the hell was he gonna do about the money?

"How much do you have?"

He looked up to see Callum standing in the kitchen doorway.

"A little over five grand," he said, trying not to wince as he straightened up. "If I sell my car, I'll get another grand, maybe less."

"That leaves you four grand short."

It might as well have been four hundred grand. Close was not good enough. Close was not gonna solve anything.

Callum moved aside as Ally appeared in the doorway, moving through into the hall. She made her way towards him slowly, powering her wheelchair with light, even strokes.

"I have two thousand dollars from my inheritance, from Gran. I want you to have it," she said, stopping beside him. "You can pay me back if it makes you feel better."

He stared at her, his blood pressure rising. He shouldn't need her help, or her money. He should be taking care of this on his own. It was his mess, not hers.

"No. I'll figure out a way to do this myself."

"So, you're gonna find four grand in forty-eight hours?"

Callum shook his head. "Are you kidding me? What are you gonna do, rob a bank? This is like déjà-vu. Pull your head out of your ass for a change!"

Jack struggled to keep his frustration in check.

"I'll figure it out."

"How?" Maggie asked from behind Callum. "How are you gonna raise four grand? Tell us how and we'll back off."

"I don't know yet, but I'll fix it."

If he had a job this would be so much easier but no bank on earth would give him a loan if he had no means to pay it back.

"Bullshit you will, because there is no other solution," Callum said roughly. "I've got about a grand in the bank and can borrow more. Ally has two. Take it and you can pay us both back. Whatever it takes to make this go away, that's what you're gonna do."

Jack glared at him, his pride insisting he throw it all back in their faces but his head screaming that he was out of options. Frustration built inside of him, pushing his lungs up into his throat. Callum was right. This was about more than just his pride. The smart thing to do was to acknowledge that doing the right thing wasn't always easy. So why the hell did it feel like he was being trapped into doing the wrong thing here? Wouldn't the right thing be to handle this himself, without getting anyone else involved?

"Jack, please."

The heartbreak in Ally's voice turned his stomach.

"You're not alone anymore," she said. "You don't have to do this by yourself. Let us help, please?"

You're not alone anymore.

Her words sank in slowly, leaving footprints on his heart. He couldn't hurt her again, not now. He had to do the right thing. And if the right thing meant borrowing money off his friends, then that's what he must do.

He imagined a hand on his shoulder, squeezing tight, encouraging him and he closed his eyes.

I feel you, Dad. I'll make it up to you, I promise.

Opening his eyes, he reached for Ally's hand.

"Thank you."

He looked over at Callum, Maggie and Jane standing by the kitchen doorway.

"Thank you," he repeated, addressing Callum. "I'll pay you back, I promise."

"It's gonna be okay," Ally murmured.

She sounded so sure, so confident, he almost convinced himself that he believed her.

The night was quiet and still. Ally had gone to bed a couple of hours earlier but Jack was on a knife edge, twitchy and restless. Every imagined little noise had him up, investigating. Callum had called him when he got home, saying that he hadn't seen anything unusual when they left, but Jimmy was no amateur. If he said they were watching both houses, Jack believed him. He checked the front door again, walking down the length of the hall in his bare feet, checking the back door for good measure. Even though he had done this a gazillion times tonight, he planned on doing it a gazillion more before the night was out.

He walked into the kitchen and sat down at the table, exhausted with the weight of responsibility. The medication that Ally had given him earlier was wearing off and he eased back against the chair, his bruised ribs aching with the movement. His brain ran in circles. How could he have been so stupid as to think that Ben wouldn't track him back here?

It was time to grow up. The only reason he was in this mess was because he had been so used to running away from his problems, the odds had been stacked against him from the outset.

After spending four years on the run from himself, he still hadn't learnt his lesson. What was it Father David had said?

"We all make mistakes. You have to learn from them or it's a lesson you'll have to keep learning over and over again."

That's what was happening to him now. He was being given the chance to learn his lesson. No more running away, no more hiding from the truth. He owed his father more, he owed Ally more and he owed himself more. Once all this was over, he was going out to find a job and he was paying everyone back.

A single brief, sharp knock at the front door startled him.

His heart raced. He waited but it was not repeated. He flew up from his seat and into the living room, peering out between the curtains onto an empty front yard, glowing in the street light. His heart battered against his ribcage as he crept to the front door. He unlocked it, opening it a crack and peering out. Nothing. Opening it wider, he glanced along the porch but saw nothing out of the ordinary. His pulse raced as his gaze swept over the front yard. Turning to go back into the house, he was about to dismiss the whole episode as part of his overactive imagination when he saw a note tacked to the front door. He yanked it off, disappearing into the house, closing, locking and double-checking the door behind him. Stepping further down the hall-way, he stared at the note in his hand.

10pm Tuesday. Lewis Street house. Come alone. Sweet dreams.

Crushing the note in his hand, he shoved it deep into his jeans pocket and walked slowly back into the living room. He sank down into the couch, his aches and pains forgotten.

He had to end this.

CHAPTER TWENTY-TWO

"The past is never where you think you left it."
- Katherine Anne Porter

*E*verything was too quiet. No birdsong, which was unusual for the hour, not even the sound of a breeze rustling the leaves cut through the early morning air. The only sound was that of Ally's footsteps on gravel, each step kicking up small stones behind her. It would have been relaxing if only she had let herself go, but somewhere in the back of her mind a voice whispered that all was not well. She ignored the twist in her gut and ran onwards, turning off at the edge of the park and heading up River Road.

The slight incline made her calves and thighs burn with the extra effort required but she didn't care. For some reason she welcomed the sensation. She heard voices up ahead and she slowed down to try and make them out. Almost instantly, she recognised Jack's voice, picking up on the panic in it that kick-started her into a full-blown sprint.

He screamed and her heart raced, her arms pumping harder as she fought to get to him. It felt like forever before she could finally see him, *and when she did, she stopped still. He was trapped inside his car, over-turned in the middle of the road. She looked for help but there was no one around. He was desperately trying to pull himself out of the car but getting nowhere. She ran to him, falling to the asphalt beside him, ignoring the stones that cut into her knees.*

He stared up at her, wide-eyed and frantic. As she reached for him, she found that suddenly their positions were reversed. She was the one inside the car and he was the one outside, trying to help her escape. What she had assumed was sharp stones cutting into her knees was in fact mangled metal, trapping her inside the car so she couldn't move. The pain was excruciating and she screamed even as he tried to soothe her, begging her to keep still while he brutally yanked at the door that refused to budge.

Smoke curled up beside her and she looked around, wrenching her neck as she strained to see where it was coming from. Jack swore loudly, a string of curses tumbling from him in a high-pitched yowl that scared her even more. She begged for help as the smoke turned into flames that licked at her, searing her skin. She screamed, renewing the struggle, ignoring the metal that dug into her knees. Her eyes stung from the smoke and the smell of burning flesh turned her stomach. She watched in horror as the flames turned the flesh on her legs a blistering red.

Jack bolted into consciousness. He sat still on the couch for a moment, his body tingling, his heart racing, as he struggled to wake up properly. What had woken him? He had no idea how long he'd been asleep but it was still dark.

Ally screamed, then - a short, sharp, sob-like scream that set his teeth on edge. He shot up from the couch and made a dive for the doorway, almost colliding with it in his haste.

He pushed open the door, peering into the darkness.

"Ally? Are you okay?"

She whimpered in the darkness as he approached the bed. She screamed again, short and shrill, suddenly thrashing about so much he wondered if someone was trying to hurt her. He grabbed for the bedside lamp, flicking it on only to see her alone in bed, pillows scattered around her. She was clearly dreaming, her eyes firmly shut, face contorted as the whimpering continued. He leaned over and tried to grab her arms.

"Hey, come on, wake up."

"I'm burning!" she sobbed, pushing him away.

"No, you're not, you're dreaming, Ally - wake up."

"My legs!"

He glanced down at her legs beneath the blankets.

"You're alright, nothing's burning."

She whimpered again, still fighting him off.

"Wake up, come on, wake up for me now."

Her eyes flew open with a sharp intake of breath, followed by a coughing fit. He pulled her towards him, rubbing her back gently.

"You're okay, you were dreaming. Just take it easy, breathe slowly, that's it. You're okay."

Trembling in his arms, his protective instinct lurched into overdrive. All he wanted was to keep her safe from harm, real or imagined. Suddenly she struggled free to reach down and push the covers off her legs. She stared at them for a moment in silence and a violent tremor shook her before she quickly drew the covers over her legs again.

"Am I dreaming?" she whispered, turning to gaze up at him in confusion.

"You were, but you're not now. You were having a nightmare."

She struggled through to consciousness.

"Are you real?"

"I'm real," he smiled, his heart swelling.

He saw the light slowly returning to her eyes as the tension in her body eased. She wrapped her arms around him and he pulled her in close. They sat, safe in each other's arms, for the longest time. It felt so familiar, so comfortable, his body relaxed into hers. All thoughts of Jimmy and his previous life were washed clean away and he found himself wondering how he could have lived without her all this time.

"I think I can feel them sometimes," she whispered. "My legs. Just for a few seconds, when I wake up."

"Can you?"

"I don't know if it's... it feels so real."

He tried to imagine the torture of fleeting sensation.

"What were you dreaming about, just now?"

She pulled him closer, fitting herself even more tightly into his body.

"The accident."

He smoothed her hair gently with his fingertips, remembering his conversation with Callum.

"You thought your legs were on fire."

"It felt like they were burning."

"Can you still feel them?"

"No," she sighed. "It's gone now."

He held her tight.

"I've never had a dream like that before, where my legs were on fire."

He gently rubbed her back.

"What do you think it means?" she whispered, vulnerability oozing out of her and soaking the air around them.

"I don't know," he mumbled, remembering the night of the accident and the fumes that had turned his stomach and forced him into making a choice that changed both their lives.

Did she remember too, somewhere deep down in her subconscious?

"It's gonna be okay," he said. "I promise. I'm here now."

He held her until his arms began to go numb. When her slow, rhythmic breathing indicated that she had fallen asleep again, he gently eased them both back onto the pillows behind him and closed his eyes.

The night of the accident came back to him in Technicolour and he let it play out this time, conscious of every move he made. From leaning over to turn the radio down to dragging Ally out of the car and across the damp grass, he relived all of it. The pain in his chest had nothing to do with Ally leaning against it and everything to do with a decision he made that night that he would never forget.

---

*A*lly woke up slowly, her back aching. After a few minutes, the ache turned into tiny fingers of pain, like razor sharp daggers burying themselves deep in the vertebrae. Opening her eyes, she realised she was in Jack's arms, half-lying and half-sitting against the headboard. He breathed slowly and evenly beneath her and every rise and fall of his chest caused the daggers to dig deeper. She could stand it no longer. She braced her hand on the mattress as she tried to move but a sudden stabbing pain in her spine forced out a gasp of surprise, stopping her in her tracks.

Jack squirmed sleepily beneath her and the movement buried the daggers deeper still, settling them in her bones until she didn't care about anything but making the pain stop.

"Jack, wake up," she hissed through clenched teeth, her chin quivering as she tried not to cry out.

"What is it?" he murmured groggily, stretching the arm that wasn't draped over her.

She sucked in a breath, the pain instantly intensifying with the movement.

"You need to move."

"What?"

"Please, you need to move," she pleaded, not caring how she sounded anymore. "Need to lay flat."

He froze, then began to ease out from under her.

"Slowly," she ordered, sucking in the curse words that were building beneath the pain.

"Okay."

That one word was infused with both confusion and fear. She knew she would have to explain this later but right now she needed to do something.

As he moved slowly from beneath her, each tiny position change was agony. She cussed liberally in her head although she was incapable of saying much aloud.

After what seemed like an eternity, he sat next to her and she was sprawled on the bed, half on her front and half on her side, in utter misery.

"What can I do?" he said gently.

She tried to breathe evenly, clenching her teeth, staring at the pillow she was half-buried in. She wanted to get the pills herself but she couldn't reach them from this position so she sucked it up and took the help he offered.

"Pills," she breathed. "Table, behind me."

Jack climbed off the bed carefully as she lay there, even the tiny movements caused by breathing sending pain rocketing through her spine.

"They're not here," he said desperately. "Oh wait - I think they're still on the coffee table. I'll get them."

Careful to keep her breathing shallow, it felt like he was gone forever. When he finally came back with them, he knelt down on the floor beside the bed with the bottle of pills and some water.

"How many?"

"One," she ground out through teeth clenched tight against the pain.

"Just one? Are you sure?"

"For now."

He uncapped the bottle and she released the sheet she had clutched in her fist to take the pill from him. Carefully slipping it onto her tongue, she fought the urge to cry out against the pain that simple movement caused. He handed her a glass of water and she slurped at it, spilling some on the pillow beneath her but swallowing enough to take the pill with it.

"Now what?" he murmured.

She pinched her eyes shut.

"Wait."

She felt him slip his hand into hers and squeeze gently. She hadn't meant it as a request, merely a statement of fact. If she were in her right mind she would have insisted he leave her alone to deal with this but she wasn't in her right mind. The pain overwhelmed her, sucking up every other emotion she had, including humiliation, and viciously discarding them. Jack whispered something that she didn't catch over the blood rushing in her ears. The only sense that hadn't deserted her was touch, and she felt him softly stroking the side of her hand with his thumb. She concentrated on his gentle, smooth strokes as the pain slowly receded.

Eventually, she opened her eyes. Jack sat on the floor, his head resting on the bed, still holding her hand. His face was drawn tight with anxiety and a wave of love rose from deep within her belly as she felt herself fighting off tears.

"How are you feeling?"

"Better," she sniffed, trying to recover her self-control.

"Did I do this? Because if I did, I'm so sorry."

"It's okay," she murmured, meeting his worried gaze out of the corner of her eye. "I should have known better than to fall asleep all twisted up like that. It's my fault, not yours."

"You said you had back pain sometimes but I didn't expect this. I thought... well, I don't know what I thought, to be honest."

He looked so miserable, she wanted to smile, to sit up, to tell him that she was fine. But she wasn't capable of any of that yet.

"It's the metal rods," she mumbled into the pillow. "Hurts sometimes."

"Can you see them?"

"See what?"

"The metal rods."

"No. Just the scar."

Jack's gaze flitted to her back for a brief instant.

"Can I take a look?"

The aftermath of the pain and the effect of the medication wore down her defences. She reasoned that it was only a scar and she was hardly in a position to argue.

"Knock yourself out."

He squeezed her hand again before letting it go, moving carefully around the edge of the bed until she couldn't see him anymore. Slowly, she moved her hand to the hem of the t-shirt she slept in and pushed it up. Anxiety worked its way through the haze of medication like a cold knife. She waited for him to say something - that the scar was huge, that it was ugly, that it looked painful - but he didn't.

Instead, he gently pushed the t-shirt higher and the cool morning air hit her bare skin. His fingertips touched her back, so gently it almost tickled. The area around her scar was hypersensitive and she knew immediately when he was near it. She sucked in a breath.

"I'm sorry," he said quickly. "I didn't mean to hurt – "

"It doesn't - hurt, I mean," she swallowed. "The pain, it's not coming from my scar."

She held her breath as his fingertips floated over her skin with incredible tenderness, electrifying the nerve-endings.

Why wasn't he saying anything?

Then he was lowering her t-shirt again. The seconds stretched out, her heart pounding against her tender spine so violently, she wondered if he could see it.

He crawled around the edge of the bed, settling into the same spot as before, reaching out to enclose her hand in his again.

"That's pretty impressive." He squeezed her hand, offering a weak smile. "But I thought it'd be bigger, for some reason."

That was it?

She looked deep into his eyes. If he was hiding something from her, she couldn't see it. Wasn't he bothered by any of this? Or was he just getting better at hiding it? Suddenly, she had a burning desire to know.

"What do you see?" she asked. "When you look at me now?"

"What do you mean?"

Her pulse raced. It was too late. She couldn't take it back now.

"I want to know how you see me."

He was obviously shocked. She couldn't blame him. She was shocked too, but she had to know. She took a deep breath and tried again.

"Do you feel sorry for me? Do you feel guilty, when you look at me? Does it turn you off, seeing this, seeing me like this?" The words tumbled over one another. "The scar, the meds, the metal rods. The nightmares and the giant hole in my memory. The fact that we can't hold hands when we walk down the street together anymore - that I can't do a lot of the things we used to do together. The way I look, the way other people look at me – "

Her breath caught in her throat, her lungs unable to keep up with her mouth.

"Should any of that matter?" he said, interrupting her as she was about to launch into another list.

But did it?

He held her hand tight and she found herself hanging on just as tightly.

"I don't know what it is you're asking me, exactly, but I think you're one of the most incredible people I've ever met. I fell in love with you the moment I saw you, did I ever tell you that? Now, when I look back on it, I think you kind of scared me. You were so confident, so much more adventurous than I was - you weren't afraid of anything. You took risks and you threw yourself into things, heart and soul. We were opposites; when I was scared, you were brave. When I was reluctant, you were already committing. You took me places and showed me things that I never would've seen if it weren't for you."

Tears filled his eyes and his expression took on an exquisite tenderness that made her heart ache for him.

"And then I let you down in the worst possible way," he whispered. "But you gave me a chance to make it up to you, even when I didn't deserve one. So, you want to know how I see you? Beautiful, courageous, determined, generous, incredibly gracious and *graceful* and so much more, I don't think there are even words that cover it."

She felt so light-headed, she couldn't tell if it was from the medication or from the sheer love she saw in his face.

"So, you don't mind... about all of this?" she whispered, choking back tears.

"I mind that it hurts you, and I mind that you thought it would make any difference to the way I feel about you. I also mind that you still feel like you have to hide things from me. But I hope you'll come to trust me again, because all I want is to be here, with you. Nothing else really matters."

There was no mistaking the sincerity in his heart, in his eyes, in his words.

"It's like we're starting all over again isn't it?"

"Yeah, I guess it is," he said, resting his chin on the bed.

She wanted to climb into his arms and have him wrap his body around hers.

"You don't have to worry about this thing with Jimmy," he said. "I'll work it out. It'll be over soon, I promise."

She nodded into the pillow. The pain had driven out all thoughts of Jimmy and the whole sordid mess but now that the pain was receding, the worry seeped back in again. Once all this was over, she would ask him more about what had happened to bring things to a head like this, but first they had to get through the next two days.

"How's your back?" he asked.

"Much better."

"Good."

He smiled, one of those rare, sweet smiles that lit him up from within and made her forget where she was and what she was doing. They would get through today, and tomorrow night the money would be in Jimmy's hands and all this would be over.

*J*ack stared at Ally's empty bed. Beneath it, a pile of cash was crammed into a canvas sports bag, hidden from prying eyes. He felt like he was in a dream world.

Callum had been in touch with Mrs. Watson again and she had reported that nothing seemed out of place in the neighbourhood, which should have set his mind at ease. Instead it had the opposite effect. He was paranoid that they were there in the shadows, watching. He refused to leave Ally's side.

"Look, you need to relax," Callum said from behind him. "Keep it together. It's nearly over."

The sentiment was so similar to what Ben had told him the day his father died that he cringed.

"You messed up," Callum said. "Big deal. It's just temporary, we can deal with temporary."

"We?"

"It's like Ally said, you're not on your own anymore, you don't have to deal with any of this shit alone."

Jack threw him a quick look over his shoulder.

"Thanks."

"Come on, let's go over the plan again."

Jack scrubbed his hands through his hair, sighing.

"I'll take the money over to the house," he said. "You stay with Ally. I'll call you when they're gone."

"See? Sounds simple doesn't it?" Callum insisted. "The only

thing I'm not over the moon about is the fact that you're going over there alone."

"I don't have any choice. I'm hardly in any position to make demands."

"I know but you've got no back-up. What happens if it all goes south somehow?"

"It won't."

"How do you know?"

"Because I know Ben," Jack insisted, with slightly more confidence than he felt. "He's a businessman. That's what this is about, Jimmy said as much. I stepped all over his street cred when I took off. He wants his money so he can tell everyone I didn't get away with it. It's business, that's all."

"Then relax. If it's as straightforward as you say it is, it'll be fine. Come on, we've still got a few hours before you need to head over. Let's get something to eat."

*P*ulling up outside his house, Jack felt the tension coiled inside of him, searching for an outlet. He wanted this over and quickly. He glanced at his watch. He was ten minutes early. As he made his way up the front path, his gaze swept the front of the house and up the street on both sides. Nothing was out of the ordinary but it didn't help to dispel the knot of apprehension in his stomach.

He unlocked the door and walked into the hall, closing it behind him. Switching on the hall light, he walked into the living room with the bag of money and stopped dead.

Jimmy and his gorilla were standing in the middle of the room, watching him. Jimmy glanced down at the bag he was holding and Jack immediately put it down on the floor, stepping away from it. He fidgeted with the keys in his hand, prepared to use them as a weapon if the need arose, but Jimmy just smirked at them pointedly.

"How did you get in here?" Jack demanded, with more bravado than he felt.

"Irrelevant," Jimmy said, indicating the bag at Jack's feet.

"It's all there." Jack shoved the bag towards them with his foot, his heart racing. The gorilla picked it up and unzipped it, showing the contents to Jimmy.

"You don't need to count it," Jack said, eager to get them out of the house.

"I won't. If it's not all there, we'll be back. I'm sure you know that."

They eyeballed each other in silence.

"So that's it then? We're done here?" Jack said.

Jimmy smiled and Jack's blood ran cold.

"Not quite."

CHAPTER TWENTY-THREE

"You pierce my soul. I am half agony, half hope...
I have loved none but you."
- Jane Austen

*C*allum checked his watch again, tapping his foot nervously. He should have heard from Jack by now. He got up and peered through a crack in the curtains, scanning the street in front of Ally's house.

"Call him," she said from her place at the kitchen table. "If you don't, I will. It's been forty minutes. How long does it take to hand over a bag of cash?"

Not bothering to argue, he dug his phone out of his pocket and dialled Jack's number. As he listened to it ringing, he shrugged helplessly across the room at Ally.

"Something's wrong," she said.

Callum disconnected the call, then dialled again.

"Who are you calling?"

"Maggie and Jane. While I check up on him, you three are gonna have a quiet drink at Barney's."

She started to object but he cut her off.

"You'll be safer in a room full of people," he explained. "You all will."

---

*C*allum pulled up slowly behind Jack's car. So, Jack's car was here. He wasn't sure if that was a good or bad thing yet. Keeping his wits about him, he made his way up the front path. In the darkness, the light from within the house illuminated the fact that the front door was ajar. Odd. He crept up the stairs onto the porch but nothing else seemed out of place. Still, he couldn't help the anxiety that sat in his throat. He gently pushed the door open and a cold chill stung the back of his neck.

The hall table had been overturned and lay on its side, contents spewing out of the single drawer.

"Jack?" he called tentatively, panic overwhelming his need for stealth.

No reply. Broken glass crunched beneath his feet as he made his way through the hall and into the living room.

"Are you here?"

He stepped over a dining room chair lying on its side in the living room doorway. More upturned furniture greeted him. Then he noticed a boot, partially obscured behind an overturned armchair.

His heart stopped as the image sensors in his brain put two and two together.

He covered the short distance in a millisecond, dropping to his knees beside him as his heart threatened to leap out of his chest.

Jack lay face down on the floor, out cold.

*C*allum checked his watch again. God, how he hated hospitals. The smell of the place was enough to make him feel sick. He glanced up as the outer doors opened and Maggie, Jane and Ally made their way into the waiting room, blinking in the harsh light. Maggie rushed straight over to him, grabbing him by the arm.

"What the hell went wrong? How is he?" she demanded.

"Keep your voice down," he warned, eyeballing the deputy who was talking to someone at the reception counter. Callum had managed to answer all of his questions without once telling him the truth. He didn't want to screw it up now. Once again, he crossed his fingers that Jack's insistence on keeping the cops out of it was the right thing to do.

"I knew it couldn't be as simple as he said," Ally said, staring up at him with tears in her eyes.

"Let's go and sit down," he said, squeezing her shoulder gently as he indicated the bank of plastic chairs on the far side of the room. "The doc said someone would come and get us when it was okay to go see him."

"What did the doctor say?" she asked, not easily placated.

He sat down beside Maggie and Jane and leaned forward, breathing out noisily.

"In a nutshell? A bruised kidney, a couple of cracked ribs and a moderate concussion."

"Ouch," Maggie winced.

"The concussion seemed to be the thing they were the most worried about," he said, wanting to prepare her. "He said there's some swelling to his brain. He might be out for twenty-four hours or so. They're pumping meds into him to keep him under, something about giving him a chance to heal."

Ally nodded silently, her gaze wandering to the door that led into the emergency room. Callum read her mind. If they could just see for themselves that he was okay, it would make this whole nightmare seem much less terrifying.

"So that guy, Jimmy - any sign of him?" Maggie asked tentatively.

Callum shook his head.

"None. If I were to take a guess, I'd say they grabbed the bag, did a number on Jack and trashed the place before they left."

They watched people come and go, mostly in silence. Callum kept a close eye on Ally, but her gaze was levelled on the door. There didn't seem to be much point in talking.

---

*A*lly was determined to stay calm and remain positive but as the curtain surrounding his bed was pulled aside, revealing the full extent of what Jack had been through, she was tempted to do the complete opposite.

Jack lay propped up on the bed, his previous bruises blending into insignificance faced with the cuts and bruises that now marked his face. Ally shuddered as she slowly moved around the bed towards him. A padded bandage was wrapped around the side of his head. What had done that? A boot? A fist? A weapon of some sort? She choked back tears as a hand squeezed her shoulder.

"Hey, come on," Callum murmured. "He's gonna be okay."

Jack was pale, a cannula clipped to his nose and disappearing behind his ears. He looked like a rag doll that had been kicked around endlessly before finally being thrown on the scrap heap, unloved and unwanted.

Except he was loved and wanted.

The realisation presented itself with such force, fighting its way up from the centre of her soul, that she felt light-headed. She took a moment to fight the sensation of falling. She wheeled forward, reaching for Jack's hand and holding on tight. She willed him to squeeze back, to show some sign that he was with her in more than just body. There was nothing, no sign of recognition.

Outside the curtain, the emergency room buzzed with urgency as medical staff called out instructions and demanded answers as they went about the business of saving lives.

Inside the curtain however, all was quiet.

---

*C*allum glanced in the rear-view mirror as they drove away from the hospital. The cluster of buildings, dominated by a single, concrete, multi-storied structure that seemed to dwarf the surrounding area, loomed in the distance. A shiver crawled up his spine as he tore his gaze away from the building and tried to concentrate on the road ahead.

Ally sat silently in the passenger seat, her mind clearly somewhere else. He half expected her to tell him to slow down. She didn't. In fact, she had barely said a word since they left the emergency room.

It was almost two o'clock in the morning and fatigue wrapped its warm arms around him. He didn't see any sign of the car he had seen a few days prior, and convinced himself that after what happened to Jack, Jimmy and his henchman had probably high-tailed it out of town. Still, he was reluctant to leave Ally alone. They knew where she lived and the image of what they had done to Jack was still fresh in his mind.

Pulling into her driveway twenty minutes later, he killed the engine. The security light came on, bathing them in cool, white light. He glanced over at her.

"Do you mind if I crash on your couch tonight? I'm wrecked."

She shook her head but other than that, made no move to get out of the car.

"How are you doing?" he asked. "You've been pretty quiet."

"I'm fine. Just tired."

He followed her up the front path to the house then took the keys off her and unlocked the door. She didn't argue as he put his finger to his lips then set about checking each room thoroughly. Satisfied finally, he came back to the hallway to find her closing the front door and locking it.

"Sorry. I just wanted to be sure."

"Thanks," she said quietly.

"I don't know about you but I could really do with a drink. You got any whisky or anything lying around?"

"I think there's some in the cabinet in the living room."

He found the whisky and poured them each a healthy dose as she made herself comfortable in the armchair. Handing her a glass, he sank into the couch.

"I hate hospitals. Just the smell is enough to make me want to puke."

"He didn't even look like himself tonight," she said. "I hardly recognised him. Did I look like that, after the accident?"

He saw no reason to lie.

"Not beat up like he is. In fact, you barely had a mark on you. That's what made it so hard to believe, I think."

What might've happened if she had been conscious throughout the accident and its aftermath? What if Jack had given her a choice that night? What if he had said, "Ally, I smell gas. I can either move you to safety or we can stay right here. What do you want me to do?" What would her answer have been?

He glanced over at her but she was staring into the glass in her lap. She seemed so far away from him. Was she thinking about that night too?

"You know that saying, 'everything happens for a reason'?" she asked.

"Yeah."

"Do you believe it?"

Too many holes in that theory for his liking.

"Not really, no. Why, do you?"

"I don't know. Sometimes I think I do. Other times I'm not so sure."

"Discuss," he said simply, taking a swig of whisky while he waited for her to continue.

"I could've died that day but you saved me."

He felt as if he'd been kicked in the chest. He didn't like thinking about that day, much less talking about it, and he knew she felt the same way. Why bring it up now?

"I don't think I ever thanked you," she said. "I wasn't too grateful at the time, I know that, but I am now. I feel like I was given a second chance. If you hadn't found me..." She took a shuddering breath, her head still bowed. "And I think maybe I had to lose Tom to get Jack back. Maybe this is how it had to be?"

Tom had been on his mind, too. Sitting at the hospital, waiting for the news from the doctor, he would have done anything to have been able to talk to him.

"I miss him, too."

"What do you think he would've said, about what's been happening these past few days?"

Callum shook his head, staring somewhere into the distance, between the present and the past.

"I think he'd have wanted to help, just like we did."

They lapsed into silence.

"After I... after that day, I spent a lot of time thinking," she said. "I wanted so badly to be stronger, but I didn't know how. I was lost, and tired - so tired. I kept thinking about my Dad. I was afraid that if he was watching over me, like Gran said he was, he'd be ashamed of me, of what I did."

She seemed so young suddenly. So fragile.

"It took a while," she said, her voice barely above a whisper. "But I finally realised that sometimes you have to have a little faith that things will get better, that this isn't how it ends, that there's more to come."

He saw her as she was that day, lying on her bed, surrounded by photos and an empty pill bottle. His blood ran cold.

"I guess you have to hit rock bottom before you can start climbing again," he mumbled. "I think that day was your rock bottom. It changed you. Just when I thought you'd maxed out on courage, you proved me wrong."

He sighed, running a hand down his face. He was too tired and too damn sober for a conversation like this.

"You make me want to be a better person, did you know that? Someone like me, with all the crap I've done, when I'm around you, you make me feel like I'm better than that, that I can be more than just that guy."

"What guy?"

"The guy who drinks too much," he said, holding his glass aloft. "The guy who screws everything up. The guy who uses his fists more than his brain – *that* guy."

"Is that how you see yourself?" she frowned, wiping her eyes.

He shrugged, thinking of his father and how much he hated how similar they were, despite Tom's influence. There were some things you couldn't escape from.

"Do you know how sad that makes me?" she asked. "That you see yourself that way? You're not that guy, not to me. You literally saved my life, and I'm not just talking about that day. I'm talking about every day, in a million different ways. You're always there for me, whether I need you or not. That's not something I thank you for often enough."

"You don't need to thank me," he said quickly, uncomfortable at how the conversation had turned.

"Yes, I do. I didn't thank Tom enough and I should've. I don't want to make that mistake again."

He glanced up as she wiped her eyes again.

"He knew," he said. "Just like I do. You didn't have to say it. He already knew."

She nodded, her chin trembling as she fought for control. Maybe it was the whisky, or the late hour, or the fact that he was just so damn exhausted, but there was something niggling at him that had to be said, and after four years, now seemed like the right time.

"If you blamed me, even just a little bit, for what happened to you, I get it."

She stared at him, dumbfounded.

"What? Why would I blame you?"

"Because if I hadn't been in the car, you would've been sitting in the passenger seat, right beside Jack. You would've walked away, just like I did."

His gut wrenched as the words burst out of him. Buried as they had been for so long, it was terrifying and strangely liberating to hear himself say them now.

"It happened the way it happened," she said, shaking her head. "That's all."

"But if I hadn't been there – "

"You don't know that. Maybe everything happened exactly the way it was meant to happen?"

There it was again, that strength, that courage. Acceptance. It was a loaded word.

He got up and crossed to the cabinet, topping up his glass with a generous measure.

"Another shot?"

"No, thanks."

He capped the bottle and sank down on the couch again, leaning back into the cushions. The events of the past few days were beginning to weigh him down. He glanced over at Ally, who had leant back in the armchair, looking the way he felt. They should get some sleep. It was going to be a long day tomorrow.

Neither of them moved.

*A*lly picked up Jack's hand, stroking his fingers. She had always loved his hands. They were large, strong and square, almost the exact opposite of her own. Right now, though, they were limp and still, just like the rest of him.

Callum came back into the room with two polystyrene mugs of coffee from the vending machine down the hall.

"Here you go," he said, handing one to her.

"Thanks."

Callum took a seat on the other side of the bed, sipping his coffee.

The morning had been long. Maggie and Jane had spent a couple of hours with them, but they had decided that having four of them hanging around in the small room, just waiting for him to wake up, didn't make sense.

Jack's doctor had visited about an hour ago, on his rounds. Apparently, he'd had a quiet night, his stats were good and they should expect him to regain consciousness anytime now. They'd been warned that he might be disorientated, confused and even nauseous when he woke up, but all of that was normal and should pass quickly.

In the meantime, all they could do was wait.

*J*ack's hand twitched in Ally's. She looked over his bed at Callum, wide-eyed.

"He just squeezed my hand."

Callum sat forward, watching him. Jack's eyeballs moved erratically beneath his lids. Ally immediately reached for the call button on the pillow beside Jack's head. Two nurses obliged soon afterwards, all professionalism and calm. They confirmed that he was indeed waking up but warned them that it could be a while before he came back to full consciousness.

Once again, they settled in to wait.

The minutes turned into hours, but eventually he began to show further signs of regaining consciousness. The call button was pushed once more and two different nurses arrived this time. Giving them room to work, she and Callum reluctantly retreated into the hallway.

Ally could hear Jack responding to them, moaning and squeezing a hand on demand. Her heart soared as she peeked into the room. The nurses checked him over and made notes on his chart, talking to him all the while.

Waiting for the all clear to go back in, Ally fiddled with her grandmother's ring. Finally, the nurses came out into the corridor. One disappeared with a quick smile, while the other laid a comforting hand on Ally's shoulder.

"He's awake and he's doing fine," she smiled. "He seems a little anxious but that should pass soon. Just go with the flow, don't worry if he's not making too much sense. He's likely to get pretty tired so he might drift off to sleep but you're welcome to stay. The doctor will be around later to check on him."

"Thank you so much," Ally smiled gratefully.

The nurse disappeared and Ally re-entered the room. Jack stared blankly at the ceiling as she wheeled slowly towards him, fighting back tears of relief to see him awake finally.

"Hey stranger," she said gently, pulling up beside his bed.

His eyes grew wide as he looked her up and down, staring at her as if he had never seen her before in his life. She put it down to the meds and wheeled closer.

"I'm so sorry," Jack croaked.

"You don't need to be sorry for anything," she soothed, reaching up to take his hand.

He shrank away from her.

"Just relax, you're gonna be okay," she insisted, thrown by his reluctance to let her touch him.

"I'm sorry," he mumbled again.

She looked to Callum for back up and he shrugged, frowning.

"Take it easy, dude. Do you know where you are?"

"Hospital," Jack mumbled.

"That's right," Ally said gently. "And you need to rest now."

"Didn't mean to hurt you."

Tears gathered in his eyes and his voice was cracked and dry. Her heart went out to him.

"Hey, I'm okay, I'm not hurt," she said.

"Didn't know what else to do," he muttered, agitated. "Couldn't just leave you there!"

Ally's heart began to pound as Jack's face twisted into a tortured grimace.

"What's he talking about?" she mumbled, turning to Callum.

"Was trying to save you!" Jack choked, getting more and more worked up.

He grabbed a fistful of blanket but he didn't take his eyes off her. A chill ran through her, like a thousand pin-pricks piercing her skin.

"I don't understand."

Callum's hand was on her shoulder.

"I think he's talking about the accident."

"Was so scared, should've waited, but then the gas... please don't hate me!" Jack sobbed, distraught.

"I don't understand," she mumbled again, looking to Callum for clarification.

Her heart began to pound. Something was wrong. Something was very wrong.

Callum sat down on the edge of the bed beside her, pale and drawn.

"What happened that night?" she whispered, tearing her eyes

away from Jack to fix them firmly on Callum as the floor felt like it was falling away beneath her.

"It's like I told you before," he said. "The car flipped and we ended up banged up against a tree, upside down. I went off to find some help and Jack stayed with you, in the car."

She listened to the part she knew, impatient for him to get to the part she didn't.

"When I got back, he'd dragged you out of the car and was kind of lying on the grass with you on top of him, trying to keep you warm. We could both smell gas - he said he was afraid the car might go up, so he had to move you. He didn't want to Ally, he had to. He didn't have a choice."

Her blood ran cold as the fractured pieces of the puzzle finally slotted together.

"Gas!" Jack blurted out, squeezing his eyes shut, his face contorted into a twisted grimace.

I had a spinal injury and he dragged me out of the car.

Fumbling for the rims of her chair, she felt like she was in one of her nightmares. No matter how hard she pushed, she didn't seem to move. Her arms refused to work, the room swam in front of her. She had to get out of here before she suffocated.

"Ally, wait!"

And then she was finally moving; away from Callum's words, away from Jack's haunted expression, away from everything.

CHAPTER TWENTY-FOUR

"Courage is being scared to death...
and saddling up anyway."
- John Wayne

*J*ack couldn't wait to get out of the hospital. Staring at the ceiling for the past couple of days had just added to the sense of helplessness. He felt surgically removed from the world.

Again.

While he lay in there, flat on his back, Ally was somewhere out there, refusing to take his calls and ignoring his voicemail messages. After packing his few possessions into the bag Callum had brought in for him, he zipped the bag shut.

"You ready?" Callum walked towards him, reaching out for the bag.

"Yeah."

He let Callum carry his bag as the orderly arrived with the wheelchair to deliver him safely to the front door of the hospital.

The orderly chatted happily, seemingly oblivious to the sombre mood, as he pushed him towards the reception area. All Jack could think about was how it felt to be sitting in a wheelchair, having someone else in control. The ache in his soul magnified.

He couldn't think of a single thing to say as he carefully eased himself into the car and they finally pulled out of the parking lot and headed for Callum's house. Callum drove in silence, for which he was grateful. His head pounded but he was reluctant to take any medication. Anything that dulled his senses felt like cheating. He deserved this. He had deserved it from day one. It was time to pay up.

"Have you heard from her?" he asked, his eyes firmly on the road, sunglasses shading them from the harsh light that aggravated his near-constant headache.

"No."

His heart sank. If she wouldn't talk to him, how was he going to explain? Assuming, of course, that he miraculously found the right words.

"Did you call her again?" Callum asked.

"She won't take my calls."

And why should she? He had lied to her.

"Do you need anything from your Dad's place?" Callum asked, as they turned onto the main road back into town.

He shook his head sullenly. What he needed most was Ally.

"Doc said you need to take it easy. No texting, no games and no reading for at least the next week. Are we gonna have any problems with that?"

"I'll cope."

He stared out the window. He hated the idea of the restrictions more than the restrictions themselves. Honestly, any form of visually stimulating exercise seemed to increase his headache so he wasn't going to waste his breath arguing about it.

"I've tried calling her too. She won't pick up."

Jack glanced over as Callum spoke. Even though his attention was on the road, his body language belied his anxiety. His knuckles glowed white where he hung onto the steering wheel, his jaw locked tight as he stared straight ahead.

"I know Maggie's with her, so she's okay, but I really wish she wasn't so damn stubborn."

"I'm sorry I got you into this," Jack mumbled. "I wanted to tell her the truth, but not like this."

"It was my call not to tell her. I screwed up, too. She's bound to be pissed off but I wish she'd just let us explain. I mean, you weren't exactly yourself the other day."

Jack stared at the road ahead. The cold, hard truth was he hadn't been 'himself' for four years. The closest he had felt to his old self had been these past few weeks, when he was with Ally. Despite all the changes, when he was with her he felt like anything was possible again. It was a bittersweet realisation given that he may have now lost that feeling forever.

"Maggie's pissed at me, too," Callum said. "So is Jane. Feels like everyone's pissed at me right now."

"Welcome to my world."

Callum glanced at him sharply but Jack ignored him, too exhausted to bother modifying his behaviour or apologising for it. They drove the rest of the journey in silence.

By the time they got back to Callum's house, Jack was nearly asleep. The simple act of getting out of the car required a major commitment on his part and he struggled to keep his eyes open behind his dark sunglasses. His head pounded and his body ached and he couldn't be bothered fighting either anymore. Callum grabbed his bag from the back seat and carried it inside and again Jack let him, too tired to argue.

As he sank down on the bed in Callum's guest bedroom, all he could think about was closing his eyes and shutting out the world. Blissfully, Callum understood and left him to it. The last thoughts that floated through his addled brain before he drifted off to sleep were restless ones.

When he awoke a couple of hours later, darkness had descended. He lay on the bed and stared at the ceiling, listening to the sounds of the house around him. He could hear Callum in the kitchen and the faint aroma of cooking food made his stomach rumble. The TV was on in the living room, turned down low. He wondered what Ally was doing.

He fidgeted, his ribs aching as he tried to get comfortable. Gingerly, he eased over to one side and pushed himself upwards, carefully swinging his legs over the edge of the bed. He dragged a hand down his face, a shallow sigh easing out of him. His body wanted to slouch from exhaustion, but his ribs hurt less when he sat up straight.

The smells emanating from the kitchen finally overcame him. He made his way to the bathroom, his full bladder demanding release. As he washed his hands afterwards, he caught sight of his reflection in the mirror and stopped, mid-soap.

He was a wreck. His eyes were hollow and one was bright purple with bruising that was only just beginning to fade. The gash on his scalp stung and another on his forehead was held together with a thin strip of tape.

The largest wounds were ones that couldn't be seen. His soul seemed to physically ache and he could almost feel it withering inside of him again. This time though, it was a thousand times more painful.

He tried to push the thought out of his mind as he finished washing his hands and made his way out to the kitchen.

Callum glanced up as he appeared in the doorway. He was in the process of dishing up the best pasta Jack had ever seen. His stomach growled again as he watched, his mouth almost literally watering at the sight of it.

"Good, you're awake. Dinner's ready."

Callum indicated the meal with a flourish. This was real food. Hospital food didn't count. They headed into the living room and

Jack carefully lowered himself onto the couch, wincing at the sharp stab of pain in his ribs.

"Do you need the painkillers?" Callum asked, setting his plate down on the coffee table in front of him.

"Nope," he lied, sitting up straighter than he would have ordinarily. "Don't fuss. I'll grab them if I need them."

Callum shot him a wary glance before sinking gratefully into the waiting armchair. Jack was envious at the freedom of movement he currently lacked.

"Sorry," Callum said, through a mouthful of pasta. "Didn't mean to hover."

Jack shook his head slightly, not daring to risk anything more for fear of aggravating his headache.

"No, I'm sorry, dude. I didn't mean to bite your head off."

"It's fine," Callum said between mouthfuls. "I do fuss, Ally tells me that all the time."

Just the mention of her name set Jack's teeth on edge. Eager for some semblance of normality, he was grateful when they settled into a quiet, contemplative mood with the TV making up for the lack of conversation.

It wasn't long before the hum of the TV started to annoy him however and he reached for the remote, turning it down slightly.

"Sorry," he mumbled. "Do you mind? "

Callum shrugged. Jack tried to get more comfortable. He longed for the simple things, like lounging on the couch. Slowly feeling himself drawn towards the self-pity that had hounded him recently, he tried to snap out of it. Lounging on the couch was hardly a necessity. He was sure Ally would agree with that. She had to put up with far more in the way of inconveniences than he would ever be able to imagine and she wasn't complaining about it.

He remembered watching her get out of the pool. She had more grace in her little finger than he had in his entire body. Far from making him feel better, the realisation just made him feel unworthy. Suddenly, dinner felt like lead in his stomach and he put the plate down on the couch next to him.

"Dude. It's gonna be a long night if you're just gonna sit there staring at the TV like that," Callum said.

Jack rubbed his eyes, not having the energy for evasive manoeuvres. Honesty came easily when there was nothing left to hide.

"I don't know what to do," he admitted. "She won't talk to me, won't let me explain myself, and I don't blame her. I should have told her earlier. I just don't know where to go from here."

"She just needs some time."

Time. That was how they had ended up here in the first place. Time didn't always heal. Sometimes it wounded.

Jack stared at the coffee table in front of him.

"I just can't help feeling that I've run out of second chances, y'know? And if that isn't bad enough, I've dragged you into this and now she's not talking to you either."

"You haven't dragged me into anything," Callum frowned. "I could've told her what really happened that night but I didn't. I screwed up too. You don't have the monopoly on mistakes, y'know. We just need to give her time to work through this, then when she's ready to talk about it, we'll talk about it."

"How can you be so sure?"

"Because that's how it works. You don't think this is the first time I've been in the doghouse do you?" Callum smirked half-heartedly. "You should know me better than that."

Jack eased himself back into the couch with a grimace.

"You're not the one who dragged her out of the car that night. I am."

"You're right. I'm just the one who kept it from her."

They eyeballed each other over the coffee table.

"I stand by what I've always said; it wasn't your fault. You're taking this all on your shoulders and you're making some wild assumptions based on what *might* have happened," Callum insisted. "I understand that you feel some sort of guilt over that - honestly dude, I really do. But taking into account the fact that the car was leaking gas and the very real possibility that it may have exploded into a fireball with her inside it, I would have done exactly what you did. You had no choice. When in the hell are you gonna let yourself off the hook for that?"

Callum's words hit him square in the gut and sucked the air right out of his lungs. Hadn't Ally said the same thing to him just recently?

"You were trying to save her life," Callum said, leaning forward. "You did the right thing, the *only* thing."

"I should've told her earlier."

"Yeah, you should've. But what's done is done, you can't live in the past. You've gotta do what's right for her, and you, right now. Leave all that shit back there, where it belongs."

Callum's even gaze penetrated through the haze of confusion and self-pity that Jack found himself swimming in.

"The only way she's gonna get past this is if you do, simple as that."

Jack took a deep breath, allowing the words to sink in. It made sense. Connections burst into life like a mini firework display inside his head. Before Jimmy turned up, they were getting on fine and it was because he had pushed all the negative, self-pitying guilt to the back of his mind. But then Jimmy turned everything on its head and she almost got hurt. Because of him. The fireworks dimmed and the void suddenly became bigger and blacker and far more frightening than before.

"All I've done is make things worse by being here," he said. "I never should've come home."

"For Christ's sake!" Callum rolled his eyes.

Jack's stomach spun in circles. Suddenly he wanted to throw up, but Callum wasn't finished.

"Hey - you haven't been here the last few years, you haven't seen what I've seen. She needs you. She may not have said so in words but she sure as hell has in every way that counts. She's been different these past few weeks and that's down to you. Maybe you've been so wrapped up inside your own head that you haven't noticed it, or maybe you just don't know how bad it really was for her, but she's changed and I have no doubt it's because you're here. You've brought her out of herself more than anyone else ever could, including me."

Callum's blue eyes shone with an intensity that begged him to understand. Jack thought he saw something else in there too, something that looked a hell of a lot like sorrow.

"Don't you get it?" Callum pleaded. "She needs you. She's always needed you. Maybe that's why she's taking this so hard. She's been fighting for so long to not need anyone, to be independent, that it's second nature. You need to show her that it's okay to need you."

***

*A*lly sat at her kitchen table, staring at the cup of cold coffee in front of her. Questions ate away at her, one after another after another.

Why hadn't anyone told her about what happened that night? What would make Callum keep something like that from her? Had dragging her out of the car caused her injury, or made it worse? How should she feel about all of this? Should she be angry, and if so, at who? Jack or Callum or both of them?

She pushed the cup of coffee away with a sweep of her hand, folded her arms on the table in front of her and laid her head on them, closing her eyes. She heard movement from the kitchen doorway but couldn't muster the energy to look up. A warm hand rested on her shoulder, squeezing gently. Long hair that smelt vaguely of oranges tickled her ears as Maggie draped an arm around her shoulders and enveloped her in a hug.

"You need to talk to them."

"And say what?" she murmured, not bothering to lift her head. Maggie didn't answer.

---

*C*allum knocked on Ally's front door with more confidence than he felt. The longer he stood there, the more he felt the weight of what had happened pushing down on him. When Maggie answered the door, she reached up to give him a quick hug, any residual anger and disappointment forgotten.

"Good luck," she whispered.

He nodded, releasing her. She picked up her handbag from next to the hall table and made a hasty exit, closing the front door quietly behind her. Drawing a steadying breath, he walked into the living room.

Ally sat on the couch, staring at the floor. When she looked up at him there was an air of helplessness about her that screamed at him over the silence.

"Hey," he said tentatively.

"Hi."

He made his way over to the armchair opposite her and sat there, perched on the edge. Now that he was here, he wasn't sure he was doing the right thing. Nothing in her expression encouraged him. She looked lost and broken and he couldn't help but feel responsible for that, at least in part.

"I'm sorry," he said gently, fearful of making things worse. "I should've told you long before now."

She glanced down at her hands.

"Why didn't you?"

He drew in a deep breath and exhaled slowly, going over that night for the thousandth time and dwelling on his reasons for not telling her what really happened. They were many and varied but the main one was obvious.

"Because I didn't want to hurt you. You had enough to deal with, it just didn't make sense to lay any of this on you then."

She nodded but she didn't look up.

"Would it have changed anything?" he asked. "If you'd known back then?"

"I don't know," she said, finally raising her head to look at him with haunted eyes that cut him to the bone. "How could I know that now? It's impossible to tell but at least I would've known the truth."

She was right. His high-handed attitude of 'it's not my place to tell her' now seemed self-serving at best. He ran his palms down the front of his jeans nervously.

"He thinks it was his fault," she said flatly. "That's why he left."

He nodded, feeling sick to his stomach.

"And you knew this."

Reason flew out the window. He wished he could have also known then the pain it would cause her now by not telling her. He would have sucked it up and told her the truth then and maybe she would be stronger for it. He scrambled for the words to explain but they tumbled out before he could think straight.

"By the time I realised he wasn't coming back, it was too late," he said. "Too much time had passed. I thought that telling you then would just make things worse."

She hung her head and he was grateful for the reprieve, as cowardly as he knew that was.

"I'm sorry," he said. "I really am. I've never been more sorry about anything in my life. I was only trying to spare you from this but I can see now that I was so wrong. I don't blame you if you hate me."

She sighed as if the weight of the world were on her shoulders, clasping her hands together under her chin.

"I don't hate you," she said, looking over at him. "Of course I don't. I just... I don't know. I guess I just wish I could turn back the clock y'know? Go back to before all of this happened. Things were so simple then weren't they?"

The pain and hope in her eyes was almost unbearable and all he could do was nod.

"But we can't," she said, her hands falling into her lap in a gesture of defeat. "So, I guess we're stuck here, trying to make the best of everything."

"Jack loves you."

She glanced away from him, as if she couldn't stand to hear it, but he had to continue, for all their sakes.

"He's hurting, Ally. He was in an impossible situation that night. He had a split second to make a decision and he made the best one he could. I would've done exactly the same thing, and so would you, if the situation had been reversed."

His words hung in the air between them and he waited anxiously, his hand flexing nervously around his closed fist.

"I know that, and I don't blame him," she murmured finally, looking up. "But it doesn't seem to matter either way because he blames himself, he said so."

"It's tearing him apart."

"I know, but there's nothing I can do about that."

Her gaze settled somewhere between the two of them, seeing things he couldn't.

"You could talk to him?" he said.

"I don't know what to say."

"Tell him what you just told me."

"What if it doesn't make any difference? What if he can't let it go?" She fixed him with a heartbreaking stare. "I can't lose him again but if he can't let it go, I can't be around him. I don't want to be like some kind of trigger for this stuff he carries around inside of him."

Callum stood up and walked over to sit beside her on the couch. He wrapped his arms around her and pulled her close.

"You need to try," he said. "You'll never forgive yourself if you don't."

———

*J*ack stood on the lawn in the rain, staring at his Dad's house. His hair stuck to his head and his clothes were soon soaked through but still he couldn't bring himself to go inside. Callum had told him that the place needed some tidying up after Jimmy had trashed it and he couldn't face that, not yet. It was just another reminder of how he had messed everything up.

Instead, he got in his car and drove over to Ally's. He had no idea what he was going to say to her but he had to see her. Even if she yelled and screamed at him, it was better than this silence. When he pulled up outside her house, her driveway was empty. It felt as if his lungs were collapsing. The message she was sending was pretty damn clear. He had pushed her too far. There were no more second chances. He had his one shot to get this right and he blew it.

With no idea what to do or where to go or how to fix anything, he headed for the one place he hoped he could find some peace.

He pulled up outside the cemetery gates and cut the engine. In the sudden silence, the rain drummed a steady beat against the roof of the car. On such a grey, wet day he hadn't expected the cemetery parking lot to be so busy but misery loves company. Three other cars were parked outside the gate. One of them, he realised as he looked closer, was Ally's.

What was she doing here? Was she looking for the same thing he was?

He got out of the car and started up the central walkway, trudging through the steady stream of water running down the concrete path. The weather suited his mood, easing the near-constant ache in his head from the concussion, although the ache in his heart seemed to grow. With each step, new anxieties and self-doubts flooded through him. He had no idea if Ally was visiting his father's graveside but it seemed like a good bet. What reception would he get if she was? He almost turned back to the car and waited for her there but he pushed on.

When he finally saw her, he froze. She was standing in front of his father's grave, head bowed low, soaked to the skin. An involuntary shiver ran through him that had nothing to do with the weather. Water dripped from his eyelashes and he blinked, running a quick hand over his eyes to clear them. She didn't move for the longest time.

A million thoughts rattled through him. Most of them didn't even have words attached to them, just fleeting emotions, racing through his subconscious, leaving emptiness in their wake.

Grief. Love. Guilt. Shame. An all-encompassing desire to turn back time.

He didn't even realise he had started walking again until she looked up and their eyes met. The rain made it impossible to tell for sure but he thought she was crying. She slipped an arm out of one of her crutches and smoothed her wet hair back from her face.

"I didn't know you'd be here," he said, willing his voice not to break. "Just in case you think I'm following you or something."

She slid her arm back into her crutch and shrugged helplessly.

"I just wanted to... I don't know. I think I just really needed to talk to him."

Her eyes were red-rimmed and dark with a soul-crushing intensity that hurt him to look at. He tore his gaze away from her to stare at his father's grave. It was still covered in flowers, some of them now dying, some fresh and new. He still had trouble relating this mound of earth to his father. He half expected him to come up behind him and put his hand on his shoulder.

"Callum told me what happened, the night of the accident. That's why you left, isn't it?"

It stung to hear her say it, much more than he thought it would. She knew. He should feel relieved, some sense of having done the thing he set out to do should have flooded through him. Instead, he felt as if he stood on the edge of a very high cliff, waiting for her to push him over. In answer to her question all he could do was nod.

"He said the car was leaking gas."

He nodded again, his head pounding. She moved so she was facing him, and there was no escape from her penetrating gaze. She stood up straighter, tilting her chin in defiance. Where she found the strength to do that, he didn't know. It was all he could do to remain upright when his entire body wanted to curl into a ball, his back to the world. Rain trickled down her face, softening her expression, but her eyes shone out at him like beacons.

"I know I've said this before," she said. "But I want you to really hear me this time. It wasn't your fault. There's no blame here, Jack. Do you understand what I'm saying?"

She was willing him to believe, he could feel it. He desperately wanted to but letting go of the guilt was like closing his eyes and jumping into the abyss.

"I can't fix this for you, just like you can't fix what happened to me. You don't need me to forgive you, you need to forgive yourself," she said, her eyes now an intense blue, piercing his soul. "When you came back, you told me you'd do anything to make it up to me, remember? You promised me you'd what-ever it takes. Well, this is what it takes. This is what I need from you. I need you to let go of everything that happened that night. I need you to stay, but not with that hanging over us."

The pain was excruciating. He felt as if he were being pulled in two different directions, physically split down the middle. Guilt over what he did that night was such a big part of who he thought he was; without it he was lost. Taking the guilt out of the equation, what was left?

"Please," Ally begged, her chin quivering. The strength he had seen in her just moments before seemed to melt away. "I *need* you."

And then it was blindingly clear. He was here to make a difference. He came back because he needed to clear his conscience, make up for what he had done. He had promised her he would, he had promised his father he would. It was time to let go of the words and let his actions speak for themselves.

"I'll do anything for you," he whispered.

And he meant it.

CHAPTER TWENTY-FIVE

"No man is an island."
- John Donne

*J*ack unlocked the side door to his father's garage and reached around the corner for the light switch. As bright, white light bathed the interior, he breathed a sigh of relief. Unlike the house, the garage was untouched. Flashes of that night rushed in on him.

Jimmy throwing him across the room. A boot in the ribs. Smashing glass. Splintering wood.

If he was going to repair what was broken, he needed tools and cleaning equipment, which was why he was out here. Looking around now, it felt like an oasis; calm, quiet, tidy.

He ran his hand over his father's car, the paint smooth and cool beneath his fingers. Tools were neatly lined up and hanging from the pegboard behind the workbench. Labelled cardboard boxes stood stacked up against the far wall.

A shape, covered in a pale sheet, at the far end of the garage caught his eye.

It couldn't be. Could it?

Even though his mind told him it was impossible, he found himself gravitating towards it just to be sure. He reached out and pulled the sheet away, doubling it back over itself to reveal the gleaming black body of his Ducati. He backed away from it slowly, as if it were some kind of hologram that might disappear if he blinked.

"Jack?"

Callum's voice in the doorway startled him but he couldn't tear his eyes away from the bike.

"I... I don't understand," he mumbled, shaking his head.

"What?"

"Did you know about this?"

"Know about what?"

He dragged himself away from the bike and turned to Callum, searching for the words to explain himself.

"I needed money," he said finally. "A couple of years back, and I asked him to sell it for me. He said he did. He sold it, sent me the money."

Callum frowned, his gaze flitting from Jack to the bike and back again.

"Then what the hell is it still doing here?"

"Beats the hell out of me," Jack ran a hand through his hair, frowning at the bike. "I don't understand. Why did he say he sold it if he didn't?"

Callum left the doorway and leant against the car, folding his arms.

"Maybe he wanted you to have the bike *and* the money?"

That sounded like his father, alright. He leant back against the car beside Callum, deflated.

"You two spent a lot of time on that bike. Maybe he just

wanted to make sure it would be waiting for you when you came home?"

The hollow ache in Jack's chest intensified.

"He never gave up on you."

Jack stared at the bike, sleek black body gleaming under the bright white light. The plan had been for him and Ally to take a cross-country trip, opening their eyes to the world outside of this town. The irony of it.

"I'll sell it," he said.

"Like hell!"

"I can use the money to pay you and Ally back."

"Think again, dude," Callum grunted. "Tom obviously wanted you to have it. He knew you loved it, that's why he kept it. You can't just get rid of it, that's like insulting his memory. I don't want anything to do with that blood money and I'm pretty sure Ally wouldn't either."

"The trip across country, that was our dream, mine and hers."

"So, find another dream."

He made a good point. Standing up straight, he walked over to the bike and pulled the sheet the rest of the way off, dropping it onto the garage floor. He ran his hand over the glossy paint.

It was a message from beyond the grave. His father hadn't given up on him. Somehow, he knew that one day, he would do the right thing.

---

*B*arney's was bustling. All the pool tables were taken and music blared out of the jukebox even though it was barely five o'clock. Jack watched absentmindedly as Harry took order after order, the bar humming with the promise of the night ahead.

By contrast, their corner table was sombre, removed from the surrounding melee. A black cloud hung over them, heavy with grief. The lack of animated conversation and hijinks set them apart from the other tables.

There was a bottle of whisky in the centre of the table, a full glass beside it.

"For Tom," Callum had said solemnly, setting the bottle down next to it.

Maggie had arranged for the beautiful wreath that they had lain on his father's grave barely an hour earlier. They had all insisted that he have the honour of placing it himself and it had taken all he had in him to do so. It felt final, like he had closed a chapter in his life. The disconcerting part was that he didn't feel ready to say goodbye just yet. He wasn't sure he would ever be ready for that.

Before long, one by one, they began to make their way home. Maggie left first, her eyes still red-rimmed as she hugged them all goodbye. Jane followed not long after. Jack squirmed in his chair, his ribs still tender as he tried to get comfortable. He glanced over at Ally. She gave him a half-hearted smile that he saw right through.

"Let's get out of here," he said over the music, indicating the door.

She nodded, reaching for her crutches as he stood up. He stretched, easing his cramped body, then put his hand on Callum's shoulder, leaning down again.

"You wanna blow this popsicle stand?"

"Think I'm gonna stay a while."

Jack could barely hear him over the music but his expression was clear enough. Callum pushed his chair back and stood up to gather Ally into a warm embrace. As he turned, Jack offered his hand and, after a moment, Callum took it.

"Thank you," Jack mouthed, not bothering to shout this time.

Callum pulled him into a brief hug, which both surprised and overwhelmed him. As they drew apart, Callum grabbed the back of his neck and pulled him close again.

"Don't let her go this time," he said, just loud enough for Jack to hear.

Surprised, Jack could only nod. The words played on his mind as he took Ally home.

---

*J*ack had been quiet ever since they left Barney's. Ally could relate. Her shoulders ached after the lengthy walk up to Tom's grave from the cemetery gate but the ache in her heart was worse. She could only imagine how he was feeling.

She had not been looking forward to today. With everything that had been going on since Tom's death, there had been little time to grieve for him. Now, she felt that need welling up inside of her, demanding to be set free.

She tried to concentrate on the coffee she was supposed to be making but the kitchen counter blurred in front of her.

"Hey," Jack said gently, walking over to stand behind her, wrapping his arms around her.

She sniffed back more tears, nodding, although not brave enough to try and speak. He seemed to understand and she wasn't surprised when he rested his chin on the top of her head, pulling her closer. She should be comforting him, not the other way around, yet she had the feeling he was seeking comfort as much as giving it. She closed her eyes and leaned back into his chest as the tears slipped down her cheeks.

"It's okay," he whispered into her ear.

She had no idea how long they stood there like that. After a while, she realised she wasn't the only one crying. Jack's chest heaved behind her as the sorrow seeped out of him. She felt herself giving in to it, too, feeling safer somehow, with Jack behind her.

Trust me.

The first time he had said it to her, she had fought her head and gone with her heart. Now, with his arms around her, it felt as if both head and heart were in sync finally.

As the tears and raw grief subsided, she turned in his arms. He put on a brave face, despite the red-rimmed eyes, smoothing her hair and tucking it behind her ear.

"He loved you, so much," he whispered.

She sighed, nodding. The feeling was very mutual.

"He loved you, too. You know that, right?"

He didn't answer, instead kissing her gently on the forehead, and a moment later, on the lips. She closed her eyes as his lips covered hers, salty and warm. It still felt surreal, like it was happening for the first time. His kiss felt different now, compared to before. Sweeter, somehow. Knowing. Patient.

---

*J*ack leaned against the kitchen table as Ally finished making coffee. All he wanted was to be near her. With the chaos that seemed to follow him wherever he went, she was the tranquillity he craved. When he was around her, anything seemed possible.

As if to illustrate his point, she moved between table and counter, transporting coffee mugs and a pot of hot coffee. Every move was no doubt carefully coordinated but she made it seem effortless.

He rubbed his eyes, tired and sore from crying. He should be embarrassed about breaking down in front of her but he wasn't. It felt right, to grieve together. It was one of only a handful of times that anything had felt right since he got home. It wasn't lost on him that Ally was the common denominator.

He dug his hand into his pocket, pulling out the small heart pendant on a thin gold chain. The memories lodged in his throat.

Two of his greatest loves, tied up in one small trinket. He glanced up to find her staring at him, wide-eyed.

"I found it at the house," he said, as if reading her thoughts. "It must've been in a drawer or something, but I found it on the floor in the hallway when we were tidying up. What I don't understand is how it got there."

Her eyes flew to the pendant in his hand.

"I didn't know what else to do," she said in a small voice.

Jack's fist closed tight around the heart. So many memories.

"You were wearing it that night," he said.

She leaned back against the kitchen counter.

"I thought it was gone, lost forever, but Callum found it. It was in the car. He went to the scrap yard after it was towed and there it was, hooked in the carpet. The chain was broken but the heart was still there."

The chain was broken.

Jack shuddered. It must've been ripped off her when the car rolled. Visions of that night sent a cold chill crawling up the back of his neck.

"When I realised that you weren't coming home, I gave it back to Tom. I'm sorry, I just thought that he should have it. I couldn't keep it. After you left, it didn't feel right."

The necklace was a symbol of the love he had abandoned. He understood, as much as it hurt.

"He would've been grateful."

"I just felt like…" she sighed, "It was the right thing to do. It was your mother's, after all."

He opened his fist and stared at the necklace again, recalling vividly the night he had given it to Ally. It wasn't big or expensive but it was his mother's and it had sentimental value far beyond the physical.

"It was yours, after it was hers," he said, looking over at her. "And I'd really like you to have it back."

He walked towards her holding the necklace gently, as if

holding it too tightly would break it. His heart raced the same way it had when he had given it to her the first time, all those years ago.

"Are you sure?" she whispered, beautiful blue-green eyes shining.

"I'm sure."

He unfastened the clasp and gently pushed her hair aside. His fingertips brushed against her skin as the pendant settled itself beneath the hollow of her neck.

"That's better," he said, as she slowly turned to face him.

She caressed the pendant gently, as if afraid it might disappear again. He reached up to do the same, capturing her fingers in his, the tiny gold heart safe in both their hands.

---

*A*lly lay on the floor in her living room, a bundle of nerves. She checked her watch for the third time in five minutes, willing time to slow.

"You're doing the right thing," Callum said, rotating her right hip and leg slowly outward, then inward again.

She wasn't so sure now. Panic gripped her insides. She hoped he could see it so she wouldn't have to say anything. He was so good at reading between the lines normally, why wasn't it working now?

"I'm serious. You know you have to do this, you owe it to him and to yourself. Just try to relax."

It wasn't that easy. While Callum bent and stretched her useless legs right in front of her, Jack was on his way over to her house right this minute. She should never have let him talk her into this. He didn't know what he was getting into. She did. That only made it worse.

"You invited him over, remember?" Callum reminded her, rubbing it in as he lay her right leg down and picked up her left.

In theory, at the time, it had seemed like the sensible thing. She couldn't keep hiding the range-of-motion exercises from him forever. But in practice - actually inviting him over, so he could see - that was something else entirely.

"I don't think I can do this," she said, silently pleading for understanding.

"Sure you can."

The message was clear; he wasn't going to help her out here. She was on her own.

A knock at the door stopped her heart momentarily. Callum laid her leg down gently on the floor again.

"I'll get it," he said, getting up.

As he left the room, she couldn't even bring herself to beg him not to open it. She tried to relax but her body had other ideas. Every muscle was taut. She was balancing on a knife edge.

Fight or flight?

She desperately wanted to disappear but she could already hear Callum and Jack talking in the hallway. In a moment or two, it would be too late.

"So, how was your first day at work?" she heard Callum ask. "Monty can be a bit of a tough nut, but from what I've heard, he's fair."

"Yeah, he's tough. And I'm still waiting on my final medical clearance so it was just light stuff today. But it's a job and I'm grateful. I'll take whatever I can get. It's not like I can afford to be picky."

Her heart pounded so violently, she could feel every beat reverberate inside her chest.

"Sounds like you deserve a beer, then."

"You read my mind. Where's Ally?"

"Living room."

Jack appeared in the doorway, smiling and relaxed. The exact opposite of how she felt. She smiled up at him from her place on the floor but her face felt like clay.

"Hey," he said. "Sorry I'm late. I got held up filling out some forms and stuff at work."

"Hi. No, it's okay."

Which was a complete lie but she found herself saying it anyway. She wanted to say something else - ask him how his day went, somehow distract him from what was happening, but the words just weren't there.

"We're almost done here actually," Callum said, walking past him to kneel on the floor at her feet. "Grab yourself a beer from the fridge. Sounds like you've earned it."

"I won't argue with that."

Ally focused her attention on Callum, afraid to look at Jack. He must be able to feel this, the mood change, the strange vibe in the air? Thankfully he headed for the kitchen, giving her the opportunity to breathe again.

Callum had her right leg in his hands, pushing her knee up towards her stomach slowly. Their eyes met for a moment and with a brief nod of his head, he tried to reassure her. Her emotions were so near the surface, she didn't know whether to laugh or cry.

She became aware of Jack standing in the kitchen doorway, watching them. Callum glanced over at him and the silence in the room became even more uncomfortable. She wanted someone to ease the tension but she knew it couldn't be her. She was too busy concentrating on breathing to try anything as complicated as speaking. What was he thinking? She was too scared to even look at him to see if she could read his expression. Callum repeated the same movement a couple of times and then switched to her left leg. Jack walked over to the armchair nearest him and sat down.

"So, this is what the yoga mat is for?" he asked.

She stubbornly refused to look at him but she saw him take a sip from his beer bottle out of the corner of her eye. Callum waited for her to answer him but she couldn't.

"Three times a week, twenty-minute sessions," he said instead, her knight in shining armour.

"So, what is it you're doing, exactly?" Jack asked.

Enough was enough. There was no way she was going to drag this out any longer than she had to.

"I think we're probably about done here, aren't we?" she said, pushing herself up onto her elbows as Callum laid her leg down on the mat again.

"I'll go get a beer and take it outside," he said, standing up. "I think you guys need to talk."

She glared at him as he left the room, directing all her frustrations at him, even though she knew it wasn't his fault. Right now, she felt so lost, she barely recognised her own living room.

She pushed herself upright and sat there, staring at her hands clasped tightly together in her lap, wondering how she was going to explain this. Then Jack was sitting on the floor beside her, reaching over to rest his hand on hers.

"What's up?" he asked softly.

She stared at his hand on top of hers. Two weeks ago, she was holding his hand in the hospital, begging him to wake up. Now here he was, wanting to talk, and she had no idea what to say to him.

Couldn't he see for himself? She was sitting on the floor wearing lycra exercise pants that should be tight and curve-hugging but instead were loose-fitting and shapeless. He had just watched Callum throwing her legs around like they weren't even attached to her body anymore. Couldn't he *see*?

"I can't read your mind," he murmured, squeezing her hand. "You need to talk to me. Please?"

Maybe it was just as well he couldn't read her mind. It was such a mess in there, she was having enough trouble under-standing it herself. She took a deep breath that seemed to rattle around inside her chest. Nothing she had planned to say came out of her mouth. None of the carefully prepared speech, explaining about the range-of-motion exercises and why she needed them. Instead, what came tumbling out were the fears and insecurities she'd been hiding for so long.

"I knew they weren't telling me everything," she said. "In the hospital, Callum and Tom, they told me that it was the meds I was on that were making my legs numb but I knew. I don't know how. Maybe it was the look on their faces when they said it but I knew even before they told me the truth. I was so scared. I couldn't see beyond tomorrow. Then one day, a long time later, I woke up and realised what living like this for the rest of my life really meant. This is it, this is what it's going to be like, always."

She took a shuddering breath.

"I freaked out. I just... I didn't know how I was going to handle it. Forever, y'know? It's a long time. And then I saw what it was doing to everyone else. It hurt so much to see them like that. I hated it, I felt responsible for it. So, I just hid the pain and the fear and everything else, just shoved it down deep where they wouldn't see. It sounds weird but it gave me a sense of power, of control, when I didn't have control over anything else."

Jack's thumb stroked the side of her hand and she took a moment to organise her thoughts before continuing.

"It's funny, you think about all the big things first, the stuff you'll never be able to do again. Walking, running, dancing, that kind of stuff, the obvious stuff. But it's the other stuff that takes longer to sink in. I'll never stand up in the shower or wear a pair of four inch heels or high-dive at the pool or have normal energy levels. I'll never be really, truly independent."

Jack squeezed her hand and she took a deep breath, letting it out slowly. She could feel the tears building behind her eyes. She had to get this over with, before she lost it completely.

"The muscles in my legs and hips need to be stretched regularly to stop them from permanently contracting. Wearing my braces helps but it's not enough so Callum stretches them for me. They're called range-of-motion exercises. I love him for helping but I hate it too, y'know? Watching him just... it kills me. It makes me feel so – "

Her breath caught in her throat and she shook her head.

"What?"

She couldn't bear to say it aloud.

"So, this is what you meant when you said that Callum helps you with massage and exercise?"

She nodded, sniffing back the tears she was determined she would not let fall, not this time.

"I can't pretend I have the first clue how that feels," he said, his voice thick with emotion. "But like I told you the other night, when I look at you I see a strong, capable, courageous, beautiful, determined and stubborn woman. That's who you are. All the rest - wheelchair, braces, crutches, pain meds, massage, this range-of-motion stuff and probably a whole lot of other stuff I don't even know about yet - that's not who you are, that's just something that happened to you. It doesn't define you as a person. You're still you."

Tears burned her eyes and she couldn't bring herself to look at him. To do so would mean showing him how much her heart had been aching to hear this from him.

"This is probably gonna come out all wrong so please don't hold it against me, but I really want to help. I really want to do something for you that's not just you letting me help for the sake of making me feel better about it. I want to *really* help, Ally. I want to be part of your life, not just standing on the outside, watching. I'm not saying I want Callum to step aside or anything but I'd really like to be able to help you with stuff like this."

She looked up at him, shaking her head, sure the raw terror that rose up inside her was written all over her face. He looked as close to tears as she was and before she could speak, he pulled her into his arms.

"Do you trust me?" he whispered into her hair.

She could feel his heartbeat, strong and fast. They sat locked together on the floor, although inside her head, she squirmed and wriggled, searching for an answer.

"That's not what this is about," she mumbled into his shoulder.

"I think it is. Do you trust me, yes or no?"

She pulled away, staring at him in pure desperation. It felt like the entire universe was holding its breath. Slowly, she nodded.

"Then let me help. Please?"

She had said she wanted him to stay. She wanted him to be a part of her life again. *This* was her life now, for better or for worse. No more secrets, no more hiding things from each other.

Afraid to speak in case she lost it altogether, all she could do was nod.

The great release she'd been expecting didn't come. Instead there was a quiet acceptance, an inner sigh of relief, a relinquishing of some of the fear she had been holding onto for so long.

She leaned into him again and he wrapped his arms around her, pulling her close.

CHAPTER TWENTY-SIX

"And ever has it been known that love knows not its own depth until the hour of separation."
- Khalil Gibran

Ally reached for the step nearest her and pulled herself onto it, her shoulders submerged in the water. She held onto the edge, watching her legs take on a life of their own as they bobbed in the water in front of her.

Callum swam towards her, his stroke long and powerful, strong shoulders propelling his arms through the water. He stopped near her, treading water, blinking as he wiped the water from his face. He shook his short dark hair like a dog, roughing it up with his hand.

"Don't tell me you're tired already," she smiled.

"Pacing myself," he winked.

Over his shoulder, Jack slowly made his way towards them. He was obviously still recovering from his injuries but his stroke was smooth and even, if a little short. She loved watching him swim, sleek and rhythmic. His body seemed longer in the water, his feet kicking up a trail of white water behind him, elongating him. He dove under a lane marker and gracefully popped up on the other side.

A few moments later, he pulled up beside Callum, blinking to clear the water from his eyes. His hair looked jet black when it was wet and he roughed it up exactly like Callum had done, so that it formed spikes all over his head. She had to fight the urge to reach out and run her hand over the glossy locks, smoothing them down again.

"I haven't swum laps for years and I still managed more than you," he said, pushing Callum good-naturedly. "And I'm carrying an injury."

"Hardy-har, funny boy. I forgot about that damn competitive streak you have."

"That's a good one, coming from you," Jack grinned. "Rough night last night?"

Callum flipped him the bird and headed towards the steps, splashing Jack in the face as he passed him.

"Real mature, dude," Jack said, wiping the water from his face with a smile.

Callum reached down to squeeze Ally's shoulder.

"And on that note, I'm outta here. I'll see you guys tomorrow night."

Ally's insides turned to jelly. Tomorrow night Callum would be showing Jack how to perform the range-of-motion exercises. Even though she had agreed to Jack learning the ropes, she still had echoes of apprehension settling in her stomach like butter-flies. As if reading her mind, Callum winked at her as he exited the pool, heading towards the bench that held his towel.

"If you're worried about tomorrow, don't be," Jack said, and she turned back to him.

The exquisite tenderness in his expression made her heart sing. He leaned forward and took her ankles in his hands. She watched him run his hands up her calves, trying to mentally substitute the image for the sensation that went along with it. He moved in closer, his hands sliding over her knees and up the outside of her thighs, finally taking her by the waist and pulling her off the step into his arms as he took her down into the pool with him.

Breathless, she draped her arms around his neck. The warm water washed over them as he moved them in lazy circles. She was almost afraid to breathe in case she broke whatever spell had been cast over them, the pool fading into the background.

Then his lips were on hers and, closing her eyes, she let herself go. His warm, wet lips pressed gently against hers, his tongue easing them apart to gain access to her mouth. Chlorine tickled her taste buds as his arms encircled her waist, pulling her even closer.

Slowly, he pulled away and she opened her eyes, not wanting to let go of the moment. He smiled at her, the kind of smile that said he wanted her - all of her. She was captivated by it.

"Can you feel that? Can you feel how much I've missed you?" he whispered, nuzzling her neck.

Alarm bells began to ring, loud and clear. She couldn't feel anything but his chest pressed tight to hers, his arms wrapped around her.

She shook her head. His smile faded and he began to run his fingertips over her back, sending shivers through her.

"Then let me tell you," he said, barely missing a beat. "I've missed being this close to you, holding you like this. You're so beautiful." He leaned in to kiss her again, softly this time, and mercifully brief as she struggled to keep a thought in her head. "I love how silky your skin feels when it's wet."

He ran his hands over her shoulders and she literally felt herself melting beneath his touch. She was afraid to move in case it should make him stop. He smiled again and she tried to smile back but the alarm bells in her head began ringing once more.

She could feel the fantasy draining away, disappearing down the plug hole, leaving her with a reality that petrified her.

Everything was different now. The question was, how different?

Jack began to move backwards and the water swished around them until they were at the side of the pool and she was reaching blindly for the edge.

"What's the matter?" he asked, still holding her.

Panic overwhelmed her, robbing her of the words. All she could do was stare at him pitifully.

"What is it?" he soothed, worry settling into the creases around his eyes. "Did I come on too strong? I'm sorry, I didn't mean to scare you."

She reached deep down inside and reminded herself that she was stronger than this.

"There hasn't been anyone since the accident." God, she hated how pathetic that sounded. "I don't know how to... or if I can even... I don't want it to be weird, for either of us. I don't want you to be disappointed."

His expression softened and he cupped her cheek with his hand.

"You could never disappoint me. When the time comes, we'll work it out. I promise."

He pulled her closer. Letting go of the edge, she gave herself over to him.

---

*I*t was a quiet Saturday morning and the sun was already beating down as the clean-up at Tom's house began. Everyone had insisted on helping out, even though Jack was sure he could handle it himself. Apparently, that wasn't an option.

They piled into two cars and headed over there, determined

to put the place back into some kind of order after Jimmy's visit. Jack had mostly avoided the house since he'd got out of the hospital, a couple of quick visits reminding him far too vividly of that night. But as much as he had appreciated Callum's hospitality, he wanted his own space again. A part of him also realised he was avoiding the house for another reason, too. It was time to start getting used to the ghosts, not hiding from them.

He and Callum righted the furniture while Ally, Maggie and Jane helped clear up the contents of the spilled drawers and the broken glass and debris in the living room and hallway. After a couple of hours, the house was habitable again and he was starting to feel as if things were finally coming together.

The only thing missing was his father. He knew that would take a lot longer than a couple of hours to come to terms with.

"Hey, look at what I found," Ally smiled, holding up an album cover.

She sat in an armchair by his father's 1960s radiogram, holding a bunch of albums on her lap.

The smile came slowly, bringing memories of good times with it. The cover was of the 1974 album *Hollies* by The Hollies. It was one of his favourites and she knew it.

Ally's smile grew into a grin.

"Shall I put it on?"

Before he could answer, Callum piped up from the other side of the room.

"Absolutely. Love that shit."

The mood in the house seemed to lighten, like the house itself had been holding its breath until now, and they began reminiscing together as the tracks on side one played on. As the haunting opening guitar of *The Air That I Breathe* began, Jack walked over to Ally, holding out his hand.

"Dance with me?"

He was aware of three other pairs of eyes in the room, all watching.

She nodded without hesitation and he stepped in to help as she draped her arms around his neck. A thrill of excitement buzzed through him as the music filled the room. From the look on her face, she felt it too. He carefully took hold of the braces he could feel beneath her jeans to pull her legs up and rest her feet on top of his. The combination of the physical toll on his still-healing body and the thrill of the moment sent a rush of adrenaline through his system.

"You okay?" he whispered.

She smiled, words completely unnecessary.

He began to move slowly from side to side, his hands cupping her backside to keep her close. Although she couldn't feel his hands, one glance told him that she knew exactly where they were and she liked it. He smiled, his gaze wandering.

Callum sat on one of the dining room chairs, his forearms resting on his knees, watching solemnly. Maggie and Jane leaned against the wall near the kitchen, Jane's arm around Maggie's shoulder. Maggie wiped her eyes quickly, smiling back at him.

Ally buried her head in his shoulder and he pulled her closer. Things had changed so much these past few weeks. He felt like he had been strapped to the front of a rollercoaster, head-first. So many changes, so many fears faced, so much he had learnt; about himself and about her; about what he needed and what he wanted and the difference between the two.

The single biggest regret he harboured now was that his father wasn't here to see them all together like this. He wanted to share everything with him, from the largest things to the smallest. His heart physically hurt thinking about it and he knew it was something he was going struggle with for a while yet.

For now, though, he was just happy to be dancing with Ally in his arms.

CHAPTER TWENTY-SEVEN

*"A kiss is a lovely trick designed by nature to stop
speech when words become superfluous."*
- Ingrid Bergman

Ally woke early, as usual. Over her morning coffee, an idea came to her that she couldn't ignore; she would have a barbeque that evening, for Jack. It was long overdue.

Too early to make phone calls to invite everyone over later, she ended up in her studio, staring at the blank canvas she had placed there a few days before. She stared at it for a long time, the events of the past few weeks playing on her mind. Finally, she picked up a brush and began to paint.

Slowly at first, almost shyly, she waited for the ideas to stop swirling around in her head and solidify into something she could use. Then she began to work in earnest. The more she painted, the more the ideas came, until by the time she eventually put down the brush a couple of hours later, the wisps of an idea had blossomed into a fully-fledged plan. Satisfied with her efforts, she smiled at the canvas, forcing herself to take a break in order to gain some perspective. She already looked forward to coming back later to work on it.

She showered, changed and made the phone calls over another coffee, filling everyone in on the plan. Maggie and Jane arrived mid-afternoon and by the time Callum and Jack arrived, the majority of the food was already prepared. She directed Callum to clean the grill, bribing him with a beer, and Maggie and Jane set about preparing the table outdoors for the barbeque.

Jack came up behind her while she was at the kitchen sink and swept her hair aside, kissing her neck.

"You smell good," he murmured.

She smiled, shying away from him as she struggled to concentrate.

"It's not me, it's the food."

His fingers lightly traced the line of her neck down to her shoulders, sending sparks of electricity shooting through her.

"Nope," he whispered, nuzzling her again. "Definitely you."

She wriggled away from him again, holding onto the counter to stop herself from toppling sideways.

"I can't concentrate if you're going to keep doing that," she scolded, only half joking.

He backed away, hands in the air, smiling.

"Okay, okay. Sorry."

He moved next to her instead, putting his bottle of beer down on the counter and turning to lean against it, facing her. Watching him curiously, wondering what had come over him suddenly, he indicated the tiny heart pendant she wore and smiled.

"I've missed it," she said.

He reached up to run his fingertips over the heart at the hollow of her neck, his touch feather-light against her skin. She shivered with anticipation as his eyes rose to meet hers. As he leaned closer, she held her breath until his lips were on hers.

Everything else faded; the room, the house, the world. All of it, gone. Nothing mattered anymore.

"For Christ's sake, will you two get a room?" Callum groused, stomping into the kitchen and throwing a filthy rag into the sink. Ignoring her blushing silence, he continued.

"Grill's clean. Where's the meat?"

She cleared her throat, willing her cheeks to return to their natural colour as she indicated the fridge with a nod of her head.

"In there."

"Need a hand?" Jack offered, picking up his beer from the counter again and throwing her a crooked smile.

"Yeah, that'd be good. We'll take it in turns. First, I'll flip the meat, sup on my beer and talk bullshit, then we'll swap. Sound like a plan?"

"Works for me."

Jack followed Callum out the door into the backyard. Ally smiled, watching them through the window. They seemed closer, these past few weeks. Callum was more tolerant, Jack had begun sharing snippets of his recent past. It was a show of trust, from both of them, and she could see the bond of friendship between them growing stronger because of it.

Something they all agreed on was that things could never go back to being like they were. There was still common ground, though. They would find a new normal. It was a slow process and she didn't expect miracles but she could see that the bridges weren't all burnt beyond repair, hers and Jack's included.

They sat around drinking and eating for most of the afternoon, moving from outdoors to indoors once night fell. Eventually, the number of yawns outweighed the number of stories and by mid-evening, Jack and Ally were alone.

Sitting in her living room, listening to the music while Jack got them both another drink, a warm glow washed over her. She was tired but there was also a fair measure of anticipation fuelling her too. She wished every day could be like this one. Jack came back with two bottles of beer, handing her one as he sank down into the couch beside her.

"Hey, remember this?" she smiled, half-turning towards him.

He listened for a second, then grinned, rocking out to Lynard Skynard's *Sweet Home Alabama*. She giggled in spite of herself, light-headed suddenly. To see him happy was a tonic in itself. Everything else seemed to fade into insignificance.

"I just poked my head into your studio," he said. "Is that a new painting on the easel? The paint still looks wet."

"Yeah it is, I started it this morning. I just woke up and suddenly I knew what I wanted to do. It's for the exhibition."

"Really? That's pretty cool," he said carefully. "Are you happy with this one?"

"Yeah, I am. It feels right this time."

"Glad to hear it," he smiled, raising his bottle. "To you, then. And to the exhibition."

She returned the smile, clinking her bottle against his.

"I know it's gonna be amazing," he said, taking a sip.

She blushed, cradling her beer in her lap. Jack sank back into the cushions beside her, his shoulder touching hers. She glanced over at him, as he stared up at the ceiling with a contented sigh.

"Happy?" she couldn't help asking, guessing the answer.

He turned to her, smiling lazily.

"More than you'll ever know. I haven't enjoyed myself like this for a long time."

"Me neither."

His smile faded as his gaze wandered slowly over her lips, her flushed cheeks, the lock of hair that had fallen forward over her eyes. She was comfortable under the scrutiny for the first time in a long time. She lapped it up, watching him watching her.

She let her mind wander, her gaze following suit. The soft fullness of his lips, the tiny freckles that dotted across the bridge of his nose and cheeks, only visible this close, the gentle creases in the corners of his eyes. Slowly, he leaned towards her, eyeing her lips and yet pausing ever so briefly to gaze into her eyes, delving deeply, asking the silent question that she felt herself answering just as silently. She may have even nodded, she couldn't be sure, but a slow, delightful smile played on his lips as he leant in.

He kissed her softly at first and she closed her eyes. She lost herself in the moment, drawing him deeper and making her forget where she was and how she came to be here. Suddenly, none of that seemed to matter anymore.

His hand curled around her neck and he pulled her closer. The kiss intensified and she reached for him, locking onto his forearm to seal the bond. He relieved her of her beer bottle, reluctantly withdrawing to slide it onto the coffee table next to his, the glass bottles clinking against each other. With both hands now free, he leaned closer, cupping her face tenderly, gently probing inside her mouth with his tongue. A slow shiver ran through her as she responded, giving herself over to the sensation of his hands on her. His body was so close to hers she could feel his heart beating, his breath warm and sweet. Time seemed immaterial as her mind emptied.

Then she was floating - literally.

Her eyes shot open. She was in his arms and he was carrying her through to the bedroom.

"Jack," she whispered breathlessly, doubt creeping in as she watched him negotiate the living room doorway.

"Don't worry," he said huskily. "Just trust me."

Struggling desperately to ignore the insecurities that were clawing up through her stomach, she nestled into the side of his neck. His cologne was woody and fresh and she tried to concentrate on how good he smelt rather than what might happen next.

Jack pushed open the bedroom door with his foot and her heart began to pound harder. He carefully set her down on the edge of the bed. Reluctantly letting him go, she grabbed handfuls of the bedcovers. Anxiety coiled inside her, tightening the muscles across her shoulders and back, her mouth clamped shut as she stared at the floor. Her breathing became heavy and laboured. She wanted to do this, but the admission alone terrified her. As if reading her thoughts, he sat down next to her and reached for her hand, his body radiating warmth.

"We don't have to do this now if you don't want to," he said gently, his eyes locking onto hers in the dim light of the bedroom. "We can wait."

She willed her heartbeat to slow down.

"I don't want to wait." If she waited, she might never do this. "But this is all new to me. I don't know what to do."

He squeezed her hand.

"It's all new to me, too. Don't worry, we'll work it out. Let's just take our time, okay? We'll find a way through this."

"Your ribs," she mumbled feebly.

"They're fine. Don't worry."

He leaned over to capture her lips with his once more, reminding her that he wasn't about to give up easily. She closed her eyes and tried to forget everything else, concentrating on his lips on hers as his fingertips stroked her cheek. Her skin felt like it was on fire, everywhere he touched suddenly coming to life as he drew her in deeper. Anxiety disappeared in a heated rush and the last four years faded into the background.

He eased her back onto the bed, caressing her ribcage, sending shivers of pleasure through her. Pulling away long enough to lift his t-shirt off over his head, their eyes locked. She unbuttoned her shirt as he slid his arm beneath her back, lifting her as she shrugged it off and pushed it aside. Hungry for him, she grabbed his face with both hands, pulling him down on her, losing herself in another long, deep kiss.

This was all that mattered. Her and Jack, just like it was before, just like it would always be. This moment in time, this blending of minds and bodies, this was what she had been waiting four years for. She was stronger now and so was he. They had weathered the storm. This was their reward for trusting that fate would bring them together again.

He rolled over onto his back suddenly, kicking off his shoes and unbuttoning his jeans. He tugged at them, arching his back and kicking his legs to get rid of them. He rolled onto his side and reached for her jeans, unzipping them slowly, his eyes flitting back to hers. She grabbed the bedcovers and rolled to one side, then the other, as he inched them down her hips and over her thighs. She raised herself up onto her elbows and watched, her heart racing. He winked, smiling as he peeled her jeans away, easing them down over her knees and then her calves, forgetting in his haste that she still had her shoes on. She couldn't help smiling as he frowned, momentarily stymied.

"I got this," he said smugly, climbing down onto the floor at the foot of her bed.

She grinned as he divested her of her shoes before dragging her jeans down and depositing them on the floor.

Then the bubble burst. Reality rushed in as she stared down at her legs, still enclosed in braces. Definitely not sexy.

She silently cursed them for destroying the fantasy. He climbed up to sit down on the bed beside her, reaching over to lay his hand on her ribs as she dared to look at him, wondering what he was thinking, afraid to ask.

He stroked her skin, his touch so feathery soft that it electrified her nerve endings and completely obliterated any self-conscious thoughts she had. She almost whimpered with pleasure, closing her eyes again, leaning her head back, her hair tickling her shoulders. His hand moved slowly downward and she raised her head again, opening her eyes as his touch faded. The sensation turned to pressure alone, the warmth gone. A moment later, she watched his hand move towards her underwear but she felt nothing.

"You can't feel that, can you."

It wasn't a question.

"I'm sorry."

"Don't be sorry," he murmured, his hand moving back up, suddenly alive on her skin again. "We need to talk about these things, okay?"

She nodded, her heart swelling again at the tenderness in his eyes, the thoughtfulness in his actions.

"Can you show me how to take your braces off?"

She searched his face for any sign that the mood had altered, that he might have changed his mind. All she found there was a deep desire, turning his eyes to molten pools of green, dark and dangerous. Her breath caught in her throat. It had been years since she had seen that look.

She nodded, her arms suddenly trembling beneath her weight. She pulled herself back towards the pillows behind her, before leaning forward to unfasten the Velcro strap over her right thigh with trembling fingers that refused to co-operate. She was hyper-aware of Jack watching her every move. After a few moments, he reached for the strap over her left thigh, pulling it gently to undo it. She glanced over at him in surprise and he caught her look.

"What? Did I do something wrong?"

"No," she said hesitantly. "I just didn't think..."

"I want to be as comfortable with this as you are and that means I need to know how these work."

He glanced down at her braces and she saw he had loosened the strap and his hand rested on her thigh. She imagined she could feel it on her skin, warm and gentle as she knew it was.

He reassured her in a way she had both become used to and looked forward to. He kissed her, snaking his hand around the back of her head to draw her closer. She closed her eyes, her hand floating up to latch onto his arm, grounding her, chasing away the insecurities that threatened to ruin the moment. Then he released her, caressing her hair as they drew apart.

"What's next?" he asked huskily.

It took a moment for her to remember what he was talking about. Her trembling fingers found their way to the second strap across her leg and pulled it open. He followed her lead, talking quietly, offering reassurance.

"These ones next?" he asked, indicating the straps across her shins.

She nodded, wishing they could skip all this and go back to when they were lying on the bed, fully clothed, immersed in fantasy, hiding from reality.

They unfastened the final straps at the same time. She pulled the straps out of the way and eased her leg out of the brace. Jack watched closely then followed her example. Her heart nearly burst at the tenderness in his movements, his face a picture of concentration as he gently eased her leg out of the brace and laid it down on the bed. She watched his hands as he worked, her gaze travelling up his strong forearms and biceps and along the smooth shoulders, remembering how it felt to be held by him. His chest, smattered lightly with chestnut-coloured hair, seemed to gleam in the soft light that shone through from the hallway. She hadn't suggested he turn the light on because she didn't want him to see too much of her own body but now she realised that in her vanity, she had cheated herself out of seeing his.

"Can you turn the bedside light on?" she asked, before she lost her nerve.

His eyes seemed to sparkle with mischief, even in the dim light, but he smiled and obliged, murmuring "Thank God."

As light flooded the room, she momentarily regretted her decision, but when he crawled back to her side again, his chest was mere inches from her and her doubts were forgotten. She smiled, reaching up to touch it, loving the shiver beneath her fingertips when she did.

He slid down beside her again, smiling crookedly as his hand captured hers.

"Ah. And here was I thinking the light was for my benefit."

She smiled up at him and he pulled her close. He was firm and solid against her as his lips pulled her under again. Her senses dipped and soared alternately, leaving her breathless. When they drew apart, he indicated the braces lying next to her on the bed with a nod.

"Is it okay if I put those on the floor?"

She nodded dumbly, not even really hearing the words, just the sentiment behind them.

I need to get closer to you.

As he picked up the brace closest to him, she opened her mouth to warn him t steer clear of the locks but it was too late. He yelped in pain, diving off the bed and taking the brace down with him, disappearing in a heap on the floor. Before she could stop it, laughter bubbled up inside of her and she quickly clamped her hand over her mouth. Powerless to stop, she hunched forward, giggling uncontrollably, watching gleefully as Jack jumped up from where he had landed on the floor, furiously shaking the brace loose and giving it a filthy look as it clattered to the ground.

"Son of a bitch!"

The sight of him in his boxers, beautifully-shaped chest gleaming, his good hand clamped tight over his wrist as he belted out a stream of obscenities, did not help her.

"Are you okay?" she finally managed to spit out, still giggling but trying valiantly to stop.

He shot her a dirty look, pacing backwards and forwards in front of the bed. After a few moments, the obscenities died down.

"Freakin' health hazard," he muttered under his breath, plopping down beside her on the bed, shaking and flexing his hand.

"Let me see," she grinned, finally able to control the laughter as she reached over to grab his shoulder and pull him around towards her.

He turned obligingly, displaying a pathetic, wounded expression that any five-year-old would've been proud of. She cleared her throat, wiping the smile off her face as she reached for his hand. Inspecting his reddened finger, she was willing to bet it hurt like hell but there was no way she was going to let that ruin the mood now.

She raised his finger to her lips and kissed it, looking up at him through lowered lashes.

"Better?"

"Yeah... a little."

A smile tugged at the corner of his mouth. She reached over to gently push the other brace off the bed. He gave it a wary look as it clattered to the floor, muttering under his breath again. She lowered herself back onto the bed as he stretched out beside her, propping himself up on one elbow to gaze down at her.

Her skin tingled under his gaze, anticipation flowing through her. He reached over to run his hand over her midriff. She moaned gently, shuddering as he slid his fingertips over her belly and up to her sternum before lightly cupping one full breast through her bra. Tenderness morphed into pure desire and he leaned over to kiss her again. She closed her eyes and lost herself in the feel of his hand on her skin, his lips caressing hers before moving down to her jaw and neck, working their way down her body to between her breasts. His hand travelled down her side, finally stopping to rest in the hollow of her waist. She tried to lean into it, enjoying the feel of it, moaning softly.

"Can you feel that?" he murmured throatily, kissing his way back up to her lips.

She nodded, incapable of speech.

"Show me how far I can go," he whispered, squeezing her waist. "I don't want you to miss out on anything."

Without thinking, she searched out his hand with hers and moved it slightly south, stopping when she felt the warmth of his hand become mere pressure on her skin. He covered her lips with his, forcing them apart, exploring with his tongue until she began to respond in kind, deeper and harder.

The hand beneath hers moved back to the hollow of her waist and she released it, reaching out for him, wanting to feel him, smooth and strong and so close to her. In return, his hand never left her torso, moving over every inch of her upper body, front and back, removing her bra so effortlessly she almost didn't notice until she was shimmying out of it.

He slid his hands around her, pulling her up to him. Her arms found their way around his neck before trailing down his back. She could feel the muscles in his back working beneath her fingers and she moaned with pleasure, hardly believing that any of this was real anymore.

He set her back down on the bed, his lips nibbling a trail down to her breasts. He reached down to remove his boxers with one hand, frantically yanking them down and wriggling out of them. He kicked them to the floor, his hands and lips back on her in a heartbeat.

Lost to the world, hands buried deep in his hair, she barely registered that he had leaned down to remove her underwear. They drew apart as he pulled them down her legs and dropped them off the end of the bed.

Crawling back up the bed towards her like a cat, she watched breathlessly as he ran his hands up her shins, over her knees and then up her thighs, her brain making the connection that her body couldn't. Seeing the sheer desire in his eyes, the substitution was automatic and almost indistinguishable.

He continued his journey upwards, caressing her hips, her stomach, her breasts, as she shuddered with pleasure beneath him. She felt claustrophobic, his body warm and damp on top of hers, her breathing ragged as she reached for him. Her hands traced the hills and valleys that formed his chest and shoulders, mapping his body, committing it to memory once more. She wanted him so badly now, she was almost beside herself.

He kissed every inch of her and she found herself wishing she could arch her back, just to get closer to him. It wasn't enough to be with him anymore, she wanted to be part of him.

Suddenly her nerve-endings were on fire. He had lit a match inside of her and it was burning so hot, she could barely catch her breath. She felt like she might implode at any moment. Giving in to the sensations that had hi-jacked her mind and body, she didn't care what happened next.

After spending so long worrying about this, she had the overwhelming sensation that this was exactly where she was meant to be.

EPILOGUE

"An invisible red thread connects those who are
destined to meet, regardless of time,
place and circumstance.
The thread may stretch or tangle,
but never break."
- Ancient Chinese Proverb

ONE YEAR LATER

*A*lly woke up slowly, teasing reality before she decided if
it was really for her. A few moments passed before the
realisation hit her.

I'm getting married today.

She had personally helped to organise a thousand things for
the wedding this afternoon; flowers, seating arrangements, the
church, the cake, the menu, the champagne. Yet they weren't the
first things that came to mind.

What if I can't do it?

She wanted to walk up the aisle so badly, she had spent the

past several months learning how. Of course, Jack knew nothing of this. It was going to be a surprise. But would the real surprise be falling flat on her face in front of their friends and family?

Callum's voice rang in her ears.

"You won't fall - you can't, it's a physical impossibility. I'll be on one side of you, Maggie on the other, remember? You'll have both our arms to lean on and we'll be holding you so tight we might actually cut off the circulation to your hands. Personally, I'd be more worried about that if I were you."

She took a deep breath, letting it out slowly.

Physical impossibility.

So was what she was planning to do this afternoon. Months of practicing with a sheet tied around her waist so she couldn't see her legs. Trusting her body was doing what she was telling it to do, without actually being able to see it respond. She was probably crazy for even thinking this would work but she couldn't back down now. She wanted to see Jack's face as she walked up the aisle to be with him; no crutches, no wheelchair. Just this one time, she wanted to do things the same way everyone else did. If it never happened again, she was fine with that. But it had to happen today.

She pushed herself upright, throwing the covers back and transferring into her wheelchair. The butterflies in her stomach increased as she laid eyes on her wedding dress, hanging silently on the wardrobe door. She wheeled over to it slowly, reaching up to touch the soft white silk folds that fell from the waistline. When she wore it, she felt like a princess.

She was getting light-headed thinking about it. The plans - both public, that Jack knew about, and private, that he didn't - were set in stone. It would be fine. It had to be. It was their wedding day.

She used the bathroom, then headed for the kitchen, eager for coffee. Maggie would be here soon and the chaos would really begin. Before that though, she needed some quiet time.

Rounding the kitchen doorway, she stopped dead.

Jack stood leaning against the kitchen counter, arms folded across his chest, smiling at her.

She stared at him, wide-eyed.

"What are you doing here?"

"And a good morning to you too, fiancée. I thought I'd come by and make your last 'first cup of coffee of the day' as a single woman," his smile faded and he scratched his chin. "Did I get that right? That sounded better in my head."

"You can't be here, Jack - its bad luck!" she sputtered, glancing around as if someone might see him and throw him out.

"Yeah, well, that's where my lack of belief in superstition comes in handy. Don't really care, as it happens. I had to see you." He shrugged, the smile back. "I didn't like sleeping without you next to me last night. The day started all wrong, so I thought I'd come over and re-start it, if you know what I mean."

"But… my dress is in the bedroom. You can't see my dress!"

"Don't panic, I don't plan on going anywhere near the bedroom. I just wanted to see you, that's why I waited in here. Knew you'd come in for your coffee eventually."

He walked over to her, bending down to scoop her out of her wheelchair and into his arms. The butterflies in her stomach took flight as she draped her arms around his neck, breathless suddenly.

"What has gotten into you today?" she murmured, anger and fear dissipating as he pulled her closer.

His smile faded and the green of his eyes seemed to deepen.

"I missed you. And I wanted to make sure you were okay, that you hadn't changed your mind or anything."

Her heart melted and she reached up to stroke his cheek. He hadn't yet shaved this morning, and the stubble was rough beneath her fingertips.

"Of course I haven't changed my mind."

He rolled his eyes, throwing his head back with a theatrical sigh.

"Whew! That's a load off!"

She grinned, grabbing his chin between her thumb and forefinger.

"Here's your last chance to kiss me as your fiancée," she said, smile fading. "Next time, it'll be as your wife."

He didn't need any more encouragement, covering her lips with his. She closed her eyes, burying her fingers in his newly trimmed hair, and tried to remember to breathe. She hoped it would always be like this between them - that his kiss would always have the power to soothe the worry in her heart and her soul. It seemed to last forever, which is exactly what she wanted right now; to lose herself in Jack's arms, his lips on hers, making silent promises she intended on making sure he kept.

The thought of walking up the aisle towards him wasn't as frightening as it had been earlier. Callum was right. She had been practicing for months. Everything would be fine. And at the reception, she would dance in his arms in front of everyone, light-headed from the champagne. She couldn't wait.

"Wow," he mumbled, licking his lips.

She smiled.

Just you wait till you see me at the church.

"As much as I want to hang around here and see where this leads, I should probably get going, right?"

"You should," she said as he deposited her carefully back in her wheelchair. "Maggie'll be here soon and while you might not be superstitious, she is. She'll kill you if she finds you here and I want you to make it to the church in one piece, otherwise this very romantic gesture of yours will've been a total waste of time."

"Very good point. I guess I'll see you later, then?"

He looked as if he wanted to say more. She waited but he didn't elaborate.

"You will," she smiled, trying to put him at ease. "I'll be the one in the white dress."

That seemed to do it. He winked, his lips tilting into that lazy, crooked smile that melted her insides.

"Great, thanks for the tip."

She nodded graciously.

"One more thing, before I go," he said, his expression softening as he reached down to smooth her hair back from her face. "You look so beautiful today."

She smiled up at him as he leaned down to give her one final, reassuring kiss.

The End

Did you enjoy Absolution? Want to know more about Callum and see what happens next? Then please check out the next book in the Absolution Series: Sliding Down the Sky. The prologue is up next. Read on!

SLIDING DOWN THE SKY

ABSOLUTION SERIES #2

PROLOGUE

"The sense of loss is such a tricky one,
because we always feel like
our worth is tied up into stuff that we have,
not that our worth can grow
with things we are willing to lose."
– Tori Amos

CALLUM

I spent a good part of my life hating my father. I hated the booze, I hated the way he treated my mother, and I hated the way he looked at me. I hated the man he was. I was as scared of him as I was ashamed of him. Then came that day, the day everything changed.

I remember that moment as if it were yesterday. Like all the moments in my life that shaped me into the man I am, they linger. They burn through my veins like neon, lighting me up from within. It doesn't matter how deeply I try to bury them, I know they're there. They carve scars deep into my heart and soul. Much like my tongue might caress the gap where a tooth used to be, my brain goes over and over these moments until they finally become part of my history. I don't realise it at the time, but I will never be the same again.

Life can be stripped down to a few critical moments. We rarely recognise these moments as they're happening. It's not until much later, when the storm has passed, and with the benefit of hindsight, that we finally see them for what they are.

I was just like him.

The realisation itself was a dye, tainting everything. It leaked into my actions, my moods, the very essence of who I thought I was, until there was no point fighting it anymore. The situation I now found myself in was simply a culmination of all of that.

Jail cells had a particular smell, and this one was no different. A unique blend of vomit, urine and misery, overlaid with the not-so-delicate scent of bleach.

So far I'd managed to keep the booze down. I should've eaten, but that would've been counter-productive. My goal, if I'd been thinking clearly enough to have one, was to get rip-snorting, memory-erasing, coma-inducing drunk – drunk enough to forget about everything – but I couldn't even manage to do that right. I should've been disappointed in myself, but I couldn't even muster up the necessary disgust anymore.

The room seemed to tilt and I leaned forward to keep up with it, my head in my hands. I tried not to think. I didn't want to think, but even when you don't want to think, it happens anyway. Just like when your heart hurts so much, you convince yourself that this is it – it can't get any worse. Then someone twists a knife and you find a new level of pain.

That's what had happened to me tonight. I'd found a new level of pain, and it was cutting me to ribbons.

I swallowed back a combination of vomit and tears, my

nostrils twitching as I fought against the impulse. I was not going to throw up or cry. I just wasn't. I wished I had my phone. How many calls had I missed? What was going on out there?

I was in the cell with a couple of other guys, one much older, sleeping it off on the bench that ran across the opposite wall. The other guy was younger than me. I looked up at him out of the corner of my eye. He'd barely moved in the hour since I'd been thrown in here, and he hadn't uttered a word. He was like me – the strong, stupid type. He just sat there, his back to the wall, watching everything. He didn't look drunk, but then some of us hid it well. Instead, he looked like a simmering volcano. That look in his eye was all too familiar.

Like me.

Like Dad.

Only, my anger was waning. Teetering on the brink for so long, I could feel it burning away, taking with it the soul-destroying sense of betrayal and even the confusion. Now, I was just broken. Broken, and drunk, and too exhausted to search for a way out of this mess.

I sank my fists into my hair and pulled tight. It was pure distraction, like stomping on my foot to take my mind off a sore thumb. Maybe, if I ripped my hair out by the roots, it'd take my mind off the ache in my chest.

Self-preservation kicked in though, and I let go, choking back a sob that sounded more like a gasp. I wanted to sink into a deep ocean of self-pity, allowing the water to swallow me up without a trace, but I didn't have that luxury.

I was wasting time. I had to get out of there. I had to get the hell out of there and see her, before it was too late.

I lurched to my feet, the floor leaning sideways as I hurled myself at the bars.

"Hey!" I shouted. "I need my phone call!"

Nothing.

"Can anyone hear me?"

"You're wasting your time."

I turned, still hanging on to the bars to keep my balance. The younger guy regarded me from across the cell, his eyes narrowing as if I was something he'd just scraped off his shoe.

"I need my phone call," I said again.

"You have to wait, just like the rest of us. They'll be back."

He was right. I should've known that. This wasn't my first rodeo. My heart sank and the despair was instant and absolute, wrapping cold arms around me and squeezing so tight, I had trouble breathing.

While I sat there, suffocating in self-pity, she could be dying.

She could be dying, and I wasn't there.

A NOTE FROM THE AUTHOR

I hope you enjoyed Absolution and the first chapter of the next book in the series (out now!) Sliding Down the Sky. Please go to my website (www.amandadick.com) for links to purchase or visit your favourite retailer store (or if you're reading this on an ereader, click here!).

I'm so grateful to each and every one of you for taking the time to read this story, one that I've put my heart and soul into. Please consider leaving a short review online wherever you purchased this book from - each and every review helps this book to find an audience. To an independent author such as myself, this is critical.

Thank you so much!

CLAIM YOUR FREE BOOK!

If you enjoyed the story, you might also be interested in signing up for my mailing list. I'll email you once every 1-2 months to notify you of my latest release, a sale or a fun giveaway (I promise not to share your email address or clog up your inbox, and you can unsubscribe at any time) and let you know how progress is going on my next book.

And as an added bonus, everyone who signs up for my newsletter also gets a FREE copy of my second novel, a stand-alone called **Between Before and After**.

Just go to my website (www.amandadick.com) and sign up there – your free book will be winging its way to you within minutes!

ABOUT THE AUTHOR

Amanda Dick is a night-owl, coffee addict, movie buff and music lover.

She believes in love at first sight, in women's intuition and in following your heart. She is rather partial to dark chocolate and believes in the power of a good vanilla latte.

What lights her fire is writing stories about real people in trying situations. Her passion is finding characters who are forced to test their boundaries. She is insanely curious about how we, as human beings, react when pushed to the edge. Most of all, she enjoys writing about human behaviour - love, loss, joy, grief, friendship and the complexity of relationships in general.

After living in Scotland for five years, she has now settled back home in New Zealand, where she lives with her husband and two children.

Please visit her website for more information (www.amandadick.com) or connect with her online here:

facebook.com/amandadickauthor

instagram.com/amandadickauthor

goodreads.com/amandadick

bookbub.com/profile/amanda-dick

PLAYLIST

Black – Pearl Jam
Mrs Potter's Lullaby – Counting Crows
Sweet Home Alabama – Lynard Skynard
The Air that I Breathe – The Hollies
Stand Up – The Feelers
It's the Only One You've Got – 3 Doors Down
The Hard Way – Thirsty Merc
The Lost Boy – Greg Holden
Eyes for You – Nathan King
The Road I'm On – 3 Doors Down
Rewind – Paolo Nutini
Make You Feel My Love – Adele
Crawling Back to You – Daughtry
Homesick – Thirsty Merc
One Foot Wrong – Pink
Your Arms Feel Like Home – 3 Doors Down
Deciphering Me – Brooke Fraser

ACKNOWLEDGMENTS

It takes a village to publish a book and these are the residents of my village.

First and foremost, my husband Willie and my children, Georgia and Cameron. Without their understanding and patience, this book would never have been finished. Thank you for making dinner, walking the dog, doing the dishes, attempting to keep your rooms tidy, for responding to frantic requests for peace and quiet and for dragging me (kicking and screaming, at times) out of my studio and reminding me to eat. Love you always.

Going right back to the beginning of this journey - 2010, I believe? - thank you Lisa Horton, for your encouragement. You were the first person to read this story and I know without a doubt that I would never have had the courage to share this with the world if it hadn't been for your passion for this story and these characters. Without your enthusiasm, this would still be on a flash drive somewhere, probably buried in a box full of other flash drives.

The best beta-reader, friend and cheerleader a girl could have. Yes, I'm talking about you, Tara Horak! Thank you for your insight, encouragement, questions, musings, thoughtful comments, generosity and enthusiasm, and for your belief in me (no small thing). Love ya!

Sarah Widdup - editor, guru, Sensei - I didn't find you, you found me. How lucky am I! Thanks for being you, and for making this journey that much more fun just by having you along for the ride. Our late night conversations still make me giggle. I'm pretty sure not all editors are as cool as you, so I kinda feel like I won the lottery here - twice.

Huge gratitude goes out to everyone who helped me raise the money to re-release the second edition (their names are listed under the Dedications page at the front of this book). Without them, this book would still be waiting to make its appearance! Thanks to my Pop, Claude Pettigrew. It was your love of books and reading that set me on this path. Love you and miss you always.

Lastly, a disclaimer: I am not an expert on spinal cord injuries in general or paraplegia in particular. I have no background in the medical field. In researching Ally's injury and the possibilities for her mobility, I have learnt more than I could possibly have imagined about both subjects. This story is not meant as a textbook or manual and I hope that any mistakes or omissions are interpreted purely as poetic licence or ignorance rather than deliberate errors. To all of you who have shared your stories; you have my admiration and heartfelt thanks.